THE HUNTER'S SORCERESS

For more information contact:
Alessia Ann
www.alessiaann.com
Cover design by: © Trinah Kei – Beauxif Graphics

ISBN: 978-1-7776482-7-5 (Paperback)
ISBN: 978-1-7776482-6-8 (eBook)

First Edition: December 2023

THE HUNTER'S SORCERESS

ALESSIA ANN

ALSO BY

ALESSIA ANN

The Primordials Series:

Spellbound
Honeymoon In Hell
Fallen

For all my readers who are still single
because the man of your dreams is fictional.
I feel you.

ONE

Luna

"What is your deal today, Sinclair?" Quinn asked, jabbing her elbow into my side to get my attention.

I shrugged, irritating my best friend with my sullen mood. I couldn't help it, though. I was down in the dumps today. My time at Deadwood High was coming to an end. Graduation was only a month away, marking the beginning of life after high school.

I knew it was coming, of course. I wasn't an idiot. I'd been training my whole life for this, preparing for the day I finally turn eighteen and officially join my coven as a working member of our society.

Although I was proud of my heritage, I had grown a little too accustomed to human life. As a witch under the age of eighteen, I was still considered a Witchling—a minor who got to enjoy the advantages of mundane life just a little while longer. Cheerleading, football games, school dances.

All privileges that would soon expire.

As graduation grew closer, the more my heart ached. For weeks, other seniors gushed and raved over what colleges they would be attending in the fall. That wasn't in the cards for me either. There was no Ivy League school in my future, even though I had both the grades and funds to make it happen. It was a stupid thing to be bummed over, especially since my chosen career path wasn't something I could study at Harvard or Yale.

Still, the FOMO was real.

Quinn nudged me again, throwing her arm over my shoulders. "Cheer up, babe. Your birthday is coming up."

Quinn Nightshade. My best friend since damn near birth. She was also the worst necromancer to have ever graced the Nightshade line. Her coven practiced the darker arts, dabbling mostly in resurrections and blood magic. All talents Quinn severely lacked. The girl, Hecate bless her, couldn't even resurrect a dead rabbit if she tried.

And she has. Many, many, many times.

As kids, it was a running joke that she was adopted. How else could we explain why a born and bred necromancer couldn't *necromance*? Still, she got an A for effort. The blonde-haired beauty was many things, but a quitter she was not. She was determined to figure her shit out, even if it meant raising a hundred deformed zombie-rabbits from their graves until she got it right.

I sighed, shooting her a dull look. "Don't remind me."

"Aw, don't be like that. This is a big year for us." She glanced around before dropping her voice to a whisper.

"What do you think our first mission will be?"

Pursing my lips, my pout deepened to toddler status. "Who the fuck knows. They probably won't give us one until after graduation." Quinn's birthday was only two weeks after mine, allowing me the honor of being inducted into the fold first.

Our people were mercenaries by trade, selling our goods and services to the highest bidder—humans and immortals alike. We didn't discriminate. Humans were our most gullible clientele, seeking out magical resources in times of need or desperation. A cure for an illness when their prayers to God failed them, revenge against those who've wronged them, or, my personal favorite, finding their one true love. As if we were no better than fucking wish-granting genies.

It wasn't exactly an honest living but, hey, it paid the bills. And ours were higher than most.

Witches were nothing if not vain.

To say we liked nice things would be an understatement. The five covens were among the wealthiest in town, running local human businesses that acted as fronts but were successful enough to justify our lavish lifestyle. There wasn't a single person in this town who knew what we *actually* did for a living.

Quinn scoffed, rolling her bright jade eyes. The contacts she wore hid the fact that her irises were far paler than they appeared, a common trait among necromancers. The thin ocular lenses never worked for me, though. An illusion spell concealed my own bizarre gaze, altering my pupilless orbs from amethyst to light brown so they would appear normal.

"Please. You can't seriously tell me that you're sad about leaving this place. Playing pretend with the humans every day is beyond exhausting."

Normally, I wouldn't disagree. Living a double life wasn't ideal, but it had its perks. The first of which was about to come into view, just as it did every morning for the past two years.

Turning down the hallway, I led us towards the stairwell to the second floor where my locker was located. The first bell rang, a warning for everyone to get to class. We passed the floor-to-ceiling windows on the first-floor landing before making our way to the second. My heart jumped in my chest as we approached the double glass doors. On the other side, my locker was among the first few lining the wall to the left. Right opposite *his*.

And there he was. *My perk*. Malakai *fucking* Slade.

The blush rising to my cheeks quickly spread to the rest of my face, heat seeping to the back of my neck. Malakai reached up to shove something into his locker, the well-defined muscles in his arm flexing just enough to draw my already rapt attention. Dark swirls of ink coated his arms like a sleeve, adding to his mysterious appeal. I'd never been close enough to see what any of his tattoos were, but my imagination did a pretty good job at filling in the blanks. His cropped brown hair was so dark it was almost black, with a light fade running down each side. His face, as always, was clean-shaven and smooth, blessed with high cheekbones and a jawline that could put Brad Pitt's to shame.

Today he wore a fitted black tee with black jeans and classic beige Timberlands on his feet. Black was obviously his color, and he wore it well. A silver chain with army tags hung low around his neck. That, and two thick silver rings on each hand, were the only pieces of jewelry he ever wore. He was well over six-feet-tall with an athletic build, one he trained rigorously in the gym sometimes after school. I wasn't stalking him or anything, we just always seemed to find each other. Or at least *I* did.

Slamming his locker door shut, he turned on his heels, my breath hitching in my throat when his storm-gray eyes flickered in my general direction. I wasn't delusional enough to think he was actually staring at me…

Oh, Hecate, he's walking over here…

He moved with a lethal grace I'd never seen before, certainly not in any of the boys at this school. His every step was laced with confidence and control, like he owned the entire fucking building and everything in it.

My lungs included.

Grabbing my arm, Quinn guided me over to my locker just as he reached the double doors, his hand barely brushing mine as we crossed the threshold at the same time. He glanced down as I peered up, his gaze regarding me with little interest as he headed down the stairs.

Quinn shook her head and laughed as air refilled my lungs. "Are you ever going to grow some balls and talk to him? You're kind of running a little low on time here."

I shot a quick glance over my shoulder, catching sight of Malakai's dark head as he cleared the landing down to the first floor. I turned and sagged against my locker, leveling Quinn with another pout. "What's the point? He's probably going away to college like everyone else, and I'll never see him again."

Except in my dreams.

Pushing me aside, Quinn fiddled with my lock, thumbing in the combination. "You don't know that," she said, letting the door swing wide. "In fact, no one knows shit about him. Homeboy's a walking mystery."

"A gorgeous mystery," I muttered dreamily, dramatically clutching my chest. If only I wasn't such a pussy. After all this time, I still couldn't work up the courage to speak more than four words to him.

The closest I ever got was, *"You dropped your pencil,"* which he responded to with a nonchalant, *"Thanks,"* before turning in his seat to face the front of the only class we shared. Chemistry.

Ironic, wasn't it?

Seeing as how the only chemistry we had was one-sided. After moving to Deadwood nearly two years ago, and in the middle of the school year, Malakai did very little to make friends or participate in anything even remotely social. Outside of school, I rarely saw him around town. I knew little of his family, except that they ran an auto mechanic shop on the north side of town.

Quinn snatched my bag from my shoulders, replacing the old books inside with the ones I needed for my next class. Slamming my locker shut, she chucked it at me. "Time to put on your big girl panties, Sinclair. Boss the fuck up and go get that boy."

Slipping my arms through the straps, I allowed her to jostle me around until my bag was secured to my shoulders again. Then she gave me a shove, followed by a slap on the ass.

I turned to glare at her. "No way. I can't do it. He

doesn't even know I exist."

"He will once you open your fucking mouth and *talk* to him. I hear humans like that."

I planted my feet. "Nope. Not doing it." I wasn't good at talking to boys. Especially the hot ones. It was the sole reason I was still single and would probably die a virgin.

Quinn pinched the bridge of her nose. "Luna, I love you, but you are way too hot to be this insecure. You need to do this before graduation. If you don't, you'll always wonder *what if*."

Whoa, she used my first name. She wasn't playing around. But she wasn't wrong, either. "You're right," I said, trying to mentally hype myself up. "I'm going to do it. Today's the day I'm going to talk to Malakai Slade."

"Fuck yeah!" Quinn cheered, pounding her fist into my shoulder a little too hard.

"I'm doing it!"

"Damn right you are!"

Spinning around, I started marching to my chem class like I was going off to war. "And if I can't do it, I'll just conjure an illusion of myself and make her do it!"

Coming from a coven of skilled enchanters, deception was my bread and butter. And I was willing to use every weapon at my disposal if need be.

"Yeah! No...wait—what? Luna, you can't do that!" Quinn hollered after me, rushing to catch up.

I ignored her and kept marching, fanning the fire I just lit under my own ass. Yep, today was the day. Before I leave this place, Malakai Slade was going to know my fucking name.

TWO

Malakai

I drummed my fingers against the desk, my metal rings pinging against the stainless-steel countertop. The girl sitting next to me—my lab partner for today—threw a scathing look my way, the noise clearly grating on her nerves.

Like I fucking cared.

I cocked a brow at her when she refused to look away. "Can I fucking help you?"

Her eyes dropped to my fingers, the repetitive drumming still on auto-pilot. "Do you mind?"

I blinked, feigning ignorance. "I'm sorry, am I disturbing you?"

She nodded. "Actually, yes—"

"Too fucking bad. I suggest you go sit somewhere else."

Her jaw unhinged, gasping in outrage. With a huff, she

gathered her books and moved to a seat closer to the front of the class.

Good riddance.

I never liked her know-it-all ass, anyway.

Plucking my cell phone from my back pocket, I tapped the screen until it lit up. No new notifications.

Dammit. I shouldn't be here.

I pocketed the device and glared out the window at nothing in particular. This school shit was pointless. I had no business being here, nor did I fucking need it. I should be out *there* with the rest of my family. Hunting.

I was so sick of being benched all the goddamn time. At eighteen, I was already far more skilled than most, an invaluable asset to the team. Yet my father insisted on me finishing high school before taking up hunting full-time. Hence why I was currently sitting in a fucking chem lab instead of killing monsters with the rest of the crew.

Zane, my cousin, was supposed to call me as soon as they were done. They had left yesterday afternoon with a five-man team to clear out a pack of Wendigos two towns over. Zane had called to check in at the ass crack of dawn to let me know they were moving in on the nest, and I hadn't heard from him since.

That was three hours ago.

I cursed and checked my phone again, waiting for the fucking thing to vibrate. I shouldn't be worried. My father and uncle were seasoned hunters. As were Derek and Alex, the other two who had volunteered to go along.

It was Zane I was really worried about.

I loved the son of a bitch like a brother, but he was too impulsive at times. Careless. I always felt like his babysitter when we were paired together on hunts. After his brother got his heart clawed out by a werewolf last year, Zane had lost touch with reality just a smidge. At any given moment, he was liable to go off the fucking rails and get himself killed. Or worse, someone else.

Why he was chosen to go on the latest hunt over me was mind-boggling. I blew out a sigh, resisting the urge to hurl my phone across the room. A chair scraped against the floor, forcing my head up just as another body plopped down in the seat beside me.

It was *her*.

I stared, partly because I was stunned stupid, but mostly because she was something worth staring at.

Luna Sinclair, the most beautiful girl I had ever laid my eyes on, was sitting next to me. It wasn't her usual seat selection. Like everyone else, she opted to stay far away from me, no doubt due to my winning personality. I always got the sense that she was scared of me, always avoiding my gaze or shying away if I got too close for her liking.

But not today.

Today she wanted to be my lab partner.

I continued staring as she emptied her bag, meticulously placing her notebook and multicolored pens down in a neat row on the desk before slinging the straps of her brown Louis Vuitton bag on the back of her chair.

Finally turning to face me, those plump pink lips of hers tipped up into a shy smile while tucking a chunk of ginger hair behind her ear with perfectly manicured fingernails.

"Um, hi," she said, batting long, full lashes that framed

light brown eyes. Rays of sunlight pierced the windows to my right, the beams hitting her face and setting her pale skin aglow.

It took me an embarrassing amount of time to find the words to respond, my eyes still glued to her face. "Hi."

Smooth.

Her smile broadened, flashing more teeth this time. And, surprise, surprise, those were perfect too.

"Looks like we're lab partners today," she said brightly.

I nodded. "Looks like."

The awkwardness was almost too painful to endure.

"I'm Luna, by the way."

"I know who you are."

Her brows shot up. "You do?"

Is she serious? "Yeah…" I said, drawing out the word like she was stupid. "We've been in the same class all semester."

She flushed, her pale skin reddening. "Oh…right. Of course. I mean, I knew that. *Duh*." Abruptly turning to face the front, she picked up one of her colored pens and began fidgeting with it, flipping the cap on and off.

My lips quirked for the first time today. For a rich kid, she was uncharacteristically timid. I knew of her family just like everyone else. The Sinclairs owned most of the restaurants in town, everything from hole-in-the-wall dive joints that served greasy burgers to upscale establishments with escargot on the menu. I knew for a fact that she was well-off, though she didn't seem as snobby as some of the rich brats who ran in her circle.

I preferred to keep my distance from people like her. I

lived a life they would never understand. Hunted things they believed existed only in their nightmares. It was why I never approached her, never thought to even strike up a conversation.

What was the point?

In my line of work, loved ones either ended up missing or dead. A lesson I learned the hard way. Keeping to myself was the best way to avoid making unnecessary connections that could possibly result in casualties. An easy task, considering how often my family moved around.

Deadwood was the longest we've ever stayed put, but I knew it was just a matter of time before this place was in our rear-view mirror.

I spent most of class trying to ignore her, but her perfume was almost as distracting as her presence. It was citrusy, with hints of vanilla and raspberries. I found myself breathing her in one too many times, quickly getting hooked on her scent. Although her head was trained towards whatever lesson the teacher was scribbling on the chalkboard, her eyes kept skirting back to me in her peripheral, stealing looks she didn't think I would notice.

I didn't mind at first, but I was already on edge and she wasn't making it better. The next time her gaze flickered my way, I turned to meet it. "Is something wrong?" I asked, forcing back a smile when she jolted.

Light brown eyes widened in horror. "Uh, no! Sorry. It's nothing."

"Hmm." She wasn't a very good liar. "Seems like you have something you'd like to say to me."

"W-What?" she sputtered, shaking her head as her face alternated between different shades of red. "I don't."

"You sure about that? If you have something to say, just say it." I wasn't trying to be a jerk, but there was nothing I hated more than people pussyfooting around with their words.

Just spit it the fuck out.

She averted her gaze, those dark lashes fluttering down to the space between us as she bit down into her lower lip. My eyes fell to her mouth, following the movement. I caught myself leaning in, waiting for a reply. My thumb itched to smooth over that captured lip, releasing it from her clutches into mine.

When she peered up at me through her lashes again, the surprise in her gaze told me I had moved too close. I was just about to lean back in my seat when she finally opened her mouth.

"Actually…I was wondering if—"

A vibrating buzz in my pants jerked my attention away. With frantic hands, I pulled out my phone and tapped the screen to read the text notification that came through from Zane.

911. Come to the yard. Now.

"Fuck," I cursed, scooting my chair back and jumping to my feet. I blazed past the teacher to the door, ignoring the sound of my name being called.

"Mr. Slade, where do you think you're going? Class isn't over yet."

It is for me.

In my haste, I flung the door a little too hard, the knob hitting the wall behind it as I stepped out into the hallway.

I took off at a dead run, my heart kicking in my chest.

911 meant someone was hurt.

My father's face flashed in my mind. *Please don't let it be him.* I couldn't survive losing another parent. Making a quick stop at my locker to grab my jacket and keys, I hauled ass down to the first floor. Another voice trailed after me as I booked it down the hallway, a janitor telling me to slow down.

I had no time to tell him it was a matter of life or death. Reaching the parking lot, I fished the keys to my Harley from my jacket, skidding to a stop in front of the sleek, blacked-out machine that I custom built myself from the ground up. Snatching the helmet from the handlebars, I fastened it in place and climbed on, hitting the kickstand with my foot as I sat down and shifted my weight to keep things balanced. With a twist of the handle, the engine roared to life. I took off like a bat out of hell, sending up a silent prayer to a god I barely believed in anymore.

Please don't let it be him…

THREE

Luna

T *hat went well...*

I spent the rest of the day the same way I started it. Sulking. *Why did he leave like that?* It was none of my business, obviously, but that didn't stop my curiosity from burning. Malakai never came back after storming out of class that morning. He was in such a rush he even forgot his bag—which I was now lugging around as an excuse to talk to him again.

I was so close!

If only I had a few more seconds, I would've accomplished the task of asking him out. Well...not *out* out. More like an invite to my birthday party this weekend.

"You're throwing a party for your birthday?" a husky voice interrupted. Stopping, I turned to see Blake Crowley walking up behind me. I slowed my pace, allowing her to catch up.

"It's rude to eavesdrop on people's private thoughts, Crowley," I said, glaring at the young witch who skipped to my side, her crazed, vacant gaze still slightly visible through the glamour spell she wore to cover it.

There were some things you just couldn't hide.

She tipped her head to the side and smiled in that serial-killer way that was typical of her people. The witches of the Crowley Coven were clairvoyant, possessing powerful psychic abilities ranging from precognitive visions to telepathy. Those of higher rank were known to walk the veil between life and death, communicating with spirits on the daily, even calling on them to do their bidding if need be.

Needless to say, they held the award for the creepiest coven.

Blake was still young, nearing the end of her freshman year. At fourteen years old, she was shaping up to be a fine witch who was more than capable of hanging with the big dogs. Still, she could be annoying at times.

And nosey.

She smiled sheepishly, flipping her long, pink-tipped blonde hair over her shoulder. "Sorry. Didn't mean to listen in. It just happens sometimes. I thought you didn't want a party for your birthday outside of the ritual?"

I didn't. But now I was seriously reconsidering. Quinn was right. The year was coming to an end, and this might be my last chance to get to know Malakai. On the night of my eighteenth birthday, all the covens would gather for my coming-of-age ritual under the full moon. It was a tradition of the highest order, a rite of passage we all must undergo. It was customary for the covens to throw a massive soirée for the birthday girl or boy afterwards to celebrate the occasion.

I opted out.

Parties weren't my thing. Especially if I was made to be the center of it.

But that was only part of it.

Truth is, I stopped celebrating anything since the death of my parents ten years ago. As heavy hitters within our coven, my mother and father were called away on missions weekly, their skills second to none among mercenaries. My naïve, eight-year-old self had idolized them, believing them to be untouchable. Until they weren't. I still vividly remembered the day Aunt Freya sat me down to deliver the news, giving me the sugar-coated version of how my parents were slain by demons, leaving out all the gory details that would've brutally traumatized my child-like brain even more.

My heart ached at the pain their memory restored, a wound that refused to heal even now. But maybe it was finally time to start living a little. Hecate knows Quinn would be thrilled. She was depressed for an entire month after I had told her my initial plans to cancel the celebration. Sure, it would be last minute, but that wouldn't be a problem for a coven of enchanters who could literally conjure anything out of thin air.

Making up my mind, I turned to Blake, giving her the green light. "I changed my mind. Spread the word to the others. The party is back on."

Her sky-blue eyes lit up with uncontained joy. "Seriously? Yay! I'll let everyone know."

I bet you will.

Crowleys lived for gossip. Not surprising considering they had a twenty-four-seven hotline to everyone's mind. Personally, I couldn't imagine having to deal with their power.

Must be exhausting.

I watched Blake skip away, muttering to herself as she went, chatting with whatever dead entity only she could see. People were quick to part the way for her, looking on with faces that said, *there goes the weirdo again.*

If their judgmental looks bothered her, she never showed it. Or maybe she didn't care. She didn't have many human friends, anyway.

Rightfully so.

All the humans in our school thought she and her family were batshit, and it didn't help that they owned all of the funeral parlors in town either. They even manned the graveyards, providing services and upkeep for the dead.

Is this a mistake? Was inviting Malakai to a party overrun with witches really the best way to get to know him?

I'll need to talk to the others. Let them know to be on their best behavior. It wasn't like they didn't know the drill already. No witchy business around humans. Coven Rules 101. But the ritual after-parties were known to get a little wild, which was exactly why humans were rarely ever invited to begin with.

Breathing out a heavy sigh, I glanced down at the backpack in my hand. Would he be angry with me for taking it? I could've left it with the teacher. Or even in the lost and found.

Gives me another reason to talk to him…

If he ever comes back.

I was tempted to look inside, if only for the chance to learn more about him. But that would be wrong. Invading someone's privacy was not the best way to get to know them. Huffing it back to my locker, I shoved his bag inside and slammed the door, jumping out of my skin when Quinn appeared beside me.

"Fucking hell, Quinn!"

Her jade eyes narrowed, arms crossing over her chest. "What's this I hear about a party?"

I blinked slowly. Damn. I knew word would spread fast, but I didn't anticipate it would be *that* fast. "Did Blake tell you?" The magical grapevine was a powerful thing.

Quinn scoffed. "More like she had one of her creepy dead minions whisper the invite in my ear. You want to tell me why I had to hear it from Casper instead of my best friend?"

I rolled my eyes. "Don't get your thong in a twist. It wasn't like that. I changed my mind just as Blake was listening in, so I told her to tell the others."

Quinn's frown curved up into a knowing smirk. "You changed your mind, huh? How come?"

She knew me too well. I hiked my shoulders, conveying nonchalance. "No reason."

She arched a well-shaped brow, trailing me as I started towards my next class. "So your sudden interest in a party, that me and your aunt have been begging you to have, has nothing to do with a certain six-foot-tall stud?"

I shot her a quick side-glance. "Maybe…"

"Hmm." I could almost hear the glee in her tone. "Did you invite him?"

"Not yet."

"But you plan to?"

My blush said it all.

"I fucking knew it!" she gasped, her voice raising to attention-drawing levels. "You little slut! You're totally gonna bang him, aren't you?"

"Shhh!" I hissed, yanking her into my side. "Why don't you say it a little louder. I don't think the first and third floors heard you."

Her laugh was boisterous. "I can't believe you're actually doing this. Luna Sinclair, throwing a party just to talk to a boy. Lucifer must be frosting over as we speak."

I pinned her with a glare. "Are you complaining?"

"Oh, Hecate, no! I already made some calls to get the ball rolling. I'm going to talk to the others and conjure up some—"

"No!" Coming to a halt, I turned to face her, lowering my voice as people passed us. "No conjuring anything ridiculous or overly extravagant. I want this party to be like any other *normal* high school event."

Quinn's face blanked as if she was struggling to process what I was telling her. "Um, have you met us? Extravagance is what we do, Sinclair."

"Yeah, well, I need it toned down to, like, a *five*."

Her eyes bulged. "A five!? Why don't we just throw it at fucking Chuck E. Cheese and call it a day!"

I patted her arm encouragingly before walking off. "It's this or nothing."

"I can get it down to an eight!" she called after me. "Anything below that, I make no promises!"

I waved her off and kept going, my gaze drifting over to Malakai's locker. Now all I have to do is get him to come. All of this will be for nothing if he says no, resulting in me being miserable at a party I didn't want in the first place.

Passing the floor-to-ceiling window in the stairwell that overlooked the parking lot, I searched for his bike. I could recognize it anywhere. Pick it out of a line-up of a hundred different makes and models if I had to.

Was that sad? It felt sad.

I wasn't even a gearhead. Part of me wondered what he would think if he knew I was *this* obsessed with him, if he knew just how deep my crush ran.

Pulling my phone from my bag, I checked the time. Two more hours until school was out. If he wasn't back by then, I would have to wait until chem class tomorrow to return his bag and pop the question.

Wonderful.

"Guess I won't be sleeping tonight..."

FOUR

Malakai

I skidded to a stop as I turned into the auto yard, my bike leaving tread marks on the pavement as I wheeled it around to line up with the six other vehicles parked outside the main garage.

The lot was pretty spacious, the other side filled with cars and bikes similar to mine. Some belonged to other hunters, while others were dropped off by customers for repairs. My father had opened Slade Auto shortly after we moved to Deadwood. Growing up, I spent most of my time under a hood, up to my eyeballs in grease and motor oil until I was old enough to properly fire a Glock. Then it became a juggling act. Between running the shop and hunting motherfuckers down, it was a miracle I even had time for school.

But the whole *education* thing wasn't up to me. I could've done without it. It was a requirement my mother had demanded long ago, one my father decided to follow through on after her death.

Other than being a decent source of income, Slade Auto also functioned as a base for hunters to gather after or before jobs.

Like now, for instance.

Dismounting my Harley, I sprinted towards the main building just opposite the garage, barreling through the front door into absolute chaos.

"What the fuck…"

The place was packed. I recognized most faces but some were new. The front entrance led straight into a rec area, furnished with a restaurant-style bar that ran along the wall and pool tables that had seen better days. Tables and chairs lay scattered, occupied by injured bodies or people patching them up.

I spotted Derek on a nearby couch with a slash in his side and a bottle of Jack clutched to his chest. He took a healthy swig, wincing as Alex stitched him up. To my right, I found Zane at the bar, pouring vodka over a nasty gash on his forearm before wrapping it with gauze.

How the hell did a five-man job turn into this?

Making my way through the crowd, I clapped a hand on Zane's shoulder to get his attention. He turned to look at me with blood dripping down his face. His dark hair was matted with the stuff, soaked from a fresh head injury he was sporting.

"What the fuck happened?" I said, looking him over. I immediately reached for more gauze from the med kit he had laid out, wadding it up and pressing it to his skull to stem the bleeding.

He hissed but still managed to offer up a crooked smile, coffee-brown eyes glinting. "Can't you tell? It's a fucking victory party, kid."

I hated when he called me that. Like being two years older made him wiser than me or some shit. Too bad he was the furthest fucking thing from it. "The Wendigos did this?"

He shook his head as I got to work patching him up. "Yeah. We got bad intel. Thought it was just going to be a pack of them, but it was a hell of a lot more. We retreated and called in reinforcements. Clint and his crew were only an hour out. When they got on scene, we moved in, cleared the fuckers out in one go. Shit got pretty dicey for a minute, though."

I frowned, scanning the room for my dad. "Why the fuck wasn't I called in?"

Zane reached for the vodka, downing another mouthful before answering. "No point. You wouldn't have gotten there in time, Kai."

"Where is he?" I demanded.

Zane uncurled a finger from the neck of the bottle and pointed to a room across the hall. "Patching up my old man. His leg got jacked pretty bad. They're both okay, though."

I blew out a breath, relief flooding me. "I should've been there."

He scoffed. "Then you would've been beaten to shit like the rest of us."

"Not necessarily," I muttered under my breath.

Zane smirked arrogantly, bracing back on his barstool. "Cocky bastard. Remind me again why you couldn't come?" He snapped his fingers. "Oh, that's right, your pops had you doing more *important* things. So, enough about me. What'd you learn at school today, pretty boy?"

"Fuck off," I grumbled, applying a little extra pressure as I bandaged his head.

He flinched. "Ow, bitch!"

"You good?" I needed to check on my dad.

He waved me off, tipping the vodka bottle to his lips. I beelined straight to the next room, bursting through the doors just as Uncle Luke's screams rang out.

"Son of a bitch!"

The surly hunter was sprawled on his back on top of what usually served as our dining room table with the bottom half of his pants torn to shit. His exposed leg was a gruesome sight, bloody and mangled down to the bone. Dad stood hunched over him with a pair of surgical forceps in his hand, trying to pry something loose from Uncle Luke's raw flesh.

"Hold him still!" he barked at the other two males holding my uncle's upper body down. "I've almost got it!"

Got what?

I rounded the table to my father's side. He didn't acknowledge me, nor did I expect him to. I quickly looked him over. He was covered in blood, but none of it seemed to be his own. Aside from a few minor bruises that had already turned purple, he was in pretty good shape.

Looking down, I watched as he carefully positioned the forceps, taking hold of something fat and curvy embedded deep inside Uncle Luke's thigh, four inches from his knee. When the forceps slipped, he tossed them aside and slapped the back of his hand against my chest, getting blood on my shirt.

"Get me the bigger forceps, son."

I moved on instinct, like the good soldier that I was. A fold-out leather carrier with surgical tools strapped to the inside was already rolled out on the floor. Spotting the bigger instrument, I plucked it from the case.

"Alcohol?" I asked the other two hunters in the room. They were identical twins, Vick and Vince. I'd met them before. They were members of Clint's crew and damn good hunters from what I've heard.

Vick, I think, nodded before snatching up a bottle of Grey Goose and tossing it to me. I caught it with one hand, the clear liquid sloshing around inside. The seal was already broken, half the contents gone.

Such a waste of good booze.

After today, the place would be bone dry. Tilting the bottle, I rinsed the forceps thoroughly before slapping it into my father's awaiting palm.

Refocusing, he went back in with the confidence of a trained surgeon, which he most certainly was *not*. But he had enough experience with battle wounds to know what he was doing. The sound of the forceps delving into raw flesh made me cringe, reminding me of a pot of mac and cheese being stirred.

Uncle Luke reared off the table, lifting his good leg and slamming it down until a piece of wood splintered off from the edge. "Jesus fucking Christ, Allister!" He fought against the twins who struggled to restrain him.

I mean, could you blame him? This was a bootleg surgery with nothing but vodka as anesthesia.

"Kai," came my father's imposing voice. "Hold your uncle."

Jumping in, I grabbed his good leg and held it down. "Chill, Unc," I said. "It's almost over." I didn't actually know if that was true, but it was the only reassurance I had to offer the man who had been like a second father to me my entire life.

His foul mouth went into overdrive as Dad continued pulling the object out at a painstakingly slow pace to avoid damaging any vital nerves. Halfway out, I realized what it was. A Wendigo's claw.

Shit. This wasn't good.

Wendigos were vile predators that feasted on human flesh. They were extremely poisonous and highly contagious. If they managed to get their toxin into your bloodstream, you would turn in a matter of days.

Uncle Luke let out a groan once the claw was free from his thigh. Lifting his head, he locked eyes with my father. "Well? Is it laced?"

Dad remained quiet, his gaze dropping to the claw, carefully examining it with the forceps. He was checking for any traces of the green substance that would mark death for my uncle.

I held my breath with everyone else in the room.

"For fuck's sake, Allister," Uncle Luke griped. "If it is, just gimme a fucking gun. I'll put a bullet in my own goddamn head if I have to, you hear me?"

"Relax, Luke," Dad said, as calm and collected as always. He was our leader for a reason. "You're fine. The claw is clean. Looks like it wasn't trying to turn you."

The other hunter grunted, letting his head fall back on

the table with a thump. "No, the fucker just wanted to take me out for breakfast."

The twins laughed, the mood lightening immensely.

Knowing that everyone was in the clear, I finally allowed the tension to drain from my body. "How did this happen?" I asked. "Zane said you got bad intel."

Dad nodded as he got to work disinfecting his brother's leg so he could stitch him up. "When we first heard about the killings, it didn't sound like anything more than a small pack. The townsfolk we talked to confirmed as much, reporting two dead and three missing persons in the last two weeks. The body count wasn't high enough to suggest that we were dealing with any more than two, maybe three Wendigos."

I frowned. "How many were there?"

"Eight."

My eyes bulged. "You're joking."

"The ugly bastards must've been outsourcing," Uncle Luke said, his face twisting in pain as Dad threaded a needle through his gaping wound. "Hunting in different locations to spread out their kills and avoid detection."

It was unusually smart behavior for their kind, but not impossible, I suppose. "Did we lose anyone?"

"Two of ours," Vick said solemnly. "Rookies."

"Shit." I scrubbed a hand down my face. "Their bodies?"

"Gone," Vince added, his expression matching his twin's. "Couldn't even find bones to burn."

A grim silence fell over the group.

"I'm sorry," I said.

They both nodded, accepting my condolences.

"Hazards of the job," Vick said. "You know how it goes."

I did. All too well. But knowing that didn't make shit like this any easier. I turned to my father, trying to keep my own irritation at bay. "Why didn't you call me in with Clint's crew? I could've helped."

His eyes, identical to my own, flickered up to meet me before returning to my uncle's leg. "We had enough bodies, son. Besides, it would've taken you hours to get down there in time. Clint's crew was closer."

"It wouldn't have been hours if you had taken me with you in the first place."

His eyes flashed back to mine, wrinkles creasing the skin around them as they narrowed. I held his glare defiantly. I was tired of him treating me like a child when I was better at my job than most of the grown ass men currently licking their wounds.

"Now's not the time, boy." The timbre in his voice held a clear warning to back off. Let it go.

Fuck that. "This could've been avoided. I'm the best tracker we have. I would've found their nest long before you had to call in for reinforcements."

A muscle ticked in my father's jaw just as Uncle Luke chimed in. "The boy's right, Allister. He should've been there. His skills would've made that job easier and you know it."

He was the next recipient of my father's ire. "You should worry less about *my* boy and more about *yours*, Luke. This never would've happened if he wasn't so fucking reckless."

Wait, what?

Uncle Luke scowled but said nothing, letting my father

take the win. As usual. Winning was what Allister Slade did. Arguing with him was futile.

"Zane caused this?" I asked.

No one answered.

I cursed under my breath. The one time I wasn't there to babysit his ass and look what happened. I turned to leave.

"Malakai."

I craned my neck back to look at my father. His expression hardened, indicating that this conversation would continue at a later date. "If you're so keen on helping, clean and ditch the van I parked in the garage. It's stolen. We used it to bring your uncle back. Take Zane with you."

I nodded, grounding out a terse, "Yes, sir," before exiting the room. Zane was still at the bar, on the verge of killing the bottle of vodka he had pressed to his lips.

"Come on," I ordered, breezing past him. I knew he would follow. I was one of the few people the fucker actually listened to.

He stumbled off the barstool and stalked behind me. "Where we going?"

"My dad wants us to ditch the van. Where are the keys?"

I could hear him fumbling around in his pants pockets until a jingle sounded.

"I got 'em."

I held out my hand until the cool metal touched my palm. "I'll drive. Follow behind on your bike."

"Copy," he muttered.

I glanced at him as he moved to my side. "How drunk

are you right now?"

He threw me a lopsided grin, his glazed eyes darker than usual with heavy lids. "Not drunk enough."

Sigh. That was true. He'd be slurring if he was.

Walking across the lot to the garage, I unlatched the door to reveal a white van with blacked-out windows, the kind serial killers and kidnappers paraded around in. Walking around to the rear, I gestured for Zane to spring the back doors as I searched the shelves in the garage for lighter fluid and matches. Finding some, I tossed it in the back of the van, unfazed by the bloody mess that painted the walls and floor.

That was a shit-ton of DNA right there.

Staggering over to his bike, Zane pulled a pack of Dunhills from his back pocket. "You strapped?" he asked, pulling a cigarette free and holding it between his lips.

I nodded, opening the driver side door while using my other hand to feel for the gun tucked into the waistband of my—

I ground to a halt. *Fuck.* It wasn't there. *Where did I...?*

My eyes drifted shut, overcome by my own stupidity. I left it in my bag. The same bag I ditched before running out of class this morning.

With a curse, I slammed the door, causing Zane to whip around, holding his hands out as if to say, *what gives?*

"Change of plans. I gotta make a quick stop. Take the van somewhere isolated outside of town and drop me your location. I'll meet you there."

He dipped his head to light his cigarette, taking a deep

draw before blowing out a thick cloud of smoke. "Everything okay?"

I wasn't about to tell him or anybody else that I misplaced my gun. I would never hear the end of it. "It's fine." I tossed him the keys to the van. "I won't be long."

Catching them, he nodded, not pressing the issue. "Alright, then."

Swapping places with him, I walked over to my bike and climbed on, watching as Zane hopped in the van and tore out of the lot like it was his first time behind a wheel. The booze was definitely hitting him now. I'll have to hurry before he crashes the fucking thing.

Starting my engine, I blazed out of there in the opposite direction towards the school, hoping and praying my shit was still where I left it. Or got dropped off in the lost and found at the very least.

If anyone finds that gun, I'm fucked.

It was unlicensed with no serial number, a felony charge waiting to happen. Since I was no longer considered a minor, a gun charge would mean actual jail time. And the multiple hits on my already tarnished record, including aggravated assault, sure as fuck wasn't going to win me any favors in front of a judge.

Weaving in and out of traffic, I pushed my Harley way beyond the speed limit. If this day got any worse, I was liable to lose my shit on someone.

FIVE

Luna

"Would you stop pouting? You can give him back his stupid bag tomorrow, Sinclair."

Sitting on the counter in the girl's washroom, I watched Quinn touch-up her gothic makeup, kicking my dangling legs back and forth. "But the party is in three days. If I tell him last minute, he might not show."

She rolled her eyes at my whiny tone. "And three days doesn't qualify as last minute?"

I shrugged. Okay, fine, she had a point. I was just anxious to talk to Malakai again, hence why I'd been tormenting the hell out of Quinn all day. "Do you think he'll come?"

The blonde threw her head back and groaned. "Hecate, give me strength. If he says no, we'll get Anya to *convince* him to come. Happy?"

"Right," I drawled sarcastically. "Because it's every

girl's dream to have her crush coerced by her little sister to spend time with her."

Not that Anya wouldn't jump at the chance to use her blossoming abilities. At ten years old, she was the last witch in our coven to finally come into her powers. No one was surprised when it turned out to be the gift of persuasion. The little delinquent was always good at getting her way.

"Besides, what happened to *not* tricking him and doing it on my own?"

Quinn puckered her lips to apply her dark lipstick, smacking the top and bottom together when she was done. "And how's that working out for you, baby-cakes?"

"Wow, thanks for the vote of confidence, Quinn."

I mean, sure, I knew I had to get over this shy crap with Malakai if I wanted to get closer to him. *Maybe it wouldn't be so bad if I used my powers a little bit...*

Running her fingers through her blonde locks, Quinn flashed me a cheeky smile in the mirror. "I have the utmost confidence in you. In fact, why don't you go check and see if Prince Charming has returned. Lay some of that natural charm on him."

Natural charm. Yeah right. I possessed the least of that out of everyone in my coven. As enchanters, charm was supposed to be ingrained in our DNA, but Hecate must've skipped me when she was passing it out. I wasn't a smooth talker like my little sister, or a seductress like my Aunt Freya.

I knew I was beautiful. I wasn't blind. I saw the way people looked at me, my teachers included—as creepy as that was. But I wasn't a fan of the attention, all the admiring stares. At times I was tempted to throw up an illusion to make myself less attractive, but that was considered blasphemy in my coven.

You can't catch flies without honey, Luna-bear, my aunt would say. She was a big believer of *if you got it, flaunt it.*

Maybe it was time I started flaunting.

Sighing, I jumped down from the counter, hearing the last bell ring.

Home time.

"I'll meet you out front," I told Quinn on my way out. She was my ride today since Aunt Freya was busy setting up for my birthday festivities. She was thrilled when I had called to tell her the party was back on. I failed to mention the reason why, though. The last thing I needed was her giving me relationship advice.

I blushed just thinking about the sex talk she gave me when I turned twelve and woke up with blood stains on my sheets. Now *that* was a conversation no child should have to endure from the only mother figure in their life. The woman has no filter and even less shame, but she always meant well.

Stopping at my locker, I turned the dial and swung open the metal door. Malakai's bag sat on a hook across from mine. Should I take it with me? Or would that be too weird?

I can't believe I'm getting this worked up over a bag.

Making up my mind, I snatched it off the hook and swung one strap over my shoulder. Something dense and blunt hit the middle of my back. *What in Lucifer's name does he have in here?* It wasn't that heavy, but it definitely didn't feel like textbooks either.

"Not my business," I muttered, slamming the door shut and crossing the hall to the stairwell. As I passed the platform window again, I couldn't help but search for his bike out of sheer habit—

My pulse quickened the moment my eyes landed on his black Harley. *He came back.* He was parked illegally along the curb that led up the stairs to the front entrance. The only reason anyone would park there was if they were in a rush.

He must be looking for his bag.

Gathering my courage, I skipped down to the first floor, keeping my eyes peeled for any signs of him. Deciding it would be better to wait by his bike, I exited the building and made my way over to it. I stood awkwardly by the sleek machine, desperately trying to calm my racing heart.

"Pull it together, Sinclair," I mumbled to myself, drying my sweaty palms on the front of my jeans. "You already talked to him once, you can do it again."

People probably thought I was crazy, standing there talking to myself. Some shot me strange looks, no doubt wondering why I was standing next to Malakai Slade's bike like I owned it. Everyone knew it was off-limits. Rumor had it he once beat a kid within an inch of his life just for sitting on it.

I looked it over, admiring the way it gleamed in the sunlight. Although Malakai had been driving the Harley for the past two years, it was still in mint condition. Not even a speck of dust coated the polished exterior. He obviously treasured it enough to take good care of it. I reached out to touch the silver handlebar when a voice startled me from behind.

"That's my bag."

Spinning around, I came face-to-face with the man himself. I gripped the strap on my shoulder and plastered on the biggest smile I could muster. *Charming. Be charming.* "Hi." A good start. My voice didn't squeak, so I took it as a win.

His steely eyes narrowed into slits. "Why do you have my bag?"

My smile faltered at his sharp tone, not sounding nearly as grateful as I thought he would've. "You left it in class this morning. I came to return it to you." Slipping it off my shoulder, I held it out to him. "Here."

His eyes dipped to the bag, then back up at me. "Did you look inside?"

Again, that wasn't the reaction I was anticipating. Something about his tone came across as deadly. I frowned. "Uh, no, I didn't. I don't make it a habit to rifle through people's things."

"Hmm." That was all he said before taking what was his and brushing past me to his ride. I blinked, indignation washing over me as he mounted the bike without a second glance in my direction, slinging the bag onto his back as he reached for his helmet.

Okay. Rude.

The blatant disrespect had me stepping in front of his Harley, grabbing the handlebars to prevent him from taking off. "Excuse me, but when someone does something nice for you, the least you can do is say *thank you*."

He met my glare with lifted brows, surprised by my sudden boldness as much as I was. The longer I stood there, the more I started to panic.

Shit...what now?

He didn't respond right away, probably pondering his next move just as I was. Suddenly, he leaned forward, draping his forearms over the shiny metal rod that connected his handlebars, his hands dangling between us. We were closer now, the proximity causing my breath to hitch for a millisecond.

Clearing my throat, I jerked back, remembering that he didn't like it when people touched his bike. "Sorry," I murmured, my face heating.

Nothing about this interaction showcased my charm!

Biting my lip, I retreated a step, unable to meet his scrutinizing gaze. When he continued to say nothing, I turned from him, ready to erase this moment from my brain forever.

"Don't apologize," came his deep, rumbly voice. I turned back to see the corner of his lips curve into a smirk. "You're right. I was an ass before. I'm sorry."

Okay. I was definitely *not* expecting that.

I opened and closed my mouth, not sure what to say to that. *Alright, Luna, time to think like the enchantress that you are!* Clearing my throat, I mirrored his smirk with one of my own. "Yeah, you were, but I guess I can forgive you."

I mentally patted myself on the back when his smirk turned into a full-blown smile. Damn, he was gorgeous. I almost swooned on the spot, butterflies erupting in my stomach.

"Thank you for returning my bag, Luna."

I nodded, flipping my long hair over my shoulder, playing it cool like my name on his lips didn't make me want to faint. "You're welcome."

His eyes deliberately skimmed my body from head to toe before leaning back and balancing up on his bike.

Is he checking me out?

Excitement flooded me, almost making me forget the reason I did all of this in the first place.

As he started his engine, I rushed forward. "Wait!"

His head snapped up, a frown marring his face. "I'm kind of in a hurry."

"This won't take long," I said, inhaling a quick breath. "It's my birthday this weekend, and I'm having a party. It would mean a lot to me if you could come."

There. I said it.

He tipped his head to the side, a curious look on his handsome face as his brows drew down over his eyes. "Why?"

I blinked. "Sorry?"

"Why would it mean a lot to you? You barely even know me."

Shit. I should've worded that better. "Well, maybe I'd like to change that."

Was that too flirty?

He didn't seem to mind, his expression softening the tiniest bit. "I don't do parties. Sorry."

My heart sank like the fucking Titanic. "Oh…that's okay. No worries." I tried to keep the disappointment out of my voice but failed. "Maybe some other time." With that, I stepped back onto the curb, clearing the way for him to leave.

But just as the growl of his engine came to life, a finger tapped my shoulder. I turned to see Quinn standing there with a shit-eating grin on her face. "Bad news, Sinclair. I can't drop you off today. Something came up."

Huh? I frowned. "Something like what?"

She clapped me on the shoulder and strutted away, waving her hand in the air. "I'll explain later. See you tomorrow!"

"Quinn, wait!" I yelled after her retreating form. "How the hell am I supposed to get home?" She ignored me all the way to her tricked-out Dodge Charger Hellcat, the metallic purple paint with the black racing stripe shimmering in the sun as she jumped in and sped off, ignoring her brakes like they didn't work.

My jaw dropped.

She really left me. *Bitch!*

Looking around, I realized almost everyone I knew had already left for the day.

Well…*almost* everyone.

Feeling his eyes bore into my back, I turned to face Malakai. He was still parked exactly where I left him.

I'm going to kill Quinn.

"You need a ride?" he asked.

My eyes widened, the offer leaving me speechless for a second. "Didn't you say you were in a hurry?"

Pulling out his phone, he tapped the screen to check something and shrugged. "Your place is on my way. It's no problem."

"You know where I live?"

He looked at me like I was the dumbest person alive.

"Doesn't everyone?"

Oh, right…

I blushed profusely, my mouth going dry. I eyed his motorcycle and swallowed. It wasn't the *getting on* part that made me nervous, it was the *holding on* that made my stomach clench. The way he smiled at me only made the heat in my face spread to the rest of my body.

"You ever been on a bike before?"

I shook my head, losing the ability to speak.

"Put this on." He handed me his helmet and shrugged off his backpack, cramming it into a small side compartment below his seat.

Sweet baby Lucifer, am I really doing this?

Gingerly accepting the helmet, I secured it to my head and took a timid step towards him, almost recoiling when he reached out to fasten the strap below my chin, the brush of his fingertips against my skin nearly giving me a heart attack.

Be cool. Be cool. Be cool.

But the palpitations didn't stop there. Taking my hand, he helped me onto the back of his bike, waiting until I swung my leg over and properly straddled the seat before letting go. Blowing out a trembling breath, I reached back to get a grip on my seat—

"Not there." Taking my hand, he pulled my arm forward to curl around his waist. "Like this."

Hesitantly, I moved my other arm to follow suit, locking them both around him. The position shifted me closer to his leather-clad back, forcing me to inhale the dark spices of his cologne mixed with cigarette smoke. The scent oddly suited him.

"Where should I put my feet?" I asked.

From his side profile, I saw him smile. Reaching down, he gripped the back of my knee and lifted my leg until I felt a foothold, his touch making my nether region tingle.

I gulped. *Oh, my...*

I was more than capable of finding the second foothold on my own, but I didn't have it in me to stop him when he bent to repeat the action on my other leg, my eyes transfixed by the mere sight of his hands on me.

They were so big and...masculine.

Once he was satisfied with my position, he leaned forward and revved the engine, throwing a smoldering look over his shoulder at me. "Hold on tight."

I nodded against his back and did just that as we pitched forward, unable to stop the high-pitched squeal that escaped my lips. My arms tightened around his torso, my thighs practically squeezing him to death as the engine purred between my legs.

If my grip bothered him, he didn't voice it. But as we flew down the road, my hair whipping in the wind, I could've sworn I felt a soft chuckle vibrate through the cheek I had flattened against his back. Easing my grip a fraction, I allowed myself a moment to relish in this small victory.

Malakai *fucking* Slade was taking me home on his Harley.

Okay, maybe I won't kill Quinn, after all...

SIX

Malakai

Luna's body coiled around mine was more distracting than I anticipated. Coming to a stop sign, I glanced down at her hands fisted in my shirt. Something about the image filled my brain with wildly inappropriate thoughts, all of which involved her fisting other things…

Looking back at her, I smiled. Her head was pressed entirely against my back, her hair and helmet preventing me from getting a good look at her face.

"You good?" I asked.

Tipping her head up, she flashed me a tight-lipped smile. "Totally. Super good."

Shaking my head, I faced forward, hiding my amusement. "You don't have to be scared. I've got you."

"I'm not scared," she proclaimed defensively.

To prove her point, she released her death grip on my shirt, her hands flattening against my stomach instead.

The simple action sent molten lava coursing through my veins, heating my blood to an uncomfortable degree.

Inhaling sharply, I exhaled through my nose and readjusted my grip on the throttle. Maybe offering to take her home wasn't the best idea. Zane was waiting for me. I didn't have time for this.

So why did I offer?

When her friend bailed on her, it didn't seem right to just leave her there after she'd done me a major solid without even realizing it. If she had sneaked a peek inside my bag, I was fairly certain we'd be having a very different conversation.

Trying my best to stay focused, I turned down the long stretch of road leading to her family's estate, passing a sign that read: *Private Property*. Willow trees lined the narrow road on both sides, all the way up to a twenty-foot-tall iron fence. The entire perimeter was gated and equipped with enough security cameras to protect the fucking President.

Slowing to a stop, I put a foot down to balance my bike. This was the closest I've ever been to the Sinclair house. Beyond the fence was another stretch of road, this one unpaved and lined with the same weeping willows that stood behind me. Frogs croaked in the distance, reminding me that the area was built on top of a bayou. Why anyone would want to live near a swamp was beyond me.

Rich people, I inwardly scoffed. "Rainy season must be a bitch out here."

Luna giggled. "It's not so bad."

I searched the gate for an intercom system. "Is there a

code you gotta punch in or…"

Unlatching her arms from my waist, she sat back and unfastened her helmet. "Uh, actually, that's okay. I can walk from here."

As she shifted to climb off, a deep wave of disappointment crashed into me, already missing the firm press of her breasts against my back, the feel of her hands on my body. Shaking it off, I narrowed my gaze past the gate. There were no houses anywhere in sight.

Shaking her auburn hair free of my helmet, I frowned as she handed it back to me. "You sure? I don't mind driving you to your door. Seems like a far walk."

Why was I pushing this? I had places to be, for fuck's sake!

But I wanted to see her home safely. My eyes fell to her lips as she pulled the bottom one between her teeth, hands slipping into the back pocket of her jeans. Her hair glowed brighter in the afternoon sun, the reddish tones standing out in stark contrast against her milky skin. She ran her fingers through the wind-tousled strands, combing out the knots that had formed on the drive over. The soft tresses fell neatly back into place as if they hadn't been spoiled to begin with.

Had she always been this beautiful?

I mean, I always knew her to be pretty, but right now she was something else…

When my staring became too much for her to bear, she looked away, her cheeks flooding with color. "It's not that far, really. The road is deceiving. There's kind of a hill just beyond the trees. Thank you, though. For the ride."

Glancing beyond the gate, I couldn't see any hill, but I

took her word for it. "Alright, then," I nodded, slipping my helmet back on. "I guess I'll see you around."

And there was that smile again, the one that did weird shit to my chest, my heart skipping beats like it was about to malfunction. That couldn't be normal, right?

She ducked her head and stepped back against the gate, looping a slender hand around one of the metallic bars. "Come to my party Saturday night and you definitely will."

Yeah. My heart really shouldn't be beating like that.

Spinning my Harley back the way I came, I turned to look at her, a slow grin stretching across my face. "I'll think about it," I said, not wanting to make any promises I couldn't keep.

She smiled, honey-brown eyes sparkling. She had dimples. Why have I never noticed that before?

"Good." She raised her hand in a little wave. "Goodbye, Malakai."

My name falling from her lips had me gripping my handlebars extra tight. I didn't want to leave. I wanted to stay, to spend more time with her, get to know her. But that wasn't an option.

"Later."

Forcing myself to turn from her, I took off before she managed to change my mind. The urge to glance back was strong, but I resisted. I had no place for this in my life right now. No place for *her*.

I cursed as reality sank in. As tempted as I was, no good would come from me starting a relationship with Luna Sinclair. Besides, I wasn't her type. She may like the idea of me—the bad boy with the motorcycle and tattoos—but she had no fucking clue what came with the package.

If she did, she'd want nothing to do with me...

Rich girls like her wanted nice guys they could bring home to their parents and show-off to their friends. I wasn't good for any of that. Unless she was interested in some casual, no-strings-attached sex, I had fuck else to offer her.

But she seemed like too nice of a girl for a quick hit-it-and-quit-it romp in the sack. As much as I was feeling her, it didn't seem right to do her like that.

No. It's best I stay away...for both our sakes.

Passing the *Leaving Deadwood* sign, I headed out of town, following the location Zane had sent me. It was dark by the time I found him. He was about an hour out, parked along a lonely strip of road off the interstate. Pulling up beside the white van, I rapped my knuckles on the window to get his attention.

He was sleeping.

He jumped at the sound, reaching for the Glock in his lap. When his eyes landed on mine, he shook his head and rolled down his window. "You scared the piss out of me, asshole."

"Then don't fall asleep on the job next time, dipshit."

He scowled, looking like absolute crap with deep bags under his eyes. I kind of felt guilty dragging him all the way out here after he had just returned from a grueling hunt, but I wasn't the one calling the shots. Besides, he was better off here with me than stuck at home with our fathers, who he managed to piss off yet again with his reckless behavior.

He rubbed his tired eyes, slipping a cigarette between his lips. "I wouldn't have fallen asleep if you had gotten your ass here sooner. Where the hell were you, anyway?"

"I had to take care of something. It wasn't that long, don't exaggerate."

"Yeah, whatever," he scoffed, dipping his head to meet his lighter, the flickering orange flame burning the tip of his cigarette. Taking his first pull, he turned to blow the smoke out the window. Then he froze, his gaze fixating on me, lids lowering into a squint. "What the fuck is that?"

I turned, assuming he was talking about something behind me. "What?"

Reaching forward with his cigarette in hand, he plucked something from my helmet with his thumb and index finger.

"This," he said, holding up a long string of auburn hair.

Fuck.

Watching the single strand blow in the wind between us, I quickly dismissed whatever theories my cousin was about to bombard me with. "It's nothing."

Zane cocked his head to the side, analyzing both the strand and my face like they were clues on one of our hunts. And then a grin split his face wide open, as devilish and mischievous as the glint in his eyes. "Nothing, huh? And what exactly were you and '*nothing*' doing?"

I rolled my eyes, purposely ignoring the question. "Come on. Let's get this done. Follow me."

I pulled off from the road, driving deep into the field before deciding on a spot. We were surrounded by farmland, with no signs of life for at least another fifty miles.

Bringing the van to a halt, Zane threw it in park and hopped out, strutting towards me with the same stupid smirk on his face.

"Don't," I warned. As much as I loved the guy, he was the last person I wanted to confide in about my love life.

"Oh, come on!" he whined, pitching his cigarette to the ground and stomping it out. "Who's the girl, stud?"

"Your mom," I deadpanned, making my way over to the van to retrieve the lighter fluid and matches from the back.

Zane barked out a laugh. "You couldn't handle my mom, dude. That's why she left my dad. Poor bastard couldn't cut it either."

Unscrewing the tin, I doused the inside of the van with fuel before coating the outside, making sure it was good and soaked.

"You need counseling. Gimme a cig," I said, throwing the empty canister aside and backing away.

Reaching for his Dunhills, Zane flipped open the top of the pack and passed it to me. Pulling one free, I placed it between my lips and lit a match, striking it against the rough part of the little box it came out of. I brought up my hand to cup the flame, shielding it from the wind as I lit the business end. I took a deep drag and then tossed the still-lit match onto the hood of the van. It went up in flames in no time, the inferno quickly spreading from the front to the back, effectively destroying every piece of evidence linking it to us.

We stood there for a while, just watching it burn.

"Did you fuck her at least?" Zane asked, breaking the peaceful silence I was enjoying. He was like a dog with a fucking bone.

"It wasn't like that."

His brows shot up into his hairline. "Oh? What was it like, then?"

Tossing my cig, I started towards my bike. "Why the sudden interest in my sex life?"

He chuckled, trailing behind me. "Cause you haven't fucked anyone since Clint's daughter. Call me curious."

I whipped around, forcing him to stop in his tracks when we nearly collided. "You didn't tell him about that, did you?" My tone was harsh, making it clear that I wasn't fucking around.

Zane actually looked offended for a second, his face twisting in disgust. "Why the fuck would I do that? I ain't no snitch."

No. He wasn't. But he was different these days, so I couldn't be too sure.

Accepting his answer, I climbed onto my bike and tossed him my helmet. "Good. Cause I'd hate to have to shoot her old man if he ever comes at me for defiling his little girl."

Snorting obnoxiously, Zane climbed on behind me. He hated riding bitch, but he didn't have a choice tonight. "Little girl, my ass. Sarah Donavan's been gargling dick since she was in braces."

"I don't think that would help me with Clint," I drawled. Hunters were a temperamental breed. Although we ran in close-knit circles, that didn't exempt anyone from getting their ass beat if they started crossing lines they weren't supposed to. Clint was my father's oldest living friend and ally, and me messing with his daughter would be viewed as a form of disrespect, making the whole *Brothers in Arms* thing null and void.

Don't shit where you eat, is what my father would say. It wasn't good for business. For anyone.

Driving back out to the road, Zane clapped a hand on my shoulder. "So, the redhead. Did you fuck her?"

Sigh. It was going to be a long ride home.

SEVEN

Luna

When Malakai disappeared down the road, I exhaled the breath I was holding. It was a bad idea, letting him drive me home. But when the opportunity to spend more time with him presented itself, I couldn't turn it down.

Dropping my hand from the iron bar, I walked through the gate, the illusion dissipating around me. None of it was real. Not the perimeter-lined gate, not the security cameras, none of it. The illusion *was* the security. It was intimidating enough to keep humans and other unwanted trespassers off our land.

And it didn't stop there.

The spell continued on for miles, just an isolated stretch of road lined with trees that led to absolutely nowhere. If someone was to get past the front gate, I would feel the trigger—having designed the spell myself–

–allowing me time to bend and shape the landscape accordingly. In truth, there was no road leading up to the house. The black and gray stone manse stood just beyond the fake gate, immersed within the swamp.

To humans, the great stone manor appeared posh and elegant, a home fitting for some of the richest folks in town. But, in reality, it was covered in moss and thorn-filled vines, built around a marsh pit infested with crocodiles and snakes. The same willow trees that lined the road surrounded the property. The soft glow of torches embedded in the ground illuminated the long pathway to the door.

It was the kind of place that screamed, *Witches Live Here!* All we needed was a neon sign on the front lawn.

Each coven occupied a different corner of Deadwood, each property just as remote and protected by magic. It was prime real estate as far as any of us were concerned.

Bypassing the façade, I sauntered up the cobblestone steps to the front door. The snakes that lay in my path slithered away, allowing me to pass. The door itself was over ten feet tall and made of pure iron, engraved with an image of our Dark Goddess, Hecate. The design was intricate with three versions of the Goddess standing back-to-back.

The Mother, the Maiden, and the Crone.

Each one held a different object in her hand—the middle a dagger, the left a snake, and the right a torch. Before entering, I lifted the pendant hanging around my neck from a thin gold chain to my lips and kissed it. As I always did.

Hecate's wheel.

The moon-like symbol consisted of a circular labyrinth with a star in the middle. The symbol was sacred to my people, representing all that which Hecate holds dominion over. The earth, sea, and sky. There wasn't a single witch among the five covens who would look upon her image without paying homage.

Slipping the pendant back beneath my shirt, I pressed onward, the door opening for me. Although the outside looked terrifying, the inside was the very definition of modern-chic, everything new and up-to-date. Waltzing across the front foyer over the large depiction of the triple moon painted over the floor—a full moon flanked by two crescents on either side—I turned into the kitchen.

The smell wafting up my nostrils made my mouth water.

Aunt Freya must be cooking.

And she wasn't alone.

I should've made a detour after the first moan, but it was too late. I entered the kitchen to see Aunt Freya leaning back against the wooden peninsula, her hands white-knuckling the edge with her head flung back in what appeared to be ecstasy. From my vantage point, I could see one of her legs thrown over the strapping shoulder of a male who was currently on his knees with her skirt draped over his head, blocking his face from view. But I already knew who it was.

William Blackwell.

Leader of the Blackwell Coven and the greatest elemental witch I'd ever seen. Most Blackwell witches had the ability to control one single element—wind, water, earth, or fire. Two, if they were skilled enough.

William, however, could control them all. He was their messiah, and for good reason. He and my aunt were somewhat of an item, although their relationship was very much on a need-to-know basis. Only a select few knew of their ongoing hook-ups, myself included.

Unfortunately.

Honestly, I would've been happier not knowing.

I cleared my throat loudly, making my presence known. "I guess I won't be eating in here anymore."

Aunt Freya tipped her head back to look at me, her ruby-red lips curving into a shameless grin. "Luna-bear! You're home."

Nodding, I plopped down on a barstool across from the happy couple. "I am. Hello, Mr. Blackwell."

Moving with little urgency, William Blackwell calmly removed his head from between my aunt's thighs and gently placed her leg back onto the floor. Smoothing down her skirt, he wiped his mouth with the palm of his hand and stood to his full height.

"Good afternoon, Luna. I do hope you're well," he said with his old-world accent.

Ever the gentlemen.

His smile was innocent and polite, like I didn't just catch him ravaging my aunt with his mouth in the middle of our kitchen. And not for the first time, might I add. I'd caught them in far more blush-worthy positions, and each time the man remained utterly unabashed.

Maybe they really are meant for each other.

I often thought of them as the Ken and Barbie of the five covens. Like my aunt, William was extremely attractive. Tall, brawny, and charming. They both had dark features, raven-black hair and fair eyes beneath thick lashes. His were cerulean while hers were the same as mine, amethyst and pupilless.

Giggling like a witch barely out of her teens and *not* over three centuries old, Aunt Freya used her thumb to clean what was left of herself off her lover's face. "William just dropped by to help me set up for your party, Luna-bear. It was very sweet of him to offer his aid, especially so last minute."

Ignoring the dig at my indecisiveness, I propped my chin on my palm and shot them both a dry look. "Oh? Will the party be held under your skirt, then, Aunty?"

William ducked his head and chuckled, receiving a playful glare from my aunt. "Forgive us. We merely got distracted," he said.

I smiled and shook my head. I'd grown immune to their vulgar displays months ago. "I noticed."

Narrowing her pupilless gaze at me, Aunt Freya leaned across the island, lessening the gap between us. "I noticed a few things myself. Like you out front with that boy. Care to share, love?"

I gaped. She saw that? "How did you—"

Her smirk was catty and oh so typical of her. "Oh, sweetie, I see everything."

The swamp creatures. Of course.

I'd forgotten all about them. Enchanting men wasn't the only gift my aunt possessed. She could enthrall animals as well, controlling them to do her bidding. The creatures of the swamp were practically her little spies, reporting back every detail no matter how small.

I guess Ken and Barbie weren't the only ones who had

been distracted...

I should've known better.

"Which one of the little critters ratted me out? The snakes?"

"The crows," Aunt Freya admitted, straightening her disheveled clothes.

Dammit. I didn't even clock those beady-eyed bastards flying around. They had always been the most discreet of my aunt's henchmen.

Falling mute, I sat there fidgeting as they both gawked, waiting for an answer. When Aunt Freya cocked a brow, I caved. "He's just a boy from school."

"You don't talk to any boys at school," she declared bluntly, shaming me in front of William. "Especially not ones like *that*."

Blushing, I puffed out my cheeks. "I do so talk to boys. Lots of them."

Reaching out, she bopped me on the nose like a child. "Boys in the other covens don't count, love."

"Freya, leave the child be," William said, jumping to my defense. I always did like him.

"I'm merely taking an interest in my niece's love life. Is that not allowed? Especially since I've never seen you take much of one yourself, Luna-bear."

Biting the bullet in hopes of ending this embarrassment, I came clean. "It was Malakai Slade."

All sound drained from the room. A beat later, my aunt's eyes widened with utter glee. "*The* Malakai Slade?"

I nodded curtly, feeling my face heat just from the mention of his name.

William's gaze darted between us, trying to keep up. "Who is this Malakai?"

"Luna-bear's future husband."

"Aunt Freya!"

She shrugged, brushing off my mortification. "What? Isn't that what you have scribbled all over your notebooks? Luna *Slade*, I believe it was."

Oh, dear Goddess...

Dropping my head in my hands, I hid my flaming face from view.

Aunt Freya chuckled. "Stop your dramatics. You've walked in on William and I acting out every position in the Kama Sutra, yet discussing this human boy sets your cheeks ablaze."

William cleared his throat and mumbled, "Surely not *every* position. I could still think of a few…"

"Oh, Hecate!" I cried, springing off the barstool and storming towards the exit.

"Hold it, young lady."

Freezing, I turned back.

Both she and William wore identical smiles, relishing in my discomfort a little too much. "Tell me, why the sudden change of heart concerning your birthday?"

"Yes, I too am curious," William said. "You made it quite clear to us all that you would partake in nothing more than the ritual."

I began fidgeting again. Now was as good a time as any to ask. "Since I'll be graduating soon…I figured it'd be a good way to close out the year and spend some time with my human friends before they go off to college."

There was a lengthy pause.

"You wish to invite *humans* to your birthday?" Aunt Freya asked as if unsure whether or not she heard me right.

I nodded nervously. "Just a few, yes."

"Luna," William chimed in softly. "You know that will be difficult."

"It would be just for the after-party," I rushed to explain before they could officially shoot me down. "And only for a few hours. They probably won't even stay that long."

A light frown marred my aunt's beautiful, forever youthful, face. "The risk of exposure is too great, Luna. You know that."

Feeling the *no* coming on, I pushed harder. "Please, Aunt Freya. I'll work the illusions myself. I promise I won't let anything slip." My illusion skills were unmatched, equal to none within our coven—not even hers.

She paused, contemplating my request. Her silence gave me hope. "How many humans will attend?"

I only wanted one, but that would look too obvious. "Eight. Ten tops." My human circle wasn't that big to begin with. The number was more than manageable.

Aunt Freya smiled. "I take it motorcycle boy will be in attendance as well?"

Chewing my lip, I nodded. Then I waited. And waited...

"Very well," my aunt said with a sigh. "No more than ten, though. Do you hear me?"

I bounced on my feet, giddy with excitement. "Yes, ma'am."

She flicked her hand dismissively. "Go on, then. The others will be over shortly to discuss your plans. I'm sure they will be willing to lend a hand."

Squealing, I ran from the room, more excited for my birthday than I was this morning.

"You shouldn't encourage her and the human boy," I heard William's voice echo as I neared the staircase leading up to my bedroom. I stopped to listen, my foot paused on the first step. "Mortals can never understand the life we live, nor can they be a part of it."

"It's just a crush," Aunt Freya insisted. "I'm sure it will pass. She's graduating, let her have her fun. After Saturday, she will no longer be a Witchling. Her new life will begin, and this boy will be but a blip in her old one."

My new life…

My mood took a dive at the reminder, putting me back in the same sour headspace I was stuck in that morning. Having heard enough, I crept my way upstairs, shaking my aunt's words from my head.

If Malakai was meant to be a blip in my life, I would make damn sure he was a memorable one.

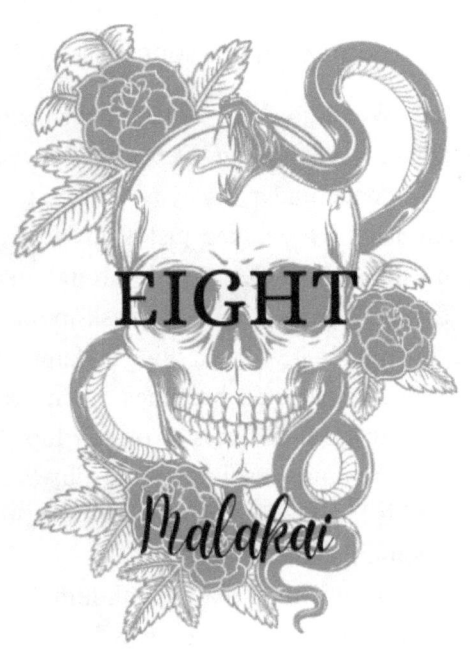

EIGHT

Malakai

"**Y**ou sure you're okay?" I asked Zane for the third time as we trudged through the dense forest located two towns over in Gravenhurst.

We were investigating a potential hunt. Some of the townspeople had reported strange occurrences in these woods, hikers wandering in and never wandering back out. Rumors of it being haunted were beginning to spread. But it was far more likely that something sinister was going on.

Since today was Senior Ditch Day, I convinced my dad to let me take this one, dragging Zane along for the ride. No one fought me on it. They were all still pretty pissed at him for going rogue on the last mission and nearly getting his old man killed. I assumed he felt guilty about the whole thing.

Maybe that's why he's been acting so fucking weird.

Since the Wendigo hunt, Zane had been restless. Barely sleeping, hardly eating. Deep, dark circles took up permanent residence under his eyes, and he'd been more irritable than usual. He walked just a few feet in front of me, using his machete to clear a path through the shrubs.

"Jesus fucking Christ, Kai. If you ask me that shit one more time, I'll impale myself on this goddamn machete."

I ducked to avoid some branches he missed, freeing my own machete from the holster on my hip. "Could've fooled me. You're doing a shit job at this, by the way."

He swung his head back to level me with a glare. "You wanna take point, then, asshole?"

"Fine," I said, switching places with him. "Ladies with their periods should hang back, anyway."

He slapped my back lightly with the flat side of his blade. "Blow me."

Laughing, I continued hacking, keeping my eyes peeled for any signs of danger. "You didn't have to tag along if you didn't want to, you know."

He snorted. "It's better than being benched back at the yard avoiding death stares from your pops."

"What the hell happened out there, anyway?" I didn't know the details, only that Zane had broken rank. He got quiet, forcing me to glance back at him. "Well?"

His coffee-brown gaze hardened into steel. "When your pops ordered us to retreat the first time, I told him it was a bad idea. The longer we waited, those monsters would've killed more people. So, I went back in...before Clint's crew got there."

My eyes flared. "You didn't."

His lips twisted into a deep scowl, anger shining in his

eyes. "I had it under control! I rigged the cave they were nesting in remotely with dynamite. All I had to do was play bait long enough to lure the lot of them inside. The explosion would've done the rest."

It wasn't a terrible plan. Wendigos were vulnerable against fire. "Why didn't you just let everyone in on your plan?"

"I did!" he said, frustrated even now with the outcome. "Your pops shot me down, and mine agreed with him. Said it was too dangerous and we wouldn't get close enough to rig the cave in time. So I did the shit myself. Would've worked too, if everyone hadn't shown up when they did."

Though I understood his side of things, it didn't matter. "You disobeyed a direct order, Zane. Did you really think that shit was going to go over well?"

He grunted out a tsk. "It was a dumb fucking order. I saw another way, and I took it. I was steps away from luring every single Wendigo into that cave when I heard the gunfire. The herd scattered after that, forcing us to take them down one by fucking one. It wasn't my fault my old man got hit, or that Clint lost two of his own. Everyone just wants someone to fucking blame, and I'm the easy target. Well, fuck that. I ain't apologizing for doing my goddamn job."

Sighing, I scrubbed a hand down my face. The OG's in the hunting community weren't good at taking suggestions from young bloods. My father and uncle especially. They gave the orders and we were expected to follow them.

No questions asked.

But the older we got, the more that *good little soldier* act was getting played out. Although Zane was reckless, his instincts were solid. He was a damn good hunter, but that didn't exempt him from following orders like the rest of us.

"They'll get over it. Give it—" I froze, catching sight of a set of tracks in the dirt. I bent to inspect it.

"What is it?" Zane asked, peering over my shoulder.

"It's human," I said, examining several other footprints. Some were barefoot while others wore shoes.

"More hikers, probably. You'd think they would stay *out* of the woods people keep vanishing in. I swear, some motherfuckers deserve to be eaten alive."

I rolled my eyes. "Nice, Zane. Whoever they are, we need to find them and get them out of here until we can figure out what's going on. We're not even sure if this is our kind of case yet. Might be nothing."

Following the tracks to a steep ridge, we both came to an abrupt halt at the sound of low, thumping music coming from the other side. Voices overlapped one another, laughter and shouting and…splashing? Pressing our backs against the slope, we discreetly peered over the ledge.

It was a watering hole. A rather large one with a tumbling waterfall at the helm. There were at least forty people present, all teenagers in swimsuits and flip-flops.

Fuck.

I recognized some of the faces in the crowd. They were all seniors at Deadwood High.

"Looks like a party," Zane murmured.

"They're from my school. It's Senior Ditch Day."

"Seriously?" He slapped my arm with the back of his hand. "Why the hell didn't you go?"

I looked at him like he was missing brain cells. "Because I'm here working a job with you, genius."

"No shit. This could've waited, though. Hell, we'd probably have better luck after dark, anyway."

"Or *now*, since it's like a fucking monster buffet out there," I hissed, stating the obvious.

He blinked, understanding dawning. "Shit."

"Exactly."

He poked his head back over the ridge. "How do you want to handle this? They won't just clear out if we ask nicely."

Pinching the bridge of my nose, I unhooked my holster and handed it to him along with my machete. "Wait here. I'll go see what I can do."

"Bring me back a beer."

Ignoring him, I jumped the slope and made my way down to the party. Things were in full swing, the booze flowing. Nearly everyone had a red plastic cup in hand. Most of the girls were either sunbathing or floating around on inflatables in the water while the jocks were busy doing keg stands. The music was loud but not deafening, coming from a handful of Bluetooth speakers mounted on rocks near the water's edge.

This was a disaster.

Out of all places, why the hell would they choose to have Senior Ditch Day *here*?

There were no cars parked nearby, which meant everyone likely parked near the roadside and hoofed it up the trail. Zane and I had rode in from the opposite end, missing the crowd altogether.

How the fuck am I supposed to get everyone out of here? They were all sitting ducks, waiting to be hunted by whatever may be lurking in these woods and making people go *poof.*

More than a few curious stares landed in my direction. Not surprising. This was the first time anyone had ever seen me at a party, of any kind, since my arrival at Deadwood High. Nothing about this was my scene, and every single person here knew it.

"Hi, Malakai."

I stiffened at the sound of her voice, not expecting to run into her way out here. Slowly, I turned, coming face-to-face with Luna Sinclair. Time seemed to stand still as I took her in. She was dripping wet. Tiny droplets of water cascaded down her pale skin. She stood before me barefoot in nothing but a two-piece red bikini. Her bottoms sat high on her hips, held together by strings on either side, the V shape drawing my eyes to the apex of her thighs. Forcing my gaze higher, I admired her toned stomach, accentuated by a belly-button piercing I never knew she had. The little studded jewel was silver and pink and sparkled in the sun. But it was the swell of her breasts that had me panting for breath, the perfectly rounded mounds sitting snug in her bikini top that was definitely too small for her, her nipples barely concealed.

One pull on those strings and she'd be naked...

Forcing myself to meet her honey-brown gaze, I sucked in a sharp breath. Her auburn hair was wet, sticking to her supple skin in the most exotic way. Beads of water clung to her lashes, glistening under the bright afternoon sun, making her look like a goddess.

I swallowed. *Fuck me.*

All the blood in my body rushed south, making my cock swell.

Slanting her head, she shot me a blinding smile, dimples and all. "Earth to Malakai. Hellooo."

Snapping to attention, I shifted on my feet, trying desperately to mentally soften the growing stiffness in my pants. "Hey," I gritted out. "What are you doing here?"

A stupid question, but it was better than staring at her in silence like a pervert.

She ran a hand through her wet hair, gathering it to one side so she could wring the water from it. "Same as everyone else. Ditching. I'm surprised to see you here."

I averted my gaze in dire need of a distraction. Just the sight of her wet and in that fucking bikini was enough to make me nut right now if I wasn't careful. "Likewise."

"I'm glad you're here, though."

Taken aback, my eyes snapped back to her face. "You are?"

Why did that make me strangely happy to hear?

She nodded shyly, color filling her cheeks. "When you didn't show up for class, I didn't think I'd see you at all today."

I balked at that. "You went to school today?" I was fairly certain she was the only senior who did.

The color in her cheeks deepened as she sputtered. "I mean, just for an hour...or two." She pulled on a lock of her hair, twirling it between her fingers. Her eyes flickered to mine, then swiftly looked away.

I studied her closely. This was the second time in two

days she'd gone out of her way to seek me out. Why else would she go to class before ditching to come here?

She was looking for me.

Before, I had chalked her sudden interest in me up to casual flirting. No big deal. Most girls at school were curious about me, I simply figured she was one of them.

But now...

Does Luna Sinclair actually like me?

NINE

Luna

Inner sexy, Luna. Find your inner sexy, I reminded myself encouragingly.

Flirting and seduction came so ridiculously easy for everyone else in my coven. Not me, though. Nope. I was a bumbling mess.

He probably thinks I'm stalking him or something. I blushed at the thought. Goddess, help me, this was embarrassing. I wanted to kick myself for practically admitting that I'd been looking for him. He wasn't stupid. He knew as well as I did that seniors never went to class on Senior Ditch Day—aside from the overachievers who wanted to impress colleges with their perfect attendance records.

But Malakai didn't like parties. He said so himself. After showing up to class only to find his seat empty, I'd hung around for a while until Quinn popped her head into my second period and pulled me out, insisting we ditch with everyone else.

Maybe lover boy will be there, she'd said. Jokingly, of course.

But low and behold...

I thought I was daydreaming when I first laid eyes on him, that I had somehow crafted an illusion upon myself, reaching a whole new level of pathetic-ness. But it really was him. In a matter of seconds, I rolled off my inflatable seahorse into the water and booked it for the shore, leaving behind a confused Quinn.

Glancing over my shoulder, I spotted her straddling my seahorse, staring back at me with a wolfish grin on her face. When she started humping the air-filled creature, I shot her a glare and turned back to Malakai.

"So," he said, lips curling mischievously. "Is there a reason you were looking for me?"

I didn't miss the way his eyes roamed my body, running over my exposed skin. I resisted the urge to cover my chest, feeling insecure under his gaze. I had a good body. Aunt Freya always encouraged me to show-off more of it, buying me clothes I had too much shame to ever wear.

Like today's outfit, for instance. Quinn had stolen the trashy swim suit from my closet with the intention of us coming here. And although the price tags had been attached, it was a couple years old and about two sizes too small. I begged her to take me home so I could change into something that actually *fit*, but she refused, insisting I looked mega-hot in the skimpy getup. That didn't stop me from adjusting the tiny triangles over my nipples every ten seconds to make sure I wasn't flashing anyone the goods.

But the appreciative glint in Malakai's smoldering gaze was making me reconsider my stance on modesty.

Clearly, he liked what he saw.

Now's my chance.

If there was ever a time to grow some of that swagger the rest of my coven liked to whip around, this was it.

Taking a step forward, I peered up at him from beneath my lashes and smiled. "Do I need a reason?"

His eyes grew hooded as he bridged the gap between us with another step. "I'm not someone you want to get close to, Luna."

His words shocked me almost as much as the heat pooling in his eyes, his pupils dilating. His fists balled at his sides as if he was restraining himself. Did he want to touch me?

I certainly wouldn't mind.

"I think I can decide that for myself, Malakai," I said, putting extra care into batting my lashes and holding eye contact despite my inner awkwardness.

Flirting was a lot of work.

I panicked slightly when his brows lowered, his expression morphing into one of irritation. "What exactly do you want from me?"

Huh?

My confidence faltered at his harsh tone, forcing me to take a step back. Had I done something to upset him?

I sputtered, timid Luna creeping back in. "I…just thought that maybe we could…"

"Could what?" he pushed, releasing an exasperated

breath like I was nothing but a bother to him. "Be friends? Date? I'm interested in neither. All I can offer you is a good fuck. Nothing more."

Ouch.

Using an illusion, I hid my wince, not wanting him to see the pain his words had inflicted. I replaced the image in his mind. To his eyes, I remained stoic, my expression the epitome of don't-give-a-fuck.

His words matched up flawlessly to the persona he'd been crafting from day one. The badass loner who didn't give a shit about anyone but himself. The disappointment that sank into the pit of my stomach left me feeling hollow and…foolish. Foolish to think my silly little crush actually had a chance of going somewhere, of becoming more than just the scenarios that occupied my mind.

At least I tried. Better to know the truth now than to be left wondering later.

Nodding sharply, I expanded the distance between us by a few more feet. "Good to know, but I'll pass on the fuck. Sorry to have bothered you. See you around." I turned from him, ready to storm off when his hand shot out and latched onto my arm. I slowly lowered my gaze to where his hand met my elbow, then lifted it to glare at him. "Let. Go." It was a warning, not a request.

I may not be as bold as the rest of my coven, but I refused to tolerate disrespect. From *anyone*.

He dropped his hand along with the attitude, his tone softening. "Look," he said. "You shouldn't be out here. It's dangerous."

Come again?

"Dangerous?" I said, blinking slowly.

He nodded, his expression grim.

I took a mental snapshot of the area, seeing nothing but a bunch of high school seniors blowing off steam. Over by the waterfall, Quinn was getting ready to do a cannonball off the rocks from above, the crowd below cheering her on.

"Yeah. Super dangerous," I mocked with a straight face. "Maybe we should call the sheriff and inform him of the perilous situation we've found ourselves in before someone gets hurt."

He scowled. "I'm serious. None of you should be here. People disappear in these woods. It's not safe."

I paused. He was being serious. "How do you know that?"

He grunted as if the answer was obvious. "Don't you watch the news? It's not a secret."

Tilting my head, I crossed my arms over my chest. He followed the movement with his eyes, his gaze lingering for half a second before shifting back up into face territory. "If it's so dangerous, why are you here?" This conversation was ridiculous. Why was he trying to convince me to leave when he'd just shown up himself?

Just as he opened his mouth, a loud bang rang out. Then another, so loud I almost mistook it for fireworks. But when the third one boomed through the forest, I knew exactly what it was.

Gunshots.

"Gun!" someone hollered. Screams quickly followed.

My head whipped in every direction as people started to panic. Those in the water sprinted for shore, rushing to get back down the trail that led to their parked cars. Only

Quinn and two other witches from the Hollow Coven—Cara and Lea—remained, drifting on their floaties without a care in the world.

They wouldn't run and neither would I. Whoever fired those shots had no idea that *we* were the most dangerous things out here.

More than one person shoved me as they sped past, hauling ass to safety. I turned, expecting to hear an *I told you so* from Malakai, but he wasn't there.

He was gone.

I searched the dwindling crowd, but he wasn't among them. *Did he really just...leave me?* My disappointment grew.

The man hears gunshots and saves himself. How chivalrous.

It was a mistake getting to know him. He was a far cry from the man I thought he was. From the one I'd *hoped* he would be. His harsh words still stung, leaving a gaping hole in my chest.

Be friends? Date? I'm interested in neither...

If that was true, then why the sudden concern for my safety?

None of it made sense. I was so sure he felt what I felt. The way he looked at me...all the signs were there. How could I have been so off base?

"What in the seven hells was that?" Cara said, coming to stand behind me. Quinn and Lea joined us next, finally dragging themselves from the water.

I shook my head. "Sounds like a gun. Probably nothing. A lot of people go hunting in these woods. Deer, caribou, shit like that."

"Should we check it out?" Lea asked, carrying both my seahorse and her turtle. Only the four of us remained in the glade. Everyone else had cleared out faster than a stampede.

Quinn scoffed and started towards the trail. "Fuck that. Where there's guns, there's humans. Let them handle their own. Unless someone's paying us to investigate, I'm out."

Cara laughed. "Would you listen to her? Hasn't even gone on her first mission yet and she's already talking big."

"With the monsters she resurrects, she'll be *creating* jobs for us to go on," Lea jested.

"I'll remember that when one of you bitches gets popped in the field and needs me to work my magic!"

"I'll stay dead, thanks," Cara snickered. "I rather not end up like one of your Zombieland rabbits."

Quinn shoved a middle finger in Cara's face, her pale eyes shifting over to me as I trailed behind the three, periodically glancing over my shoulder for any signs of Malakai. "Sinclair, you alright?"

"I'm fine." My clipped tone suggested otherwise.

"What happened with lover boy?"

Wish I knew.

I shrugged, not feeling very chatty. Quinn knew me well enough to drop the subject as we neared her Dodge Charger. The car was the last one sitting along the dirt road, putting an abrupt and miserable end to Senior Ditch Day. The other girls took the time to deflate their floaties before getting in. I couldn't be bothered. I tossed mine over my shoulder, not caring where it ended up.

Accepting the pink towel Lea flung at me, I wrapped

the terry cloth around my waist and slid into the backseat, letting one of the other girls take shotgun. I ignored their concerned glances, turning my head to stare out the window as we drove off.

Aunt Freya was right.

Malakai Slade wasn't the guy for me. It was time to put silly crushes and mortal life behind me and finally become who I was always meant to be. To embrace my place within the coven.

Suddenly, I couldn't wait for graduation to be over with.

TEN

Malakai

I watched Luna and her friends leave before rounding on Zane. "What the fuck was that?" I hissed.

He shrugged, gun in hand. "You were taking too long to clear the place. My way was faster."

"And if the cops show? Someone probably called it in already, dumbass."

He returned my gun and machete before continuing into the shrubs. "We better hurry, then."

This fucking guy. "It's this rogue shit that keeps getting you in trouble, Z," I said, following behind him.

He barked out a laugh, shooting me a knowing smirk over his shoulder. "You're just pissed I interrupted your little one-on-one date back there. Is that the chick that had you running late the other day?"

Ignoring the question, I searched the area as we moved, looking for clues. Truth be told, I *was* a little pissed at the interruption. Something about Luna Sinclair had latched onto me and wasn't letting go. I actually enjoyed being near her, a rarity in itself considering I wasn't much of a people person. There was an undeniable attraction between us, one I couldn't let fester for too long.

Which wouldn't be a problem after what I'd said to her. I cringed recalling the way her face fell. My words were harsh, but necessary. I didn't need her in my life any more than she needed me in hers.

"I'll take that as a *yes*," Zane prattled on. "She's hot. From the looks of that awkward ass conversation you two were having, I'm guessing you haven't fucked her yet. You should. A sweet piece of ass like that will get tapped real quick if you don't move on it."

My eye twitched. The fact that Zane had even *looked* at Luna irked the shit out of me. My fingers curled into a fist, eager to connect with his face.

I exhaled a slow breath. *Stop it.* I barely know the fucking girl!

Drowning him out, I stooped down to examine a set of tracks in the dirt. "These are fresh." I pinched the soft soil between my fingers. "An hour, maybe less."

"Human?"

I caught sight of more to my left, but they were different. "Starts out human but changes into something else. Looks like hooves." I followed the trail off the beaten path, the terrain growing treacherous.

"I got your six," Zane said, gripping his gun in one hand and his machete in the next.

The trail led us to a small campsite where a single tent

was pitched. The firewood was cold, covered in ash and soot. A duffle bag sat on a nearby log, ripped open with its contents thrown about. Slowly, I reached for my gun, flipping off the safety and pointing it towards the tent. I nodded for Zane to cover the other side, which he promptly skirted around to.

The tent was already unzipped. Moving in, I slipped my barrel between the flaps and peeped inside. "Fucking hell," I muttered.

"What is it?" Zane asked.

Dropping my gun, I opened one side of the flap to reveal the carnage inside. The smell hit us right in the face. We both recoiled, covering our noses.

"Urgh," Zane grunted, mouth opening and closing on a gag. "That shit is foul."

A human corpse lay inside, a male, by the looks of it. His flesh had been torn from his bones, blood and guts coating the tent walls. Zane covered me as I crawled inside, inspecting the body carefully. The small patches of flesh that remained intact were already beginning to rot, but it was the teeth marks embedded in the skin that piqued my interest.

Something had eaten the poor bastard alive.

"So?" Zane called. "What are we dealing with?"

I backed out, drawing my flashlight from my holster. It was getting dark. "A Ghoul, I think. It would explain the human footprints that suddenly changed." Ghouls could shapeshift into their victims after consuming them, using the disguise to lure more people to their deaths. "It's most likely wearing this guy's face now."

"Which means the fucker should be close."

I nodded, walking over to the duffle covered in bloody handprints. "Looks like it went shopping before it took off." I followed another set of tracks towards the treeline. "This way."

"Should we call it in?"

I shook my head. "One Ghoul shouldn't be a problem."

Zane didn't argue, just fell into step beside me. As we approached the edge of the clearing, a pair of glowing yellow eyes blinked in the shadows beyond the trees, the setting sun shrouding the area in partial darkness. I held a hand out, signaling for Zane to stop. We both stood with our guns raised, aimed and ready to go.

And there it was.

I kept my hand up, waiting for the right moment to move in. It was a standoff. The creature was waiting for us to make the next move so it could strike.

That wasn't going to happen.

A minute ticked by. I could practically feel Zane twitching beside me. I shifted my gaze in his direction. Sweat beaded his brow as his finger jerked over the trigger of his gun. He cracked his neck from left to right as if trying to get himself right.

Strange.

This wasn't like him. Sure, he was a trigger-happy kind of guy, but he was never this anxious before a fight. Like me, he thrived when faced with danger with a steady hand, even if he lacked a steady head at times. Something was off with him…

I had no time to dwell on it, though, as the creature finally pressed go and came running. I quickly closed my hand into a fist once the Ghoul was within range, signaling for Zane to open fire. We pumped it full of lead, slowing it down just enough. Emptying my clip, I dropped my gun and reached for my machete.

"Hold!" I yelled.

Zane held his fire, allowing me to get close. The creature jerked back as the last slug hit its shoulder. It rebounded swiftly, lunging for me with its mouth jarred wide. Needle-like teeth dropped down from black gums, protruding in front of the human ones it wore as a disguise. I evaded the advance, pivoting behind it as I brought my blade up and swung, taking its head clean off. It hit the ground with a thump. The body went down next, dropping to its knees before collapsing on its front.

Zane approached with his flashlight, shining it on the Ghoul's face. "Doesn't look like a guy to me."

Frowning, I used my boot to tip the head up into the light. He was right. It was in the middle of shedding its skin when we found it, appearance partially that of a female with red hair. The facial features were not yet recognizable, twisted and distorted by the creature's true form.

"It must've gotten to someone right before we found it."

"Probably one of the kids from that party we broke up," Zane said, throwing me a look. "Isn't that girl of yours a redhead?"

My head whipped up, sending him a death glare for even suggesting what he was about to.

He held up his hands defensively, silently declaring he didn't want no smoke. "Hey, I'm just saying. The hair looks the same, don't you think?"

I took a closer look, inspecting whoever this was supposed to be. The body was still that of a male's, but the head was definitely female. And yes, the hair was…similar.

A strong sense of dread gripped me, twisting my gut. No. It wasn't possible. "I watched her leave."

"They all ran down the same trail after I fired off those shots, Kai. It could've easily snatched and killed one of them in the commotion."

Fuck. He was right.

And it was too dark to search for a body now. Even if we found one, it would be mangled and stripped bare, beyond recognition just like the guy in the tent. There would be no way to know for sure…

Spitting out a curse, I reached into my back pocket and tossed Zane my lighter. "Burn the bodies. We'll come back in the morning to search for more."

"Where are you going?" he hollered as I walked off.

"I'll meet you back at the yard." I didn't wait for his reply, just continued down the path leading to the main road where we parked our bikes. Zane was seasoned enough to handle clean-up duty on his own. I couldn't get Luna out of my head.

That hair…

It wasn't the same shade of red as hers, but it was too dark to be a hundred percent sure.

And I needed to be sure.

Reaching the road, I jumped on my bike and took off, circling back to the area closest to the watering hole to check for any abandoned cars.

It was almost a relief when I found none, that is, until I caught sight of an aqua green inflatable shaped like a seahorse abandoned on the side of the road. I remembered seeing quite a few floating around in the water earlier, but I hadn't paid attention to Luna's.

Did she even have one?

Revving my engine, I drove faster, my mind racing. She was fine. She had to be. I was just overreacting, being paranoid.

I managed to cut what would've been an hour's drive down to thirty minutes, breaking every traffic law imaginable to reach her house in record time. Passing the sign that read: *Sinclair Manor*, I swerved down the long road leading to her gate.

Parking my bike, I approached the iron barrier. How the hell was I supposed to get past it? Looking up into one of the cameras mounted at the very top, I waved. "Hello? Is anyone there?"

No answer. There was no speaker or intercom system either.

"Goddammit."

Cursing myself for not asking for her number sooner, I took a step back, prepared to scale the fucking gate. I jumped as high as I could, latching onto the bars that ran horizontally across the middle to propel myself further up. But just as I reached the top, about to hop over, things started to move.

Letting go, I jumped down, landing on my feet as the gate split wide down the middle. And that was when I saw her. Luna sauntered down the hill on the other side, wearing a pair of white cut-off shorts that hugged her curves and sat sinfully low on her swaying hips. Her fitted red halter top left her toned stomach on display, her crimson hair blowing in the wind behind her.

I grew nervous as she approached, my heart beating abnormally fast. She was very much alive and well. Not a scratch on her. *Thank God.* A suffocating weight lifted off my chest, one I didn't quite understand.

She came to a halt in front of me, hands tucked in the back pockets of her shorts. Flawlessly shaped brows drew down over her confused gaze. "What are you doing here, Malakai?"

Words escaped me.

Her skin held a dewy glow, looking so incredibly supple and smooth I wanted to reach out and touch her. Just once. An act I doubt she would appreciate after how we had left things.

Clearing my throat, I took another shot at those words. "I just wanted to check on you...make sure you were alright."

Her eyes narrowed, a quiet anger simmering in their depths. "Oh, now you care? I couldn't tell by the way you ghosted me earlier."

I winced. Fair.

I should've left it at that. I should've turned my ass around and walked away with her thinking I was exactly the asshole she thought I was. But I couldn't fucking do it. I still wanted that touch, wanted to feel her skin against mine so desperately my cock twitched at the thought.

I wonder what her lips taste like?

Anxious to find out, I stepped into her space. Adrenaline gripped me, my eyelids growing heavy as I loomed over her, tempted to just take what I wanted. To her credit, she didn't back down, tipping her head back to hold my gaze as if I didn't intimidate her in the slightest. Gone was the meek girl who fumbled over her words the first time we spoke.

"You're right," I admitted. "I'm sorry. Like I said, I just came to check on you. And I was hoping..."

To fuck you. Ravish you. Ride you so hard that you'll be screaming my name for hours from those plump little lips...

All wildly inappropriate thoughts dancing on the tip of my tongue, begging me to give them life. But I bit them back.

Luna leaned in, shortening what little distance still separated us. Chewing on her lower lip, she reached for my hand, her sudden boldness surprising me, the soft graze of her fingers coaxing mine to intertwine with hers.

"Hoping for what?" she murmured softly.

I couldn't deny the spark her touch ignited, electrifying my blood until it sizzled in my veins. She was so close I could feel the warmth coming off her body, a warmth I wanted to smother myself in.

I swallowed. *Fucking hell.*

The effect this girl had on me was unreal. I knew it was a bad idea, but, for the life of me, I couldn't recall the reasons *why*.

Tugging her closer, a charming smile pulled at my lips, any thoughts of backing off fleeing from my brain.

"That you'll let me take you for a ride."

ELEVEN

Luna

Is he serious right now?

I wasn't sure which was harder to believe. That Malakai Slade just tried to break into my house, or that he did it for the sole purpose of checking on me.

Why would he do that?

I was so shocked to see it was him who triggered the alarm on my illusion that I didn't have time to throw on proper clothes. The moment I saw him scaling the gate, I rushed outside before my aunt could notice, weaving an illusion to conjure up a more enticing outfit that didn't consist of a tank top and long pajama bottoms covered in little black cats...*with* the matching slippers.

"Where?" I asked. Though, to be honest, I really didn't care. I'd go anywhere with this man. No persuasion needed.

He shrugged like it was no big deal. "Just for a ride."

Nerves and excitement clashed all at once, forming a ball in the pit of my stomach. It didn't change the fact that I was still pretty pissed at him for earlier. I wanted an explanation, one way or another.

"Sure. I'd love to."

I didn't miss the grin he tried to mask as he turned and led me over to his Harley, tossing me his helmet as he got on. Clasping his shoulder, I climbed on behind him, and I wasn't shy about holding on this time either, my hands locking around his waist comfortably.

He swung the bike around, taking us back down to the main road. Aside from his headlights, the roads were shrouded in darkness. Living this far into the swamplands meant little to no street lights, which would change the further we got into town. But he missed the exit. It wasn't until we neared the mountain slopes that I realized where he was taking me.

Lookout Peak.

It was a hiking trail located near Nightshade territory on the outskirts of town. No one ever went there, mostly because it was surrounded by cemeteries—human and animal alike—and there was a long-standing rumor that the land was haunted. Rumors that Quinn herself may have accidentally started.

She frequented these graveyards regularly, as most young Nightshades did to practice their necromancy. It was morbid, sure, but morbid was kind of their coven's thing.

Kids would wander around these parts for shits and giggles, to prove to their friends that they weren't scared of ghosts and monsters. That is, until they stumble upon one of Quinn's fucked up practice dummies and take off running with piss streaming between their legs.

I had half a mind to shoot her a text to make sure she wasn't out here trying to raise the dead. Nothing like a little terror to ruin a date.

My eyes widened at the thought. *Oh, sweet Lucifer...is this a date?*

My heart pounded, beating against my chest like it wanted out. Malakai spared a fleeting glance over his shoulder before returning his attention to the road. Did he notice? Could he feel the thumping against his back?

Pulling my shit together, I held tight as he took the trail all the way to the top of the mountain, the ride growing bumpy. When he finally came to a stop, it was at the end of a cliff overlooking Deadwood. The entire town was lit up, hundreds of lights glimmering in the distance under a star-filled sky.

Unwinding my arms from around his waist, I sat back and pulled off my helmet, shaking out my hair. I waited for him to kill the engine before hopping off and taking a few short steps to the edge of the cliff. I cringed, seriously regretting my choice of footwear as jagged little rocks dug into the soft soles of my fluffy bedroom slippers.

My feet will be sore after this...

"You shouldn't stand so close," he said, taking my hand and tugging me back from the edge. "It's dangerous."

I smiled, allowing him to guide me back to his bike. His genuine concern for my safety was beginning to give me the warm and fuzzies. If he could see what I was actually wearing right now, he'd probably freak.

Turning to face me, he leaned back on his bike, bringing me to stand between his spread legs. He refused to release my hand, so the position was unavoidable.

Not that I was complaining.

Our joined hands dangled between us with only the tips of our fingers intertwined. One little tug would've been enough to separate them, a move neither of us were attempting.

I cleared my throat to cut the lingering tension. "So…why'd you bring me out here?"

His fingers squeezed mine as he held my gaze, a slow smile stretching across his face. My breath hitched. Why did he have to be so unbelievably sexy all the time? It was ridiculous. No other boy made me feel this way.

But he wasn't like most boys, was he?

He was hardened, rough around the edges as if he'd lived a longer life than your average eighteen-year-old. He carried himself like an immortal would, wholly confident and self-aware. A man who knew exactly where his place was in this world instead of stumbling through it like the rest of us.

"I wanted to apologize to you properly."

"You already did that."

His smile grew, head tilting slightly. "I didn't like that one. You deserve better."

Dipping my chin to hide my flustered face, I smiled. "You were kind of a dick."

He nodded, the intensity in his piercing gaze making me squirm a little. "I was. I never should've come at you like that. I was out of line."

"So why did you?"

His expression gave little away, making me wonder if he was always this serious.

"Just having a bad day, I guess. I didn't mean it. Any of it."

I chanced a step closer, giving our hands a little swing. "I'll forgive you…under one condition."

His eyes darkened, lashes lowering as they flickered between us, taking note of the little distance remaining. "What's that?"

"Tell me the real reason you went to that party." It was bothering me. I just couldn't wrap my head around it. "You told me those woods were dangerous, that you saw it on the news. So why go?"

He remained perfectly stoic. "When I heard the party was in Gravenhurst, I went out there to warn everyone that it wasn't safe."

My brows shot up. *Interesting*. I didn't expect his response to sound so rehearsed, like he'd practiced the excuse before coming here. But why would he do that? "Hmm. I didn't realize you were such a good Samaritan."

He shrugged offhandedly. "I'd hate for something to happen knowing I could've prevented it. I don't do good with shit like that on my conscience."

The sincerity behind his words struck a chord with me. I never pegged him as the do-gooder type. "Wow. That's surprisingly…*sweet*. I didn't know you were…"

"A good guy?" he finished with a slow grin.

I blushed, ashamed of my own judgmental thoughts. I knew next to nothing about him, and I had no right to assume anything. "I'm sorry, I didn't mean—"

His chuckle eased my guilt. "Don't worry about it. I

know I have a reputation for being a hard-ass. I don't blame you for thinking the worst of me."

"I've never thought the worst of you," I blurted without thinking, my eyes flaring wide immediately afterwards.

Malakai flashed me another panty-melting smile, and, I swear to all hell, I nearly fainted.

"Is that so?" His voice dropped to a purr, the sensual undertone making me gulp. "What do you think of me, then, Luna Sinclair?"

Breathe. I needed to breathe. My lungs had stopped working. Like, literally stopped providing me with oxygen. Was he moving closer? He seemed closer.

Using the hand that wasn't connected to his, I reached over to rub the goosebumps from my arm. "Um…well, I think—"

"Are you cold?"

I stared dumbly at him. "Me? No, not really…"

But he was already shrugging out of his jacket and draping it over my shoulders. It was big and heavy when it landed on me, encasing me in his scent.

Cigarette smoke and earthy cologne.

Suddenly, I could breathe again, my lungs back online and urging me to inhale as much of him as I could, my nostrils flaring. He pulled the two halves of the jacket tighter around me, drawing me closer between his legs until I was pressed flush against him. A muscle feathered along his jaw as he studied my face, the moment so extremely intimate it was making me hot in places I shouldn't be, craving things I shouldn't crave.

Somehow, I found my voice, as choked as it was. "I

think I have a lot to learn about you, Malakai Slade."

Stone-gray eyes fell to my lips. "Call me Kai."

Giddiness filled me. Everything I wanted was happening. Right here, right fucking now. Maybe my enchantress skills were improving. A brazenness I never felt before overtook me, spurring me on, putting a temporary hold on my inhibitions. Leaning forward, his lips called to me like a magnet, and he did nothing to stop it.

"Are we on nickname terms now?" I whispered, terrified of breaking the spell we were under.

I actually saw him swallow, his body molding against mine. "Only if you want to be. What can I call you?"

I smirked like a seductress would. "Whatever you want."

Was that my voice? It was huskier than before, heavy with a lust I had zero shame feeling. I was flagrantly throwing myself at him, taunting him to take what I was freely giving.

And he wanted to. It was obvious by the way he was looking at me, like he wanted to ravage me on this cliff. Or up against his bike…

Reading my mind, his arm snaked around my waist and lifted me, my feet leaving the ground as he spun me to take his place on the bike. I gasped as he leaned over me, his lips so close we shared breaths. His fingers splayed across my lower back as his other hand gripped the handlebar of his Harley. I held my position, waiting for his next move.

"Luna." His voice was low and guttural, a tone no man had ever used to utter my name before.

"Yes?" I was breathless, the word coming out on a pant.

"Can I kiss you?"

Raising my hand, I dared to touch him, my thumb dragging down his bottom lip as I stroked his jaw. "I don't know, *Kai*, can you?"

His eyes flashed dangerously right before he slammed his mouth against mine, claiming my never-been-kissed lips for himself.

TWELVE

Malakai

I was trying to be respectful. I really fucking was. But she was making it *hard*. She didn't know me well enough to provoke me like this, to test the boundaries of a relationship we'd barely established. But neither of us seemed to care.

I took her mouth roughly, showing little restraint. If she wanted me to stop, all she had to do was push me off. Or slap me. Whichever she preferred—

She moaned, the throaty sound sending me mad. Her arms came up to circle my neck, pulling me deeper into her embrace.

Fuck.

I gripped the handlebars to keep us both upright. Parting her lips with my tongue, I deepened the kiss, anxious to get a taste of her at last. When my tongue met hers, she recoiled for a split second, seeming unsure for the first time. Not wanting to scare her, I slowed things down, sliding a hand under the curtain of her hair to clasp her nape. I took my time caressing the shy appendage, coaxing it out to play.

Soon enough, she was mimicking my actions, rolling her tongue against mine. Without breaking the lip lock, I hoisted her up, splitting her legs apart to straddle me as I moved us to sit on my bike.

We kissed until our lips were red and swollen, the heat between us so overwhelming she shoved off my jacket, no longer needing its warmth. Easing back, I dragged my lips down the column of her throat, sucking her skin hard enough to leave bruising hickeys. I wanted to mark her. To have the satisfaction of knowing she'll look in the mirror hours later and remember the feel of my mouth on her.

She eagerly tipped her head to the side, granting me better access. She was panting now, her arousal so potent I could almost taste it on her skin. And I was right there with her, brimming with a desire I'd never felt before. I'd been with other girls, sure, but none had ever made me feel this…uninhabited.

Slipping my hands past the hem of her shorts, I jerked her closer by her thighs, aligning my crotch with her center. I resisted the urge to grind against her, to let her feel just how painfully hard she'd made me in such a short amount of time. Doing so would only push me over the edge, taking what little was left of my fragile control. Her skin was even smoother than I imagined, a stark contrast against my calloused hands that had decapitated a Ghoul only hours ago.

Grasping my jaw, she dragged my face back to eye level and clamped down on my bottom lip with her teeth, sucking it into her mouth. "Touch me more," she groaned, reaching down to move one of my hands from her shorts to her stomach.

My cock jumped at the command. With the patience of a saint, I allowed her to guide my hand where she wanted it. "Here?" I asked, my voice strained, my thumb flicking over her belly button ring.

"Higher," she whispered, hand dipping under my shirt to do some exploring of her own.

I clamped down hard on my jaw, breathing through my nose for restraint. She was a spicy little thing. I didn't expect this passion from her, this unquenchable heat burning between us. Her fingernails raked over my abs when I found her breasts.

She wasn't wearing a bra.

God, help me.

"You're killing me," I groaned into her mouth, squeezing her left breast. The soft mound was the perfect handful. Not too big, not too small. I kneaded it with care, my thumb rolling over her perky nipple. But when her hips gyrated against me, bumping my erection, I fucking lost it. Shoving my hand further beneath her shorts, I swept over the curve of her ass and touched the lace lining of her panties, not caring that I was stretching the fabric. Pressing forward, my lips distracted her as I moved to lay her down on my Harley, my fingers shifting her panties to the side—

Her palms flattened against my chest and shoved me back. "Wait…"

Shit. I retreated immediately, pulling my hands from underneath her clothes and leaning back. "Fuck. I'm sorry...I got carried away."

She remained horizontal with her auburn hair splayed across my bike. Her honeycomb eyes were glazed over, a dazed expression on her astoundingly beautiful face. Her reddened lips were slightly parted, panting to catch the breath I'd stolen from her.

I bit down hard on the inside of my cheek, mentally scolding myself when I almost reached for her again.

She said stop. Settle the fuck down!

Rubbing a hand down my face, I tried not to focus on the painful throbbing in my pants, the head of my cock beating against the zipper of my jeans.

When she smiled up at me, the beating intensified, promising a serious case of blue balls in my future.

"You apologize a lot."

Her smile was so contagious I found myself emulating it. "Yeah. You have that effect on me."

Her lashes fluttered against her flushed cheeks. "Hmm. I wonder why."

I held her gaze, unable to look away as if in a trance. "I think you know why, Luna."

The tension between us grew overwhelming, our chemistry indisputable. She moved to sit upright, relaxing her legs so that they were no longer straddling me. Clearing my throat, I stood from the bike and offered a hand to help her off. And as we stood face-to-face, all I wanted to do was get her horizontal again.

I rather liked her on her back...

Shaking the depraved thoughts from my head, I

grabbed my discarded jacket off the ground and held it open for her. "I should get you home. Here, put this back on."

"Such a gentleman," she muttered with a bashful smile, turning to slide her arms through the sleeves that were far too big for her. Gathering her silky locks in one hand, I pulled it free from the collar, my fingers gently brushing her nape in the process.

She shuddered, and I barely stopped myself from leaning in and dropping a kiss on her neck, my mouth eager to get back on her any way it could. "Only with you, it seems."

She turned to face me, lips twitching. "I must have *quite* the effect on you, then."

"You do." That much was fucking obvious.

Her smile grew impish. "Enough to get you to come to my party tomorrow night?"

Ah, yes. Her birthday. I had no intention of going when she'd first invited me. But now...

"I'll be there."

Her eyes flared. "Really? You'll come?"

"I might be a little late, though. I help my dad run the shop on weekends." And hunt. A fun fact she didn't need to know. The logical part of my brain was telling me not to go down this road with her. Not to get attached.

It's just a party, I kept telling myself. Probably the last one I'll see for a while. After graduation, I'll have less downtime between hunts. Less time to do anything that didn't involve slaying monsters. *Might as well take advantage while I can.*

Especially if it meant *she* would be there.

She beamed up at me as if I'd just made her day. "Not a problem. Our parties tend to go until morning, so you're welcome at any time."

I stepped into her, unable to keep an appropriate amount of distance between us. I brushed my fingers across her jaw, hooking one under her chin to tilt her face closer to mine. "You'll probably be too busy to spend any time with me, seeing as how it's your party and all."

I smirked at the bob in her throat. *Seems like I have an effect too...*

"I'll make time," she murmured, already pushing up on her tiptoes to meet me halfway.

Our lips brushed. Just a soft caress, no tongue. After the second and third pass, I needed more. Fuck. What was it about this girl that turned me into a greedy bastard?

All I wanted was to be on her all the time, touching and kissing every inch of flesh my lips could reach. Kissing her harder, I had to mentally check myself to keep things strictly PG.

Chill the fuck out, Slade.

But she didn't seem to mind, slinking her arms around my neck to pull me closer. This kiss was more intimate than the last. More deliberate. We took our time exploring each other, our mouths working together in synchronized harmony. I was in no hurry to wrap things up, and neither was she.

God-fucking-dammit, I thought, wrapping both arms around her waist and lifting her off her feet so I wouldn't have to bend. I fought the impulse to lock her legs around my waist again, content for now just having her pressed against me. But the longer we kissed, the more riled up I became.

"Luna…" I growled in warning.

"Mmm," she murmured, lips still moving against mine.

"We need to stop."

Her eyes fluttered open to look at me, her lips still puckered. "Why?"

"Because I'm going to fuck you if we don't."

Okay. Maybe that was a little too much honesty.

Smiling coyly, she pulled back, her arms going slack around my neck as I returned her feet to the ground. "Yeah, you're right," she said, nibbling on that bottom lip I just had in my mouth a second ago. "We should stop. I've never really…I mean, I don't usually…do this."

I frowned. *Do this?*

Her demeanor abruptly shifted from hot-and-bothered to standoffish, fidgeting with her hair as a means to avoid eye contact.

What the hell just happened?

Then it clicked.

"Are you a virgin?"

Doe eyes snapped to mine instantly, then dropped to her feet, twirling a lock of hair between her fingers. She shrugged, muttering, "Kind of."

A smile fought to take over my face. God, she was so fucking cute. "Kind of? How are you *kind of* a virgin, Sinclair? Either you are or you aren't." I was only teasing, of course. I didn't mean for it to come across as condescending as it did.

Dropping the lock of hair, she cut her eyes at me. "I am. And don't call me Sinclair. Only Quinn calls me that."

I recoiled at her tone, knowing I had inadvertently killed the mood. Reaching out, I tugged her forward by the opening of my jacket and dropped a kiss to her cheek, letting my charm wiggle me back into her good graces. "I didn't mean anything by it. And I don't care that you're a virgin."

She blushed, the tension draining from her shoulders. "Sorry. I didn't mean to snap at you."

Chuckling, I mounted my bike. "Don't apologize. I liked it. You're hot when you're angry."

She shook her head and smiled, climbing on behind me. "Will that be your excuse for pissing me off from now on?"

I tossed her a grin, throwing in a wink for good measure. "Maybe. Put your helmet on."

"Yes, sir," she mocked before strapping in.

Damn. I liked the sound of that. I had half a mind to tell her to save it for the bedroom, but chose to let the words die on my tongue instead. Best not to make sex jokes with someone who's never had it.

Revving the engine, I went rigid when her arms circled me, her breasts squishing against my back. The vibration against my crotch wasn't helping matters either. I was painfully hard and in need of a release.

But for tonight, my hand and a cold shower would have to do.

THIRTEEN

Luna

As the Harley rumbled to a stop near the front gate, I took extra care to disguise what was happening all around us, throwing up illusions to prevent Malakai from hearing or seeing anything out of the ordinary.

Because it was all out of the ordinary.

The Sinclair Manor was abuzz with activity. Everyone was working tirelessly to prepare for tonight.

The ritual.

From my vantage point, I spotted three of my cousins carrying an altar through the bayou, yelling at each other to lift it higher.

"You're dragging on your end, Tidus!"

"Well, maybe if Marcus would put his fucking back into it, I wouldn't have to drag!"

"Would you both shut up and move your asses!" Clay hollered over the bickering. "This fucking thing is heavy."

For fuck's sake, I groaned. The three were relatives on my father's side and complete morons. Why they didn't ask one of the witches who could levitate the thing into the bayou was beyond me. Casting a spell to drown out the noise, I made sure the only thing Malakai could hear were crickets.

Dismounting from the back of his bike, I stiffened at the sight of Aunt Freya standing on the other side of the gate with her arms folded. When our eyes met, hers lowered into a glare.

I was late.

The ritual was scheduled for three in the morning—the witching hour—and it was now nearly midnight. *Shit.* Time had gotten away from me.

And to make matters worse, my entire coven was littered about the place, nearly a dozen cars parked on the front lawn. Some were carting food and liquor into the house while others, like my cousins, were setting up for the ritual, donning black cloaks as they made their way deeper into the bayou.

Most were focused on the task at hand, but quite a few were more interested in the human whose bike I was just straddling. I could feel their eyes burning into me, my aunt's the most scalding. None of them had ever seen me with a boy before. Especially not *this* close to home.

Keeping the illusion of nothing-to-see-here well in place, I turned to face Malakai, my neck burning at the thought of saying goodbye to him in front of everyone.

Would he kiss me?

I wanted him to. But a part of me was also dreading it. "Thanks for tonight," I said quietly, trying to keep our conversation as private as possible. "I'll see you tomorrow."

"Tonight, you mean."

I blinked. "What do you me—"

Taking me by the waist, he pulled me in for a kiss. His lips were a solace against mine, soothing my nerves and making me forget all the eyes currently on us. Eyes he couldn't see. I melted against him, cupping his face as he devoured my mouth.

It ended too quickly; my eyes still closed when he pulled back. "Happy birthday, Luna," he whispered softly.

Of course. It was midnight. The fact that he was the first person to wish me happy birthday planted a smile on my face so wide it made my cheeks hurt.

"Thank you," I murmured back, my nails lightly scratching his jaw as we reluctantly parted. Goddess, help me. I didn't want to let him go.

My aunt cleared her throat, my head turning in her direction. She impatiently tapped her wrist, even though she wasn't wearing a watch.

Time to go.

"You okay?" Malakai asked, following my line of sight. He frowned, seeing nothing.

"I'm fine. Just thought I heard something. I better get inside. I need my beauty sleep for the party."

His fingers brushed my cheek, those intense eyes of his studying my features as if memorizing them. "No, you don't. You're all set in that department."

I was straight swooning on the inside, wanting nothing more than to throw myself at him again. "Give me your phone."

He didn't hesitate to follow my command, reaching into his jacket pocket and handing me his Android. I quickly punched in my number and hit send, ensuring I'd have his as well. Then I saved it under *Luna* with the kissy lips emoji and handed it back to him, along with his helmet.

"Call me."

With a lopsided grin, his eyes sluggishly trailed down my body and back up again as if saying goodbye was the last thing on his mind. "I plan to. Goodnight, Luna."

"Goodnight, Kai."

I stepped back as his bike roared to life, watching as he spun around and sped off. I waited until his taillights were but a dim glow in the darkness before heaving a tremendous sigh, forgetting that I wasn't alone. The catcalls and whistles that echoed all around were a blaring reminder of my audience.

Groaning, I turned to face the firing squad.

"A happy birthday, indeed!"

"Damn, who's the eye candy?"

"Looks like someone went and bagged themselves a hot piece of mortal ass."

"How's the D? I hear mortal men can't get it done."

"I'm more of a werewolf girl myself."

"What the fuck is she wearing?"

The chatter went on for a while, voices overlapping as the gossip wheel started spinning. I answered nothing as I made my way over to Aunt Freya. Her annoyed façade was cracking, amusement leaking in as she took in my attire from head to toe.

"Please tell me you didn't let him see you like this,"

she deadpanned.

I rolled my eyes. "Of course not."

"Good. I was beginning to wonder if I've taught you nothing." Stepping forward, her hand shot out, pinching my chin hard between two fingers. Then she squinted, taking a good long look at my swollen lips and flushed skin. "Judging by the size of that hickey, I take it you must really like this boy."

In spite of the indignity heating the back of my neck, I couldn't keep the dumb, dreamy smile off my face. I nodded, needing her to understand that this was more than just a silly crush. "I do, Aunt Freya."

Sighing, she shook her head and smiled. "I guess I'll have to meet him, then. Now go wash up and get ready for the ritual. Quinn is waiting for you inside."

Meet him?

That meant she approved! That she wouldn't give me a hard time about him anymore. It wasn't forbidden for a witch to date a human or anything, but it did make life more…complicated. I knew I was jumping the gun, but it was comforting to know Aunt Freya would have my back with the coven if things with Malakai…progressed. If we ever became something more, I would need their consent to tell him our secret. To loop him into the fold. But that step required complete trust on both sides, and neither of us was there yet.

Still, the prospect of it excited me. I threw my arms around Aunt Freya and squeezed, squealing in her ear. "Thank you, thank you, thank you!"

She laughed and hugged me back, then pushed me off towards the house. "Yeah, yeah. Now get going. You have less than three hours. And do something about that hickey."

I skimmed my fingers along my neck. "Is it really that bad?"

She scoffed loudly, making me regret I even asked. "I'm pretty sure astronauts can see it from space, my love. Now get."

Blushing, I skipped off to find Quinn, dashing into the house and up the stairs to my bedroom. I found her sprawled out on my bed, one knee crossed over the other as she scrolled through her phone.

"There you are," she said without looking up. "I found you the perfect look for the party. That human of yours is going to nut his pants."

I grinned wickedly, closing the door so I could spill my guts to my BFF in private. "He almost did tonight."

That got her attention.

Her head whipped around, her stunned expression morphing into one of complete horror as she assessed me from head to toe. "What the fuck are you wearing?"

"I didn't have time to change."

"You were with him dressed like *that*? What the fuck is wrong with you! You're supposed to be seducing the man, not scaring him off."

Glaring, I strode past her to my bathroom, stripping out of my clothes as I went. "Rude. I conjured something up, obviously."

"Something crippling hot, I hope," she said, jumping up and tailing me to the shower.

Flicking on the water, I adjusted the temperature and shrugged, throwing her a cocky grin as I stepped under the hot spray. "He didn't have any complaints."

"You little skank!" Quinn beamed from ear to ear. "You're washing off his cum right now, aren't you?"

Rolling my eyes, I reached for the soap, getting good and lathered. I wish I could've worn his scent a little longer, bask in it for just a few more hours. But I had to be cleansed for the ceremony. My aunt, along with the other elders, were sticklers for tradition. "It didn't go *that* far. I wasn't ready."

He sure was, though. He came insanely close to venturing where no man had ever ventured before. I blushed, ashamed of my own purity. Malakai, on the other hand, was overtly confident in all things sexual. He was a man, through and through. It was easy to let him take the reins, let him guide me through my own carnal desires. He made me feel like the seductress I was meant to be, bringing out a confidence I never knew I possessed until I was using it on him. I mean, the way I threw myself at him...

I cranked the faucet to cold when my skin grew unbearably hot.

"Oh, you're ready," Quinn mused gleefully, shuffling about the bathroom with haste. I couldn't see what she was doing since the glass walls of the shower had grown foggy with steam. "You're just scared."

True.

If I had let him, Malakai would've taken me right there on his Harley. And as much as that terrified me, it also left me tingling with anticipation.

Rinsing off, I shut off the water and stepped out, barely catching the towel Quinn tossed at my face. She stood in front of my vanity mirror with everything I needed for the ritual laid out across the counter. Without a word, she unraveled the black cloak she held in her hands, holding it open for me to step into.

She was taking her role in this seriously, no doubt following my aunt's instructions to a tee.

I sighed, taking everything in.

This was it. My official induction into the coven. Something in my chest ached, and I knew it was the hole where my parents should've been. The void no one will ever be able to fill. They were supposed to be here for this, to see me through this day.

My eyes prickled with tears.

Inhaling sharply through my nose, I reminded myself of all the people I still had in my life. They would see me through this. And Malakai would be waiting for me on the other side.

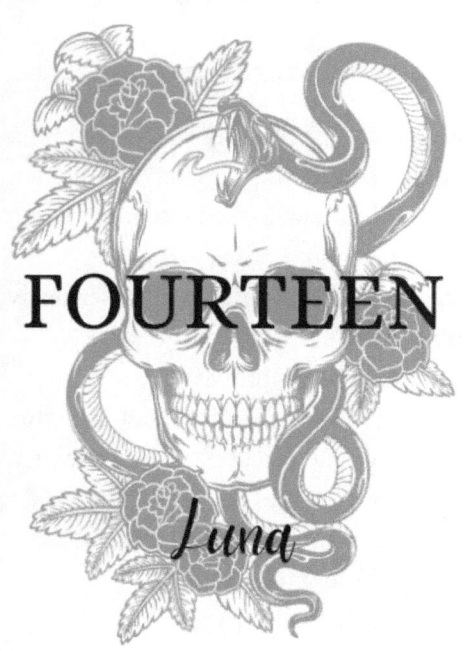

FOURTEEN

Luna

I waited at the entrance of the bayou. My gaze held captive by the shimmering full moon. It hovered high in the sky, deep within the swamp.

That was my destination.

Reaching under my cloak, I brought my necklace to my lips and kissed it.

Show time.

I could feel Aunt Freya approaching me from behind, her presence soothing. I didn't turn to look at her. I wasn't allowed. All I could see was the flickering flame of the torch she held in her hand, the light casting a warm glow over me.

It was then my sister, Anya, skipped into view several feet in front of me. She was like my mini-me, our features so similar it was like looking into a mirror. Our only differences were her chubby, child-like cheeks and short curly hair that was far redder than mine. Our black cloaks were the same, only I was naked under mine. She held a torch in her hand as well, acting as my guide to the altar alongside my aunt. Despite her age, it was her sacred duty to fulfill this role as my closest blood relative. Even at her young age, she was well on her way to becoming a fierce witch. It was a shame our parents never got to see her grow up. She was just a baby when they were killed, taken before she was even old enough to recall their faces. If all was right in the world, it would've been my father standing at my back and my mother at my front.

But the world sucked.

Anya smiled, giving me a little nod. Her silent way of telling me I've got this. I shot her a wink as Aunt Freya's hand came down on my shoulder, giving me a firm squeeze of reassurance. I appreciated it. Appreciated them.

"Walk."

I complied with my aunt's order, letting her guide me as I took my first steps into the bayou. Giving me her back, Anya followed suit, matching our languid pace. No words were exchanged as we walked, the percussion of the swamp filling the silence instead. Crickets chirping, frogs croaking, snakes hissing.

The trek was ten minutes, max, bringing us to a three-way crossroads where the rest of the Sinclair Coven were gathered. All twenty individuals were dressed identically, their faces hidden under long cloaks. Most were distant relatives who I rarely interacted with outside of special occasions like this one. I was still a little bummed that Quinn couldn't be here.

Coven members only and all.

But at least she was allowed to help me get ready. She did a stellar job on my makeup, giving me that smoky-eye look, complete with glitter and wingtips drawn across my upper lids. I never went this dramatic with the glam, but even I had to admit I looked like a whole-ass snack. Even my hair was styled differently, slicked back and straight as a blade. Quinn had doused it in so much gel that I was itching to get it washed and back to its normal waviness.

Smack dab in the middle of the crossroads sat the polished wooden altar, a raised dais carved in the image of the Strophalos—Hecate's Wheel. It was identical to the one I wore around my neck. My sister and aunt guided me forward, halting before the three small steps leading up onto the platform.

Passing off her torch to another member, Anya was given something else in exchange, the object concealed by a black silk scarf. Holding it with both hands, she turned to face me, blocking the steps to the altar.

"Kneel, blood of my blood," my aunt commanded.

Lowering to my knees, I kept my eyes on Anya. With great care, she unveiled the object in her hands, the discarded scarf floating to the ground. It was a crown crafted from the bones of our ancestors—the first of our bloodline—with black roses woven intricately around the base. Without being told, I bowed, accepting the weight of it onto my head.

"Rise."

Pushing to my feet, I held my head high as Aunt Freya reached around to the tie at my collar. She pulled it loose, the cloak falling from my shoulders. As the rest of the coven circled the dais with their heads bowed, I willed my arms to stay by my side. I so desperately wanted to shield my naked body, even though no one except for my aunt and sister were looking.

"Proceed," Aunt Freya said.

Anya took that as her cue to step aside, allowing me to pass. I took the steps one at a time to the top of the dais. Approaching the center, I kneeled once again, sitting back on my legs and resting my hands on my thighs. The coven began chanting in Latin, their voices low. It was like a hum that caressed my skin, the breeze picking up around me.

The moon seemed to shine brighter as a murder of crows circled overhead, casting a shadow over me. I moved my hands to lay on the dais, palms up at my sides, waiting for the next step to commence.

I heard the hiss before I felt them, the white pythons slithering their way onto the platform. Their beady eyes were blood-red and solely locked on me. One approached me from each side, coiling up my arms and around my shoulders. Slowly, they switched sides, crawling back down the opposite arm and stopping at my wrists. They were heavy, weighing at least thirty pounds each and ten feet long. But I held my position, showing my respect by remaining serene.

Their presence actually brought me a great deal of comfort, aiding in my desire to show less skin. And they were warm, their thick bodies shielding me from the cold.

"Speak the vow." My aunt's voice grew distant as she rejoined the others, taking her place at the head of the crowd. Anya joined her soon after, leaving me to do this part on my own.

I gazed up at the moon as if speaking to Hecate herself. "Blessed be to Hecate, our Dark Goddess, the Mother, the Maiden, the Crone. With my blood, I pledge my soul unto thy service forevermore."

I repeated the words two more times in Latin. At the end of the third, both pythons let out a giant hiss before rearing back and striking hard and fast at my wrists. Their fangs ripped into my veins, my eyes rolling to white as an immense power consumed me. The pain was an afterthought, barely registering in my mind. The three faces of the Goddess flashed before me, her essence flowing in and around me. The feeling was addictive, like a drug I never knew existed.

One by one, I felt a connection to each member of my coven being sown, my soul tethering itself to theirs. Their chanting grew louder as my blood filled the crevices of the wheel, flowing through each section of the maze until complete. Unclamping their jaws from my wrists, the snakes nuzzled the wound as if apologizing for the pain they caused before slithering away.

I swayed slightly, their missing weight combined with the blood loss making me woozy. Suddenly, several hands were upon me, holding me steady as I pushed to my feet.

But no one was there.

I was still alone atop the platform with the coven spread out around me. Yet I could feel them. *All* of them. They were a part of me now, in a way they weren't before.

I didn't think it would feel like this. That I would feel this...*whole*.

When the chanting stopped, Aunt Freya came forward, climbing the steps onto the dais with a dagger in her hand. Standing before me, she held the dagger by the hilt between us, the gleaming blade pointed down.

Then she smiled. "Do you, Luna Sinclair, blood of my blood, vow to honor, defend, and protect this coven until your dying breath?"

Reaching out, I used both hands to clasp the blade, squeezing until my blood dripped down the cold steel. "Yes. This I vow." Releasing the blade, I held my bleeding palms out for everyone to see.

The crowd erupted into cheers, marking the end of the ritual. When Aunt Freya pulled me in for a hug, I threw all of my weight onto her, exhaustion kicking in.

"Your parents would be so proud," she whispered into my ear, helping me down from the platform. I nodded into her shoulder, finally allowing the tears from earlier to fall.

Someone held out my cloak. Anya, I assumed.

Once I was no longer rocking my birthday suit, I sighed in relief. I did it. It was over. I was now officially a working member of the coven. Soon I would be sent out on missions, thrust into the dangerous world we lived in. This was the part I'd been dreading for so long.

So why was my heart racing with excitement? Or maybe it was the adrenaline still pumping through me.

As we made our way out of the bayou, music could be heard coming from the manor, the bass so loud it could wake the fucking dead.

I spotted Quinn first, standing there with a big ass grin on her face. She held her arms out wide as if she expected me to run into them.

Fuck that. My tired ass wasn't running anywhere.

"Time to party, bitches!" She timed her words perfectly, fireworks blasting into the sky a hot second later, courtesy of the Blackwell Coven. A bunch of them stood on the roof of the house, lightning and fire flying from their fingertips into the sky. My cousins ran to join in, their cloaks wafting behind them as they raced to cast illusions over the sky.

The party was already underway with all five covens present. Cars and limos pulled up one by one, everyone dressed to the nines and carrying extravagantly wrapped gifts. Pigs were being roasted on spits right on the front lawn as another group started setting up for beer pong.

Wiccan style.

This version didn't require a table. Red cups levitated in the air, constantly rotating to make for harder targets. And they weren't filled with human beer either. Witches' brew was way stronger.

But this was just the beginning. A pre-game before the real chaos kicked off. I'd warned everyone to keep things as 'human' as possible. For now, they were free to do as they pleased since the human guests wouldn't be arriving until much later.

Quinn ran to collect me from my aunt. I was glad to see Cara and Lea with her as well. I could use a Hollow right about now. Their coven was chalked full of healers who could cure just about anything.

Quinn held me up as both girls got to work, hovering their hands over my bleeding wounds. "Shit," Quinn muttered. "You're making me wish I wasn't next, Sinclair. Shit looks like it fucking hurts."

I smirked, resting my head on her shoulder. "It wasn't so bad. I could use a cookie and a juice box, though." The blood loss was getting to me.

"All done," Cara and Lea announced at the same time.

I glanced down to find my wounds gone, both puncture marks and cuts replaced by smooth, untarnished skin. I smiled up at them. "Thanks, guys."

"C'mon," Quinn said, throwing an arm over my shoulders and steering me towards the house. "Let's get you cleaned up. You got a beefcake to seduce later. You can't greet the man all covered in blood."

That's right. Malakai was coming.

A smile broke out over my face. I had no interest in the party. All I wanted was another hot shower and my bed. The coven could have their fun.

Mine would come later.

FIFTEEN

Malakai

T he gate was wide open when I pulled up, a surprise in itself. Luna had never invited me beyond the iron barrier, so I had no idea what was waiting for me on the other side. I was always the type to drop a girl to her front door, since I was well aware of the dangers that lurked in the night. But since she had insisted against it, I never pressed the issue. Her reasons were her own. I had no business prying.

Fuck knows I had my own secrets she wasn't privy to.

Bypassing the gate, I frowned driving down the pathway to her house. The road was the same as before, unpaved and lined with willow trees. Luna had claimed her house wasn't a far walk beyond the gate. Just over the hill, she'd said.

But it was a little further than that. More like over a hill and around a very long, very sharp, bend. It was no wonder I couldn't see it from the road. The entire area was drenched in darkness and surrounded by woodland. I couldn't see shit until it was right in front of me.

She'd rather hike back to her house than let me see her to her door?

It didn't make sense. Unless she didn't want to be seen with me.

Understandable. I was never the guy girls rushed to take home to meet the parents. But if that was the case, why invite me to the party? It was on Sinclair property, meaning I was bound to meet members of her family at some point.

Pushing it from my mind, I gawked when the house came into view. *Holy shit...*

I knew she was rich, but *this…*

It was a fucking mansion; the kind only pop stars could afford.

"The restaurant biz must be booming," I muttered to myself, looping around the three-tier fountain in the middle of her massive driveway. The structure was unique, each tier resembling a circular maze with water flowing from one down into the other. They even had their own lake that ran alongside the house. Hundreds of fireflies floated above the water, creating a serene ambiance that didn't quite mesh with all the over-the-top extravagance only yards away.

The place was already crammed, the roundabout driveway lined with cars. It was easy to nab a spot on my bike, though, parking it in front of the fountain where no one else could fit. The music was so loud it shook the foundation, the bass vibrating through my boots the moment my foot touched the pavement.

I reached into my pocket for my phone, debating if I should call Luna or not. I had no idea where to go. I felt out of place, like I didn't belong here.

The stares didn't help either.

A handful of people standing on the front porch were eyeing me hard. I recognized a few of their faces from school. They were a part of the rich crowd that Luna rolled with.

The Crowleys and the Nightshades.

They were the creepy motherfuckers always hanging around graveyards and cemeteries. One of their families owned all of the funeral parlors in town. I couldn't remember which.

The lot of them turned and whispered something to each other, doing little to hide the fact that I was the topic of conversation. As I approached the front steps, the chatter ceased. I ignored them, their heads turning with me as I sauntered straight into the house. The doors were left open, people coming and going as they pleased.

It was like walking into a nightclub.

A professional DJ booth was set up right at the entry, the place dark with strobe lights flashing in time with the music. I made my way through, searching the crowd for Luna.

How many rooms does this fucking place have?

I had lost count. People were dancing in some, while others served as designated areas for eating and drinking. I cocked my brows at the massive banquet table packed with food. In the middle sat an entire fucking pig with an apple stuffed in its gaping dead mouth.

Jesus. These people are serious.

Each room had its own bar, stocked with endless amounts of alcohol, all top shelf. Were her parents cool with this? I knew for a fact that not everyone here was of legal drinking age. Then again, the rich didn't give a fuck about shit like that, did they?

Giving up on my search, I was about to reach for my phone when a gentle tug on my sleeve drew my attention. I turned, my gaze dropping to the little girl standing a foot behind me, her features a carbon copy of Luna's.

She beamed up at me with dimples in her chubby cheeks. "Are you looking for my sister?"

I quickly glanced around before looking back at her. She seemed to be the only kid here. "Depends. Is your sister Luna?"

Stupid question, but figured I'd ask anyway.

She bobbed her head, ginger curls bouncing. "I'm Anya."

"Nice to meet you, Anya. I'm Mal—"

"Malakai. I know."

Pause. *She told her family about me?*

"Luna just went upstairs to change. Marcus pushed her into the pool." Her sing-song tone suggested that she was thrilled to be relaying this information to me.

"Who's Marcus?" And where can I find him so I can drown him in retaliation?

She swung her little body from side to side, honey-brown eyes an exact replica of Luna's. "Our annoying cousin. Luna got so mad at him. He ruined her fancy makeup, so I made him walk into the alligator pond when no one was looking."

My head jerked. *What the fuck did she just say?* "What do you mean you *made* him?"

Her smile fell, almost as if realizing she'd made a mistake. Then she was talking again, her lips moving slower this time. "You misheard me. Forget I said that." Her voice held a melodic tone, a bout of vertigo overtaking me. It only lasted for a second before I was back to normal.

Shaking my head, I blinked down at Anya. "Sorry, did you say something?"

She smiled, big and bright. "I said I can take you to Luna, if you'd like."

"Oh." I must not have heard her over the music. "That'll be great. Thanks."

"No problem. This way." She sauntered past me, heading for the grand staircase behind the DJ booth.

Several eyes watched me climb the stairs, making me wonder if I was even allowed up here. When we reached the top, Anya stopped and pointed to a door down the hall.

"Last one on the left is hers."

Without another word, she turned and skipped back down the stairs, humming a tune as she went.

I frowned, watching her go. *Weird kid.* Walking to the end of the hall, I stopped at Luna's door and raised my hand to knock.

No answer.

I tried two more times before turning the knob and poking my head inside. "Luna?" When I heard her shuffling about, I let myself in, closing the door behind me.

"Anya, is that you?" she called from another room. The bathroom, perhaps. The door was left slightly ajar, warm light spilling through the crack. "I told you I'll be down in a—" She rushed into the bedroom, stopping short when her eyes landed on me. "Malakai?"

Fuck. Me.

I swallowed hard, eyes dropping to the tiny towel wrapped around her shapely body. Her hair was wet and dripping down her back, damp strands sticking to the side of her flawlessly smooth face. She gripped the front of the terry cloth with both hands as if afraid it would fall.

I prayed that it would.

Clearing my throat, I stepped further into the room. "Sorry. I knocked."

She flushed, her lips tipping up into a bashful smile. "You came."

"I told you I would." I moved closer, the urge to put my hands on her already weighing heavily on me. "I heard there was a pool incident."

Her brows wrinkled. "Who told you that?"

"Your sister. Cute kid."

"I should've been downstairs to greet you. I'm so sorry. I hope no one gave you a hard time."

I didn't care enough to mention the stares. "Not at all. Nice place you got here. Glad to see I finally made it past the front gate." It wasn't meant to be a dig, but I was curious.

She bit her lip, looking a little guilty. "I'm not ashamed of you or anything, if that's what you're thinking. My family can be pretty meddlesome at times. I guess…I just wanted to keep you to myself for a little while longer."

My heart skipped a beat in my chest. God-fucking-dammit! *What the hell is happening to me?* I was never a relationship kind of guy, but Luna Sinclair was making me wish I was.

Sauntering forward, I reached out to tuck a wet lock of hair behind her ear, satisfaction rippling through me when she leaned into my touch.

"I know the feeling," I muttered, eyes falling to her luscious lips. "But from now on, I'll be dropping you to your door. It's a far walk and I don't want anything happening to you."

A puff of air left her lips as she stared up at me, those long dark lashes of hers fluttering against her cheeks. "From now on? You plan on dropping me home often, then?"

"I do." I was finding it harder and harder to stay away from her. To keep things 'casual' like I did with most girls. Hooking a finger under her chin, I tilted her head up, bringing her lips closer to mine. "Any complaints?"

I grinned when she gulped, her lids drifting shut. "None that I can think of at the moment."

I brought my lips down over hers, just a soft caress at first, warming them up for a proper taste. Keeping one hand on the towel, she brought the other up to hold my jaw, surrendering herself to me. Taking her by the throat, I walked her backwards until her back hit the wall. She groaned into my mouth, our tongues warring as I went in on her. She caught my bottom lip between her teeth, giving it a firm suck before letting go.

Hmm, she has a biting fetish, does she? I ran my

tongue over the indentation left behind, tasting blood.

She was getting braver.

I liked it.

Bracing a hand to the wall, I dropped my head to her neck, placing open-mouth kisses down the side of her throat. "Are you having a good birthday?"

She made a sound that resembled a yes, her head falling back for me. "I am now. I wish you could've seen me earlier, though."

I kissed lower, tracing over her collarbone. "Why's that?"

"I dressed up for you."

I dragged her towel up an inch from the bottom, my fingers grazing her bare ass as they dipped underneath. "I prefer you like this."

"I'm naked under this, you know."

"I'm aware." I wasted no time lifting her off her feet by her ass, her legs instinctively winding around my waist.

Abandoning her death grip on the towel, her arms slung around my neck. I carried her over to the bed, her forehead touching mine. I sat with her straddling my lap, the towel riding up just enough to position her exposed flesh over my erection.

I cursed my jeans, needing them gone ASAP.

She shifted nervously, pressing herself closer to me. "I've never been naked for anyone before," she admitted self-consciously, but did nothing to stop me.

Quite the opposite.

She seemed comfortable in my lap, with nothing but a towel protecting her from all the scandalous things I wanted to do to her, her body pressed so closely to mine I could look down past her shoulders to the curve of her back and get a spectacular view of her ass—which currently sat in my hands.

I dug my fingers into the supple flesh. "You're not naked, Luna. Not yet, anyway."

She sucked in a sharp breath and bucked her hips, effectively grinding against my cock.

"Fuck!" I hissed, white-hot pleasure ripping through me.

"I'm sorry!" She jerked back, thinking she'd done something wrong. "I didn't mean—"

I yanked her back, leaning in to growl in her ear. "Do that again."

Smiling, she resumed her position, this time bearing down on her knees as leverage to rock back and forth on my lap. She was a quick learner, allowing me to guide her until she was confident enough to ride me on her own.

"Shit. Yeah...just like that," I grunted, keeping our foreheads locked and eyes connected. She held onto me for dear life, fingers tunneling in my hair as she rolled her hips, chewing on her lip to keep from making a sound. But I wanted to hear her. Grasping her hips, I applied more force to her thrusts, wrenching a cry from her lips.

"Oh, sweet Goddess," she moaned, panting against my face.

Sweet Goddess? *Never heard that one before.*

Her rocking grew frantic, her breathing labored as I forced her to ground harder against me, the rough fabric of my jeans rubbing against her sensitive clit. She was probably soaking wet. I yearned to touch more of her.

"You like this?" My voice was pure gravel, thickened with lust.

Her head nodded vigorously, unable to speak.

"Want more?"

My cock nearly jumped out of my fucking pants when she nodded again, prompting me to shove my hand fully underneath her towel. She jolted when my fingers found her slippery folds, a soundless moan parting her lips. Leaning back, she attempted to look down, wanting to watch the show.

"Look at me," I commanded. When her eyes flipped to mine again, I could've sworn they were a different color, her pupils blown so wide it appeared as though she had none. Then it was gone, back to normal like it was never there.

Strange.

Brushing it aside, I refocused on my hand between her legs. "You're so fucking wet." Her juices coated my fingers, dripping down my palm. "I need you to come for me." My fingers slid up and down through her folds, teasing her entrance with the tip every so often.

The way she tensed each time I breached her opening didn't escape my notice. She wasn't ready to be penetrated, not yet, and I wasn't about to force it on her. So I found her clit instead, using a single finger to lightly rub it in slow, circular motions until she was a writhing mess on top of me.

Her grip in my hair tightened, her head rolling back on her shoulders in complete bliss. "Oooh...fuuucck."

Pride consumed me. I loved that I was the first to do this to her. To give her this high. I rubbed faster, working her harder, grazing my teeth up along her throat as her hips continued to rock with wild abandon. She rode my hand with fluid ease, grinding against my palm as I flicked her little nub. Her erotic moans were close to sending me over the edge. I fought every instinct telling me to throw her down and fuck her ten ways from Sunday.

Soon.

When her body tensed, I knew she was close. I pushed her to the brink until her body trembled, ready to explode. "That's it," I murmured, driving her clit so hard my hand was vibrating against her sweltering heat. More moisture pooled. "Fucking come for me."

She cried out, her muscles seizing, wringing tight before going lax as she came undone, collapsing against me. She panted hard, struggling to catch her breath.

Pulling my hand from between her legs, I made her watch as I licked my fingers clean from base to tip, doing nothing to stifle the satisfied groan that rose to the back of my throat. "You taste good." Like honey and milk. But I mostly said it to see her blush.

Success.

Her face was on fire, her skin just as heated to the touch. Her lips found my cheek, showering me with kisses until she reached my lips. "What about you?" she asked softly.

"What about me?"

Her hands trailed down my chest and over my stomach to my crotch. She shifted back to caress the bulge that sat between us. I shivered when her fingers brushed over the head, making me gnash my teeth until my jaw hurt.

"You were like this last time, too."

"Hmm." It was the only sound I trusted myself to make.

"Maybe I could..." She reached for the zip on my pants, pinching the metal tab to pull it down.

I caught her wrist. "You don't have to do that."

She was nervous again. I could tell by the way she tensed, an uneasiness about her. Brows creasing, her eyes flickered back and forth between me and my raging hard-on. "But you didn't get to...you know."

Jesus. She couldn't even say the word. She was so fucking cute. My lips quirked. "Come?"

She nodded despite her blush, reverting back to her shy self. Leaning forward, I pecked her pouting lips. "I'm a big boy. I'll survive."

"But—"

"How about you take that towel off for me instead," I smirked, laying back on her bed with my hands tucked behind my head.

She stared down at me, blinking as if my request made no sense. "My towel?"

I nodded. "I want to see you. *All* of you."

She hesitated, pulling the top tight across her chest after it had fallen slack during our activities. Did she really have to think about this?

"Luna," I said, my voice deepening. "I've already *felt* all of it. Now I want to *see* it. Drop the fucking towel."

Her dark lashes lowered, expression growing lustful at the command. I was quickly learning that she enjoyed my roughness. She responded to my dominance with submission, reaching for the knot of her towel.

She kept her eyes on me the entire time, studying my reaction as she let the cloth unravel and fall to her waist. I followed its descent down with my eyes, watched it bunch at her waist, and slowly made my way back up, taking my time to drink her in. I honed in on her toned—surprisingly athletic—stomach first, memorizing the flawless path to her ample breasts. Her pert nipples were dusted dark against her pale skin, puckering out as if to say hello. My tongue shot out to wet my lips, wanting nothing more than to taste those little buds along with the rest of her—

Her room door burst open, slamming into the wall behind it. "Luna, we've got a prob—Oh, fuck! Shit—My bad!"

I bolted upright, throwing my arms around Luna to shield her nakedness from our unwelcome guest.

Twisting her upper body, she shot a glare over her shoulder at the person still standing in her doorway. "For fuck's sake, Quinn!"

SIXTEEN

Luna

"What the hell, Quinn!" I hissed, shoving the blonde out into the hallway and closing my bedroom door behind me with Malakai still inside.

Her smirk was wicked, not looking guilty in the slightest. "My bad. I didn't mean to interrupt *sexy time*, but we've got a problem."

"It couldn't wait?" I was already anxious to get back inside, to continue where me and Malakai had left off. But Quinn shook her head, effectively dashing my hopes.

"A Blackwell was attacked in the woods, not far from here. Said she thinks it was a Wendigo."

I frowned. "She *thinks*?"

"She said it looked weird, like it hadn't fully turned yet. She managed to burn it a little, but the fucker got away."

I cursed. "Which means it's still roaming around."

With an array of witches partying in the vicinity. "Why are you telling me this? Go tell one of the elders."

She snorted as if to say, *do I look stupid?* "Do you really think I'd be here cock-blocking you if that was an option? Most of them left already, and your Aunt Freya disappeared with William hours ago."

I rubbed my face. Of course she did. They were probably off fucking somewhere, knowing them.

"I can't find your sister either."

My head snapped up at that. "What?"

"Her and two other Witchlings were playing near the swamps earlier and now they're gone. We can't find them anywhere—"

Turning, I barged back into my room. The bed was empty. Looking over, I spotted Malakai standing on the balcony that overlooked the pool in the backyard. I double-checked that my illusion was still in place to make sure he was seeing what I wanted him to see. A *normal* pool party with people in modest swimsuits doing *normal* things. *Not* half-naked witches running around conjuring mini tsunamis to hurl at each other and levitating themselves onto the roof to use it as a diving board.

As I stepped out onto the balcony, he spoke without looking at me. "Nice pool," he drawled, the dryness in his tone suggesting he had other opinions he was keeping to himself.

It was, indeed, a nice pool. The freeform monstrosity was backlit with pink and purple lights shining from the bottom, illuminating the water with a colorful glow. It spanned the length of the entire yard, complete with waterfall slides and a separate section for the jacuzzi. He couldn't see the stone statue of Hecate that rose up from the middle, or the snake-like construction lining the outer edge.

As he gazed out over everything, I had a hard time gauging his reaction. His stare was blank as if unimpressed by the display. It made me wonder for the first time what he must think of me. Of my wealth. Did he think I was just some spoiled rich girl living in the lap of luxury without a care in the world? Frivolous and shallow-minded.

Pushing the thought aside, I laid my hand on his back, forcing him to turn and look at me. "I hate to do this, but there's something I need to take care of. Not sure how long I'll be."

He frowned, concern drawing down his brows. "Everything okay?"

"Yeah, it's just my sister. She ran off into the woods and now no one can find her. I need to go look for her."

He stepped forward, his whole demeanor changing as if he was ready to go to war for me. "I'll help you look."

Smiling, I cupped his cheek, caressing it gently with my thumb. "Thank you, but I've got it. I'm sure she didn't go far."

He gave a reluctant nod before turning his head into my hand and laying a sweet kiss on my palm. I sighed at the gesture, those dreamy gray eyes of his melting me into a puddle of goo.

"I'll wait for you," he promised, leaving me speechless.

"Really?"

With a grin, he leaned in, stealing a chaste kiss. "I

came here for you. And I'm not ready to say goodnight yet. If you don't mind, that is."

I was beaming like a moron, unable to help myself. "I'd like that. I promise I won't be long. You can hang out here or go back down to the party if you want. There's lots to drink and eat, please help yourself."

Springing back up on my toes, I gave his lips another quick peck before dashing back into my bedroom and throwing on the first set of clothes I could get my hands on. Then I was back in the hallway with Quinn.

"Let's go," I told her, practically flying down the stairs and out of the house. Bella Blackwell—William Blackwell's niece—was waiting for us outside, my cousins Tidus and Clay beside her.

"Why is Bella here?" I asked Quinn.

"She's the one who burned the Wendigo. Figured she could help."

Fine by me. The more bodies the better. Without a word, I marched past the group and headed towards the woods, taking the lead. They all flanked me, falling in line with two on each side of me.

"What's the plan?" Clay asked from my left.

I glanced over to Bella, my years of training sending me into battle mode. "Do you remember where you saw the creature?"

She nodded, brushing dirt from her face. She was a little banged up, but nothing serious. "Yeah. I can take you."

"You get scratched?" Quinn asked, giving her a cautious once-over.

She scowled at the necromancer as if she had just

insulted her. "Of course not. I ain't no rookie, Nightshade. The fucking thing just caught me off guard. Came out of nowhere."

No, she most definitely was not a rookie. Only a year older than myself, Bella was among the strongest fire elementals in her coven, her uncle's pride and joy since he had no children of his own. We weren't the closest of friends, but if she wanted to help, I wasn't about to turn her away.

"We should split up," I suggested. "Cover more ground." No one knew these woods better than us. "Whoever finds Anya or the Wendigo first will signal the rest of us. Bella, you're with me."

Without a word, Quinn and Tidus branched off in different directions, leaving only Bella at my side.

"This way," she said with a jerk of her chin, taking me deeper into the woods. She lit a fireball in her palm, using it as a torch to guide us through the darkness. "I bet this isn't how you thought you'd be spending your birthday, huh?"

"I had other ideas."

She tossed a smirk over her shoulder at me. "All involving that human, I bet."

At my surprised look, she said, "I saw Anya taking him upstairs earlier. She came back down alone."

I blushed, knowing I was caught. "His name is Malakai."

"He's cute."

"He is." Look at us, bonding over boys. The sharing ended there, though. I preferred my business to remain just that. *My* business. "Did you see my sister after that?"

She shook her head, her glossy dark hair swaying behind her. "No, sorry."

My stomach turned, imagining the worst. As capable as Anya was, she was still just a child.

"This is it," Bella announced as we approached a large clearing. "This is where it attacked us."

The area was littered with discarded plastic cups and empty beer bottles from the party. In the middle sat a makeshift bonfire with fresh smoke tendrils swirling in the air. I bent down to touch the scorch marks burned into the ground, spotting the footprints alongside it. Instead of the deformed hooves of a Wendigo, the prints were that of a boot.

Male, by the looks of it.

I looked up at Bella. "Quinn mentioned that something was off with the creature?"

She nodded. "That's right. It was still in human form, not fully transformed. I thought it was just a stray human until I saw the face and claws."

Standing, I scoured the area. It could be anywhere. "You got anything sharp on you?"

Frowning, Bella patted herself down. "Just this," she said, pulling out a small pocket knife.

"That'll do." Taking it, I flipped the blade upward and held out my other hand, palm up.

"What are you—"

Slowly, I pressed the serrated end into my skin, drawing a bloody line across my palm. "Wendigos are attracted to the smell of blood. We have a better chance of it coming to us than us going to it."

Something resembling respect crossed Bella's features

as she looked me up and down. "Smart." Then she turned her attention to the woods, keeping her eyes peeled and hands out for any signs of movement.

We stood there for a solid ten minutes, my hand oozing blood. I held it high in the air, allowing the wind to catch my scent and set the trap.

Then we heard it. Rustling in the trees.

A figure emerged from the shadows, crouching low on all fours before standing to its full height. The male that stepped forward was fairly tall, wearing dark jeans and a leather jacket that was down to one sleeve—courtesy of Bella. The side that was ripped away revealed burn marks running down his tattoo-covered arm, the ink now defaced by char. His forearm was bandaged by some kind of gauze, the fabric tattered and singed as well.

I bet that's where he got infected.

"That's where I got him," Bella muttered, backing closer to me.

Whoever this guy was, he was turned recently. A few days at most. Aside from the jagged, razor-sharp fangs overlapping his lips and the knives he was rocking for fingernails, his appearance was still that of a human's. His dark brown eyes were rimmed red and crazed as if he hadn't slept in days. Cranking his jaw wide, he snarled at us, body tensing like he was ready to lunge. His head kept twitching like the human was fighting to take back control.

But that was a losing battle.

The infection had already taken root. There was no saving the poor bastard at this point. His hunger was visible, froth dripping from his twisted mouth. Relief flooded me when I realized he hadn't fed yet. If he had, his transformation would've been complete by now.

Which meant there was a good chance Anya was safe.

"We need to put him down before he turns someone else," I said.

Bella nodded, her amber eyes sparking like a match before igniting the flames that shot down her arms and into her hands. "Just say the word."

I locked eyes with the beast. This was going to be quick. "On my signal."

Planting our feet, we waited for the attack. The standoff was a short one. He was faster than your average human, but not quite up to Wendigo speed. He took off at a dead run, lunging for us without any thought like the mindless savage he was quickly becoming.

I allowed him to get close before pushing an illusion into the forefront of his mind. He stopped short three feet from us, his eyes deceiving him into thinking we'd vanished. All he could see was an empty field with no one to eat. His head whipped from side to side, searching.

I glanced at Bella, giving her the go ahead with a single nod. She wasted no time. Taking one step forward, she slammed her hands into his chest with brute force. Fire surged from her body into his, spearing his chest like a blade and engulfing his body within seconds.

He screamed and stumbled back, arms and legs flailing as he hit the ground rolling. His roars gradually faded from that of a howling animal to a human in pain as the flames burned away his flesh. Wendigos were most vulnerable to fire. Though a silver blade or bullet to the heart could easily do the trick, fire was the most effective way to ensure they stayed dead.

As the flames died down, so did the screams. I waited a beat before approaching the body from the right, Bella taking the left. He wasn't moving. Only his eyes remained intact, peeled wide and frozen in place. His flesh was charred to the bone, not even an inch of skin remaining on his corpse.

I reached into his mind, finding it blank. "He's dead," I confirmed just as a murder of crows flew overhead, cawing as they passed. *Tidus.* I sighed with relief. "They found Anya."

I finally allowed myself to breathe. Two crises averted. *Thank the Goddess.*

"Check this out," Bella said, directing my attention back to our roasted friend. She crouched down, picking something up from the ground. "This must've dropped from his pocket when he fell." She held up a wallet, the blackened leather still in good condition.

She tossed it to me. "Let's see who this guy is," I said, flipping it open.

If he was a local, some serious damage control would need to be done to keep the whole *monster-on-the-loose* thing on the DL—

My eyes widened at the sight of mystery man's driver's license. Then my heart joined the party, hammering against my rib cage like it was one beat away from bursting.

No…fucking way…

It wasn't possible for my luck to be *this* shitty…it just wasn't. My hand shook as I pulled the plastic card free from the wallet, holding it closer to my face as if that would change the name printed in bold letters beside a picture of what this guy used to look like before we burnt off his face. If I squinted and looked close enough, there was almost a resemblance, one that wasn't strong enough to be noticeable at first glance, or even a second. Easily overlooked. The name, however, not so much.

Zane Slade.

SEVENTEEN

Malakai

I tipped the green Heineken bottle to my lips and turned from the pool bar. I kept to myself, observing the party from afar. The place was a madhouse.

The few faces I knew from school had already called it a night, leaving behind the rich townies and a wide array of unfamiliar faces.

Outsiders, probably.

Someone squealed as they were tossed into the water, causing a chorus of heckling laughter to erupt. Keeping far from the pool's edge, I made my way back onto the terrace. The last thing I needed was for someone to try that shit with me. It would only end with the muzzle of my gun pressed to their forehead, or my fist breaking their nose.

My unwillingness to engage in any and all social interactions was exactly what kept me from turning when a presence approached me from behind. I had zero interest in small talk with strangers. Yet they continued to linger, eyes burning into the back of my skull. Ignoring whoever it was, I kept my eyes trained on the foolishness taking place around me. Drinking competitions, daredevil stunts, and make-out sessions that were seconds away from turning into full-blown orgies.

"Not your style?" The voice was too sultry and smooth to be a teenager's.

Finally caving, I turned to see a woman standing behind me with a cat-like grin on her face. She was beautiful, in her late thirties, at least, with long midnight-black hair and light brown eyes. Her floor-length black skirt had thigh-high slits on each side, flashing nothing but skin as she sashayed closer.

The tiny hairs on the back of my neck prickled, the same way it did when a monster was near. When danger was imminent. I fought the urge to step back as she invaded my personal space. I was at least a head taller than her, but she didn't seem intimidated by that. She carried herself with enough poise and confidence to fill that lake everyone called a swimming pool behind me.

Her smoldering gaze slowly raked down my body in a way that made me surprisingly uncomfortable. I've never been one to shy away from a little female attention, even when it came from a more...mature audience. But her critical assessment of me felt more invasive than admiring.

She made a short humming sound, those ruby lips that looked like they belonged on a siren stretching even wider across her face. "I definitely see the appeal," she drawled evenly.

"Excuse me?"

Her throaty chuckle was just as alluring as her voice. "Malakai, right?"

I stood a little straighter, my chin jutting out. "Who's asking?"

Why was I being so defensive? Her very presence made me uneasy. If Zane was here, he would've dropped at least five pickup lines on her by now. But I wanted her gone.

Something in her eyes flickered as she held out her hand for me to shake. "Freya Sinclair. Luna's aunt. Pleasure to meet you."

It felt like I'd been doused with a bucket of ice water. Luna's *aunt*? The back of my neck heated. *Shit*. I was just rude to one of Luna's relatives…

So much for good first impressions.

Clearing my throat, I humbled myself and accepted her outstretched hand. "I'm sorry, Ms. Sinclair, I didn't mean to be rude."

Pulling back her hand, she waved off my offensive behavior. "No need to apologize, doll face. I like a man who can hold his own, especially if he wants to date my niece."

I was stunned stupid for a second. *Date?* I haven't even asked her out yet. "Luna's mentioned me, then?"

Her shrug was lazy, eyes blinking in the most unbothered way. "She didn't have to. I've seen you drop her off."

Ah, yes. The security cameras on the front gate.

Not wanting to make this more awkward by asking her

what else she'd seen, I quickly changed the subject. "You have a beautiful home, Ms. Sinclair."

She crossed her arms over her chest, bringing a hand up to toy with the gold necklace hanging low around her neck. Both the chain and pendant were similar to the ones Luna wore. I never paid much attention to the pattern until now. It was oddly familiar...

Catching my gaze, she tucked the pendant beneath the collar of her shirt. "Thank you. I'd offer to give you a tour, but you've already seen plenty, haven't you?"

From her impish tone, I gathered she already knew I'd seen the inside of her niece's bedroom. And judging by the glint in her eyes, she knew exactly what we had been up to. I suddenly felt the need to explain myself, to justify my intentions. "Ms. Sinclair—"

"Call me Freya," she waved again. "Ms. Sinclair was my evil cunt of a mother."

Okaaay, then...

My palms started sweating. She was just as intimidating as my old man. *I'd love to see the two of them in a room together.* Now *that* was a show I'd pay to see. Clearing my throat, I began again. "I care about your niece...*a lot*. I would never do anything to hurt her."

The truth behind my words surprised even me. Never in my life have I waited around for a girl before, much less at a party where I knew absolutely no one.

Freya rocked back on her heels as she stared up at me, her eyes looking as though they had the power to peer into my soul. "Hmm. Big words have little meaning," she said. "Only actions will tell."

I nodded, agreeing with her. "Mine will." I wasn't sure

where my confidence was coming from, or the sudden interest to prove myself to this woman. As much as I didn't *want* to hurt Luna, there was no guarantee I wouldn't. And given how often my family moved, I couldn't even guarantee how long I'd be sticking around for.

But I knew I wanted her. For now, that was enough.

Flipping her long locks over her shoulder, Freya turned from me. "I guess I'll be seeing you around, then. You kids behave." With that, she sashayed back into the house, but not before stopping at the threshold and craning her neck back to look at me. "Oh, and don't forget to use a condom, doll face. Raising kids can be a real pain in the ass."

Her words were loud enough to turn several heads on the terrace. Snickers sounded, followed by low whistles. Stunned stupid once again, I watched her disappear into the house. Shaking my head, I downed the rest of my beer and chucked the bottle into a nearby trash bin. Clearly, Luna was the only normal person in her family. If that was her aunt, what were her parents like?

Hell, even her sister seemed a little...odd.

Sighing, I pulled out my phone to check the time. Over an hour had passed and still no sign of her. *Where the hell is she?*

I frowned, scrolling through my notifications. Eight missed calls from Zane?

The last one was over three hours ago. *Fuck.* I had left my phone on silent. I quickly found his name in my contacts and hit send. Straight to voicemail. *His phone must be dead.*

Worry began trickling in. Zane never blew up my phone unless something was wrong. Good thing I was able to track his ass. *God bless Google Maps.* In our line of work, keeping tabs on each other wasn't an invasion of privacy. It was a safety measure—the life-or-death kind.

Even if his phone was dead, I'd still be able to see his last known location. Opening my map, I tapped on the icon with his face to pull up his information. His last updated location was showing…

I squinted down at the screen. *That can't be right.* According to the map, he was somewhere nearby. Close to me. Maybe he was looking for me?

That was even more worrisome than him blowing up my phone. Something was wrong. Weaving through the crowded mansion, I beelined for the exit until I was standing out front next to my bike. Hoping on, I quickly shot Luna a text:

Sorry, had to bail. Family emergency. I'll call you later.

I didn't want to leave without seeing her, but I had to make sure Zane was alright. Honing in on his location, I took off, bypassing the front gate and making a left at the end of the long path leading to the main road. I didn't have to go far. Within five minutes I found his bike on the side of the road, tipped over on the shoulder.

Shit.

I parked my Harley behind his and rushed over. It looked like he took a spill. Is that why he called? Was he hurt? I searched the area, finding his phone just a few feet away. He must've lost it in the crash. But there were no other tire marks except for his. No blood either.

A good sign, at least.

"Zane!" I hollered, hoping he was close enough to hear me. No answer. Spitting out a string of curses, I turned on the flashlight on my phone. It was pitch fucking black out here. There were no street lights near the bayou, just bush and swamp. Shining the light on the ground, I searched the gravel for footprints.

If his bike was still here, then so was he. No way would he leave it behind. There was only one set of footprints leading from his bike into the woods along the road. Why would he go in there? Why not just flag someone down and hitch a ride back to town? Guilt turned my stomach for not seeing his calls sooner.

Heading back to my bike, I lifted the middle console and pulled out my gun. Better safe than sorry. Taking inventory of how many bullets I had in the chamber, I flipped off the safety and started towards the treeline. I kept my gun aligned with my flashlight, making sure I could see what I was aiming at as I began my trek. I followed his footsteps for a while, noticing how chaotic they grew.

Why did it look like he was running?

The dread growing in the pit of my stomach worsened the further I followed his prints into the swamp. Pretty soon I found others, a group of them all scattered together in a clearing. There was an outed bonfire in the middle and some blood splattered on the ground. Not enough to be fatal, but enough to tell me something had gone down. A brawl of some kind.

Then I saw it.

A piece of black leather stomped into the ground. Going down on my haunches, I pulled it from the dirt. It was a sleeve. Or a piece of one, by the looks of it. My fist clenched, crumpling the torn fabric in my hand. It was Zane's. I didn't want to believe it, but my panic-stricken mind wouldn't allow me to come up with another alternative.

The deep-seated fear spreading through me made me want to call out again, but I bit my tongue. There was a good chance that Zane wasn't alone. And neither was I.

Continuing on, I followed the last of the footprints through a cluster of willow trees. I moved quietly, keeping the light on my feet as I made my way through.

"What should we do?"

I jerked to a halt, going perfectly still to listen for the faint voice that was barely audible to my ears. Shutting off my flashlight, I inched forward a few more steps, making as little noise as possible. The trees provided good cover, keeping me hidden as I tried to listen in.

"I don't know," came another voice. "Fuck.... FUCK!"

"Calm down, Luna. We didn't have a choice."

I stiffened, my blood running cold. *Luna?*

Creeping forward, I came to an opening in the treeline. Ducking behind a thick bark, I poked my head out just enough to scope out the area. And there she was. It was Luna alright, standing shoulder-to-shoulder with another girl. The two were looking down at something, but it was too dark to make out what. The smell of smoke carried on the wind, and not the delicious barbeque kind. It was rancid and foul, the odor stinging my nose.

What the hell are they doing out here?

Luna told me she needed to look for her sister, but why

would a kid wander out into the woods in the middle of the night by herself? Especially when there was a party going on back at the house.

"How did this even happen?" Luna said. "For all we know, there could be more of them."

More of who? I thought, crouching low in an attempt to get closer.

"Let's just go back," the brunette said. "My uncle and your aunt will know what to do."

"We can't just leave him here," Luna hissed, stepping aside to reveal the body lying on the ground at their feet.

The moonlight overhead helped me out by casting a silver glow over the clearing, illuminating the horror my eyes couldn't believe. The body was badly burnt, barely recognizable. But I knew. Right away I fucking *knew*.

Zane.

The height and build were a dead match. I feared to move any closer, to confirm what I already knew to be true. I couldn't assess his injuries from here, but there was no chance in hell anyone could survive burns that severe.

That...*brutal*.

He was gone.

The pain in my chest left me feeling dizzy, cold sweat breaking out over my forehead. The hand gripping my gun shook uncontrollably. The air in my lungs stalled. I squeezed my lids shut, warding off the tears that burned the back of my eyes. *No... This can't be happening.* My heart thundered, beating so hard it pulsed in my ears, on the verge of bursting my eardrums.

"I can just finish him," the brunette suggested next. My eyes popped open just in time to see her hold out her hand. Flames appeared, spiraling above her palm until it morphed into a sphere.

What...the fuck...?

Luna reached out, clamping her hand down on the other girl's forearm. The show of magic didn't seem to faze her, not even a little bit.

"No," she shook her head, her tone strict. "It's not our call to make. If he's a member of the town, the coven will need to decide how best to cover this up."

Bile burned my throat on its way up, threatening to spill from my mouth.

Coven.

They were witches. All of them.

Rage heated my blood, hardening my pain into revulsion. She lied to me. Has she been playing me this entire time? Did she know who I was? What I did for a living?

Christ. I almost fucked a witch.

I wasn't sure which was worse, the disgust or the disappointment mixing with my fury. How did I fucking miss this?

Steeling myself, I rose from my crouched position and adjusted the Glock in my hand. It wasn't trembling anymore. A numbness washed over me, one I welcomed. Without giving it another thought, I slid from behind the trees and stepped out into the clearing with my gun cocked.

EIGHTEEN

Luna

"**D**on't fucking move."

The sound of his voice sent a wild rush of panic flooding through me. A click echoed. Everything seemed to move in slow motion as I turned my head, catching sight of Malakai standing on the other side of the glade with a gun in his hand. He had it raised, pointed directly at me.

What the hell was he doing with a gun?

He seemed a little too comfortable holding it, like it was an extension of his arm or something. He closed in on us, moving with the unusual trained precision of a military soldier. My eyes shifted over to Bella, who still had a fireball blazing in her right hand.

How was I supposed to explain this away?

Wetting my suddenly dry throat, I took a tentative step forward, holding my hands out to the side where he could see them. "Kai, I can explain—"

He surged forward, jerking the weapon at me. "I said don't fucking move! Don't make me say it again, *witch*!"

I recoiled at the hatred in his voice. He spat the word like a curse, as if my very nature sickened him to his core. *He knows*. The coldness that radiated from him could ice over the entire swamp. How long had he been here? How much had he seen?

Clearly, he'd seen enough to know what was up.

"Please," I said carefully. "This isn't what you think it is."

He scoffed/laughed, a cruel sneer twisting his lips. "Is that right? So you and this bitch," he waved his gun at Bella, "didn't just kill my cousin?"

I could feel the blood draining from my face. My eyes flickered to the body on the ground. Cousin. This guy was his cousin. Could be worse.

At least it's not his brother…

I immediately scolded myself for the thought. *I'm a terrible person.* I didn't know how to fix this, how to make it better.

"He attacked us. He left us no choice."

His jaw clenched, eyes darkening into storm clouds as he stared me down. I stared back, unable to look away. He looked like an entirely different person with that gun in his hand, like a stone-cold-killer on a mission. I didn't recognize him, didn't know who he was anymore.

"Now *I* have no choice," he said forebodingly, reaching into his pocket with his other hand.

I tensed when he took out his cell phone and tapped something on the screen. Who was he calling? The police? They wouldn't be able to help him. Although the authorities might prove bothersome in a situation like this, it'll be easy to wipe their minds and send them on their way. The same would be done to him. Anya wasn't the only witch with mind manipulation abilities within the coven.

"Drop the phone," Bella demanded, sparking more flames in her hand, "Or I'll fry you like I did your cousin."

I whipped a glare at her. "No you fucking won't!" That wasn't happening. Not on my watch.

Her amber eyes narrowed in outrage. "Are you fucking kidding me? He's seen too much as it is."

"Just let me handle this—"

Bang!

I flinched as Bella dropped, a bullet hitting her right between the eyes.

"No!" I screamed, dropping to my knees beside her fallen form. Blood pooled around her head like a halo of death. So much blood. It took me a minute to feel the splatters on my face, to realize it was hers. Her lifeless eyes were still open, her mouth slightly ajar as she stared back at me. "No, no, no, no…" Hot tears sprang to my eyes. I turned to look at Malakai. His expression hadn't changed. He showed no sorrow for what he'd done, his eyes as cold and cruel as they were before. "H-How could you…?" My voice quivered, choking on my sorrow.

The sinister smile that touched his lips sent an icy chill down my spine. "How could I *what*? Drop the bitch who dropped my cousin? It was pretty fucking easy, actually."

I remained on my knees as he moved closer, his gun

still raised. Would he shoot me next? Even after everything that's happened between us?"

I had the power to end this, to stop him. But the thought of using my powers to hurt him—as much as he deserved it—made my chest constrict painfully. I couldn't stop the fat tears from rolling down my cheeks as he came to stand in front of me, his gun inches from my face. I stared down the barrel, tilting my head up to meet his hateful gaze head-on.

"Why are you doing this?" I choked on the words, struggling to get them out. "I thought you...cared for me."

Something in his expression changed for the briefest of moments. A flicker of...regret, maybe?

He cocked his gun again, making me flinch. "You lied to me." He actually sounded hurt, as if *he* was the victim here.

"I couldn't tell you. You weren't exactly honest with me either."

For someone who just stumbled upon two magical beings, he wasn't as freaked out as most humans would be in his position.

Quite the opposite, in fact.

He was all poise and control. I could tell by his bravado that this wasn't his first time taking a life. No. Someone who was *that* comfortable killing and *that* good of a shot already had a few bodies under their belt.

"Who are you?"

"How many of you are there?" he countered, completely ignoring my question.

"I don't know what you're talking about." Did he really think I would rat out my coven? He had no idea who he was messing with.

He inhaled a deep breath as if searching for patience. "Don't make this harder than it has to be, Luna."

Now it was my turn to scoff. "You're kidding, right? You've already made it impossible. You have no idea who you just killed."

He was finished and didn't even know it yet. The Blackwells would kill him for this, make him suffer for days before putting him out of his misery.

The thought made me queasy.

He cocked a brow, unimpressed by my shady warning. "Oh? It isn't *Sabrina the Teenage Witch*, is it? And to think, I didn't even get an autograph."

Had he always been this much of an asshole? It was like his personality did a complete one-eighty from normal to psycho. I couldn't wrap my brain around it, couldn't comprehend the horrible things he was saying and doing.

"You should run," I warned him. He didn't deserve a pass, but it was the closest thing to one he would get from me. If he ran now, he may yet live. As much as my heart was breaking, seeing him dead would only shatter it into pieces I would never be able to paste back together.

His laugh was dark, his smirk as mocking as it was cruel. "You've got that backwards, sweetheart. I'll even do you a favor and give you a head start."

Seriously? He was starting to piss me off now. My tears instantly dried as I leveled a scornful glare at him. "Don't say I didn't warn you, *sweetheart*."

Then I unleashed my power.

Digging into his mind, the first thing I altered was the

gun in his hand, twisting it into a snake.

"The fuck!" He stumbled back a few paces, eyes bulging as his grip loosened around the handle of his gun. He didn't notice it drop to the ground, or me kicking it away. He was too busy shaking the imaginary snake from his hand.

I needed to get out of here, needed to get Bella's body back to her coven. Grabbing her under the arms, I dragged her backwards against me. *If only I could levitate.* It would've made this escape attempt a hell of a lot easier. I cursed my lack of upper body strength as I hauled her back towards the pathway we came from. Enchantresses weren't physically strong, but what we lacked in muscle we made up for in willpower.

"Get this fucking thing off me!" Malakai bellowed, rolling on the ground as he tasseled with his empty hands. For the sake of being a bitch, I made the snake grow, coiling around his limbs as it expanded and thickened, weighing him down to the point of suffocation.

Once I was out of range, the illusion would fade, freeing him. But then what? He knew what I was now...who my people were. He'd met my sister, knew our faces.

Lucifer's balls. This was bad. Really fucking bad.

How many of you are there?

That single question left a strong feeling of dread lingering in the pit of my stomach. Everything about him had been so vengeful in that moment, so... terrifying. I'd never felt that from a human before, that level of danger. If he was angry enough over his cousin's death to put a bullet in Bella without any hesitation or thought, there was no telling what else he was capable of.

I really know how to pick 'em.

Sweat dripped down my face as I continued to heave Bella's body down the path, her dead weight making my arms go numb. At this rate, Malakai was going to catch up to me. Setting her down, I searched her pockets for a phone. I'd left mine back in my bedroom.

Yes!

Finding hers, I tapped the screen. Password protected. *Fuck.* I didn't know Bella well enough to know what her password might be. I made several attempts before getting locked out. *So much for that,* I grumbled.

Projection was my only other option, but I wasn't sure I could pull it off in my weakened state. I had already exerted too much energy in the last twenty-four hours, between the ritual and the party and now this? I needed time to recharge. Time I didn't have.

Dropping to my knees, I closed my eyes and concentrated. Visualizing a raven, I projected it outward until it appeared in front of me. The bird was bigger than average, with blood-red eyes and black feathers that gleamed blue under the moonlight. I sent it flying, praying to Hecate that my aunt or someone from my coven would notice it before it vanished.

My mental range would only allow it to go so far before dissipating into nothingness. Moving projections were far more difficult to maintain than immobile ones. They required more power and focus…all things I was severely lacking in my tired and frantic state.

I gritted my teeth, feeling like my head was about to explode. *Just a little further…*

Wetness trickled down my nose the more I pushed, the metallic taste touching my lips—

"This way!" a male voice hollered. Several footsteps followed the command, tramping through the swamp as a unit.

That was fast.

Overcome with dizziness, I dropped my projection, the raven fading from my mind's eye.

"Check the tracker again!" Someone else shouted.

I frowned, using the back of my hand to wipe the blood from my nose. *Tracker?*

As the footsteps grew louder, I realized that whoever was coming, wasn't coming to save me. Grabbing Bella under her arms again, I dragged her off the beaten path, maneuvering the both of us until my back braced against a tree. Resting her against my chest, I stood perfectly still, projecting an illusion to make us invisible.

In under thirty seconds, a flock of people came barrelling through the woods, heading in the same direction I left Malakai. There were five of them, all dressed in black camouflage clothing and wearing masks that obscured their faces from the nose down. They moved as a tactical unit, following a formation they were all familiar with.

Like soldiers.

Like Malakai.

I quickly ruled them out as cops when I didn't spot any police gear. No shiny badges and logo that read: *Deadwood P.D.*

These were *his* people.

It wasn't the police Malakai had called. It was *them.*

The one leading the pack kept glancing down at his phone, directing the others with hand signals. They were packing too, well-equipped with guns, knives, and ammo strapped to their chests, and Goddess knows what else. Instead of flashlights, they all sported green tinted goggles over their eyes.

Night vision.

Holy shit… Who are these people?

Waiting until they were out of earshot, I took a breath and readjusted my grip under Bella's arms. I didn't have the energy to push out another projection, but I was getting out of these fucking woods…one way or another.

NINETEEN

Malakai

Son of a bitch!

I couldn't breathe. Whatever this thing was, it wasn't a goddamn snake! It kept growing until I was coiled into a cocoon. I couldn't move, my body paralyzed as it grew tighter and tighter, locking off my airway. I gasped, struggling to pull down even the tiniest morsel of air.

She's killing me.

I tried to tell myself that the throbbing in my chest was strictly because of the enormous python slowly crushing me to death. That it had nothing to do with Luna Sinclair. I should've put her down when I had the chance, but I couldn't do it. I choked. How the hell did I end up here? Conned by a fucking witch?

And to think I was actually starting to fall for her. *So stupid...*

And now my stupidity was going to be the death of me. Just like it was for Zane. My eyes watered at the reminder, or maybe it was the lack of oxygen going to my brain. My vision grew fuzzy as the light-headedness kicked in.

"Kai!"

Dad?

A set of hands jolted me upright. "Snap out of it, son!" My father demanded in his usual drill sergeant tone.

I opened my mouth to tell him I couldn't, that I didn't have much time left. The others were with him, hovering over me in a semicircle. Why weren't they doing anything? Couldn't they see I needed help?

I opened my mouth, barely wheezing out, "S-Snake..."

My father's brows knitted in confusion.

"What the fuck is he talking about?" someone muttered.

Then my father's face relaxed as if he finally understood. "Sorry about this, boy," he said before cocking back his fist and clocking me a solid one in the face.

The punch swiftly landed me on my back, blinking up at the sky in bewilderment. The unbearable weight holding me down lifted, fresh air filling my lungs again.

"You alright, Kai?" Dad asked.

I sat up, frantically patting myself down. The snake was gone. "Where did it go?"

"Where did *what* go?" a voice I recognized to be Alex's asked.

Someone clapped my hand and pulled me to my feet. Derek.

"The giant fucking snake that was wrapped around me," I said, still searching for it. "It was just here."

They all looked at each other as if I'd lost my mind.

My father's hand clamped down on my shoulder. His gaze roamed over me, searching for injuries. "There was no snake, son. We came as soon as we got your S.O.S. Found you on the ground gasping for air. You were alone."

I paused. Then it clicked. "Fucking witch," I growled, scrubbing a hand down my face. "She must've gotten into my head."

"Witch?" the others echoed.

I nodded and filled them in, deliberately leaving out my connection to Luna. She was mine, and I intended to deal with her myself.

"How many?"

"You got a bead on their location?"

"What kind of abilities are we looking at?"

I opened my mouth to answer their questions when one of the guys, Felix, called out, "Hey, we got a body over here."

They all turned, ready to investigate. I tensed, my stomach plummeting to the floor. I had to tell them. They needed to hear it from me before they went over there. Before they saw for themselves...

"It's Zane." I didn't know how else to say it.

Everyone froze, heads snapping in my direction. I was thankful I couldn't see their expressions, their faces all covered by masks and night vision goggles.

Except for my father. His eyes and nostrils flared all at once, color draining from his face. "What did you just say?"

I swallowed, the words getting lodged in my throat as I tried to force them out. "I tracked him here earlier when I couldn't get a hold of him and found his bike on the side of the road. But by the time I got here…it was too late. Found the witches standing over his body. He was already—"

Brushing past me, Dad rushed over, dropping to his knees next to his nephew. The others followed. I didn't look. I *couldn't*. It was too much. Their sobs only added to my guilt, to the part I played in Zane's death.

God, how was I supposed to tell Uncle Luke that his last remaining son was dead? Gone to join his brother only a year after his death.

I didn't flinch when my father reappeared in front of me. Tears soaked his cheeks, a ruthless scowl distorting his face. "Tell me everything," he demanded, his voice shaking with uncontrollable rage. At that moment, he wasn't my father. He was my leader.

I felt numb, the words flowing out of me as if I wasn't attached to them. "There were two witches when I got here. One possessed fire-like abilities, the other some sort of mind manipulation power." I was careful not to mention Luna by name, protecting her for the time being.

"Did you recognize either of them?"

I hesitated a fraction of a second before answering. "No, sir."

He paused, those battle-hardened eyes analyzing my every tick and twitch, searching for tells. He knew them well. "What else do you know?"

I had to give him something before he found out on his

own. Allister Slade was nothing if not resourceful. "I think they came from a party the Sinclairs were throwing. This is their land."

He nodded. "I know. I saw the sign on our way in."

Case in point.

"Were you at this party?" He didn't blink, and neither did I.

I maintained eye contact, keeping a straight face at all times. "No, sir." Revealing I was there would mean revealing *why* I was there. And with who.

"Was Zane?"

"No, sir.

"Then what the hell was he doing out here?"

Fucking Christ! "I. Don't. Know," I gritted out, my patience growing thin. "Like I said, I tracked his phone and it led me here. When I confronted the witches, they admitted to killing him. I popped one of 'em and the other got away." That was all he was getting out of me.

His brows creased as he looked around. "Where's the body?"

I blinked, taken aback. "What?"

"The witch you said you killed, where's her body?"

I searched the glade, finally realizing the bitch was gone. I spat out a curse, stabbing my fingers through my hair. "She was just here. I got her right between the eyes. There's no way she walked away from that."

Witches may be immortal, but they weren't immune to death. They could be killed just as easily as any other creature, especially with the warded bullets we loaded into our guns that nullified all magic. We melted and molded them ourselves, etching the runes into the metal of each slug by hand.

One of the guys walked over, pulling off his mask and goggles. It was Clint. "Found his gun," he said, holding out my Glock. "A single bullet was discharged."

I took it from him and checked the chamber before flipping on the safety and tucking it into my waistband. "Yeah, the one currently in that bitch's head, wherever she is."

Clint nodded, respect shining in his eyes. "We'll find her. You did good, putting one of them down."

My father nodded in agreement but said nothing. He was never one to dish out praise. "You three," he barked at Alex, Derek and Felix. "Take Zane's body back to the truck and wait for us."

I closed my eyes and swallowed, fighting to get down my own saliva. Zane's body. I wasn't ready to hear shit like that, to accept that this was real life and he was really fucking gone.

Dad returned his gaze to mine, still in leader mode. I would get no words of comfort from him tonight. "Take me and Clint to the Sinclair house. We'll scope it out from the woods, see what we can find. If the witches came from there, maybe the one who got away went back."

She definitely did, I thought, once again keeping quiet.

"You get a good look at them?" Clint asked, reaching into his pack and handing me an extra pair of goggles.

"Only one," I lied. "It was dark."

If he thought I was being dishonest, he didn't call me out on it.

"Lead the way," my father said.

Slipping on the goggles, I took point, keeping my eyes

sharp for any signs of Luna. Part of me prayed she got away. The last thing I wanted was to run into her with Clint and my father at my back. The thought of either of them putting a gun to her head as I had left me feeling unsettled. And I hated myself for it.

I wasn't even sure what I would do once I got my hands on her...

It didn't take me long to find a set of tracks in the dirt. Drag marks. *She took the body.* Why would she do that? Why not just leave it behind and save herself?

If she was physically dragging her friend's corpse around, that meant she didn't have the power or strength to lift it. *All she has is her mind tricks.* Good to know.

I followed the tracks until it led to an opening in the treeline. Holding out my hand, I signaled for Clint and my father to stop and take cover.

We were here.

Dad sidestepped to the left while me and Clint took the right, putting our backs against a set of trees to keep ourselves hidden. I couldn't hear anything. No music, no chatter, no signs that there was a party happening.

Was it over?

Signaling with a closed fist for them to hold their positions, I crept forward to get a better look.

What the fuck?

It was gone. The entire Sinclair compound was gone. All that stood in its place was an empty lot surrounded by swamp and weeds that looked like they had been growing there for years.

I moved in, Clint and my father slowly trailing behind me. I shook my head. "This...can't be right."

"Did you take a wrong turn?" Dad asked.

No, I didn't. Something wasn't right. The hair on the back of my neck stood on end. We were being watched. I could practically *feel* her eyes on me.

This was her power. It had to be.

"I guess I did," I lied yet again, not wanting to alert Luna that I was on to her little game. "We should come back at first light with more bodies and fresh eyes. We'll cover more ground."

My father gave me a look but agreed nonetheless. He wasn't stupid. He knew I was hiding something. "Fine," he said. "Let's go."

As we turned to head back, I threw one last glance over my shoulder. *I'm coming for you, Luna. Just you fucking wait.*

TWENTY

Luna

*T*hat was close.

My head swung, the forest around me spinning like a freaking merry-go-round as I dropped to my knees. I held the projection until Malakai and his people were far out of sight, blood dripping down my nose from the overexertion I forced my body to endure. I was reaching my limit, my energy levels running on reserves from using my powers all night.

"Luna!"

I couldn't answer, could barely catch my breath as Quinn's face appeared in front of mine moments after I collapsed on the front lawn.

"Bella…" I managed to wheeze out. "Help…her."

I could hear footsteps approaching, people running, voices overlapping.

Quinn turned her head to yell at someone. "Get

Freya!" Then her pale blue orbs were back on me. "What the hell happened, Sinclair?"

The question alone made my eyes water. I didn't know where to start. How was I supposed to explain that the boy I brought into our home just put a bullet in one of our own?

And was about to do the same to me.

I squeezed my eyes shut, willing my tears away. *This is all my fault.* None of this would've happened if I hadn't thrown that stupid party to get closer to Malakai. I brought him here. Exposed him to my people...to our secrets.

And now Bella was dead.

I heard my aunt before I saw her. "Luna, baby, are you alright?" She dropped to her knees beside me, pulling me into her arms.

William wasn't far behind, his voice booming over everyone else's as he tore through the crowd that was already forming. "Bella? Bella!"

I turned my head into my aunt's chest, unable to bear the look of absolute distraught on his face at the sight of his niece lying dead at my feet with a hole in her skull. It was my final tipping point, the floodgates opening as a sob broke loose.

"I'm sorry..." My lips trembled. "I didn't mean for this to happen, Aunt Freya."

She cradled my head to her bosom, stroking my hair in that same soothing way my mother used to when I was little. "Shh," she hushed, "it's okay, my sweet girl."

My lids cracked just in time to see William hoist Bella into his arms, her lifeless head flopping back on her shoulders as he stood to his feet.

"Summon the necromancers!" he ordered, the crowd parting for him as he took off.

Necromancers? I looked up at Aunt Freya. "Can they save her?" I asked, hope filling my broken heart.

She brushed some hair from my face, offering me a reassuring smile. "They'll try. As long as her soul hasn't crossed the veil yet, there's a chance. You did the right thing bringing her body back with you."

A shaky breath left my lips. Good. That was good.

"Luna, you need to tell me what happened. Who did this?"

I paused, dreading what would happen once I confessed the truth. I still wanted to protect Malakai, even if it meant dealing with him myself. "There was a Wendigo on the loose in the swamp. We went looking for Anya when we found it and killed it, but then..." I hesitated, weighing my options before making a split-second decision. "These people showed up, armed from head to toe and wearing tactical gear. They moved like soldiers and wore masks. I couldn't see their faces."

Aunt Freya frowned. "How many?"

"Five, maybe six."

"Did they see you use your powers?"

She cursed when I nodded. "They didn't seem scared. Just angry."

"Angry about what?"

I shrugged. "The Wendigo we found was newly turned. I think he was one of them. They weren't too happy about us putting him down, so they killed Bella. Kept asking if there were more of us."

Okay, so I was leaving out some major details. Guilt and shame stabbed at my conscience. I was such a traitor. Letting the enemy go free because of a silly fucking crush.

Aunt Freya remained quiet, the wrinkle in her brow deepening as she thought long and hard over what I was telling her. Did she believe me?

I looked over at Quinn who stood just behind my aunt, her eyes narrowing in curiosity. She knew I was withholding information. She was always better at calling me out on my bullshit than anyone else. I shot her a look, silently begging her to keep her observations to herself. She nodded, reading me loud and clear.

"They sound like hunters."

My eyes snapped back to Aunt Freya's, flaring wide. "Hunters?"

Sighing heavily, she helped me to my feet. "We deal with them from time to time. Humans who like sticking their noses in our business instead of keeping it in their world where it belongs. They think anyone or anything who isn't human deserves to be in a grave six feet under. Nuisances, the lot of them, but they can be dangerous. Especially the ones who know what they're doing."

I'd heard stories of hunters killing our kind before, but I'd never met any until now.

And now one has seen me naked.

My stomach flipped inside out. I wanted to scream my frustration into the universe but swallowed down the urge when it rose. *This can't be happening*...

"Is there anything else?" Aunt Freya asked as if sensing my deception.

I made sure to look her in the eyes when I shook my head, feeling like the treacherous piece of shit that I was. *Hecate, forgive me.* I took a vow less than twenty-four hours ago to protect my coven, and now I was the sole reason they were in danger.

Aunt Freya studied me closely, her expression somewhat skeptical. "Very well," she finally nodded. "I need to call a meeting with the other coven leaders. If there are hunters in town, everyone must be warned. Go get some rest."

Rest? I didn't need any rest. "But I can help—"

"No. I'll take it from here, Luna-bear. If I need you, I'll call you." Giving my shoulder a firm squeeze, she turned and marched back to the house, yelling at everyone who didn't live there to go the fuck home.

Her words, not mine.

The party was clearly over.

"Now will you tell me what the fuck is going on?" Quinn asked once the coast was clear.

"It was Malakai," I admitted numbly. It still didn't feel real, the words foreign in my mouth. "He was one of the hunters."

Quinn's jaw dropped. "You're joking."

I wish I was. "He was the one who shot Bella. The Wendigo we killed was his cousin." Turning, I pinned her with a stern look. "You can't tell anyone, Quinn. Promise me."

Looking around, she zipped closer, lowering her voice to a whisper. "Have you lost your fucking mind, Sinclair? You need to tell the others. What if he comes after you again?"

"I can juice up the security around the property. He and his people won't be able to get inside."

She threw her hands up as if I was missing the point. "And what about the rest of us? If he knows what you are, it won't be long before he starts making connections to identify other coven members. We all go to the same school, for fuck's sake!"

"Aunt Freya is meeting with the coven leaders now. They'll come up with a plan to protect every—"

Grabbing my shoulders, Quinn gave me a hard shake. "You aren't listening! You need to protect *yourself!* You can't lock yourself away forever. He's a fucking *hunter* and only we know about it. That information can help the others find him and his people faster. Doesn't his family own a mechanic shop or something—"

I slapped a hand over her mouth. "Keep your voice down! I know, okay? I'm going to handle it."

She shook me off with a glare. "Handle it *how*? You can't just go after them by yourself."

"Not them," I deadpanned. "Just him."

She scoffed, rolling her eyes to the heavens. "Then what? If you really wanted to kill him, he would've been dead already, worms eating his eyeballs as we speak. But he's not! So, what's the grand plan here, Sinclair? Get Anya to wipe his mind?"

Damn Quinn and her bullshit detector!

She huffed out an exasperated sigh when I said nothing, confirming her suspicions. "That won't guarantee his life, Luna. If he's with the other hunters when the covens track them down, he's as good as dead and you know it."

She was right. All I was doing was endangering everyone the longer I kept this from them.

Rubbing my temples, I turned from her. "I just...need to be alone for a while."

She didn't follow me as I walked back to the house, making my way inside and up to my bedroom as calmly as possible. I was on the verge of a breakdown, and I didn't need an audience to witness it.

Closing the door behind me, I leaned against it and slowly slid to the floor, my chest heaving up and down, hyperventilating to the extreme. The room spun, forcing my eyes shut to ward off the dizziness. *Breathe, Luna. Just breathe.* I repeated the mantra over and over only to break apart anyway, succumbing to my grief. Bringing my knees to my chest, I curled into a ball and cried. Sob after sob wrecked me until I was a trembling mess, hot flowing tears drenching my cheeks until my eyes began to swell.

Sniffling, I looked up to see a neatly wrapped little box sitting in the center of my bed, the sight momentarily putting a pin in my pity party.

I frowned. *Who put that there?*

Curious, I sauntered over. The packaging was simple, with white wrapping paper and a light purple bow stuck to the top. It fit nicely in the palm of my hand and even had a note attached to the bow, hanging by a rope-like string. Perched on the edge of my bed, I flipped over the note to see who it was from. My pulse quickened.

> *Happy Birthday Beautiful. I hope*
> *to spend more of them with you.*
> *Xoxo - Kai.*

My hands shook as I unwrapped the packaging one corner at a time. By the time I got to the black velvet box underneath, my heart was like a wrecking ball in my chest. I took a staggering breath before lifting the lid to reveal the gold charm bracelet cushioned inside. It was beautifully crafted with three little dainty charms dangling from gold links.

I touched the first charm. A backpack. It looked almost identical to the one I returned to Malakai the first day we spoke. The second was a motorcycle—his Harley. I couldn't even think of the bike without remembering the way he kissed me while straddling it. The way he made me feel...

And the third was the number eighteen—for my birthday. Each charm represented memories we both shared, memories that were now tainted and ugly. I didn't realize I'd put the bracelet on until it was already strapped to my wrist, the smooth gold links caressing my skin.

The tears returned, prickling my eyes as I struggled to keep them at bay. Why did it have to be him? And why did it hurt *this* much? We were just beginning to get to know each other, yet the pain felt as though I was losing something special. Something I would never be able to find again.

A ping rang out. Looking towards my dresser, I spotted my phone right where I had abandoned it earlier. The birthday messages were probably pouring in from people who had no idea what had gone down tonight. Needing a distraction, I picked up the device and scrolled through all my messages, my lungs deflating when I got to the last one.

From Malakai.

Seeing his name pop up on my screen had the same effect as the gift he'd left for me. Tingling excitement. And what I read next made me hate myself for it.

You can't hide forever, witch.

TWENTY-ONE

Malakai

I ignored my father's scrutinizing gaze as I packed the car, throwing everything I needed into the backseat.

"Is there a reason why you can't fill me in on this plan of yours?" he asked, arms folded as he leaned against the bumper. The car was a loaner, one of Clint's. We'd been staying with him and his people for the past three days since the auto yard was no longer safe. It wasn't that hard to convince my dad to clear out since almost everyone in Deadwood knew that we owned the place.

Including Luna.

I still hadn't told anyone about her, nor did I intend to. I shared whatever information I had on the Sinclairs and those associated with them without mentioning her name. No one needed to know.

She was mine.

As much as I tried not to, I still wanted her.

Damn her!

Though I wasn't entirely sure what I was going to do once I caught her, I knew her capture would lead us straight to the other witches who were obviously hiding in plain sight. We've had eyes on the Sinclair property for days now, but there was no activity, no one coming or going. And just like in the woods, we couldn't get eyes on the house, only the iron gate that secured the area—which was now electrified and at least ten feet taller. Something that was impossible to do overnight.

It was an illusion, obviously. One of *hers*. How I didn't realize it sooner was beyond me. And though I knew it wasn't real, it still *felt* real, a barrier we couldn't get past.

Throwing in the last bag, I shut the door and turned to face my father. "Some of these witches may be mind-readers. The less you know the better." It was a plausible enough excuse to stop him from asking questions. "If my plan works, you'll be able to get inside the Sinclair house. Just keep an eye out for the signal."

"What's the signal?"

"You'll know it when you see it." If Luna was truly the one crafting these illusions, then taking her off the board was our way in. "Split the guys up if you can. We need eyes on the Nightshades, Crowleys, Blackwells, and the Hollows too."

Luna hung around that crowd way too often for it to be a coincidence. Either they knew something, or they were witches themselves. And the fact that they had all been MIA from school—herself included—since the night of her birthday only solidified my theory. She was avoiding me, protecting her people.

Not for long.

My father frowned, eyeing me closely. "You really think all these families are made up of witches?"

I shrugged. "Call it a hunch."

Again with that skeptical look. I could tell he wasn't buying the shit I was feeding him, but he seemed to trust me enough to let me run this. A surprise in itself. Especially after what happened to Zane...

I shook his face from my mind.

We had only put him to rest two nights ago, burning what was left of him on a hunter's pyre. It almost didn't seem right, burying him the same way he'd been killed, consumed by flames. But that was our way—a hunter's funeral. Uncle Luke was still in shambles, drinking his way to the bottom of every whisky bottle he could get his hands on, throwing fists and slurred curses at anyone who tried to pry it from his grip. Each night before passing out in a drunk stupor, he would rant and rave about how he never got to say goodbye to his son.

None of us did.

I thought it would've eased his mind to know that I killed the bitch who killed Zane, but it didn't. Nor did it ease mine.

I want them all dead! He had screamed the night we brought Zane home, his body burned beyond recognition. *Every fucking last one of them!*

Can't say I disagreed with him.

But you do, a voice echoed in my mind. The same one that kept telling me I couldn't kill Luna. I blocked it out.

Because I had to. For Zane.

"Well, if your *hunch* is correct," Dad said, following me over to the driver's side door. "We'll need to call in more reinforcements. We've never dealt with witches on this grand of a scale before. It'll be a bloodbath."

I nodded, already anticipating that. "Call them. Get everything ready. I'll be in touch."

Locking eyes with me, he clamped a hand down on my shoulder and pulled me in for a quick hug, clapping me on the back. "Be careful, son."

I forced a tight-lipped smile, trying to make it as reassuring as possible. "I will. I learned from the best, remember?"

He chuckled and stepped back. "Keep your tracker on."

"Yes, sir."

Ducking inside the borrowed Ford Fusion, I threw it in drive and sped off, glancing at my father in the rear-view. I felt like shit for keeping the truth from him, but there was no other way.

This was between me and *her*.

Parking a mile down from her house, I waited until Derek was in position before texting Luna the staged photo I took with a little help from Clint's daughter. Sarah Donavan and Quinn Nightshade had similar body types, close enough that it'd be pretty hard to decipher who was who with a bag over their heads.

Sarah posed for the picture late last night without much coaxing, even letting me bound her hands and legs without complaint. Clint rarely involved his precious little girl on hunts, and she was itching to earn her stripes, a weakness I exploited by insisting her aid would help bring down a town full of witches.

After sending the picture, along with a message—*Better come and get her while she's still breathing*—I called Derek.

He picked up on the first ring.

"Do it," I ordered.

"On it."

Within seconds, my cell phone crashed. *Good man.*

Derek was a brilliant hacker. MIT didn't know what they were losing when he turned them down to hunt full-time. There wasn't a piece of tech in existence he couldn't hack his way into. In this case, he fucked over anyone within a fifty-block radius of my location, downing all communication devices. No service or network.

Temporarily, of course.

It would be back up within a few hours. That was all the time I needed. I knew this was a long-shot. If these witches had other *magical* forms of communication, my plan would be dead in the water. I'd encountered enough of their kind to know that most of their abilities were unique to the individual user. Luna's was illusionary based. I wasn't sure what else she could do, or Quinn for that matter.

Here's hoping they're not telepathic.

The sun was already setting when I arrived. Under the cover of darkness, I popped the trunk and rolled out the spikes across the road. If Luna decided to go after her friend, she would have to come this way. These roads were often deserted, seeing less traffic than the ones closer to town.

I sat and waited patiently, prepared to be out there all

night if I had to. But luck was on my side. Within thirty minutes, I spotted a pair of headlights headed in my direction. I was parked off-road with no headlights on, my windows tinted heavily enough to keep my face hidden. It helped that the road was pitch black, so dark no one would be able to see me until *after* crossing the spikes.

I grew anxious the closer the vehicle got, the steep slope of the road pushing it past the speed limit. Or maybe the driver was just in a rush to get to where they were going. There was no way to tell if it was her or not. Truth be told, I'd never seen Luna behind the wheel of a car before. Did she even know how to drive?

Damn. I never even considered that.

I held my breath as the vehicle hit the spikes, tires screeching loudly as they popped. The car spun out, doing a donut in the middle of the road before coming to a full stop. The headlights faced away from me, doing me a favor as I jumped out and hot-footed it over to the driver's side.

It was a nice car. A sleek black Audi R8, two-door with tints darker than mine. Exactly the kind of car I expected a Sinclair to be cruising around in.

A shame I had to fuck it up.

Palming my gun, I used the butt end to strike the glass, smashing it into shards. The scream that followed was feminine. The girl behind the wheel had her head turned in the opposite direction, shielding her face from the shattered glass. But I didn't need to see her face. That auburn hair was a dead giveaway.

Got her.

"Going somewhere?" I drawled, aiming my gun at her

head.

When she whipped around to face me, I almost lost all common sense. It was Luna alright, but her eyes were different. Instead of light brown, a deep purple greeted me. Her irises were like crystals, blown so wide she didn't have pupils.

I'd never seen anything like it.

On anyone else, it would've been creepy. Downright disturbing. But on her, it was…mesmerizing. It suited her a lot better than the brown ever did.

She was absolutely fuming, wishing me dead ten different ways with her eyes. "You fucking asshole!" she yelled, jerking forward in her seat to attack me, forgetting she still had on her seatbelt. "What did you do to Quinn!"

I dropped the gun an inch, aiming for her neck and squeezing the trigger.

Pop!

She flinched when the dart hit her, lashes fluttering rapidly as she reached up to pluck it from her neck. "What…did you…"

Her words trailed off, eyes slowly drifting shut as her forehead fell against the steering wheel. Opening her door from the inside, I unbuckled her seatbelt and lifted her into my arms, ignoring the twinge in my chest when her head lolled against my shoulder, her body fitting perfectly against mine.

Get it together, Slade.

Walking back to my car, I popped the trunk and laid her gently inside. Grabbing my supplies from the backseat, I made quick work of binding her hands and feet before tying a blindfold over her eyes. Though the extent of her power was still somewhat of a question mark, I could only assume she couldn't manipulate what she couldn't see. If that wasn't the case, the sedative I dosed her with was strong enough to keep her weak for at least a couple hours until I could implement a more...*permanent* solution.

Giving her a quick pat down, I found her phone and dashed it. A little gift for her people to find when they come looking for her.

Reaching up to close the trunk, I spared her one last pitying look. Hesitation gripped me. Just the sight of her had me by the fucking balls. I didn't like this. Every instinct I had was telling me to untie her. To let her go.

Then I remembered Zane's charred flesh and my anger returned tenfold.

She deserved this. Her and her people.

She's nothing but a monster.

With that reminder, I slammed the trunk shut, locking her inside.

TWENTY-TWO

Luna

I woke with a start when something jerked from underneath me, jarring me back to reality. I tried to shake off the grogginess that weighed me down, my mouth so dry I could barely gather enough saliva to wet my throat. My eyelids were heavy in a way that had nothing to do with the blindfold blocking my vision.

Where am I?

The disorientation was real. So was the nausea rolling around in my stomach. *I'm going to be sick...*

I couldn't move, my arms bound behind my back as I lay on my side. I kicked out my legs, hissing when they collided with something hard and metal. "Fuck!"

My ankles were stuck together with the same shit laced around my wrists. It felt like...zip ties? I wiggled every which way to free myself, wincing each time the straps dug into my skin, rubbing it raw.

"Dammit!" I jerked upright, my head slamming into something hard. "Ow!" I fell back, turning my face into the carpeted flooring below me.

Wait. Carpet? Tight space?

Of course. I was in a car. Or the trunk of one, at least. I could feel the movement of the road vibrating against my body, accompanied by twists and turns every so often. The bumps were the worst, adding to my nausea with every sharp jolt and lurch.

How did I end up here?

The memory came with a shooting pain that pierced my cranium.

Malakai did this.

The last thing I remembered was him holding a gun to my head. Then he shot me. He actually fucking shot me! But not with a bullet. Rolling my neck from side to side, a dull ache pinched the column of my throat.

He drugged me, the bastard.

I should've known that picture of Quinn was a trap, but doubt had gotten the best of me. With hunters lurking about, all the covens were on high alert, the elders implementing strict lockdown orders until it was safe to go about our business again. Which meant no going out, especially alone. Even school was off-limits.

But it had been three days and people were getting antsy. What if Quinn decided to sneak off? I was on the verge of calling her, just to check, when my phone suddenly crashed. It was a colossal mistake to go off on my own, but I reacted without thinking.

Stupid!

Aunt Freya was going to kill me. And her car...

After destroying all four tires, Malakai had smashed the window to get to me, racking up the repair bill on Aunt Freya's Audi. I had waited for her and William to leave before snatching her keys, since the lovebirds decided to ride together. The coven leaders were meeting tonight to move forward with their plans and, despite his ill-treatment of me, the thought of them getting their hands on Malakai still wasn't sitting right.

I wanted to deal with him myself.

Guess I got my wish...

Where the hell is he even taking me? Why not just kill me and be done with it?

Rubbing my face against the carpet, I tried to nudge the blindfold off. If I couldn't see him, I wouldn't be able to get inside his head to work my magic. My illusions would be useless. Projections were my only hope, but I still needed a target—somewhere to aim them.

Did he somehow know that?

It would certainly explain my current bondage situation. Giving up on the blindfold, I tried something else.

"Hey, asshole! Let me out of here!" Hiking up my knees, I banged them against the top of the trunk, making as much noise as possible. "Let. Me. Out!"

My answer came in the form of music blasting all around me. He turned up the radio, tuning me out as he kept driving. He even sped up a little, the bumps in the road growing more frequent. I kept banging until my knee caps grew sore and tender. They would turn black and blue soon enough.

"Urgh!" My arms were getting numb in this position, a

tingling sensation settling in. *I can't believe he's really doing this.* The pang in my chest returned, the one I'd been desperately trying to ignore for days.

I inhaled a deep, soothing breath. I needed to focus. To think. I couldn't see him, or the vehicle I was crammed inside of, but I could *feel* it. It wasn't much to go off of, nor was it a skill I practiced often, but it might be enough to get him to stop the car to check on me.

Then I'll attack.

Slowing my heart rate, I twisted around onto my stomach, pressing my cheek against the carpet so I could get a better feel of the road. I envisioned it below me, the gravelly asphalt zooming by, the yellow lines separating us from oncoming traffic. The sound of other vehicles whizzing by were few and far apart, which told me the road was vacant enough to do what I was about to do next.

Concentrating, I projected the image of cracks forming in the road in my mind's eye, giant fissures forking out below me until it reached the front of the car, opening up like a crater to swallow us whole—

The car swerved, then jerked to a stop, sending my head crashing into something hard again. I groaned, the abrupt movement amping my queasiness up to a ten.

I'm seriously going to hurl...

A door opened and slammed, the force of it creating a ripple I could feel in my bones. Then a click came from above. Fresh air wafted in. I took a deep breath, hoping it would help settle my stomach a little. I could feel the presence of someone towering over me, the weight of their gaze burning holes into my body.

"Malakai? Is that you?"

He took a while to answer. And though I couldn't see his gaze, it still made me squirm.

"Stop with your fucking tricks, witch," he grated with irritation, "or else I'll hit you with another tranq dart."

I swallowed at the sound of his voice. Cold. Just like that night in the woods. "Where's Quinn?" I still wasn't sure if he had her or not.

He scoffed as if my question was stupid. "Don't know. Probably hiding with the rest of your people. I never had her."

Yep. I was definitely the stupid one here. "What do you want with me, then? If you're going to kill me, you might as well get it over with. Because once my people find me, you're a dead man."

"Hmm. They'll be too busy to come looking for you, I'm afraid."

I blinked underneath the blindfold. "What are you talking about?"

"I got a better question for you." I could practically hear the smirk in his voice, gloating as if he'd already won the war. "How far is the range on your power? I assume you must have one, or else I'd still be wrestling with that snake, and that nice house of yours would still be protected. Or maybe your lack of consciousness did the trick. I can't be sure."

My lack of...

My eyes bulged beneath the blindfold, the air seizing in my lungs as my heart thumped from the lack of oxygen. My illusions. The security around the house. *No...*

He was right. How long was I out for? My spell around

the property was a fixed projection that could withstand a little distance, sure, but would've broken the second I lost consciousness, leaving everyone vulnerable if they didn't fix it in time.

I just endangered my entire family…

I shook from the realization. This was his plan all along, to lure me away to get to the others. And it worked. "W-Where am I? Where are you taking me?"

"I'm not going to tell you that," he uttered calmly. "Just know that you're hours from home. Your illusions disappeared a while ago. We've already breached your home. It's just a matter of time now."

Fuck, fuck, fuck…

As panic threatened to consume me, I reminded myself that the others were smart. Powerful. They wouldn't fall so easily. Hardening my voice, I filled it with as much bravado as I could muster. "You sure about that? When did you last hear from your people?"

His silence told me it had been a while. If he knew more, he would've been barging about it, throwing their deaths in my face to hurt me.

I grinned at the small victory, satisfied to have rattled him if only for a moment. "I see. You should hurry back. Maybe you'll make it in time to say your goodbyes before my coven slaughters all of them."

"Shut your fucking mouth," he spat vehemently.

I laughed heartily, putting on my best baby voice. "Oh, did I hit a nerve? Is the little human upset? Cry me a river and go drown in it, bitc—"

His hand shot out, locking around the front of my throat. He squeezed, his menacing voice growing closer.

"How about I drown you in one on my way back to dig graves for your aunt and sister."

I gasped. What a cruel thing to say. I guess that's what I got for throwing jabs I couldn't take. I tried not to flinch at his rough treatment, proving to him that I wasn't afraid.

"Fuck you," I hissed. "I wish I never met you."

His warm breath fanned across my face as he leaned in. "Like-fucking-wise," he growled, the words strained as if he was barely containing himself.

Was this really the same guy I was swooning over only days ago? Doodling his name in my notebook like a stupid little girl? *Never again.* From here on out, I planned to do background checks on all my crushes. No exceptions.

"You better kill me," I wheezed out when his grip tightened. "Because that's what I'm going to do to you the first fucking chance I get." A lofty threat, considering I've never actually killed anyone before.

He would be my first.

Oh, the irony.

I wanted him to be my first for so many other things...

He laughed in my face. "You're pretty brave for someone bound and gagged."

"I'm not gag—hmmm." Something soft went over my mouth, his hands working to tie it behind my head. *Prick.*

"This should keep you quiet for a while," he muttered right before a sharp sting pinched the side of my neck.

The grogginess returned full force, my lids growing heavy, my limbs growing tingly and numb.

Not again...

TWENTY-THREE

Malakai

Why the hell isn't anyone answering their goddamn phone? I thought, pulling into a motel just off the interstate. I'd been driving for hours and needed a break. Plus, Luna's sedative would be wearing off soon. I needed to get her inside and detained before that happened.

Hours had passed without an update from the crew. The last text I received was from Derek telling me that my plan had worked and they were able to breach the Sinclair house. It'd been nothing but radio silence since.

Did something go wrong?

Fishing out my phone, I tried my dad again, but the call went straight to voicemail. *Dammit.*

Choosing a parking spot closest to the ground level rooms of the motel, I hopped out and popped the trunk, checking to make sure my hostage was still down for the count. I looked around before lifting the top. The area was dark and remote, too early in the morning for people to be roaming about.

Better for me.

I peeked inside to find Luna in the same position I left her, on her side with her hands bound behind her back and her legs curled up in the fetal position. Given how long she'd been like this, she had probably lost circulation in her limbs hours ago.

I tried not to feel bad about that, pushing the guilt down as far as it could go. Pressing two fingers to her neck, I quickly checked her pulse. Strong and steady.

Good.

Closing her in again, I headed towards the motel lobby, taking count of the security cameras along the way. Only two were mounted near the front entrance, with another set located on the upper level.

Areas to avoid.

The guy at the front desk didn't give me any trouble, so focused on his word jumble he couldn't be bothered with me.

"Room for two," I said.

"One bed or two?" he muttered without looking up from his puzzle, his tone indicating just how much he hated his life.

"Two. Something on the lower floor. Near the back, preferably."

"How many nights?"

I wasn't sure. However long it took the others to get the job done. "Two, for now."

He rang me up and reached under his desk for the keys. "Room 108, straight down on the left."

Taking what was offered, I sauntered back to the car and moved it closer to the room that was thankfully situated near the back of the building with no cameras in sight. I spent some time getting everything set up, grabbing my supplies from the backseat. The bed furthest from the door would be Luna's. Pulling the red spray-paint from my duffle, I got to work drawing sigils on every door and window that could be used as an escape route. The symbols were most effective against demons but, if altered correctly, could also be used against witches, preventing them from entering or escaping any space as long as the sigil remained intact.

Once finished, I gathered Luna from the trunk, gritting my teeth against the feel of her in my arms, the way her skin heated mine with just a simple graze. God, she felt perfect. Why was this so fucking hard?

Her low, muffled groans told me she would wake soon, pushing me to move faster. Laying her down on the bed, I rolled up her sleeves and pulled a needle and syringe from my bag. Using a tourniquet, I tied off her arm and tapped the biggest vein visible, inserting the needle and drawing back on the syringe until her blood filled the vial.

I didn't need much.

I cursed myself for being so gentle with her, even going as far as disinfecting the injection site and applying a Band-Aid like a fucking nurse. Without meaning to, I caressed one of her supple cheeks, flinching when she subconsciously leaned into my touch.

Enough of this!

Leaving her side, I sat on the bed across from hers and

got to work setting up the tattoo gun I'd brought with me. Next, I infused the ink with her blood, muttering out the incantation I knew by heart over the mixture and setting it aside. It was a simple immunity spell; one that didn't require any innate magical abilities to pull off. Peeling off my jacket and t-shirt, I searched my skin for an empty spot. I'd done this so many times that I was running out of real estate.

Glancing down at my left hand curled around the tattoo gun, my eyes zeroed in on the blank canvas staring back at me.

That'll work.

Giving the area a quick clean, I switched the gun into my right hand and flipped it on. It buzzed to life, the low hum echoing in the quiet room. Dipping the needle into the concoction of ink-mixed blood, I slowly began outlining an image on the back of my hand. In between shading, my eyes flickered over to Luna. She was moving around a lot more, her head tossing this way and that as the sedative slowly worked its way out of her system.

I was just about finished with my new masterpiece when Sleeping Beauty graced me with her presence. I kept my back to her as I bandaged my hand, my tranquilizer gun sitting in my lap just in case. I really didn't want to keep drugging her. It just didn't feel…right. The tattoo was a better option, one that would protect me from her powers indefinitely.

I gave her some time to come to, watching quietly as she groaned and squirmed in her restraints. Sighing, I took the smallest bit of pity on her and removed her gag, allowing her to speak and breathe properly.

She blew out a curse on her first breath. "Fuck," she hissed, her forehead crinkling in discomfort behind her blindfold. She must have a headache—a side effect from the sedative. The dosage was high enough to kill a human.

Which she most certainly was *not.*

"The headache will pass," I assured her, the sound of my voice making her jump. "Your kind heals fast."

"Not that kind of witch, asshole," she spat, her words slurring together.

That last dose must've been too much for her. Standing to my feet, I moved closer, towering over her. "What kind of witch are you, then?" Maybe she was doped up enough to let some details slip.

Her smirk managed to be both loopy and catty at the same time. "Go ask your squad. I'm sure they've learned exactly what kind of witches we are by now." Her taunting laughter followed, a girlish giggle that grated on my nerves.

I scowled down at her glee, wanting nothing more than to hurt her. But as I reached out to do just that, I wavered, my hand freezing mid-air as if some invisible force had intervened, preventing me from doing something I'd regret.

Dammit!

When her laughter turned into coughing fits, my sympathy returned. Sighing, I reached into another duffle and grabbed a bottle of water. Ripping off the cap, I held it up to her lips. "Drink."

She shook her head. "No…way," she wheezed between coughs. "Don't…trust you."

"It's just water."

"Fuck you!"

Rolling my eyes, I clamped a hand to the back of her head and forced her mouth to the rim of the bottle. "Just fucking drink it," I grumbled impatiently, tipping the clear liquid down her throat.

She tried to twist her head away, but I held firm, forcing her to drink. She spat out the first mouthful, calming herself once she realized nothing tasted funny. Only then did she allow me to feed her more, encouraging her to take slow sips instead of rushed gulps. After she'd had her fill, the back of my fingers ghosted across her lips on instinct, catching her tongue when it darted out to lick the stray droplets of water clinging to her lips.

A jolt of electricity sizzled through me at the brief contact, leaving me jonesing for more. Laying her head back down on the pillow, I stepped away, desperately needing to get a grip on myself. This...this couldn't happen, this *thing* between me and her. Not anymore. I needed to move on from it. To banish it from my mind.

So why couldn't I stop looking at her?

Seeing her tied up on that bed had my mind crafting all sorts of depraved scenarios, all of which involved her naked and me on top of her...

And then inside of her...

"Malakai? Are you still there?"

Fuck. Her voice did nothing to quell the storm brewing inside of me, boiling my blood and chasing it south into my pants. My cock twitched, the head throbbing from anticipation alone.

She shifted on her side until she was able to sit upright, her head swiveling in my direction. Auburn hair tumbled over her shoulder, the tangled mess taking nothing away from her beauty, even blindfolded.

"I need to pee."

Of course she did. It was a long drive, after all. On the other hand, this could easily be a trap. An escape attempt in the making. Not that she could.

Might as well let her try.

My new tattoo needed testing, anyway. And, judging from what I already knew, she lacked any sort of physical strength without her powers.

Checking the seals around the exits one last time, I strolled over to her bed and untied her blindfold, tossing it onto the nightstand. She blinked hard to regain focus, her strange, hypnotic gaze landing on me moments later. We stared openly at one another, neither of us moving so much as an inch.

God, she was so fucking beautiful.

My attempt to hide my appreciation of her beauty failed miserably, my eyes taking great leisure in exploring her features. Gone were her usual doe eyes, replaced by a sultry siren's gaze and encased by lashes that went on forever.

I swallowed hard, unable to tear my gaze away. Jesus. It felt as though she was enthralling me with just one look. Maybe the tattoo had failed to do its job...

Then her eyes dipped from my face to my chest, journeying down my body until they landed on the front of my pants—getting an eyeful of the erection I was sporting. My jaw locked tight, silently commanding my body to stay right where it fucking was. I wanted to rush her. To take her down on that bed and nail her so fucking har—

"You have a lot of tattoos," she said, her voice hoarse. She must still be thirsty.

Words didn't come when I opened my mouth, so I cleared my throat and tried again. "You knew that already."

She shook her head, eyes roaming up my ink-covered arms. My muscles flexed under her scrutiny as if trying to show-off without my consent. "I've never seen them all," she said. "I was always the one getting naked when we were together."

I sucked in a breath, my cock jumping at the reminder. "I preferred it that way."

Her eyes flashed to mine. I recognized the heat simmering in their depths since I felt it in my own.

Then she smiled. "I bet you did. Too bad you'll never have me like that again."

I cocked a brow. "You think so?"

She was right, of course. I could never have her like that again, not after finding out what she was. But to hear her say it as if *she* was the one depriving *me* of what I wanted irritated the fuck out of me. Without thinking, my hand shot out, latching onto her face and squeezing, tipping her head back to look at me in the exact way I imagined she would with my cock in her mouth.

"I'd say I could make it happen again if I wanted to," I uttered darkly, glowering down at her.

What the hell am I doing?

Her pink lips turned up into a saucy smile. "Sorry, not in this lifetime. And you know what else?"

She clearly believed she had the upper hand here, and I

continued to indulge her. "What's that?"

"You shouldn't have taken off my blindfold."

TWENTY-FOUR

Luna

Nothing was happening. Squinting, I concentrated harder, pushing my mind into his only to be shoved out like an unwanted guest. Meanwhile, Malakai looked on with a self-satisfied smirk smeared across his stupid face.

My powers aren't working.

I glared up at him, wrenching my face from his grip. "What did you do to me?"

He shrugged, looking entirely too full of himself. "Not a damn thing, sweetheart."

"Bullshit!" I seethed. "You did something. My powers are gone."

Was it the water? Did he drug me again?

He scratched his chin and tilted his head as if it was a mystery to him as well. "Not sure what you mean. Maybe you're just tired. Get some rest and try again later."

"Urgh!" I struggled against my restraints, wanting nothing more than to smash his condescending face in with the nearest blunt object. "I fucking hate you! Let me go!" I couldn't believe I was drooling over him a minute ago, but the sight of him had caught me off guard in the most delicious way.

The man was the very definition of sex on legs! Totally drool-worthy.

In all of our encounters, this was the first time I had the pleasure of seeing him without a shirt on. And what a pleasure it was. I mean, I knew he had ink, but my goodness...

He was dripping in tattoos from his arms to his chest. Most were occult in nature, sigils and runes warding off demonic possession, hexes and curses. Some were protection-based, wards to keep jinns out of his dreams and sirens from compelling him with their song. He had a tattoo for almost every creature in the Underworld, a means to defend himself against them.

How many has he killed? I wondered.

Certainly more than me. I hadn't even gone on my first mission yet. But the real showstopper came when he turned around. There, from the top of his shoulders down to the small of his back, sat the image of a hooded grim reaper. The detail etched into its skeletal face was hauntingly beautiful, its boney fingers clutching a long scythe to its robed chest, the hilt replaced with a shotgun. The curve of the sleek blade reached the top of Malakai's shoulder, the steel gleaming as if it were real.

And as I shamelessly ogled him, pointlessly speculating how many hours it took for such an intricate portrait to be inked, I finally noticed the bandage on his left hand.

I frowned. *He didn't have that before.*

Growing frustrated, I tried conjuring a projection instead, wading through the intense sluggishness still weighing me down. *Stupid drugs!*

"Don't hurt yourself," he taunted, the corner of his lips curving upward in amusement.

I scowled, ignoring his patronizing comments so I could focus on conjuring a mutated, Godzilla-sized spider into existence. Its eight spindly legs fanned out, standing between Malakai and the door leading to my freedom. He followed my line of sight, his demeanor far too calm for someone facing off against a nightmare made real. Although the illusion wasn't crafted within his mind, the sight alone was enough to trigger a basic human reaction.

Fear.

But he had none.

Instead, he glanced back at me, expression blank. "Is this the part where I'm supposed to be scared?"

I blinked. *What the fuck?* He should be more than scared! He should be pissing his fucking pants!

I made the creature lunge, its monstrous mouth opening wide like it was ready to swallow him whole. But the smug bastard didn't flinch, not even a little. He simply stood there, allowing the illusion to faze right through him.

Struck utterly stupid, I gaped, my mouth catching flies as he turned to face me with a victorious grin on his face.

"I'm sure whatever that was, it was very creative. Your corporeal projections can't actually hurt anyone, can they?

They're nothing but scare tactics. Your real power relies on getting inside people's heads, tricking their brains into believing your illusions are real."

Shit. He's on to me.

I said nothing to confirm or deny his theory, though I didn't have to. He knew he'd hit the nail spot on from the dumbstruck expression on my face, the one reflecting just how well and truly fucked I was. I took another shot at getting inside his head, only to get bounced right back out.

He was blocking me somehow, but how?

I sighed, exhaustion setting in. My head pounded as if I just went ten rounds with a brick wall. Flopping backwards onto the bed, I let my body go lax, staring blankly up at the ceiling. "Okay, you win."

Silence.

I angled my head to look at him. His brows popped at my sudden show of defeat. "Oh, don't look so surprised. This is what you wanted, isn't it? Me weak and at your mercy? Well, here I am. What now, hunter boy?"

He regarded me with continued silence, gunmetal eyes lingering, contemplating. Why not just kill me and be done with it? That would've been easier than dragging me Goddess knows how many miles outside of Deadwood. My illusions would've faded away just the same, allowing his people to attack. But I wasn't about to give him any ideas.

"Do you still need to pee?" he asked out of the blue.

Huh? "Uh...yeah. I do."

Nodding, he reached into the black duffle bag sitting on his bed and pulled out an eight-inch blade with a serrated edge. I tensed as he approached, his eyes locked on mine as he leaned down to cut the zip ties holding my feet together. Then, with one knee on the bed, he leaned over my body to cut the ones around my wrists.

Is he seriously letting me go?

I wasn't sure if I should be happy or suspicious. A little bit of both, perhaps.

He stood back with the knife still in his hand, his unwavering stare trained on me. It was too soon to make a move. I had to be smart about this. Slowly, I rose from the bed, massaging the soreness from my hands. Ugly red welts circled both my wrists and ankles, embedded deep into my skin. He remained close, refusing to even step back as I stood—

My knees buckled, legs cramping after being stuffed in that trunk for so long. I was prepared to meet the ground, but it never came. A soft gasp left my lips as Malakai caught me, his brawny arms circling my waist and hoisting me back to my feet as if I weighed little to nothing.

For the first time ever, my face was pressed to his naked chest, my fingers splayed across his rock-hard abdomen. His skin was surprisingly soft despite the rough ridges of his muscles.

Clearing my throat, I shoved against him. "Don't touch me!"

He scoffed. "You're the one who fell."

"Yeah, thanks to you and your bondage kink, you psycho!"

He rolled his eyes, uninterested in fighting with me. "Whatever, witch. Go take your piss before I change my mind and let you stew in your own filth instead."

I gaped at him, my jaw unhinging.

The fucking disrespect!

I wasn't used to him talking to me like that, like I was nothing more than a nuisance. Balling my fists, I sent one flying. "How dare you!"

He dodged it, his head snapping to the side the same time his hand reached up and captured my wrist. One quick twist and my back was to his chest, my arm bent behind me at a painful angle. I hissed out a curse, unable to move as his mouth lowered to my ear, the low timbre of his voice so frightening it actually instilled some fear in me.

"Watch yourself. Don't think for one fucking second that I won't hurt you just because I haven't done so already."

"What are you waiting for, then?" I challenged, hiding my grimace with a brave face. "Just fucking do it already!"

Egging him on wasn't the best idea, but my pride had taken one too many hits to back down now. If it was a fight he wanted, then a fight he would get! I'd trained my whole life for this, preparing for this very moment. As an immortal, my body was capable of withstanding a great deal before conceding to death.

Could a human say the same?

Doubtful.

I admit, he was physically stronger than me, but that didn't make him better. As he applied more pressure, I cried out, preparing myself mentally for the crack I was about to hear.

But it never came.

"Fuck this," Malakai muttered under his breath. Then, with a shove, he released me and strutted away. The second he turned his back, I attacked, striking his leg with a firm kick. His knee buckled, sending him to the ground.

Springing past him, I bolted for the door, inches from freedom as I reached for the knob—

I flew backwards, my body hitting the floor and skidding halfway across the room. I blinked down at the ground, trying to understand how I got there.

What the fuck?

Laughter had me craning my neck back to look at the asshole himself. He sat on the edge of his bed with a shit-eating grin on his face, his gun dangling from his hand. "Try the windows next," he said, gesturing with his weapon. "I dare you."

Whipping around, I searched for the source that put me on my ass, my eyes flaring wide when I found it.

Oh, you motherfucker!

A red pentagram was spray-painted across the door, with warded runes drawn into each section of the star to prevent anyone with magical blood from crossing its threshold.

A binding trap.

The same symbol decorated the window as well. All exits were officially off-limits.

That cocksucker!

No powers and no escape. At least now I understood why Malakai felt comfortable enough to untie me. I turned my glare on him. "A little hypocritical, isn't it? A hunter using magic against a witch."

He shrugged, his don't-give-a-fuck demeanor pissing

me off even more. "You use it to inflict harm. We use it for protection."

"I've never used my powers to hurt anyone!" Not that I had to explain myself to the likes of him.

He scoffed, his eyes darkening dangerously. "Except for me and my cousin, right?"

I bit back my retort, choosing my words carefully. "That was self-defense."

With a tsk, he stood from the bed. "I'm sure it was."

I scrambled to my feet, blood boiling from his arrogance, ready to set him straight about what really happened that night. "Your cousin was a danger to everyone around him! And *you* killed my friend! Whatever harm I inflicted was well fucking deserved, you self-righteous, ignorant, pathetic excuse for a—"

He flew at me with a speed that was impressive for a human, his massive body slamming my much smaller one into the wall with such force I was shocked the drywall didn't crack. I raised my arms to defend myself, raking my nails across his face. He spat out a vile curse, easily securing my wrists above my head with one hand. The other latched onto my face, squeezing my jaw so hard I winced from the pain.

"I suggest you watch your fucking mouth, witch," he snapped, our noses almost brushing.

"Or what?" I shot back just as heated. I refused to show fear, to let him think he'd won simply because I was at a disadvantage. Aunt Freya always says that every battle has more than one path to victory.

I just had to find mine.

With murder in his eyes, Malakai pegged me with a

punishing stare, his jaw twitching, his lips thinning into a straight line. We were molded together, soft curves pressed into hard muscles. I hated the way my body responded to his, hated how my nipples pebbled beneath the thin fabric of my shirt, demanding his attention. The gray in his eyes turned liquid silver, glazed with hatred and just a hint of something else. Something wild and untameable.

It should've scared me.

But the prickle running down my skin wasn't from fear. Neither was the tingling between my legs.

No, not him!

I wasn't allowed to feel that way about him anymore. Too much had happened. *He's the enemy,* I kept telling myself. Only one of us would leave this motel room alive, and I needed that person to be me.

So I waited. Waited for him to make his move so I could make mine. But that look on his face…

I swallowed hard when that hateful gaze of his dropped to my lips, forcing my tongue to dart out for a lick. Time seemed to stand still between us, the world slowing to a stop as his thumb swept across my bottom lip, pulling it down gently before dipping inside. I couldn't stop the whimper that broke loose, a shiver crawling down my spine. I should've clamped down and bit the fucking thing right off! That would've made more sense than closing my lips around the digit and giving it a suck.

Malakai grunted, the sound caught somewhere between a pained groan and a sharp hiss. Neither struck me as disgruntled.

"Damn you," he muttered tersely, abruptly removing his wet thumb from my mouth and replacing it with his lips.

TWENTY-FIVE

Luna

I t was like a switch flipped and I couldn't flip it back. My sanity was lost, thrown away with the rest of my self-respect the longer I allowed this to continue. Malakai kissed me with such fervent passion, like a man starved. It was all I could do not to moan, not to discard my last bit of dignity for a man who was actively trying to hunt and kill my family.

But it was a losing battle.

As much as I wished it otherwise, this was still the same guy I'd been obsessing over for two years. That's what made me kiss him back, made me hook my leg around his waist and pull him closer until his erection jabbed into my lower stomach. Freeing my wrists, his hands took up residence on my ass, lifting me until our nether regions were better aligned.

The last of my dignity shredded the moment he

worked his hips against mine, his cock repeatedly brushing my pussy. I could feel the moisture pooling in my panties, my body betraying me in favor of the orgasm it knew he could easily deliver. I delved a hand into his cropped hair, clawing at the strands while the other clawed at his back, holding on for dear life as he worked me harder against his bulge, the rough seam of his jeans providing the perfect friction.

It wasn't enough, though.

When his fingers slid beneath my shorts, bypassing my panties, I welcomed the invasion. A single digit skated along my wetness, facing little resistance as it dipped inside barely an inch before retreating. Instinctively, my hips rocked against his hand, anxious for another dip.

Granting my silent request, his finger took another plunge, this time joined by a second. The strangled moan that fell from my lips made me wonder what my coven would think if they knew I was writhing like a whore with the hunter who popped a slug in Bella's head.

The deeper he pushed, the louder I moaned, the tight pinch of my walls trying to expel him. The sharp sting lasted mere seconds before it was replaced with something else—a fullness I needed more of.

Whimpering, I bit down on his lip to keep from screaming his name, the metallic taste of his blood dripping onto my tongue. Under different circumstances, I might've apologized for the infliction, maybe even kissed it better. But I had no such inclination.

If I had to bleed, he would bleed with me.

The heel of his palm rubbed my clit as he stroked my pussy, his fingers gliding in and out like they belonged there. I grew wetter with each pass, my hips moving in time with his thrusts as he ushered me to the edge of that familiar cliff I ached to plunge from.

My nails scored his back, scratching him raw, my breath coming in deep, jagged pants. I was so close, just teetering on the edge. Finally breaking our kiss, I threw my head back against the wall, not caring that I banged it a little too hard in the process. His mouth ghosted up the front of my throat, sucking and nibbling his way back to my lips as if he couldn't bear to be parted from them, taking them by force yet again.

Squeezing my eyes shut, the sensory overload was unreal, hitting me like a runaway train, my nerve endings growing too overwhelmed to function.

"Look at me," Malakai rasped against my mouth, his tone making it clear that the order was non-negotiable.

I followed the rough command like a slave. It disgusted me, but not enough to stop what was happening. The fire in his gaze somehow shot straight to my belly, consuming me from the inside out. Freeing my lips, he pressed his face against mine, his lips grazing my cheek as he uttered the filthiest things to me.

"You like being finger-fucked, don't you?"

The answer brought me too much shame to voice, so I nodded instead.

His lips curled against my cheek. "Use your fucking words."

No way. I shook my head, unable to stifle my staggering groan when his fingers sped up.

"Do you want me to stop?" he threatened, doing just that, his fingers slowing inside of me.

"No! Please…don't stop." My voice wasn't my own, so frantic and desperate I didn't recognize it.

Chuckling, he continued, his palm vibrating against my clit until I saw stars. "Scream for me," he growled.

No problem there.

I quickly found my voice and used it, moan after moan spilling shamelessly from my lips. Anything to keep this going, to keep any part of him inside of me.

"Malakai!"

Hecate help the people next door, if there were any. This place was far too cheap to have soundproof walls, and my cries of pleasure were surely loud enough to be heard by anyone within screaming distance.

"Are you going to come for me?" he rumbled, playfully nipping my cheek.

Fuck, yes.

His fingers blurred, fucking me harder, his palm slapping against my sopping wet flesh.

"What did I say before?" he growled, biting my cheek harder.

He's the devil! I was convinced of it.

"Y-Yes!" I forced out to appease him.

I was quite literally on the verge of tears, my body close to bursting at the seams. The pleasure was laced with the faintest bit of pain as his fingers probed deeper, taking a piece of my virginity in the crudest of ways. Normally, I'd object, but *no* wasn't in my vocabulary at the moment.

"Who do you belong to?"

I knew the answer without thinking, without needing to be told. It was the only one he wanted to hear, and it damn near rolled off my tongue.

"You!"

I was so close. So fucking close...

His lips moved to the shell of my ear, teasing me with his tongue. "Do you want more?"

I turned my head in search of his mouth. "Yes..." I whispered. "More. I need you."

Mad with lust, I wasn't sure what I was saying anymore, my responses on auto-pilot, so lost in him I could see nothing else. Mind you, orgasms were still new to me, but this one felt like the mother of them all, eyes rolling to the back of my head, my inner muscles cramping around his fingers as I spiraled. The high was so magnificent I barely registered the sound of his pants unzipping, or the feel of fabric sliding down my legs.

"You have no idea the things I'm going to fucking do to you, witch."

The sexy rumble of his voice almost had me, but his words quickly lifted the fog that had temporarily robbed me of my senses.

Witch. A subtle reminder that I was no longer *Luna* to him.

Eyes snapping open, my wits returned just in time to feel the blunt head of his cock brush against my still quivering flesh. Unwinding my leg from his waist, I shoved against his chest with a little more force than was necessary. "I think I'll pass, asshole."

He stumbled back, head tilting as he blinked in confusion, looking as disheveled as I felt. "What?"

I scoffed mockingly, bending down to roll my panties and shorts back in place. "It's not that hard to comprehend, *killer*. I got mine. Go look elsewhere for yours."

Sorry, not sorry.

I attempted to blaze past him, but his hand shot out, his iron grip seizing my upper arm and bringing me to a halt. Our eyes locked in a heated standoff; one I was bluffing my way through. I was at his mercy, and we both knew it.

The intensity in his gaze almost made me fold. Would he force me? He never really struck me as the type. Then again, I never pegged him as the type to put holes in people either. Clearly my asshole-meter needed some serious fine-tuning.

"Get your hands off me," I said, enunciating each word with force.

He opened his mouth to say something but reconsidered. An apology would've been nice, but I wasn't holding my breath for that. I waited for him to say something, anything, but the silence only dragged on, thickening the unbearable tension between us. Then, with one last withering look, his hand fell away, giving me the opportunity to storm off into the bathroom.

I slammed the door for dramatic effect before sagging against it, my frustration reaching explosive levels with no way to decompress. Crouching over, I belted out a soundless scream. I couldn't let him hear, let him know he was winning whatever game we were playing.

Think. I needed to think.

Combing my hands through my hair, I turned in a circle, carefully accessing the shoebox of a bathroom that was my only safe haven. It was by far the shittiest one I've ever been in. Or maybe I was too privileged to judge.

Great. No windows.

Was Hecate punishing me? Yes, she must be. This was my punishment for almost giving it up to a fucking hunter on numerous occasions like some thirsty thot! And now I was trapped with him while my coven was in danger.

Or worse.

I tried not to go there. My coven was smart. Even with me gone, no way would they allow a bunch of humans to get the drop on them.

Still, it wouldn't hurt to know for sure.

Blowing out a shaky breath, I leaned over the sink and cranked the faucet to cold, splashing my face with the frigid water. I was still a little groggy from whatever Malakai had drugged me with. And then there was the mystery behind why my powers weren't working on him. The warding prevented me from leaving, sure, but my magic should still work within its confines as long as he was in here with me.

So what gives?

Wiping the excess water from my face, I reached for a scratchy towel on a nearby shelf, my eyes catching sight of the brown Band-Aid taped to the inner crook of my arm. Frowning, I peeled it off, finding a little red dot underneath.

What the hell?

I ran a finger over the mark, the vein there slightly swollen as if…

That son of a bitch!

I damn near ripped the bathroom door off its hinges and stomped back into the room, marching right up to the devil himself. He was sprawled out on his bed without a care in the world, hands tucked behind his head as if he hadn't tried to bang me five minutes ago.

Typical.

Stopping at his bedside, I hovered my arm over his face. "What the fuck did you do to me, you sicko!"

He slowly opened his eyes, his expression beyond bored. "Don't know what you mean, witch."

It irked me to no end that he wasn't as intimidated by me as I was of him. *Because he knows I can't hurt him.* Something he evidently went to great lengths to ensure.

"You took my blood."

A ghost of a smile touched his lips. "Did I? That's a wild accusation."

My scowl deepened, patience waning. "Don't play games with me, you jerk! You did something with my blood, didn't you? That's why my powers aren't working."

"Or maybe you're just weak."

I blinked. *Weak? Weak?!*

My chest heaved up and down, my breathing growing heavier by the second, struggling to harness my mounting rage. "You have no idea what I'm capable of, you brainless mouth-breather!"

I stepped back as he sat up and regretted it immediately. So much for proving I wasn't weak. Or scared.

His eyes lethargically raked down my body with a confidence I didn't appreciate, his smirk growing to obnoxious levels. "Perhaps you should show me, then. Put me in my place."

"Ha! I did that already, remember? Luckily for you, I

was nice enough not to let you suffocate to death. I guess we all have regrets, don't we."

One by one, Malakai swung his legs off the edge of the bed and stood to his full height until he was looming over me.

Planting my feet, I forced myself to remain where I was, my hand instinctively curling around my necklace. *Hecate, give me strength.*

His eyes tracked the movement, head tilting like an adorable puppy. *No! Not adorable!*

I really needed to stop this shit.

I nearly flinched when he reached for my neck, a tattoo-covered hand closing around the front. His touch was surprisingly tender, even going as far as massaging the spot where he had drugged me twice, his thumb gently kneading the area as if apologizing in his own way. There was no ill intent behind it, no malice. He dragged his hand downward, fingers tracing over the delicate gold chain that fell to my chest.

I swallowed hard, his touch soothing my rage like a balm.

"I should've known what you were. All the signs were there," he said, carefully prying my necklace from my closed fist. "Even this. It's Hecate's wheel, isn't it? I never noticed it until now." His voice was calmer than ever, all traces of his earlier hostility absent. For a moment, he was the Malakai I knew…the one I'd fallen for. "Your beauty always distracted me. Still does."

My breath hitched, those words stunning me into silence. *He still thinks I'm beautiful?*

My hand fell away as he took hold of my necklace,

pinching the pendant between two fingers and lifting it closer to his face to inspect. Then he yanked it from my neck, breaking the clasp in the back.

"Hey!" I lunged for it, throwing myself at him. "Give it back!"

He dodged my advances, slipping the necklace into his back pocket. "Sorry, witch. Occult symbols have power. Can't risk you using it against me."

I gaped. Was he serious? "Were you born this stupid or did you take lessons? It's just a necklace! I can't do anything magical with it."

He sidestepped me when I lunged again, sending me crashing onto his bed.

"That may be the case," he drawled from behind me. "But I rather not take the chance."

Scrambling up from the bed, I got right in his face, tiptoes and all. "You can't take it. It's mine!" When he only stared back at me with zero remorse, his eyes as dead as his soul, I forced myself to utter the next word in hopes of swaying him. "Please... It's all I have left of my parents."

The reminder brought tears to my eyes. I held them back, not wanting to give him another reason to call me weak.

His stone-cold eyes softened for a second before frosting over again. "So it holds sentimental value, then?"

I nodded. "Yes."

"Is that the only reason you wear it?"

That, and to pay homage to our dark Goddess. Best to leave that part out, though. "Yes."

His gaze fell to my wrist. "Is that why you're wearing

the bracelet I gave you?" He arched a brow, eyes flickering back to mine. Then he smiled. "For *sentimental* reasons?"

On reflex, I swung my hand behind my back like an idiot, hiding what he'd already seen. My nostrils flared in anger. And embarrassment. *Urgh! I hate him!* I had slipped the bracelet on the night everything had gone to shit and forgot to take the stupid thing off.

Or maybe I just didn't want to.

Maybe I wanted to remember the sweet boy who'd given it to me instead of the monster he'd turned into. But I didn't need to explain myself to him.

To save face, I unclipped the clasp and shoved the bracelet to his chest. "I guess we both got distracted, didn't we? Keep it. I don't want it anymore."

I'll find another way to get back my necklace. I already felt naked without it. Even the spot where his bracelet laid the last few days felt…empty.

But it would remain that way.

Storming off, I headed back to the bathroom, the only other room here that *he* didn't occupy. Slamming the door shut, I braced my back against the flat surface and slid to the floor. I hated feeling this powerless. Is this what it felt like to be human?

Because it sucked.

I needed to get out of here and reach my coven somehow. If only I could get my hands on that phone of his…

Shouldn't be hard considering he couldn't seem to keep his hands to himself.

I cupped my cheeks, feeling the heat spread through

them at the thought of what his hands on me could do. The damage he could cause both physically and mentally if I let him. I could still feel remnants of the orgasm he'd given me, the aftermath leaving my legs wobbly and my clit twitching uncontrollably. I should hate his touch. Hate everything about him. But I didn't, and neither did he.

Maybe that was my way out.

In spite of everything, we were still attracted to one another. I just needed to take a page out of my Aunt Freya's book, be the enchantress she always wanted me to be.

Dreading what I needed to do, I stripped out of my clothes and jumped in the shower. It was time to break out the big guns. Guns I've never used before.

Here's hoping I don't end up shooting myself...

TWENTY-SIX

Malakai

Should I break it down?

She'd been in there a while. The shower stopped running over thirty minutes ago and Luna had yet to make an appearance. She was avoiding me, obviously, but she couldn't hide in there forever.

I never should've kissed her. What the hell was I even thinking?

I wasn't, and that was the problem. I would've fucked her right against that wall if she had let me. No use denying it. Shit, the boner currently standing at attention in my pants wouldn't let me forget it either. It was starting to hurt, too, my balls turning bluer by the second.

Cursing, I marched over to the bathroom door and raised a fist to knock. I pounded twice. "If you're not out here in the next five minutes, I'm coming in to get you, witch."

"Stop calling me that!" she hollered back.

I smirked, loving that I was getting under her skin so easily. "Oh, you don't like it? I'm sorry. What should I call you instead? Sorceress? Satan worshiper?"

At the sound of the lock turning, I expected the door to fly, but she only cracked it, poking just her head outside.

Those hypnotic, pupilless eyes narrowed "We worship the Goddess Hecate, you ass-hat. Not Satan."

"What's the difference?" I asked, though I really didn't care. It was all the fucking same to me.

She rolled her eyes. "I don't have the patience or the crayons to explain it to you."

I almost smiled. Almost. "Whatever. Get out here."

She leaned her head against the door jam, an innocent smile overtaking her face. Her skin seemed to glow, still dewy from her shower. "No thanks. I'm good in here."

"I wasn't asking."

She pursed her lips, her demeanor strangely playful. "I'm naked."

My nostrils flared at her blunt confession. "W-What?" I sputtered.

She shrugged. "I don't have any clothes."

"Put back on your old ones."

"They're dirty." She continued to pout, her batting lashes making me suspicious. "Do you have something I can wear?"

What game was she playing?

Letting out a deep sigh, I walked over to my duffle and pulled out a clean black t-shirt. Walking back, I handed it to her through the crack in the door. "Here."

"Thanks," she uttered shyly before closing herself in

again. Two minutes later, she emerged, finally stepping out to face me.

I swallowed. Hard.

Fucking Christ...

I wasn't prepared for the sight of her in my clothes. The plain tee was too big on her, the hem brushing the top of her milky thighs and the sleeves falling just short of her elbows. She kept tugging at the bottom as if doing so would somehow make it longer.

Thank fuck it wasn't.

With great effort, I barely managed to drag my gaze from her naked legs that I very much wanted hooked around my waist again. Maybe I should just take her and be done with it. Get it out of my system once and for all.

Only I knew once wouldn't be enough for me. Not with her.

Tucking a few wet strands of hair behind her ear, her eyes dropped to my crotch, taking in the arousal I did nothing to hide. She ducked her chin, a timid smile grazing her lips.

What was she up to?

"Sooo…" she said, breaking the tension building between us. "What now?"

Good question.

I wasn't sure what to do with her. I still couldn't get a hold of anyone, not my father or uncle. Even members of Clint's crew were offline. It took everything in me not to haul ass back to Deadwood and survey the damage myself, but I couldn't risk leaving Luna unattended for that long. If she were any other monster, I would've put a bullet in her by now and rejoined the others.

But that ship had sailed.

I warred with my natural instincts to do what I'd been trained to do my entire life, but every time I looked at her, I choked. All my training gone to shit over a pretty face and the promise of a tight pussy. That's what I was telling myself, at least. I couldn't accept that there was another reason behind my hesitation. *One problem at a time.*

"Get back on the bed," I ordered, reaching for another set of zip ties.

Luna visibly tensed, taking a step back. "What? Why? It's not like I can go anywhere."

"I'm not sleeping with you wandering around. On the bed. Now."

With a giggle, she skirted to the other side of the room. "Is the big bad hunter scared of the teeny-tiny witch? Seriously, I'm like half your size. I can't hurt you without my powers."

I circled her like a predator, prepared to manhandle her to the bed if need be. Excitement coursed through me at the thought of her putting up a fight, wishing that she would.

"You could go for my weapons. Don't tell me you haven't thought about it."

I would, if I was her.

She shrugged, biting her lip. "It may have crossed my mind once or twice. Firearms aren't really my thing, though. I'm a lousy shot."

"I've got knives, too."

Her smile was brazenly flirtatious, giving me pause. "I am better with those."

"I bet you are, Sorceress."

As I closed in on her, she stopped, craning her neck back to look at me as I blocked her path. "Is *Sorceress* my new nickname?"

I grinned, unable to stop myself from engaging in this pointless banter between us. "You didn't like *witch*, remember."

"Hmm," she hummed, stepping forward and lightly dragging a finger down my chest. "I much prefer hearing my name fall from your lips instead."

I blanked at that, dumbfounded by the sultry way she was eyeing me. All smiles and hooded eyes. And here I thought she would still be pissed at me for taking her necklace. What happened to put her in such a good mood?

I glared down at her from my imposing height. "You're acting strange."

"Am I? Maybe I just don't want to fight with you anymore. It's exhausting and pointless."

Interesting turnaround.

"And what do you hope to achieve with this pleasant attitude of yours? Freedom? Not happening." Snatching her hand, I guided her over to the bed. To my surprise, I didn't even have to drag her.

Sitting down without a fuss, she scooted back against the headboard and held out her hands like a good little hostage. "If it'll make you feel better, go ahead," she said innocently, an indulgent smile on her face.

Trying not to overthink her deceptively good mood, I looped the ties around her wrists and pulled them tight, lifting her hands over her head to secure them to the nearest bedpost—

I stiffened, immediately realizing my mistake.

Ah, fucking hell…

Clearing my throat, I pegged her with a hard look, barely restraining myself. "Why aren't you wearing underwear?" Her, or rather *my*, shirt had ridden up over her hips, exposing her bare slit to me.

Pouting, she rubbed her thighs together, feigning modesty. "You got blood on my panties. I couldn't wear them."

Blood?

Fuck. That's right. She was still a virgin.

I cringed thinking about how rough I'd been with her. What the hell was I thinking, fingering her like that? Guilt stabbed me, enough to make me soften. "Did I hurt you?"

I must have if she bled.

Tipping her head back, she studied me closely, her smile bashful. "It stung a little at first, but then…" she paused to wet her lips, drawing my gaze to her tongue. "It felt good. *Really* good."

Fuck. Me.

Every circuit blew in my brain, the head of my cock pulsating in agony, desperate for another chance to get inside of her. Leaning into the headboard, Luna arched her back and separated her thighs, keeping one leg down and the other raised.

"Will you touch me again?" Her voice came out breathier than before. "I won't stop you this time."

I rubbed a hand over my mouth. It watered just looking at that spot between her legs. Would it be wrong to taste her? To bury my head there until she screamed?

She didn't seem to think so.

Waiting for an answer, she shifted her legs up and

down on the mattress as if to tame her own aches and pains. Her eyes were like molten pools of purple lava, omitting flames that threatened to burn me alive. It only took one glance for me to get lost in them, happily drowning like a fool. What a crime it was, for something so beautiful to be hidden away.

Her brows knitted together as I continued to stare. "Why do you keep looking at me like that?"

Shit. Was I that obvious?

Shaking off the trance she unwittingly continued to put me in, I reached to untuck the blanket from the bed and draped it across her exposed lower half. Out of sight, out of mind.

Ignoring her pout, I took a seat on the bed across from her, leaning forward with my elbows on my knees. "Why do you conceal your eyes?" I was genuinely curious.

She frowned, head jerking back in disbelief. "You can see them?"

I nodded.

"Since when?"

"Right before I took you."

She glared. "You mean before you *kidnapped* me."

"Same shit."

"And you still see them now?"

When I nodded again, she turned away, mumbling to herself, "How is that possible?"

"You forget," I said, "your powers don't work on me anymore. Same goes for whatever spell you used to alter your appearance."

She huffed and rolled her eyes. "Yeah, you still haven't mentioned why that is."

Smirking, I began unraveling the bandage around my hand. "Let's just say I know a little blood magic myself."

The ink was still fresh, covering the back of my hand in the shape of a black crescent moon. It was the closest I've ever gotten to inking a girl's name on my skin, since Luna meant *moon* in Latin.

Her mouth dropped at the sight of it, the truth clicking into place.

"You fucking bastard!" she spat vehemently. "That's what you used my blood for, isn't it? You mixed it with the ink to create a protection ward. That's why my powers don't affect you anymore."

"That's right," I said, briefly admiring my own handy work. "A few drops of your blood and a little incantation was all I needed to make myself immune to your magic."

Her scowl deepened. I had no doubt she would attack me if she could move.

"You disgust me."

Ouch.

Ignoring the wound those words ripped open in my chest, I plastered on a cocky grin. "Funny. I didn't seem to disgust you when my fingers were buried in that tight pussy of yours."

"Fuck you!" she spat despite the blush that colored her cheeks.

I pitched forward, resting my hand inches from her face on the headboard. "Careful, Luna," I warned, finally using her name. "I'm beginning to think that's exactly what you want. You've been begging me to touch you all night."

Flinging the blanket off her lap, I slid a hand to her

thigh, giving it a firm squeeze before slipping it higher beneath her shirt. My shirt. She gasped as I ventured up past her stomach, my fingers grazing the smooth swell of her breasts.

"Stop," she whimpered, already succumbing to my advances.

Trailing my lips across her cheek, I nipped at her jaw, soaking in every little reaction I forced out of her. "What are you going to do if I don't?"

Nothing. She couldn't do a goddamn thing.

She turned her face into mine, our lips brushing. "Why don't you untie me and find out."

I chuckled. "You don't get points for bravery, Sorceress."

She yanked at her restraints. "And you don't get points for groping me while I'm tied up."

I cupped her breast, surprised to see that she had ditched her bra too. "Admit it. You wanted this. Why else would you get naked for me?"

I pinched a nipple just to hear what sound she would make. Her sharp hiss was far from pained.

"I...didn't have anything to change into." Her lids grew heavier and heavier as the fight gradually left her.

I laughed low in my throat, my hand switching to her other breast. It would be wrong to neglect it. "Keep telling yourself that, sweetheart." I was gentler with her nipple this time, toying with it at my leisure.

Her moans grew in volume, her hips jerking off the bed. "I hate you..."

"So you keep telling me," I murmured against her flushed skin, burning a path down her neck with the flat of my tongue, savoring the taste of her. I wish I could say the feeling was mutual, but I'd be lying.

I wanted this girl.

The fact that she was the enemy was irrelevant. A detail I couldn't change and one that didn't make me want her any less. The more I fondled her, the more she squirmed, causing the zip ties to dig into her skin.

"These are hurting me," she whined, wiggling her hands against the bedpost.

"Then stop moving," I muttered, sucking her pulse point at the base of her neck before dragging my mouth lower. The night was young and I had more to explore. I skipped her breasts on purpose, smiling when her back bowed off the bed to seek out my mouth. But I carried on, kissing and licking my way down her stomach, giving her navel a quick lather. Her stomach coiled inward, trying to escape my tongue lashing, but I held her down, my lips moving to her naked thighs.

She yanked at her bonds again, the headboard rattling from the force of it. "Kai...please," she begged on a whimper, the discomfort in her tone quickly thwarting the rest of my fun.

Dammit.

How was a single plea capable of decimating my resolve? Even without her abilities, the power she held over me was baffling.

Heaving a sigh, I reached for the knife strapped to my ankle knowing it was a mistake, knowing she would attack the moment I cut her loose. But I did it anyway.

She was on me in less than a second, using her weight to tackle me to the bed. I threw the knife before she could reach for it. I had no intention of using it on her anyway. She threw the first punch, fist connecting with my jaw. The force behind it was impressive, enough to leave a decent-size bruise later.

"That was for shooting my friend!" she declared, going in for another. "And this is for kidnapping me!"

I dodged the second, grabbing her hand and twisting it behind her back. When she cried out, I eased my grip. "That's enough." I sat up, forcing her to straddle me. She shoved her free hand into my face, her fingers jabbing me in the eye.

"Fuck!" The pain was white hot, her nails scratching the fleshy part of my eyeball. Capturing that hand as well, I stood with her in my arms and tossed her over to my bed. I dove on top of her, flipping her onto her stomach and pinning both hands to the small of her back. "Didn't your coven teach you how to fight?" I jeered in her ear just to piss her off.

She kicked out her legs, hitting nothing but air. "Urgh! I can't believe I was ever in love with you, Malakai Slade!"

I went still, forgetting how to breathe as if my lungs had been ripped from my fucking body.

"What did you just say?"

TWENTY-SEVEN

Luna

I wanted to die. Just wither away into nothingness right here on this crappy, stained motel mattress. It was the only escape I saw from the scolding embarrassment I'd subjected myself to.

Hours had passed since my stupid confession, and now I lay facing whatever direction Malakai wasn't in. If he moved, so did I. Anything to avoid the questions I felt looming in the air between us. After those words had so carelessly slipped from my lips, I went silent on him.

Completely mute.

Once I realized I had no hope of winning the fight between us, I gave up and waited for him to secure me to the bedpost once more. But no punishment came. Instead, he allowed me to return to my bed, zip tie free, without a word.

And that was where I remained, sulking on my side as

he cleaned his weapons on the bed next to mine. I was grateful for the peace, even with the weight of his gaze lingering on me every so often. At some point, he turned on the TV, the sound of cheesy sitcoms filling the silence.

I wasn't watching, though. That would mean turning to face him since the TV was closer to his side of the room. I opted instead to focus on the sole window in this shit-hole with a binding trap painted over it. It was storming outside, rain pelting against the glass and thunder clapping in the distance.

I wasn't sure what time it was—the clock was on his side too—but it was late. Early morning, perhaps? An entire day had come and gone without knowing if my coven was alive or dead.

My seduction plan was an utter fail.

I had hoped to snag his phone during our tussle, but the big brute overpowered me too quickly. *I should've paid more attention during combat training.* Truthfully, it was never one of my strong suits. If there was one thing this entire ordeal had taught me, it was that I relied too heavily on my powers.

But all was not lost.

Sleep would call him soon enough. He was only human, after all. I just had to wait for the perfect opportunity to strike—

My stomach growled, a long, drawn-out rumble that seemed to go on forever. I curled into myself in hopes of quelling the noise. It had been a while since I'd eaten anything, and I wasn't about to beg my *kidnapper* for food. My pride wouldn't allow it. But the grumbling only grew louder.

And louder.

I cursed my stupid hunger when Malakai shifted on his bed, the springs groaning under his weight. "You hungry?" he asked.

I ignored him, pulling the covers tighter around my body.

His hefty sigh irritated me. "You're fucking stubborn, you know that?"

An array of snarky insults danced on the tip of my tongue, but I kept them to myself. Another sigh and he stood from his bed. I tensed knowing he was about to walk over here. I wasn't ready to face him. Not yet. Not after what I'd said.

His phone rang.

Jumping up, I finally turned to face him. He hurried to pull the device from his pocket, his eyes reading the lit-up caller display before flickering to meet mine. It was someone calling with news. It had to be.

He held my gaze as he lifted the phone to his ears. "Talk to me," he said to whoever was on the other end. His facial expressions gave nothing away as he stood there listening intently to whatever he was being told. "Any casualties?"

I sat up straighter, my pulse quickening. Would he tell me if my coven had been slaughtered? Rub their deaths in my face just for the joy of watching me crumble? Dread twisted my intestines into knots, skyrocketing my anxiety.

Please let them be okay... I silently prayed, reaching for my necklace only to be reminded that it was gone.

"Okay," Malakai said minutes later. "Send me the coordinates." Then he hung up.

Coordinates for what?

"What happened?" I forced myself to ask. I needed to know. I held my breath, waiting for his answer.

Tucking the phone back into his pocket, he turned from me without a word and collected his weapons. One by one, he packed them neatly into his duffle and zipped it up, swinging the strap onto his shoulder.

"I'll be back," he said, heading for the door.

I blinked. "What?" Throwing off the covers, I followed after him. "Where are you going? You can't just leave me here."

Reaching for the door, he flipped the locks and swung it open. "I said I'll be back."

He couldn't even be bothered to look at me, the door slamming shut behind him. I rushed to grab it, but the binding trap repelled me as soon as my fingertips touched the knob. Flying backwards, I grunted as I hit the ground, landing flat on my back.

"Fuck!" I yelled to the rafters, pounding my fists into the floor.

Leaping to my feet, I double-checked the room to see if Malakai had left anything behind, a weapon I could use against him.

He didn't.

The man was thorough, I'd give him that. The room didn't even have a landline to call the front desk, only wires where it should've been on the nightstand between our beds.

Since I couldn't touch the window, I searched for something heavy enough to smash it with. But there was nothing. No chairs. No dishes. No lamp.

Bastard probably hid those too.

Still, I tried with what I could find. My shoes, the alarm clock, the remote control. Hell, I would've thrown the TV if it wasn't attached to the fucking wall. In the end, I broke everything except for the window and my shoes.

Growing frustrated to the point of tears, I resorted to pounding on the walls, screaming for help until I was hoarse, praying to Hecate that someone would hear and come to my rescue.

But my pleas fell on deaf ears.

The surrounding rooms must be vacant.

"Argh!" With one last pound, I flopped onto my bed face first and stayed there, wallowing in my misery. I didn't budge when I heard the lock turn in the door, or when it creaked open. My face remained firmly planted in the mattress even as Malakai's footsteps approached me from behind.

"Here," he muttered, tossing something down beside me. I turned to see what it was. The brown paper bag had no logo, just a grease stain and the most delicious smell wafting from it. Opening it up, I took in the glorious sight of a double bacon cheeseburger and fresh-cut fries.

My mouth watered, but I wasn't about to show him any gratitude. I was in a bitchy mood, and he was about to feel it. My eyes narrowed into slits. "You didn't even ask if I'm a vegetarian or not."

He looked bored, unimpressed by my attitude. "Are you?"

"No. But you could've at least—"

"Then shut the fuck up and eat it. I don't have time for

this."

Glaring, I chucked the bag at his face. "Rude." He caught it, preventing the contents from spilling out. "I don't fucking want it."

It was my worst lie yet.

My stomach *screamed* for it even though my pride won the battle. I turned from him as he made his way over, dropping the bag near my face so I could smell it.

"If you don't want it, I can get you something else. But you need to eat."

I scoffed, refusing to look at him. "Why do you care if I eat or not? You're planning to kill me anyway, aren't you?"

He grunted as if I didn't know what I was talking about. "If I wanted you dead, Sorceress, you would be in the ground already."

Standing, I made a show of tossing the food onto his bed, looking him dead in the eyes. "Then why haven't you? You don't need me anymore. My illusions fell, you and your people got what you wanted. So why am I still here?"

He said nothing, only inhaled and exhaled through his nose, his jaw clenching and unclenching as he stewed in whatever emotions were running through him.

When he finally spoke, his tone was clipped. "Eat your food," was all he said before turning on his heels and marching into the bathroom. He didn't bother shutting the door. I watched as he gathered my dirty clothes from the floor and shuffled back into the room, throwing them at my feet. "Get dressed when you're done."

"Why? Are we going somewhere?"

"Enough with the fucking questions!" he barked, making me jump. When I stepped back, his face changed, his anger draining, his voice lowering. "Just...do as I say, okay?"

Something was wrong. He was agitated for some reason, coming back in a worse mood than when he left. Was it because of the phone call? I needed him in a better frame of mind to ask or risk him ripping my head off. If he had information about my coven, I needed to know what it was.

Choosing my battles wisely, I quietly bent to gather my clothes and headed into the bathroom to change. When I returned, Malakai was picking up the broken pieces of the TV remote and alarm clock from the floor.

The, *are you fucking kidding me,* expression painted across his face needed no words. I simply shrugged and snatched up my discarded food from his bed. I couldn't deny my hunger any longer. Un-crumpling the bag, I dug in, starting with the burger. I picked off the onions before taking a very unladylike bite, all the while ignoring Malakai's blatant stares.

What the devil is his problem?

I savored the first few bites before diving in on the fries. They were a little dry. I checked the bag for ketchup and found none.

Urgh. Another reason to hate him.

"Problem?" he drawled, leaning his shoulder against the window sill. He had yet to move from the spot, choosing to just sit there and watch me eat.

"Nope. All good here."

It wasn't until halfway through my burger that things

got fuzzy. The room started spinning, tiny dotted spots invading my vision.

What's…happening? "Kai…I feel weird…" I lost my train of thought when I looked over to see two of him standing there, my vision growing blurry.

He didn't seem surprised by my condition in the slightest. As he pushed off from the window sill and made his way towards me, my fading senses barely registered the guilty expression he wore. Glancing down at the burger in my hands, I dropped it like it was on fire, the room spinning harder the more I tried to focus.

"Did you…drug me?" Again.

His gaze shifted to his feet as if he couldn't bear to look at me. "I'm sorry, Luna…"

His apology echoed like ripples in a pond, my body going numb as everything faded to black.

TWENTY-EIGHT

Malakai

Rain beat against the windshield, forcing me to keep the wipers on high as I drove along the highway at a snail's pace. Cars honked behind me until they grew fed up, switching lanes just to cut in front. Still, I kept my pace, using the rain as my excuse.

It had nothing to do with the witch lying unconscious in my backseat, being driven unknowingly to her doom. One look in the rear-view mirror made me sick to my fucking stomach, so much so that I was tempted to pull over and hurl on the side of the road. I didn't have the heart to lock her in the trunk again, but I kept her blindfolded and tied up just in case her sedative wore off before reaching our destination. I didn't need her attacking me while I was driving.

I gripped the steering wheel hard, the thought of what was about to happen next gnawing at me.

I never should've answered that call.

There was a moment, a split second, where I considered letting it ring, putting off the inevitable. But I couldn't do it. Now I wish I had. Though my father's voice on the other end had been a relief, his orders had me twisted up in knots I couldn't untangle.

We had to retreat. He'd said. *There were too many of them. Looks like we're dealing with multiple covens here. We need more intel. Bring the girl to Clint's compound up north. We'll squeeze her for information if we have to.*

Squeeze her for information…

It was just a polite way of saying torture her until she breaks.

My eyes flickered back to Luna in the rear-view. Fuck me. *I can't do this.* There was no fucking way in hell I would be able to stand by and watch them rip into her. If any of them even touched her…

"Fuck!" I slammed my hand into the steering wheel, my composure slipping. No one knew of our connection, not even my father. If I was to tell them now, it wouldn't go over well. Chances were it wouldn't even make a difference.

She was a witch, and that was enough to warrant the treatment she would soon receive.

Just let her go, my conscience urged.

I could say she got the drop on me and escaped. I knew I was betraying my people just by letting my mind go there. Betraying Zane. And there was no guarantee she wouldn't return with her people to finish us off. There were deaths on both sides, and no one was willing to just call it even and let that shit go.

Rubbing my forehead to ease the pounding headache forming, I pressed on the gas, picking up speed just a tad. I kept my eyes forward because nothing but doubt lay behind me.

It was mid-afternoon when we arrived at the compound. I had to hand it to Clint, the place was a fortress. Gated out in the middle of nowhere with top-notch security in the form of both tech and bodies. A handful of hunters guarded the front gate with their weapons drawn as I slowed the vehicle to a stop. There were more of them than I expected.

It's like a fucking hunter's convention out here.

I waited until one of them marched up to my window and tapped on the glass with the butt of his gun before rolling it down.

"You lost?"

"Malakai Slade," was the only answer I gave.

It was the right one.

With a nod, the hunter stepped back. The gate opened and he waved me through. My father was already standing at the top of the driveway when I pulled up. He looked like shit. His nose was busted and the left side of his face was discoloured and bruised. Shutting off the engine, I got out to greet him, trying my damnedest not to look back at Luna.

Dad looked past me to the car, catching sight of her sprawled across the backseat. "Is she properly secured?"

"Yes, sir. The sedative should be wearing off soon."

"Did she give you any trouble?"

"Nothing I couldn't handle."

I remained perfectly stoic as he studied me, searching

for any signs to indicate I was bullshitting him. "Good," he said with a curt nod. "Get her inside. Everything's been prepared."

A bitter taste filled my mouth, one my saliva couldn't cleanse. "What if she doesn't cooperate?" Which was far more likely than her blabbing all of her coven's secrets to a room full of hunters.

"Then we'll use her as bait to lure the rest of them out. I'm sure they're looking for her. We can use that to our advantage."

Once his back was turned, my expression fell, the doubt I was trying very hard to conceal creeping to the surface. Turning, I headed back to the car to retrieve Luna. Curling my hand around the handle of the back passenger door was an easier feat than actually pulling the fucking thing open. My hesitation was brief, short enough to go unnoticed by the hunters scattered about, all staring this way to catch a glimpse of the enemy being delivered to their doorstep. There would be no going back once I carried her inside. Chances were she was never getting out of this place alive.

The pang in my chest was becoming harder to ignore.

Bending down, I scooped her into my arms, letting her head fall against my shoulder once she was settled. I took my sweet time walking to the house, paying close attention to the steady rise and fall of her chest.

Once inside, another hunter—one of Clint's men—reached out to take her from me. I jerked back, a snarl pulling at my lips. Violence was my instinct of choice. *If he steps any closer, I'll break his fucking legs.*

Clutching Luna tighter to my chest, I fixed the bastard

with a glare. "What the hell do you think you're doing?"

The male frowned, looking genuinely confused. "We've prepared a room to nullify her magic. I was going to take her there."

"I'll take her myself."

"Really, I've got it," he insisted, reaching for her again.

Fucker was lucky my hands weren't free, otherwise he would've gotten pistol-whipped real fucking fast. Pivoting out of his reach, I snapped. "Are you fucking deaf? I said I've got her."

That earned me some strange looks from the guys standing in the foyer, but the amount of fucks I had to give was slowly dwindling.

"Malakai." Uncle Luke came shuffling into the room. He was finally back on his feet, walking with only a slight limp after the Wendigo attack. "What the hell's the matter with you, boy?"

Good question. I went with the most logical answer that popped into my head. "She's got some powerful mind tricks. I've made myself immune, so it's best if I'm the one who handles her." I flashed the ink on the back of my hand to drive my point across.

Uncle Luke nodded. "Alright, then. This way."

The other guy stepped back, but not without dressing me down with his eyes, making his newfound disdain for me obvious.

The feeling's mutual, motherfucker.

Following my uncle past the main floor, new faces surfaced as we walked the halls—men and women alike. There were forty, maybe fifty, of them, all readying themselves for battle. The sound of weapons being disassembled, cleaned, and reassembled chimed from all over. One room in particular housed shelves upon shelves of occult artifacts—most commonly used to fight fire with fire. Magic against magic.

Luna was right. We were hypocrites.

Many stared as I walked with her in my arms, their immense hatred for her kind smeared across their faces. Each and every one of them would kill her in a heartbeat if given the chance.

Not gonna fucking happen.

The thought was one of many that plagued me, scaring me more than I was willing to admit. Even after everything, my need to protect her was difficult to shake. I didn't want her dead, far from it, yet I couldn't see this playing out any other way.

Uncle Luke led me down a set of stairs toward the back of the house. At the bottom sat a thick, reinforced steel door with a touch-screen panel installed where the door handle should be. I couldn't see the code as he punched it in, the door popping open a moment later. Stepping through, he closed us in, the heavy locking mechanisms shifting back into place.

"What is this?" I asked, looking around at what appeared to be a dingy cellar tunnel. Lighting was minimal, running on old-school generators along the walls. About fifty yards in, the tunnel split into three. We took the one on the far right. Similar steel doors like the one at the entrance lined the walls at least twenty feet apart.

"Clint's got a good setup down here," Uncle Luke

said, seemingly impressed. "Place used to be a bomb shelter back in the day. He dug out these tunnels and extended them to make impenetrable prison cells for anything that wasn't human. Different rooms have different uses." He stopped in front of the third one in. "This one is for our little magical friend."

He punched in another code. This time, I paid close attention to each digit. *5195*

The locks clicked and turned, automatically swinging open to reveal a room fully encased in steel from top to bottom. It was giving medical lab vibes, impeccably sterile and clean. A binding trap was painted on the ceiling like a mural, covering every square inch of the space. The same trap was mirrored on the floor only steps from the door. Once inside, there would be nowhere for Luna to run.

Chains propelled down from the ceiling attached to a harness that resembled a straitjacket. But instead of leather straps, this one was made up of impenetrable steel mesh with runes etched into the metal, glinting under the dull lighting.

Magic blockers.

Jesus...

"Not bad, huh?" Clint's voice snuck up on me from behind.

I kept my back to him, worried he would try to take Luna from me. "Yeah. It's something," I said flatly, not sharing his enthusiasm.

"Go ahead and strap her in, Kai," came my father's voice, joining the party. Shooting a glance over my shoulder, I spotted Derek and Alex as well, standing out in the tunnel along the wall. When did they all get here? I was so lost in my own head that my sense of awareness was slipping.

My steps faltered the moment I lifted my feet to move, my unwillingness to go any further into the binding trap prompting someone behind me to clear their throat.

"Something wrong?" It was Clint.

Yes. Something was very fucking wrong.

I couldn't move, rooted to the spot as if the weight of Luna in my arms was keeping me anchored. She couldn't be more than a hundred pounds soaking wet, yet it felt as though she was the only thing keeping me tethered to the earth. When her head rolled against my shoulder, I had to smother the growing urge to bolt, to fight my way out of here to get her to safety. I dreaded her waking up to this, strapped to that thing.

She'll hate me. If she didn't already.

Why that mattered now was absurd. I wasn't concerned for her feelings when I drugged and abducted her to ambush her people. But I wasn't the one dictating her fate this time. It was out of my hands.

With great effort, I stepped forward, my feet like lead, so heavy I practically dragged them behind me. Clint and Uncle Luke assisted with the harness. I almost flinched when they reached to slip it around Luna.

Everything about this felt…wrong.

I saw red the moment they lifted her out of my arms, every muscle in my body flexing to cause harm. *Don't fight. Let them take her,* I repeated on a loop in my head, mentally calming myself to avoid going apeshit on everyone in my vicinity.

Luna's head lolled forward as they hooked her up, the harness compressing her arms to her body. Pulling the chain, they suspended her in mid-air until her feet were left dangling.

My jaw clenched along with my fists at my sides. Before opening my mouth, I triple-checked my tone in my head, keeping any trace of aggression to myself. "Isn't this a little much?" Her powers were bound within the circle, and I knew from our time together that she severely lacked hand-to-hand combat skills.

Ambling to my side, Alex jabbed me in the shoulder. "Did you forget what she did to your ass back in those woods? You thought a snake was suffocating you to death. Who knows what else she can do." Inching closer, he raised a hand to pull back the hair that curtained her face, tugging down her blindfold. "She ain't half bad to look at, tho—"

Surging forward, I yanked him back by his collar. "What the fuck do you think you're doing?" I growled in his face.

Alex frowned, green eyes dipping to where my hand held his jacket. "Dude, what's your problem? You've been on edge since you got here."

I shoved him back. "She's not here for you to gawk at, asshole."

"Alex," my father's booming voice interrupted, "go get the tools."

Straightening his jacket, Alex brushed past me, making sure to bump my shoulder on his way out. *Fucking hell.* I shouldn't have done that.

All eyes were on me the moment he left, flashing a

mixture of concern and confusion.

"You sure you're alright, son?" Uncle Luke asked while my father looked on with suspicion.

I cracked my neck from side to side, careful to keep my tone light. "I'm fine. It was a long drive, is all."

"Maybe you should get some rest," Clint suggested. "We can handle the girl when she wakes."

The fuck you will! "No. I want to be here."

"We don't need you for this, Kai," Dad insisted. "Sit this one out."

As much as I respected the man, I was reaching my breaking point with all his, *I'm the boss and you have to obey me,* bullshit. Looking him dead in the eyes, we squared off. "I've sat out long enough, don't you think?"

My outburst gave him pause, those unyielding gray eyes slanting back at me. "For good reason."

Brows raised, I scoffed. "And what reason might that be? Are you forgetting that *I* was the one who found the witches? *I* was the one who avenged Zane. Without me, none of you would've gotten inside the Sinclair house. If the mission failed, that shit is on *you*. Maybe *you* should sit this one out."

Neither of us moved, or blinked, for what felt like hours. I waited on pins and needles for his calm façade to break, for him to blow an ass gasket and tear me a new one right here in front of everyone. I needed a punching bag, someone to fight with, to lash out at.

But he didn't take the bait.

Instead, he nodded, crossing his arms over his chest and jutting out his chin. "Alright, then. Since you feel so strongly on the matter, you can take point."

Alex chose that moment to return with a rusty cart in tow, the flat surface lined with tools all laid out in a neat row. The two shelves below it contained bigger instruments…the chainsaw in particular was most concerning.

A soft groan made me snap my head in Luna's direction. She was stirring, head bobbing as she came to.

My palms grew sweaty, my heart beating a mile a minute. The chaotic thumping reverberated in my ears, so loud I feared the others could hear it as well.

"Well, then," someone said. I was too busy having a nervous breakdown to recognize who. "Let's get started."

TWENTY-NINE

Luna

What in the actual fuck...

I squinted down at my feet, trying to will my blurry vision into focus. *Why am I dangling?*

My feet hovered inches above the ground with zip ties holding my ankles together. *Wonderful. More zip ties.*

I couldn't move, my arms compressed in some sort of metal binding that burned my skin. The sensation was bearable, but unpleasant just the same. Slowly lifting my head, others came into view. Several bodies, in fact, all gathered around me like I was a circus act. My eyelids felt as though they were weighed down by a sack of rocks. It was a mission and a half just to peel them halfway, but I managed.

Who are these people? The only face I recognized was *his*.

Malakai.

His presence strangely calmed me, until I remembered *he* was the reason I was here. Drugged and dangling from the ceiling like a pig on a hook. Would they butcher me like one too?

I doubted anyone here would be against it

They aimed their revulsion and death stares at me like weapons that could kill if they willed it so. How anyone could feel such abhorrence towards a person they've never met was absolutely insane. I mean, what the fuck did I ever do to any of them?

Malakai's face, however, was trickier to read. A blank slate. He wouldn't hold my gaze, his attention shifting to the male who came to stand at his side.

A relative?

The two resembled one another. Same height and build. Same cold, stormy eyes. One was just an older version of the other. If I had to guess, I'd say the man was his father. My gaze travelled to the others, wondering if they were all related as well. A family full of hunters.

How quaint.

A family that kills together, stays together.

Their eyes burnt holes into my skin as if they were all waiting for me to do something *witchy*. I wiggled in my restraints, watching them all tense.

Dammit all to hell. Whatever this contraption was, it was the real deal. My entire upper body was immobile, numb with not even a tingle going through my limbs.

"Don't bother trying anything, witch," someone spat from behind me, their tone pumped with disdain. "You're trapped."

No shit.

The gigantic binding trap below me was hard to miss. The one above, however, was overkill. I wasn't powerful enough to escape one, much less two. Not to say other witches couldn't—ones with a few more centuries under their belts than me. But these dumbasses didn't know that. They didn't know that I was young and inexperienced.

Unless Malakai had told them, of course.

"Thanks," I said sarcastically to whoever had spoken up. "Don't know how I would've figured that out without you."

Malakai's eyes zipped past me, cold fury hardening his voice. "Don't!" But the order wasn't directed at me.

From the corner of my eye, another male appeared from behind me, skirting the wall with a long rod clutched in his hand. He was burly-looking, but not quite as tall as Malakai.

"The fuck do you mean *don't?*" He glared, crow's feet wrinkling his eyes. "We can't just let this little bitch mouth off whenever she wants."

Malakai walked forward into the trap. Fortunately for him, he was the only one who could. The others wisely stuck to the perimeter of the barrier, knowing my power couldn't reach them there. But if any one of them so much as dipped a toe inside the circle, they were fair game.

"Enough, Clint," the older version of Malakai said, his calm, imposing voice filling the room like he owned it. "Kai is taking point on this. Let him handle it."

The one named Clint grunted and leaned back against the wall, tossing the rod to Malakai and folding his arms across his puffed-out chest. "Handle it, then."

Catching it mid-air, Malakai shortened the extension

piece to better wield the rod, twirling it expertly in his hand. Not recognizing the device at first, my eyes bulged when a blue spark licked the tip.

No...he wouldn't...

Lifting his gaze to look at me, I stared back, fighting tooth and nail to keep my fear at bay. But he saw it. Was that sympathy that flashed in his eyes? Or maybe I was just seeing what I wanted to see.

"Why are you doing this?" I whispered.

His throat bobbed as he swallowed. "Just answer our questions and I won't have to hurt you."

I snorted out a bitter laugh. "Oh, you won't *have* to? How fucking gracious of you." Did he seriously think he would get anything other than resistance out of me?

"Give the bitch a taste, Kai," the one behind the tray piped up. He looked young, barely out of his teens.

"Yes, *Kai*," I mocked with the nickname he once insisted I use. "Give me a taste." The *I-dare-you* was implied. A small part of me wanted to believe he wouldn't go through with it, but I braced for it anyway.

I flinched when the steel end of the rod sparked blue again, the harsh crackle of high-voltage electricity sounding off. He did that on purpose, to scare me. And it was fucking working, but I refused to give any of them the satisfaction of seeing me tremble.

"How many covens reside in Deadwood?" was his first question.

I smirked, playing the villain card since they saw me as nothing else. "Too many to count. The whole damn town is flooded with them. I hope you aren't close with your neighbors. I mean, awkward, am I right?"

Malakai heaved a sigh, knowing full well I was fucking with him. "I need a number."

Scrunching my face in contemplation, I pretended to give the request some serious thought. "You know, I'm not sure. I've never really been too good with numbers."

"What abilities do they have?"

"Should I list them alphabetically or do you want bullet points?"

"Give us their location."

"Did you check up your ass?"

That earned me a crack in his otherwise stoic façade, his lips twitching into a scowl. He lunged at me, hand shooting out to latch onto my face, squeezing my cheeks between his calloused fingers.

"Do you think this is a joke?" He spoke so quietly I doubted the others could hear. "The more useless you prove to be, the higher your chances are of catching a bullet or worse. And believe me...this *can* get worse."

"What difference does it make?" I glowered. "I'm dead either way. I'd rather die alone than take my coven down with me. We did nothing to you people."

"You call killing my son *nothing*?"

We both turned our attention to the male who joined the conversation, moving along the perimeter with the others, a slight limp in his gait. His overgrown salt and pepper beard was in dire need of a trim. My gaze fell to his feet, hoping he was stupid enough to step into the circle. Just a foot inside the line would suffice.

"That was different," I said, ignoring the way Malakai's grip tightened around my face. A warning to keep my mouth shut.

Fuck that.

The other hunter stopped walking, halting just outside my peripheral. "Different?" His clipped laughter came across a tad bit crazed. "I would love to hear how roasting my son alive was *different*."

"Uncle Luke, let me handle this," Malakai told him.

Uncle Luke, huh, I mused to myself. *Look at me, meeting the whole fam.* It was like a sign from above. An opportunity I couldn't pass up. "He wasn't your son anymore. He was a Wendigo."

Well, that was one way to quiet a room.

Though they all stared at me in disbelief, my gaze never strayed from Malakai's. I'd wanted to tell him for so long, but he'd never given me the chance. I needed him to see the sincerity in my eyes, to know I was telling the truth. His vice grip on my cheeks loosened without letting go.

"I tried to tell you," I whispered softly. His renewed grief was evident. It was like learning his cousin had died all over again, the pain as fresh as it was that day in the woods. It should've pleased me to see him hurt like this. But it didn't. I detested the way my heart broke at the sight of his watery eyes, glossed over with unleashed tears I knew he would never shed in the presence of others. He had too much pride for that.

"No..." his uncle murmured, shaking his head like a madman. "That can't be true. We would've known. She's lying!"

"I'm not! *He* was the one who attacked *us* that night. His transformation was incomplete. He was one kill away from fully turning—"

"Shut your filthy fucking mouth!"

"Luke, that's enough!"

"Calm down!"

The man was losing it. I watched as the others fussed over him, trying to defuse the situation.

But I wanted it to explode.

Even Malakai was distracted, his head down, trying to process everything he'd just learned.

"I did you all a favor!" I hollered, gaining their attention once more. "I saved you all from killing him. I mean, that's your job, isn't it? Killing monsters? You should be thanking me."

I tried not to smile when the uncle brandished a hunting knife from his holster. Belting out a war cry, he rushed forward in a blind fit of rage. Right into the circle.

Releasing me, Malakai rushed to stop the fool. "No, don't!"

"Luke, no!" His father screamed next.

Multiple hands fought to grab him, but they were too late. He was *mine* now.

Locking eyes with him, I dug into his brain, nice and deep. The illusion was simple but effective. He screamed when the floor dropped out from under his feet, convinced he was falling to his death into a black abyss. He dropped his knife and fell to the ground, thrashing uncontrollably from his back to his stomach like a flopping fish out of water.

Spitting out a curse, Malakai scurried over to him, grabbed him under both arms, and dragged him from the room. The others followed, filing out one by one until I was left all by my lonesome. The steel door slammed shut. I listened as the locks shifted and turned, shutting me in. Sighing, I eyed the forgotten blade still lying within the confines of the circle. If only I could reach it.

Not that it mattered.

I needed my hands to wield it.

Squirming in my restraints again, I rocked my body back and forth in hopes of breaking something loose with the momentum. But all I managed to do was turn myself into a pendulum, my body swinging aimlessly until it slowed to a stop. Groaning, I closed my eyes and tipped my head back, sending a silent prayer up to Hecate.

Only she could save me now.

THIRTY

Malakai

W hat a fucking shit show.

Fishing out my lighter, I lit up my twelfth cigarette for the night, well on my way to killing an entire carton. I couldn't focus, could barely think straight. Not with Luna chained up inside, waiting to be executed.

And she would be. Soon.

I welcomed the burn in my lungs, leaning my head back and blowing a thick cloud of smoke into the night air. Luna's attack on Uncle Luke only served to rile the others up more, sparking heated debates on the best, most painful, way to break her. Some suggestions were a little too creative for my short fuse to handle, my trigger finger itching to off the next person who opened their fucking mouth.

Hence why I'd been pacing around on the terrace for what felt like hours, staring out over the moonlit lake as if it held all the answers.

Though the spell had worn off, Uncle Luke was still reeling from whatever Luna had done to him, constantly eyeballing the floor like it would dissolve from under his feet at any moment. I was reeling as well, but for an entirely different reason.

Several, in fact.

The first being Zane.

This entire time I had believed he was killed in cold blood. Fallen in the line of duty like any good hunter deserved. That would've been a noble death.

But this...

The others didn't believe Luna's story, but I did. I'd seen the signs. The scratches on Zane's arm after returning from the Wendigo hunt. His sunken eyes he had blamed on a few sleepless nights. His loss of appetite. He'd even tried calling me that night, over and over again, but I was too busy to answer.

Grinding my molars, an unhealthy amount of self-loathing bubbled up inside of me, ripping me apart. He needed my help, and I wasn't there for him. I should've known. I could've done something...cured him somehow. We would've figured it out.

And the worst part? None of this was Luna's fault. She was only defending herself from a threat, which is what she'd been trying to tell me from day one. If Zane had truly turned that night, then she really did do us a solid. She saved us from having to put him down ourselves.

And how did I repay her?

By putting a bullet in her friend and turning her life upside-down. All in the name of a crime she didn't commit. I didn't know how to fix this, how to make it right.

I pounded my fist into the wooden railing until my knuckles split, bruised and bloody, the pain dulling the bigger ache in my chest. I only stopped when the terrace door opened behind me. Keeping my eyes on the lake, I watched the fog roll in, taking one last drag from my cigarette before snubbing it out and lighting up another.

"You seem stressed."

I said nothing as my father came to stand beside me. He found the lake just as interesting, choosing to keep his sights on it instead of me, allowing the uncomfortable silence between us to drag on for a minute or two.

"You know her, don't you." It wasn't a question. More like an accurate observation.

I took an extra long drag just to feel that burn in my lungs again, to feel my throat closing up as I forced down the cough threatening to rock my chest. I deserved worse.

"It's complicated," I ground out, smoke streaming from my nose.

Dad took a deep breath, then exhaled. "It always is. Did you know?"

I finally looked at him, my brows dropping low. "What she was? No. I found out…after."

There was no need to say it. We both knew what I meant. After Zane's death.

He nodded in understanding. "I knew something was off when you wouldn't tell me how you planned on getting inside the Sinclair house. But I trusted your judgment. Trusted you to take care of it. But after what I saw tonight, I don't anymore."

My jaw dropped. *Excuse me?* Keeping my temper in check, the little voice of reason in the back of my head reminded me to stay calm. "I've done nothing to break your trust. I still brought her here, didn't I?"

He shook his head as if I had disappointed him. "You showed weakness in front of the others. She attacked your uncle and you still didn't shock her. Not even once."

He attacked her first!

I had to bite my tongue to stop myself from screaming those treacherous words. "Our attack on her coven was unprovoked. We can stop this now if we let her go. Avoid any unnecessary casualties."

Personally, I thought it was a solid plan.

My father's glare, however, told me he thought otherwise. "Are you listening to yourself, Kai? You let that girl get inside your head. Even if what she says about Zane is true, they're still monsters. All of them. Have you forgotten what we do to monsters?"

My temper flared at his condescending tone, the edges of my vision going red at the thought of him or anyone else laying a finger on Luna, touching what was mine.

"Luna's not a monster," I said without thinking.

The regret that washed over me was both instant and terrifying. But not because of the continued look of disappointment on my father's face. I was becoming numb to that shit. It was because I didn't want him knowing her name, or a single goddamn thing about her, for that matter.

He was quiet for some time, the muscles in his jaw flexing. Then he went in for blood, looking me dead in the eyes as he delivered his next blow. "Your mother would be ashamed of you."

Pause.

What the fuck did he just say to me? I must've heard wrong.

Slowly, the red lingering on the outskirts of my vision crept in further, ready to swallow me whole. "Come again?"

"You stand there defending a witch, when it was one of their kind that killed your mother."

Shaking. For the first time in my life, I was fucking shaking. Taking a tentative step forward, it took every bit of self-control to keep me from lunging at my own father, from crossing the line of no return. "Witches didn't kill Mom," I forced out, my jaw locking up. "She did that herself. I should know, since *I* was the one who found her with that barrel in her mouth right before she pulled the fucking trigger."

A sight not easily forgotten. No child should have to see their mother's brains paint the walls of their bedroom.

Dad snarled, his impenetrable persona cracking. "She was under a spell! A hex cast by that witch!"

I grew tired of this story. This *excuse*. The witch he spoke of was killed days before my mother took her life. Any spell or hex cast would've died along with her. Others who knew my mother told a different story. The story of a woman who just wasn't cut out for this life. The life of a hunter.

Most people weren't.

But I wasn't about to stand here and debate this shit with my father again. I had neither the time nor patience for it. Letting the jab go, I returned to the topic at hand, doing my best to steer him away from the war he was determined to finish. "We're outnumbered. This isn't a battle we can win without taking considerable losses."

Dialing it back, he averted his gaze, cracking his knuckles one by one to collect himself. "So the girl says, but she could be lying. If torture doesn't loosen her lips, then we'll use her as bait to lure her coven out of hiding. Maybe one of them will feel more inclined to talk after a little persuasion."

My heart stalled like it was one beat away from failing me. "Bait how?"

He turned from me, making his way back inside. "That's no longer your concern. I'm benching you until further notice."

My lips curled into a sneer, the sheer disrespect heating my blood. "Benching me? You can't be fucking serious."

Stopping with his hand on the door, he glanced back at me, scolding me with his eyes like I was a little boy again. "I am. Your judgment has been compromised. Stay away from the girl until I tell you otherwise."

Until *he* tells *me* otherwise?

It would be wrong to punch my own father in the face. That's what I had to tell myself as I watched him leave, as I *allowed* him to walk away without a fight. Every bone in my body thrummed with hostility. With violence.

Images of Luna flashed in my mind. She haunted me. Everything from the silkiness of her skin to the taste of her lips. And those eyes. Fuck me. I'd stare into them for hours if she'd let me. Even now they held me captive, beckoning me to her side.

I can't believe I was ever in love with you, Malakai Slade!

I winced, recalling her words. I would've thought she was fucking with me if the confession hadn't come from a place of anger, steeped in nothing but pain and regret.

I could relate.

I wasn't sure if what I felt for her was love, but it was something. Something raw and unexpected that came out of nowhere and knocked me on my ass before I could understand it.

Head in my hands, anxiety chipped away at my resolve the more her face solidified itself in my mind, finding a permanent home there. *I can't fucking do this.*

Turning, I marched back inside. It was late, prompting most to turn in for the night, except for the hunters standing guard outside. There was no one around to stop me as I took the stairs leading down to the tunnels. The door, however, would be a problem.

I didn't know the code.

I stopped as problem number two presented itself.

Derek sat manning the door, Glock in hand. He stood from his chair, his expression apologetic.

"Open the door, D," I demanded roughly.

He looked uncomfortable, unable to meet my gaze. "Sorry, Kai. I'm not allowed to let you in. Your dad's orders."

Surprise, surprise.

The pain in my jaw told me I needed to unclench before I cracked my teeth. "I'm not asking."

His eyes flickered nervously to my hand. Only then did the weight register. When did I pull my gun? The safety was on, but my thumb itched to rectify that.

Derek frowned, meeting my gaze. "You serious?"

His shock was justified. I mean, I could barely believe it myself. I had never pulled a weapon on one of my own before. Never had reason to.

Until now.

Keeping my gun lowered, I pulled back the safety. "You wanna find out?"

He gave me a once-over as if he didn't recognize me anymore, his head shaking in disappointment. *Join the line, buddy.* He wasn't the only one to feel that way…and I imagined he wouldn't be the last.

"What the fuck did that witch do to you, man?"

A fair assessment. I wish I fucking knew. How far was I willing to go for her? It frightened me that I didn't know the answer to that question. And if Derek didn't get out of my way, we would both find out soon enough.

"Last chance, D," I warned. "I don't want to fight you." But I will. The threat hung unspoken between us, like a fuse just waiting to ignite. I always considered him a friend, one of the few I actually trusted with my life.

Seconds ticked by as we faced off, neither making a move. Then he sighed, scrubbing a weary hand over the stubble on his jaw. "Fine. Hit me."

Okay. Not what I was expecting. "What?"

He dropped his gun, kicking it away with his boot. "I'm not about to tell your old man I let you pass willingly. He'll skin me alive. So hit me. And make it look good. I plan on playing dead until you get back."

Good man.

Nodding, I switched my gun to my left hand and

cocked back my right. "Thanks," I said, letting my fist fly. It connected hard with his jaw, enough to leave him bruised but still conscious. He fell to the floor.

"Fuck me," he grunted, rolling over onto his side and spitting out some blood. "Just go. The code is 1802."

Reaching down, I patted him on the shoulder before hopping over his body. Unlocking the door, I took off, veering down the tunnel that led to Luna's cell.

I needed to be quick about this. Get her out without raising any alarms. Beyond that, I had no real plan. If caught, we would be severely outnumbered and detained within minutes. An outcome that wouldn't bode well for either of us. Reaching her cell, my steps faltered at the sight of her door left slightly ajar.

Fear made my heart pound into overdrive. Someone had beat me here. Was it my father? Clint? Taking a few cautious steps forward, I switched my gun back to my shooting hand, prepared to blaze my way out of here if I had to.

A blood-curdling scream propelled me forward. Rushing in, I burst through the door just in time to see Alex jabbing the electric rod into Luna's stomach. Her scream made me sick, blood chilling in my veins as my vision tunneled into murder mode. Alex stood just outside the trap, an inch from the edge. The rod was fully extended so he could reach her at a safe distance.

One of Clint's men stood along the wall, watching with a deranged smile on his face. "I told you she would scream louder if you upped the voltage," he said with a chuckle, his laughter dying once he caught sight of me. "What the hell are you doing—"

Bang.

I fired off the first shot with zero hesitation, the bullet lodging itself in Alex's forehead, forcing remnants of his brain to splatter out the back end. I watched his body drop with no remorse. I always liked Alex. He was a comrade, a brother-in-arms. I waited for the regret to sink in, to feel some sort of shame for my actions.

None came.

The tears streaming down Luna's face wouldn't allow it. Fuming, all I felt was rage. White-hot, all-consuming rage.

Clint's man came at me, tackling me to the floor and disarming me, my gun skidding out of reach.

"Have you lost your fucking mind, boy!"

He had me pinned for half a second before I flipped him onto his back and laid into his face. I held no punches, each one driving down harder than the last. I should've stopped once I felt his nose break and his jaw shatter, but I was too far gone to care. Luna's heart-wrenching screams were on repeat in my mind, her pain stripping me of my sanity.

I needed to protect her. To put down anyone who dared to touch her. Only *I* had that right. Me!

"Malakai!"

At the sound of her voice, my bloody fist stopped mid-swing, saving the mangled face below me from receiving what would've been a death blow. Lifting my head, I met her wide-eyed gaze that seemed to soften the longer she stared, her head tilting curiously as if studying me, trying to understand where my head was at.

Her guess was as good as mine.

Strange. She was oddly calm. It unnerved me. I wanted her anger. Her fury.

I deserved it.

She should hate me.

I was no better than Alex. He may have tortured her, but I was the one who put her in those chains. Who left her vulnerable and helpless. Staggering to my feet, I walked into the circle until we were face-to-face. Reaching for her restraints, I began undoing them.

"What are you doing?" she asked quietly with no hostility in her voice.

I gnashed my teeth. Why the hell wasn't she more upset? I expected her to be ranting and raving about what an asshole I was for doing this to her in the first place. Maybe once her arms were free, she would deck me.

I would welcome it.

"I'm getting you out of here."

She remained quiet as I unraveled the mesh straitjacket from her body. As she pulled her arms free one at a time, I looped my arm around her waist to prevent her from falling since she still hovered inches from the ground.

She accepted the help, her arms slinging around my neck the moment they were freed. The sight of the thick red welts imprinted into her pale skin from the harness made me cringe.

Shutting my eyes, I held her in my arms longer than was necessary, not quite ready to relinquish my hold just yet. When her fingers clutched the hair at my nape, I cracked my lids to find her staring at me with that same inquisitive look from before.

"You killed one of your own for me." She uttered the

words as if she couldn't fathom the logic behind them. "Why?"

The way her luminescent eyes searched mine for answers had my throat closing up. I swallowed to speak. "I...I don't like seeing you hurt."

The curl of her lips suggested that she knew there was more to it than that. My breath caught when she applied pressure to the back of my head, pulling me closer.

"My hero," she murmured, her lips drawing near. The kiss was unexpected, soft and sweet. A short caress and promise of more to come.

Inwardly groaning, I restrained myself from taking her lips more forcefully. If I started, I wouldn't be able to stop.

"Come on," I said, clearing the rasp from my throat and setting her on her feet. "We have to do this as quickly and quietly as possible."

She nodded. "Just free me from the trap and I'll do the rest."

That part was simple enough. A little scratch in the paint was all that was needed. Outing my blade, I walked to the edge of the circle and bent to scrape out an opening. When that was done, I looked towards the ceiling sigil.

That one would be trickier.

Flipping the blade hilt up in my hand, I took aim and let it fly. The pointed tip grazed the edge of the circle before bouncing back, chipping away flecks of paint. It took me a few tries, but I managed to damage the circle enough to break the spell.

Taking Luna's hand, I ushered her to the edge of the trap. "Time to go."

THIRTY-ONE

Luna

S tepping free of the trap was an instant relief. The feel of my powers buzzing in my veins rejuvenated me. Sidling closer to Malakai, I peered up at him through my lashes, biting the inside of my cheek.

I still couldn't believe what he'd done for me.

He killed one of his own without so much as batting an eye. He didn't even spare the two bodies on the floor a second glance as he pulled me from the room, only stopping to retrieve his gun. The one he'd nearly beaten to death was still breathing. Whoever the bastard was, he owed me his life.

"This way," he whispered, tugging me behind him as we rushed out into a tunnel. Wherever this place was, it was underground. Rock and dirt surrounded us, and the air was musty, a clear sign that there were no windows or ventilation down here.

I kept my eyes trained on Malakai's back, my heart racing each time he turned to check on me. *His people might kill him for this.*

I wasn't sure what moral codes hunters lived by, but surely they frowned on betrayal just as much as immortals did. I was scared for him. No one had ever killed for me before. I knew my coven would, of course, if ever faced with such a scenario, but this felt different. The possession and violent rage he displayed was a side of him I'd never seen. The homicidal look in his eyes as he went to town on that guy's face…there was nothing human about it.

And it was all for me.

It was…flattering. And hot as hell.

When those two trigger-happy psychos had shown up in my cell earlier, I had sagged in disappointment, wishing it was Malakai instead. Though he was responsible for my plight, I still longed to see him. To hear his voice.

And now here he was, turning on his people to help me escape. *What changed?* I opened my mouth to ask, but shut it when I ran into his back. "Hey, why did you st—"

His hand detangled itself from mine to loop around my back, keeping me tucked against him from behind.

"What are you doing, Kai?" a voice called from what couldn't be more than a few feet in front of us.

Shit. Busted.

Leaning to the side, I peeked out from behind Malakai's big frame to see his father standing at the fork in the tunnel, gun in hand. He kept the weapon down at his side, his finger nowhere near the trigger. He appeared relatively calm, which, since meeting the man, seemed to be the only function he operated on.

Malakai's body went rigid, his arm coiling tighter around me. The veins in his neck bulged, looking like they were about ready to pop. With his other hand, he reached for the gun tucked against his back, but made no move to pull it. "I can't let you kill her," he told his father unwaveringly.

The older male sighed and shook his head. "Whatever you're feeling for her, son, it isn't real. She's an enchantress. This is what she does. She comes from a coven of illusionists and tricksters. I've seen what they can do. She's in your head, playing with you. Don't be a fool."

Enchantress, eh.

Ha! I wish. I mean, illusionist, sure…but enchantress? Not my strong suit. *He must've met Aunt Freya,* I thought with a smile.

At that moment, his eyes caught mine.

"See," he said, jabbing an accusing finger in my direction. "She's smiling. She knows exactly what she's doing, turning you against us."

"Screw you!" I yelled, stepping out from behind Malakai. "You don't know a fucking thing about—"

He yanked me back behind him just as his father raised the barrel of his gun and fired. The bullet whizzed past my ear, nicking my cartilage and shattering one of the lights embedded in the wall.

"Stay behind me!" Malakai ordered, shielding me with his body.

Of course. His father would never hurt him. The

bastard just wanted a clear shot at *me*. Something he couldn't get as long as his son stood between us.

He took two steps forward, forcing us back. "She's a monster, you know. Do you really think her people will spare you once she runs home and tells them all about what you did to her?"

"I'll take my chances." He spoke those words with such striking confidence that it made me gape up at him in awe.

Would he really?

A scowl marred his father's face, his calm façade crumbling. "Is that a chance you're willing to take with the lives of everyone here?"

He glanced over his shoulder at me with utter conviction in his eyes. "Yes," he said without breaking eye contact. It was a pledge if I've ever heard one, a declaration of love that nearly stopped my heart right there on the spot.

Was he serious? He couldn't be.

But the longer I gazed into his eyes, I knew he meant it.

Damn you, Malakai Slade...

Why is it that every time I tried to hate the man, I fell a little more in love with him?

The cock of a gun drew our attention back to the livid face of his father. "You disappoint me, Malakai." He aimed his gun at both of us now, as if he was prepared to drop two bodies instead of one. But he wasn't fooling anyone.

I clocked the way his hand trembled, the gun shaking with it. He didn't strike me as the type to hesitate before a kill, but this was his son. His flesh and blood. No way would he want that blood on his hands.

Refusing to pull his weapon, Kai shot me a look, followed by a nod. Was it weird that we didn't need words to communicate?

Returning his nod, I locked eyes with the other hunter, letting my power flow out of me as I burrowed into his mind. I was gentle, knowing Kai wouldn't want me to hurt his father—even though I was well within my right to. I filled his sight with darkness, blinding him.

Reaching up, he rubbed his eyes, digging the heel of his palm into the sockets. "Get out of my fucking head!" he roared, swinging his gun in a frenzy.

Charging forward, Kai disarmed him with ease, twisting his wrist until he dropped the gun. He kicked it away just as his father threw a blind punch. He missed, the momentum sending him tumbling forward.

Backing away, Kai watched him struggle, his expression pinched with pain. "I'm sorry," he told his father before turning to take my hand.

As we made our way down another tunnel, a scream echoed in our wake.

"There's no coming back from this, Kai!"

Our pace never slowed as Malakai quietly muttered, "I know," to himself. Only the hard clench of his jaw and his grip tightening in mine told me how difficult this was for him. When he didn't look back, I once again found myself in awe of him.

It was official.

I was hopelessly in love with Malakai Slade.

Melting on the inside, I wanted to throw myself at him

and declare my love against his lips until neither of us could breathe. But we had more pressing issues to deal with at the moment.

When a vault-looking door came into view, he finally pulled his gun, keeping it lowered as he crept closer to see if the way was clear. It wasn't locked, likely left open by his father in his haste to stop us. We both flinched when an explosion rocked the ground above, the hefty steel door vibrating on its hinges.

I grabbed the back of his shirt, clinging to him. "What was that?"

Gunshots rang out next, accompanied by distant screams.

Keeping his body in front of mine, Kai cracked the door and peered outside. "Sounds like we've got company."

My coven. They came for me.

My excitement was tampered by a deep-seated fear. A war zone lay on the other side of that door, one that Malakai and I were on opposite sides of. Would he really stand by and watch his people fall?

I couldn't, if it were me.

And I couldn't allow anything to happen to him either.

"Let me lead."

He turned to face me, brows wrinkling. "What?"

"I can use my powers to cloak us. It's the only way we're both getting out of here alive." Escaping undetected was already a bust, and fighting our way out now posed a risk for us both.

Hesitating, he looked back and forth between me and the door as if it was the last place he wanted me to be.

How sweet. His eagerness to protect me warmed my heart. "I'll be careful," I said in an attempt to ease his mind.

He nodded despite his concern. "Alright. Go. I'm right behind you."

Switching positions, I got in front and took his hand. "Stay close. I can't cloak you if I can't see you."

He flashed me a sexy crooked smile, making my heart skip a beat. "I'm not going anywhere, Sorceress."

Oh, my...

Clearing my throat, I turned from him before he could see the blush that painted my cheeks. Damn him and his charming ways! It would only make our situation more complicated. But I couldn't think about that right now.

One problem at a time, Luna, I told myself as I stepped forward, planting my palm against the flat surface of the door and pushing it wider

"Stay low," Kai whispered, tugging me into a crouched position.

The gunshots that rang out reminded me that my cloak would only make us invisible, *not* invincible. Death was still a very real possibility here. Swallowing my nerves, I gripped his hand and allowed my power to flow into him.

When he hissed, I turned back. "What's wrong?"

"My hand. It's burning."

Turning his hand over in mine, I gazed down at the crescent moon tattoo drawn on the back of his. The one infused with my blood.

Oh, no. "Shit."

"What is it?"

"I can't cloak you. You made yourself immune to my powers, remember."

Taking a beat, he pinched the bridge of his nose. "Okay, new plan. Conceal yourself until I can get you to safety."

I shook my head. "No. If my people see you—"

Freeing his hand from mine, he slid it along my jaw to the back of my neck, grasping it firmly before pulling me in for a bruising kiss.

THIRTY-TWO

Malakai

There was a fifty-fifty chance that she would slap me, but I was willing to risk it just to kiss her one last time. I didn't know if I would see her again after tonight, or if I would live to see the sun come up once her people got their hands on me.

Not that I blamed them.

If I was willing to off my own comrades to protect her, I could only imagine what her family would do to get her back. I needed to make this right.

I never should've started this fucking war.

It was all my fault.

I should've listened to her when she tried to tell me about Zane, but I was too blinded by my own grief and hatred to accept the truth. And now, as her eyes fluttered closed and her lips parted for me, I wished things were different, wished I could keep her for myself without having to deal with the repercussions on both sides.

But that was a fairytale, and I was too old and too scarred to believe in shit like that. Had seen too many fucked up endings to believe in happy ones.

Sighing contentedly, I took my time with her mouth, worshipping her, pouring everything I never said into a single kiss.

Maybe in another lifetime... I thought as we parted, my forehead resting against hers.

She cradled my face, giving my lips one last peck. "Malakai, I—"

"Shh," I hushed, my fingers brushing her cheek. "We'll have time for that later." Or not. What the fuck did I know? "We have to go now."

She nodded solemnly, sniffling with her gaze lowered. Taking her hand, I guided her up the stairs to the main floor, keeping her close. Those who knew of my betrayal were still in the tunnels, my father included. Once Luna's illusion wore off, he would come looking for me.

Would he expose my treachery to the others?

He didn't know about Alex. Not yet, at least. None of them did. It was just a matter of time, though...

Stifling my guilt, I focused on the chaos in front of me. Several hunters remained inside, manning the windows and doors to prevent whoever was outside from getting in. Derek was one of them, kneeling beside a window with a sniper rifle in his hand. Looking up, I spotted eight more hunters on the upper platform in similar positions.

"Out of the way!" one of Clint's men hollered, barrelling past me with a grenade in his hand, his finger on the pin. I tensed, waiting for him to recognize Luna, but he breezed past her as well.

Good. They can't see her.

Glancing back at her, she nodded, reassuring me that her cloak was firmly in place.

"Kai!" Uncle Luke called, running my way. He was clutching his bad leg, his limp more noticeable as if he'd been putting far more strain on it than he should. "Where's your father? It's balls-to-the-wall out there."

I shifted in front of Luna, keeping the hand holding hers close to my side to avoid drawing suspicion. "I don't know," I lied. "I was about to ask you the same thing. What's happening?"

"The girl's coven. They must've followed us here when we left Deadwood, or tracked the girl somehow. Clint's crew is outside holding the line. The perimeter is warded, so the fuckers can't get in. Doesn't look like they'll be giving up anytime soon, though."

Luna leaned into me at the mention of her coven, hugging my arm to her chest, squishing it between her soft breasts. She was getting antsy.

"How many of them are out there?" I asked.

He snorted. "Fuck if I know. No one can see a goddamn thing. Everything from here to the lake is covered in fog so thick you can't see your own feet in front of you."

Fog?

Fog had been rolling in on the lake when I was on the terrace earlier. It was them. It had to be. I needed to get Luna past the wards.

When I turned from my uncle, his hand locked onto my forearm. "Where are you going?"

"To help. Dad's probably out there already. I need to find him." The lie scalded my tongue and made me queasy at the same time. God, I was such a piece of shit for this, and soon everyone would know it.

Uncle Luke nodded. "I'll come with you."

No the fuck you won't. "I got it. You should go secure the tunnels. Make sure the witch doesn't escape."

I didn't wait for him to reply, just patted him on the shoulder and bolted towards the exit. Luna matched my pace, flanking me.

Just as we reached the door, Derek called out from the platform above. "Has anyone seen Alex?"

Well, shit.

Freezing with my hand on the doorknob, I steeled myself against the cold reality of what I'd done. By choosing Luna, I had chosen a side. And it wasn't theirs.

Blocking everyone out, I pushed on, continuing through the door with her by my side. Jesus, Uncle Luke wasn't kidding about the fog. The white mist that covered the landscape was so thick I would've lost sight of Luna if her hand wasn't linked to mine. Only sounds could be heard, faint yelling and muffled voices in the distance. My ears popped the further we ventured, all sounds dimming and growing muted as if someone was purposely turning the volume down to fuck with us.

"Is this your people's doing?" I asked her.

"Yes and no."

I threw her a skeptical look. "Care to explain."

She paused as if debating how much she should share. "They're my people, but not my coven. An elemental is doing this. They specialize in long-range combat. Your wards won't be able to protect you for much longer."

Wonderful.

"How many covens are you allied with?" When she didn't answer, my grip tightened on her hand. "Luna, I need to know." I was putting my ass on the line here. I needed to know what I was facing on the other side.

She worried her lower lip, quietly muttering, "Five, including my own."

Jesus fucking Christ.

I blew out a breath. We never stood a chance.

Cursing, I closed my eyes to think. Five covens meant we were seriously fucking outnumbered. None of us would live to see the sunrise.

Luna shifted from my side to my front, her chest molding to mine, her arms stretching up to circle my neck. Opening my eyes, I peered down at her. Her smile was meant to be reassuring, but I could see the doubt swimming in them, her uncertainty over how this night would play out.

"I'll talk to them," she said. "Convince them to back off."

Leaning my forehead against hers, I chuckled. If only it were that easy. "The witch I killed, who was she?"

Heaving a deep, miserable sigh, her eyes fluttered closed in defeat. "Bella Blackwell. Niece of William Blackwell, leader of the elementals."

"And how important are you to your coven?"

She gazed up at me with a heavy heart, like someone about to deliver bad news. "My Aunt…she's my guardian and leader of our coven."

So basically, I was a dead man.

"It sounds like I killed and kidnapped two very important witches. And unprovoked, to make matters worse. If your people are anything like mine, blood must be answered with blood. There's no way around it, Luna."

Frowning, she stumbled back a step, lashes fluttering as she blinked up at me. "What are you saying, Kai? What are you going to do?"

What I have to.

"We don't have time for this." I reached for her hand. "Can you sense what direction they're in?" Because I might as well be blind at this point.

I tried to pull her forward, but she yanked me back. "No! I won't let you sacrifice yourself!"

Horrified screams had me whipping my head in every direction, trying to discern where they were coming from. The warding around the property would only work if we stayed within its confines. But if no one could see where they were fucking walking, getting lost beyond the perimeter was inevitable.

That was their game plan. To lure us *out*, not break *in*.

And it was working.

"Dammit, Luna!" I growled, jerking her forward one more time. "We have to go!"

I couldn't let the others die like this. If these witches wanted blood, they could have mine.

She dug her heels into the dirt and used what little body weight she had to anchor herself there. "No! We'll find another way. We...we can leave together. Go somewhere where they'll never find us."

The offer left me speechless. Totally and completely baffled. She couldn't possibly mean that. Even if she did, no way was I letting her blow up her life for me. I leveled her with a glare, regretting it when she flinched.

"You don't know what you're saying."

She kicked her chin out, defiance shining brightly in her eyes. "I do."

Enough of this.

Huffing out my irritation, I bent at the waist and looped my arm around her knees, hoisting her up over my shoulder.

She shrieked, fists balling into the back of my shirt. "What are you doing? Put me down!"

Listening for voices, no matter how faint, I picked a direction and took off running. When my feet moved from grass to pavement, I knew I was headed in the right direction. I remembered from my drive up that the pathway down to the gate was a lengthy one. At one point, I veered off course, stepping on a patch of grass. The further I went, the thicker the fog grew, the mist so dense it was suffocating. Redirecting until I touched pavement again, I kept going, all the while ignoring Luna's flailing, her hands clawing and pounding at my back.

"Why can't you just listen to me for once! You have no idea what they'll do to you!"

"I have a pretty good theory," I mumbled under my breath.

Hearing me, she snorted. "Then you're even dumber than I originally thought."

Laughing, I readjusted her on my shoulder. "Ouch. That wasn't very nice. And here I thought you liked me, Sorceress."

She went quiet, her voice dropping low. "I do…"

Sigh. Just what I needed. More guilt.

Stopping, I shimmied her down my front until we were face-to-face, keeping her pressed against me with one arm around her waist and the other tucked under her ass, her feet never touching the ground. The second her lovely amethyst gaze fell on my face, I leaned in, capturing her lips.

I tasted every inch of her delectable mouth, ingraining it to memory. She was more than receptive, cradling my face and moving her mouth languidly against mine, our tongues tangling as the tiniest moan rose up from her throat. Tilting our heads to opposite sides, we deepened the kiss, greedily devouring one another as if this day was our last—which it might very well be.

Granting her a moment to breathe, I trailed a line of hot kisses to her ear. "I'm sorry," I whispered, kissing the spot below her ear. "For everything."

She sniffled, pressing her face into the crook of my neck, her arms padlocking themselves around me like she never wanted to let go.

Fuck, she felt good in my arms, the feel and smell of her making me forget where we were. It was like a dream. Like we were the only two people in the world, surrounded by a clean white slate where we could start fresh.

A nice fantasy.

If only it were real. I had no qualms about leaving this life behind if it meant I got to keep this beautiful creature who fit so perfectly in my arms forever.

Luna choked back a sob, pulling back to look at me. "I

can still fix this. Please let me try."

The tears that streaked her pale cheeks fucking killed me. I hated seeing her cry. Hated being the cause of it even more.

"Luna, I—"

An explosion rocked the ground like an earthquake. The gust of wind that hit us nearly put me on my ass, debris flying with it. Turning with Luna in my arms, I shielded her from the onslaught, caging her head against my chest.

"What the hell was that?" she said once the air had settled.

The fog wasn't as thick, thanks to the blast, allowing me to catch a glimpse of the gate up ahead. It was blown wide, the iron structure completely demolished.

Ah, fuck.

My ears finally un-popped, the volume turned back up.

"You idiot! You blew the gate!" someone yelled. A long chorus of F-bombs followed. The gate was warded, connected to the protection spell that surrounded the property. With it gone...

Slowly, the fog dissipated, revealing more hunters scattered across the lawn. One, in particular, was straddling the perimeter wall near the gate, a grenade launcher hiked on his shoulder. Blinded by the fog, the dumb fuck must've aimed *at* the gate instead of *over* it.

That was when I saw them.

Two lone figures sauntered through the debris onto the property, their gait measured and controlled. Fog swirled and dispersed around them, revealing a man and woman standing side by side. The man was tall and impeccably dressed, looking like he was about to attend a black-tie event instead of a battle. Everything on him looked tailored, from his long wool coat to his expensive-looking dress shoes. He was definitely an Italian leather kind of guy. He radiated a calm the woman at his side did not possess. I recognized her immediately.

Luna's aunt.

One look and I knew she was out for blood. An ocean of it probably wouldn't suffice. Her eyes, identical to Luna's, appeared crazed, glowing with pure menace. Her long dark hair flew about her shoulders in disarray, adding to the whole psychotic thing she had going on.

Simultaneously, the two raised their hands. To attack?

No. It was a signal.

More bodies appeared, flanking the pair and forming a unified line where the gate used to be, four on each side. There was a beat where no one moved, too afraid to even breathe. The magic in the air was potent. It felt old. Ancient.

Unlike Luna, these motherfuckers were seasoned, well-rounded killers. A handful of hunters cautiously backed away, attempting to return to the safety of the house where the wards still held strong.

But not everyone was willing to retreat.

"Attack!" came several war cries.

"Don't!" I shouted.

But it was too late.

THIRTY-THREE

Luna

This was bad. This was *soooo* fucking bad.

It was like an action movie happening in real-time right in front of me in slow motion. When the bullets started flying, Malakai threw himself on top of me, taking us down to the ground. His big body curled around me, using himself as a human shield to protect me.

Terror sliced through me at the thought of him so close to that many bullets. He was human, for goddess sake! Death came far more easily to his kind than it did to mine. I should be the one protecting him!

Yet I found myself frozen beneath him, unsure of what to do. Turning my head against his shoulder, I was graced with a pretty decent side-view of the battle from the ground. Aunt Freya and the others hadn't moved from their position, taking everything the hunters threw at them. Once the symphony of gunfire ceased, the shocked gasps that echoed came as no surprise. I knew none of those bullets had a chance in hell of landing, not while dealing with that particular all-star lineup.

Out of the ten witches who had made an appearance, five were coven leaders and the others were their seconds. Lieutenants of sorts. All powerful, unstoppable forces of nature.

Vicktor Hollow—leader of the Hollow Coven—had successfully stopped each bullet in its track with his telekinetic abilities, creating a wall of hovering ammo mere inches from their faces. Not one of his fellow comrades flinched, trusting wholeheartedly in his ability to shield them.

When the wall of bullets fell to the ground in a dead heap, someone finally had the good sense to shout, "Retreat!"

Lucy Crowley—leader of the Crowley Coven— laughed hysterically. "No, no, there will be none of that." Stepping forward, her head fell back, onyx eyes rolling to white as she began muttering indecipherable words to herself.

Several hunters were propelled backwards into the air by an invisible force. Spirits of the dead. Lucy, the most powerful clairvoyant in her coven, had a special relationship with the deceased. There wasn't a spirit in the veil she couldn't manipulate. Hunters shot and stabbed at entities they couldn't see, scrambling to get away while the dead dragged them back by their feet.

William was next. Dark clouds gathered overhead, lightning spearing the sky. I knew what was coming.

"This is for my niece," he growled, his cerulean gaze

turning electric as bolts of lightning shot down from the sky. It forked out, striking down any who tried to run. The smell of seared flesh carried on the wind, saturating the air with death and anguished screams. Fire came next, blazing up his arms as he turned and took aim towards the house.

"Wait!" I shouted, but my voice was drowned out by the chaos.

The flames flew over our heads. Malakai grunted when the heat licked his back, singeing his shirt. Still, he held his position on top of me, refusing to let me up, to put me in harm's way.

"We need to move," he said, getting to his feet and pulling me with him. "It's too dangerous here."

Then he hesitated, his eyes set behind us rather than in front. I turned to see the house consumed by rolling flames, the smoke already turning black. I felt his body stiffen when his father and uncle emerged from the blaze, crouching over to cough with their hands on their knees. Others ran out soon after, many dragging bodies with them.

Dead or alive, I couldn't tell.

Looking up at Kai, I watched the inner turmoil play out over his face. Those were his people back there, and he was abandoning them. For me.

I hated this. Hated that it had to be either or.

From across the way, I finally locked eyes with Aunt Freya. Time seemed to stand still. The relief that flooded her face at seeing me alive and unscathed quickly morphed into vengeance the moment her sights landed on Malakai.

The sound of crows cawing in the distance had me reaching for him, my hands fisting in his shirt to get his attention. "Please, you need to run. Get as far from here as you can."

Tracing my petrified gaze, he glanced over his shoulder, catching sight of my aunt. She was getting closer, a growing murder of crows circling her.

Seemingly unfazed, he returned his gaze to mine. "I don't run. Not my style."

"Dammit, Kai! Now isn't the time to be prideful!" His bravery would be the death of him.

He smirked. Actually fucking *smirked*.

Then he reached for me, his tattooed hand locking around my throat. His grip was firm but gentle, the action more sexual than anything else. Though, I seriously doubted Aunt Freya would see it as that.

With lust darkening his gaze, he licked his lips, angling his body into mine. "Do you know what my biggest regret is, Sorceress?"

The gravel in his voice gave me heart palpitations. I swallowed past the lump in my throat when his thumb teased my bottom lip, heat seeping to the apex of my thighs. "What's that?" I murmured softly, already lost in him.

He squeezed my neck harder, an unholy glint in his eyes. "That I'll never know what it feels like to be inside of you."

Holy Mother of Darkness.

Did my clit just jump?

A breathy sigh escaped my lips just as a tornado of crows spiraled around us, caging us in. There was no escape, the birds only parting to allow Aunt Freya to enter the fold.

"*You*," she seethed at Malakai, her movements slow and predatory. "Get your disgusting fucking hands off my niece, human."

I'd never seen my aunt like this before. The woman was terror incarnate, striking fear even in me. Her pupilless orbs appeared empty as if the lights were on but no one was home. Her dark hair whipped across her face, the birds growing more and more agitated from her fury, their flapping wings trapping us dead smack in the middle of a wind funnel. A few of them shot forward out of formation, pecking at Malakai until he released me, their sharp beaks cutting into his skin.

Without thinking, I threw myself in front of him, flinching when I caught a beak to the cheek. "Stop! Don't hurt him!"

All at once, the crows quieted. No cawing or squawking. Only the flapping of their wings could be heard.

Without blinking, Aunt Freya tipped her head to the side, her eyes gradually narrowing. "What did you just say?"

Uhh...

"I-I said don't hurt him. Please..."

The silence was more frightening than anything else. That, and the way my aunt was peering into my soul, trying to comprehend the words I dared to speak out loud.

"He's a hunter, Luna," she said, her voice growing increasingly louder with each offense she rattled off. "He kidnapped you. Shot Bella. Aided his people in *vandalizing* our home!"

She spoke to me like a child who lacked common sense. Each reminder had me cringing harder than the last. How did she know he was the one responsible for Bella?

Quinn must've spilled the beans.

I couldn't even be mad at her. Sworn oaths of secrecy tended to become null and void under certain circumstances. Abduction being a major one.

I fought against the urge to cower like a little girl being scolded. "He made a mistake."

Cocking a brow, Aunt Freya laughed incredulously. "Mistake? Yes, on *that* we can agree. A mistake they will *all* pay for tonight."

Stepping out from behind me, Kai held his hands up in surrender. "This doesn't need to end in bloodshed. If it's revenge you want, take me. My people had nothing to do with it."

Aunt Freya flaunted a smile so evil it made my skin crawl. "Well, if you insist." One look was all it took for her to send him to his knees, his hands gripping his head like it was about to explode.

"Ahh!"

His excruciating screams ripped a hole in my heart, my stomach sinking. Dashing forward, I faced off with my aunt. "Stop it, let him go! He saved me!"

"Saved you?" The unforgiving harshness in her voice almost made me want to back down. "For fuck's sake, Luna, listen to yourself! You're acting like a child. Do you have any idea the danger you put us all in by keeping his identity a secret? They nearly killed Anya! Did your little boyfriend tell you about that? Did he tell you how two grown men held down your ten-year-old sister and tried to decapitate her?"

I recoiled as if struck, my head suddenly spinning. *Anya?* "No...I didn't know. Is she alright?"

"She's fine. But she never would've been in that position if you had told us about *him* from the beginning," she spat, glaring down at Malakai before shooting one my way. "Quinn told us everything after the attack, after we realized you were missing. A hunter walked our halls, knew our faces, and *you* let him get away. What exactly did you think would happen, huh?"

I flinched, guilt clawing at my insides. She was right. I allowed my feelings for Malakai to cloud my judgment. I even forced Quinn to lie for me, protecting a secret I had no right keeping. But that still didn't change the fact that I couldn't let him die now.

"You're right. This is all my fault, I know that. But I can't go back and change anything now. And I can't let you kill him either. I love him."

Blowing out a frustrated sigh, Aunt Freya closed her eyes as if begging the Goddess for patience. "Oh, my sweet niece," she muttered softly, sounding sympathetic for once. "If that's true, then I'm truly sorry. Because he's dying today with the others."

I looked back to see Malakai faced-down on the ground, clawing at his skull in anguish, blood dripping from his nose. She was giving him an aneurysm. A few more seconds and he'll be dead.

Backing up until I was closer to him, I held my ground. "No. That's not happening."

Aunt Freya shook her head, eyes narrowing in

warning. "Luna, don't you dare. Nothing good will come from you protecting this boy."

"Maybe. But it's my mistake to make."

I had never used my powers against my family before, not like this. Throwing my head back, I began channeling, my power bursting forth like an explosion. The energy I expelled scattered the crows, disbanding the funnel they had trapped us in.

I turned my sights on my aunt next.

I wasn't foolish enough to think I could take her, but I didn't need to fight her. I just needed to get Malakai away from her. From all of them.

They can't hurt him if they can't see him.

Weaving my illusion into reality, I pushed the image from my mind. The ground quaked before cracking in half, a massive chasm leaving me and Malakai on one half and everyone else on the other. They all wobbled on their feet, trying to keep their balance as the earth shifted below them.

Or so they thought.

Lifting my hands into the air, I brought the ground up with it, forging a never-ending rock wall that ran east to west—so tall it vanished into the sky.

With Aunt Freya's sight temporarily blocked, Malakai slowly picked himself up from the ground, his pain subsiding.

"You need to go," I told him. "Now! This won't hold them for long." I bought him five minutes, if that. My illusions were difficult to pick apart, but not impossible. Especially not for Aunt Freya.

Frowning, his gaze flickered between me and the

group of witches I brought to an astounding halt. He caught on quick, his immunity allowing him to see past my illusions.

"Come with me," he said, his eyes pleading, causing my own to water.

I wish I could.

I forced a weak smile for his sake. "We'll find each other again. I know we will." That was my hope, at least.

For a second, I could've sworn his eyes were glossy too, or maybe my watery vision couldn't tell the difference between my tears and his.

He took a step in my direction, but I shook my head. "Don't. Please...just go."

His jaw ticked, his sorrowful gaze lingering for a short while before he nodded reluctantly and turned from me.

Squeezing my eyes shut, I concentrated on holding the wall so I wouldn't have to see him walk away. *Oh, Hecate, why did this hurt so much?* They were still closed when I heard his distraught cry.

"No!"

My eyelids flipped open just in time to see Malakai throw himself in front of me, a loud bang reverberating in my ear. His heavy body sagged against mine, forcing me to reach out and grab him, letting my illusion fall.

"Kai?" Worry set in when he leaned more of his weight on me. Gripping his shirt, I fought to keep him upright, shifting myself around so I could see his face. "Kai, what's wrong?"

His head dipped sluggishly, his expression blank as blood poured from his mouth. That was when I felt it, the wetness seeping through his shirt, soaking my hand.

My eyes widened at the bullet-size hole in his chest, red liquid drenching the front of his shirt. Then he collapsed. I caught him under his arms, going down with him.

"Kai!"

THIRTY-FOUR

Luna

This wasn't happening. This *couldn't* be happening! I laid Malakai on his back, my hands trembling as I applied pressure to his wound. But the bleeding wouldn't stop. It only got worse. There was so much blood I couldn't see straight, couldn't wrap my head around how this had happened.

"You're okay… You're going to be okay…"

I choked on sob after sob chanting those words, my own tears blinding me. The more blood he coughed up, the harder I cried.

Who did this?

I looked up to see Malakai's father in the distance. He just stood there, rooted to the spot, skin growing paler and paler as everything burned around him. The gun in his hand went limp at his side as if he no longer had the strength to lift it. Was it him? Did he pull the trigger?

The look of devastation on his face was answer enough.

He stumbled forward, making like he was about to come over here, but someone hauled him back by his collar, screaming words I couldn't hear in his face. Though hesitant to go, he allowed himself to be dragged off, holding my gaze until the very last second before turning his back. Together with the remaining hunters, they ran for the woods behind the house, disappearing beyond the treeline.

It was supposed to be me, I thought despairingly. I was the one he wanted dead, not Malakai.

He just got in the way.

"Hey…" came Malakai's weak voice, pulling my gaze. His face had already grown clammy and pale from the blood loss, his eyes struggling to stay open. He lifted a hand, barely making it to my face. I helped him the rest of the way, guiding it to my cheek and holding it there.

He brushed away my tears. "Don't cry, baby. It's okay."

Frantic, I sobbed harder. "Somebody help me!" A Hollow. A Hollow witch could heal him! Luckily for me, there was one here. "I need a healer!"

When no one came forward, I searched for them. They all kept their distance, ignoring my plea. It was Aunt Freya who eventually stepped forward, bending to kneel beside me.

"He took a bullet for you?"

I couldn't answer her, couldn't even look at her. I was too focused on keeping the blood inside his body. Going up on my knees, I used both hands to push down on his chest, blocking the blood flow. His eyes never left mine, and I refused to look away. Not even for a second.

"Vicktor, is there anything you can do?" I heard Aunt Freya ask.

Hope soared in my chest as the leader of the Hollows came forward. Vicktor was a tall, slender male. Quinn and I often joked that he was the giant among the five covens. And though he was the most reserved, he was also kind.

He gently laid his hand on top of mine over Malakai's chest.

No way was I moving.

Closing his shimmering, canary-yellow eyes, he concentrated. The warmth that filled me was comforting, his touch healing whatever minor injuries I'd sustained. The same heat pierced Malakai's chest through my hand, warming his entire body.

I waited to feel his wound close, to feel his heart rate pick up again. But it only slowed more, his lids growing heavier.

"W-Why isn't it working?"

I began hyperventilating when Vicktor retracted his hand, shaking his head with great remorse. "The bullet is still lodged inside of him. I can feel it repelling my magic. It must be warded, just as Bella's was."

A strained half-chuckle left Kai's lips. "I guess karma really is a bitch…" he muttered, making light of his dire situation.

"Can't we remove it?" I asked.

Aunt Freya rested a hand on my shoulder. Her attempt to soothe me only made me wince. "Not with magic, love."

"And he won't survive anything surgical at this point," Vicktor added. "It's too late for that, I'm afraid."

I couldn't breathe. "No...no, there has to be a way. There has to be!"

"Luna...stop," Kai forced out, his voice growing weaker, hoarser. "It's okay."

"It's not okay! You can't die!" Not today. Not like this.

He smiled, lips curling to one side. "Better me...than you, Sorceress." With a shaky hand, he reached into his pants pocket and pulled out my gold necklace, the one he had ripped from my neck. *I can't believe he still has it...*

With his last bit of strength, he held it up. "I've been meaning to give this back to you. I never should've taken it. Forgive me."

I clasped his hand instead, not caring for the trinket as I threw myself on top of him. My tears were endless, my heart breaking as I sobbed against his face, peppering it with kisses before dragging my lips to his. "Please don't leave me... Please..."

He didn't kiss me back, didn't have the strength to even keep his eyes open. His final breath felt like my own, like a part of me was dying with him. Then he went still, his head lolling to the side.

He was gone.

Cradling his head in my lap, I stared at his face for what felt like hours, praying to Hecate that this was just a fucked-up nightmare and his beautiful gray eyes would pop open at any moment. But they never did.

This was real. He was dead...because of *me*.

Some of the others knelt in front of me, trying to get

my attention, but I couldn't hear a single word that fell from their mouths. It was like watching TV with the sound on mute. Everything was drowned out, a blur, leaving me alone with nothing but my pain to keep me company.

It was the sun hitting my face that finally returned me to my senses. How long had I been sitting here?

I squinted as the rays grew brighter, burning my eyes. Then, just like that, it was gone. A shadow shielded me, a lone figure standing three feet away.

"Hey, Sinclair."

Quinn.

Her voice brought tears to my eyes all over again. It actually hurt to look at her, my neck stiff from being in one position too long.

"He's gone," I told her as if she couldn't see that for herself.

Stooping down to my level, she nodded, pale blue eyes shimmering with emotion. "I know."

"When did you get here?" My throat was dry, the croakiness in my voice reflecting exactly how I felt. Broken and exhausted.

"A little while ago. Witchlings weren't invited to the battle. They forced us to hang back. But Freya called me after…" I grimaced when she paused, mindful of her words. "Well…you know."

Yes, I did. Finally glancing around, I realized we were alone. "Where did everyone go?"

"Freya and William are waiting for us by the car. The others left. They're packing up. The elders think it's time we move on, start fresh somewhere new. Deadwood isn't our home anymore."

I nodded, growing numb to the guilt that continued to stab at me.

"It's not your fault, Sinclair." Quinn knew me too well, knew I would be blaming myself for this. "We were living in the same town as hunters. Shit was bound to pop off sooner or later."

Maybe. That didn't change the part I played in all of it, though.

Absently stroking Malakai's cold cheek, I stared off into the distance. "I want to take his body home with us. His people left him. He deserves a proper burial."

Sighing, Quinn sat forward on her knees, unslinging a tote bag from her shoulder. "Sure. We can definitely do that if this doesn't work."

I watched dumbfounded as she pulled a knife, some crystals, and a candle from the bag.

"What are you doing?"

Ignoring me, she continued about her business, placing several of the crystals around Malakai's body before plopping the last one down on his chest, directly over his gunshot wound.

"I'm going to bring him back."

I blinked. Rapidly. "Excuse me?"

With a carefree shrug, the crazy blonde pulled out a silver zippo lighter and sparked the candle, placing it down in front of her. "You heard me, bitch. Now put him down and back up."

My eyes bulged out of their sockets when she whipped out a spellbook next, titled: *The Book of the Dead.*

"You can't be serious." Clearly, this was a joke. And

not a very funny one.

Without sparing me a glance, she flipped open the book in her lap. "Deathly. No pun or offense intended."

"Quinn, you can't work a spell of that magnitude." I didn't have the energy to be polite about it. "And even if you did, magic that dark always comes with consequences."

Incredibly serious, often deadly, consequences.

"I've been practicing," she said, flipping through the pages. "Just trust me. What have you got to lose?"

Scowling, I shot forward and slammed the book shut. "My fucking sanity! If it doesn't work, it'll be like losing him all over again. I can't…" My voice cracked. "I can't go through that again."

The unblinking determination blazing in her eyes told me she wouldn't let this go without a fight. "Is it not worth trying, at least?"

I inhaled an unsteady breath, fearful of the hope blooming in my chest. My sullen gaze fell to Malakai's lifeless face. Our hands were still interlocked, melded together by his crusted blood, my necklace trapped in between. I still couldn't bring myself to put it back on.

Of course it was worth trying. He was worth everything.

"What about the bullet? It's warded and it's still inside of him. Won't it interfere with the spell?"

"A ward that small won't override a spell this big. Black magic trumps everything. Trust me."

That was enough for me. With my mind made up, I nodded. "Do it."

That was all Quinn needed to hear to get to work,

preparing the spell as I mulled over a million different scenarios in my head, envisioning all the ways this could go bad. Quinn was known for reviving zombie versions of woodland creatures. If Malakai came back...*wrong*, I'd have no choice but to kill him. Again.

What the fuck am I doing?

This wasn't going to work. I hated to say it, but the chances of Quinn pulling off a spell of this calibre were *extremely* slim. I was only setting myself up for another heartbreak.

I opened my mouth to call the whole thing off, to tell her I'd changed my mind, but she was already in the swing of things, words in Old Latin flowing from her lips—the language commonly used among necromancers.

Picking up the knife, Quinn sliced a deep cut down the middle of her palm. To her credit, she didn't flinch. Making a fist, she jerked her chin, gesturing for me to give her some space.

I hesitated, reluctant to relinquish my hold on Malakai. Quinn waited patiently as I gently removed his head from my lap and placed it on the ground. I did the same with his hand, painstakingly untangling it from mine and resting it at his side.

Clutching my necklace to my chest, I sat back on my knees and nodded for her to continue. Reaching for the knife again, she cut the blood-drenched shirt from his body and upturned her fist over his bare chest. With her blood, she smeared symbols on the surface of his skin, her chanting growing more pronounced.

In truth, I was impressed. Quinn spoke and moved with a grace I never knew she possessed. I'd never seen her take anything more seriously in my life. Regardless of the outcome, I was beyond grateful for her efforts.

As she drew the last symbol on his forehead with her fingertips, the clouds overhead darkened, the wind picking up drastically. Then her head fell back, pale eyes rolling to white as she peered up at the sky, locked in a trance. In Old Latin, she called out to the Goddess Hecate, begging her to return the life that was stolen.

> *Hear me now, in this hour, I call*
> *upon your darkest power, return the*
> *soul that has been lost, return it here*
> *without a cost. Beyond the veil, I*
> *summon thee, flesh and bone, return*
> *to me.*

All at once, the wind settled, the skies above returning to normal, dark clouds fading to white. Quinn slumped forward, catching herself on out-stretched arms to keep from crumpling to the ground. Blood poured from her nose like a river. Neither one of us spoke a word until she composed herself.

"Quinn, are you okay?"

Nodding, she pulled the sleeve of her sweater over her hand and wiped it across her nose. "I'm fine. Did it work?"

Crawling back to Malakai, I cradled his head, turning it to face me. I could feel Quinn holding her breath along with me, time standing still as we waited for him to open his eyes.

Make a sound.

Wiggle his fingers.

Anything! Any sign of life would have sufficed. But nothing happened.

It didn't work.

My last shred of hope perished, leaving only darkness in its wake, a void deepening in my soul.

"I'm sorry, Luna..." Quinn murmured softly, her lower lip quivering. "I thought I could...fuck, I'm so sorry."

Just when I thought I had no more tears to cry, I surprised myself with a fresh batch. Touching my forehead to his, I inhaled his scent while it still lingered, not yet tainted by the pungent stench of death. Every part of me ached as I slowly came to terms with the harsh, cruel reality forced upon me.

Malakai was gone, and he was never coming back.

THIRTY-FIVE

Malakai

Where the fuck am I?

A violent chill shook me to my core, forcing my eyes open. The blurriness cleared from my vision with just a few swift blinks. The razor-sharp clarity that replaced it surprised me, like waking up after a long nap with a brand-new set of peepers.

Even in the dark, everything was brighter. Crisper.

Groaning, I cranked my neck from side to side to loosen up my stiff muscles, propping myself up on my elbows. I lay sprawled on top of a...table? Wearing nothing but my jeans and shoes.

The cold slab of stainless-steel was giving mortuary vibes, the kind dead bodies were dissected on. Sitting up, I took a look around. The room resembled an old cellar or basement, musty with no furniture or windows. Shabby wooden shelves lined the walls, packed with jars of all sizes. Some had objects floating around inside, filled to the brim with strange-colored liquids.

How did I get here?

Hopping down from the table, I stifled a groan at the sharp pain that shot from my nape to my frontal lobe. *Fuck.* My head was killing me, the king of all migraines kicking my ass. Squeezing my eyes shut, I tried to remember...well, anything. But my memories were foggy, jagged pieces of a puzzle that didn't quite fit.

All except one.

Luna.

She stood at the center of my confusion, her face stamped into the forefront of my mind. All I could see were her uniquely stunning eyes and that bashful little smile she only wore for me. The last thing I remembered was holding her in my arms, her petite frame dwarfed by me. And then...

Darkness.

Why can't I remember?

Rubbing the tension from the back of my neck, I searched the darkness for an exit but found none. Impossible. If there was a way into this room, there had to be a way out. Walking along the walls, I dragged my hand across each brick, looking for a crease, a doorway of some kind. A secret compartment, perhaps.

Individual bookcases stood in the four corners of the room, the crown of each one touching the low ceiling. I paid no mind to the worn leather spines that were clumped together on the dusty shelves. Choosing the one closest to me, I laid my hand on the flat side panel and pushed.

It was surprisingly light, taking minimal effort to

move. The hidden doorway that lay behind it matched the exact measurements of the bookcase. Curious, I walked over to the other three and shifted them over in a similar fashion.

Separate doorways were hidden behind each one.

Which way do I go?

I had four to choose from and no clue where any of them led. Going with my gut, I chose the one on the south side corner of the room. The narrow hallway had no lighting, yet my eyes had no problem adjusting to the dark. A mystery I didn't have time to dwell on. The pathway was long, one with many twists and turns that led to another blocked entrance.

Another bookcase, I assumed.

Flattening my palm against the wooden surface, I pushed until warm light spilled onto my face. Another presence seemed to guide me forward, an invisible force beyond my understanding. The air was fresher here, a far cry from the funky cellar. I inhaled deep to replace the stale oxygen in my lungs, stopping short when another scent greeted me, one so powerful I could taste it on my tongue.

Wildflowers and summer rain.

I...know that scent...

It was entirely new, yet familiar.

Luna.

This was her bedroom. Of course. I *remember now.*

The French doors leading out to her balcony were wide open, the white sheer curtains billowing in the wind, dancing over her disheveled bed. I almost didn't see the figure lying in the middle of the soft mattress, completely engulfed by pillows and blankets.

With a mind of their own, my feet carried me forward. The closer I got, the more my chest burned, a piercing pain robbing me of breath momentarily. I slid my hand over the area, just above my heart, my fingers searching for something but finding nothing but smooth skin. So why did it feel like there was supposed to be something there?

Coming to a halt at the foot of the bed, I took in Luna's still form. She was lying face-down with her arms curled around her head, oblivious to the world around her—my presence included. Cocking my head, I allowed my gaze to wander, raking down her body. She wasn't wearing much, just a tank top that looked more like a lacy bra and some plain cotton panties.

Damn.

I was salivating at the sight of her, my thoughts growing lewder the longer I stared. She was freshly showered. I could tell by the wet strands of hair that clung to her back. Pulling my bottom lip between my teeth, I fought down the predator-like instinct compelling me to wrap her damp locks around my fist. To yank her head back until she notices me. Anything to wring a strangled moan from those sexy lips.

In the end, it was my pained groan that startled her enough to pop her head up and whip around. She froze the moment her gaze landed on me, her petrified expression not the one I was hoping for. In one swift motion, she kicked her feet, scrambling back against the headboard.

"Sweet Virgin Goddess!" she exclaimed, grasping her heaving chest. Her very naked chest. My eyes fell to the plunging neckline of her top. The fabric was practically see-through, putting her very pert nipples on display.

My tongue darted out to wet my lips, that predatory instinct taking hold again, this one a little darker than the last. *Need to get my cock inside of her. Fuck her until she can't walk. Make her scream for me.*

I blinked. What the fuck was that? I couldn't get my thoughts or my dick under control. It strained against my pants, standing at attention like a soldier ready to take orders. I should say something to her. Yes, words might work wonders right now.

Unfortunately, I had none.

Bringing her legs up to her chest, she continued to gawk at me. "M-Malakai? Is it really you?"

I frowned. What the fuck kind of a question was that? Who else was she expecting? Lifting a leg off the floor, I brought my knee down on the bed, moving to crawl towards her.

Her eyes filled with terror, pressing herself further into the headboard as if she wanted to faze right through the fucking thing. It was on the tip of my tongue to ask her what her problem was, but the words wouldn't come.

I already knew her feelings for me, so why this game? Leaning forward, I placed a hand down on the bedding.

"Don't!" she screamed, jabbing a finger at me. "Stay where you are!"

Sigh. This shit was getting old. Patience lost, I grabbed her ankle and pulled until her body slid beneath mine. The breathy gasp that tumbled from her lips made my eyes droop. Yes. This was how I wanted her.

Utterly weak to me.

Kicking her legs apart, I made myself comfortable between her thighs, trapping her with my body. Slipping one hand down to her ass, I brought the other up to cup her face, my thumb lovingly grazing her cheek. The gesture stunned her into submission, curious eyes slanting up at me.

Smirking, I leaned forward to brush her nose with mine, barely allowing our lips to touch as I finally dug my voice free. "Playing hard-to-get doesn't suit you, Sorceress."

She gaped, her jaw going slack in bewilderment. Her hands came up next, slowly at first, hesitating as if she wasn't sure if touching me was a good idea. She cradled both sides of my face, fingers brushing over my every feature. When she used her thumbs to drag down the skin beneath my eyes, I flinched from her grasp.

"What the hell's the matter with you, Luna?" She was acting weird, as if seeing me for the first time.

"Holy shit...it worked," she whispered to no one in particular.

When she made a grab for me, it was my turn to retreat, dodging her touch by sitting back on my knees. "What worked? What are you talking about?"

She was all smiles now, practically giddy with excitement as she crawled towards me. Her eyes glistened with unshed tears, roaming over my chest, searching. Then she laughed, her sudden joy swiftly overshadowed by the sob she tried to smother with a hand clamped over her mouth. Then she threw herself at me, a full-on, linebacker tackle, putting me on my back. I caught her around the waist, holding her as she wept, her head buried in my neck.

"I thought I lost you…"

Lost me?

I rubbed soothing circles on her back, trying my damnedest to ignore the sight of her plump bottom cushioned between my legs. "I'm right here, Sorceress." Which reminded me… "You mind telling me how I got here?"

Turning her face, she rested her cheek flat against my chest, refusing to look at me. "What's the last thing you remember?" She sounded off, running her hand up my chest and bringing it to rest on my left pectoral.

"I'm…not sure." I couldn't put my memories into words. They were too jumbled. Too messy. "I remember…you. *Us*. We were going somewhere. Together. Next thing I know I'm waking up on a table in your basement."

She remained quiet for some time before letting out the world's deepest sigh. Pushing against my chest, she sat up between my legs.

"The memory loss must be a side effect," she mumbled more to herself than to me, her gaze still lowered like a frightened child.

Her damp hair had dried into waves, spilling over her shoulder and blocking her face. Reaching out, I tucked a few strands behind her ear, relishing in the way she leaned into my touch.

"Side effect of what?"

The doe-eyed look she shot me was riddled with guilt. "Promise you won't freak out."

I cocked a brow. "My patience is fading fast,

Sorceress." The fact that she was dragging her feet in fear of my reaction didn't sit well with me. "Tell me."

She mumbled out the words so quietly I couldn't catch them, her voice an octave lower than a whisper.

Sitting up, I pinched her chin and forced her to look at me. "Say again?"

Opening her mouth, she tried again. Louder this time. "You…you kind of…died."

I paused. *Is she joking?* "I think I would remember if I'd died."

She fidgeted, absently picking at a loose thread on her blanket. "Not necessarily. The trauma can sometimes cause regression in memories, the need to block out anything painful or overwhelming. In your case…"

I scoffed. "You sound ridiculous."

When I moved to get up from the bed, she latched onto my arm. "What reason do I have to lie? You have no idea what these last twenty-four hours have been like for me…" Her voice broke at the end, face twisting in turmoil. The tears that had gathered in her eyes earlier finally fell, rolling down her pale cheeks. For the first time, I noticed just how bloodshot her eyes were, red and swollen as if she'd been crying for hours.

Fuck me. She was actually serious, wasn't she?

I couldn't deny the gaps in my memory, lost time I couldn't account for. Rejoining her on the bed, I pulled her into my lap and wiped away her tears. "Tell me everything. I'm listening."

THIRTY-SIX

Luna

The calm that fell over us was giving me anxiety, biting my nails while Malakai paced the length of my room. I still couldn't believe he was upright and walking. *Alive.*

He came back to me. Thank the Goddess.

And Quinn.

She's never going to let this one go.

It was about to be gloating-central up in here once she caught wind of this. I still couldn't believe she pulled it off. And it wasn't some half-assed, zombie version of Malakai either. No. It was *actually* him, live and in the flesh.

I was transfixed by the sight of him, bulging muscles flexing beneath inked skin as he marched back and forth. Each time he turned his back on me, I found myself staring at the grim reaper tatted across the expanse of his back, its skeletal face and hollow demonic eyes piercing through to my soul, casting judgment over me.

Perhaps it was this very reaper that brought him back to me. Brought him back without so much as a scratch. No bullet wound or scar to tarnish his skin.

He was perfect.

Well...almost.

His eyes were a *tad bit* different. The same stormy gray, only paler. Okay, *a lot* paler. It was the only thing that threw me off when I first saw him, leading me to believe he was another one of Quinn's failed attempts about to go Hannibal Lecter on my ass. My heart had stuttered to a stop when he finally spoke, teasing me as he normally would. His voice eased my pain, slowly stitching the broken pieces of my heart back together.

I cleared my throat to get his attention. He hadn't spoken a word since I filled in all the blanks for him, not leaving out a single detail...no matter how painful.

"Are you okay?" The dark stare he drilled into me made me regret my word choice. I flinched, shrinking into myself. "I mean...sorry."

I wouldn't be okay either if I found out my father killed me and a witch brought me back from the dead. Fiddling with a pillow in my lap, I averted my gaze, unable to look at him without feeling terrible.

What if he hated me for doing this to him? Though he looked perfect on the outside, there was no telling what repercussions his resurrection would bring. What long-term effects he may have to endure because of a decision *I* made without his consent. I didn't care, though. Anything was better than him being dead.

Did that make me a shitty person?

I kept my head down as his footsteps approached. He was angry with me. I could feel it. Just knowing that had me on the verge of tears again. If I looked at him now, the floodgates would open, and that wasn't fair to him. I deserved his anger. That bullet was meant for me, not him.

I could feel him looming over me, his presence more intimidating than before. "Am I still human?" he asked, his tone far too calm.

"I'm not sure. The necromancers will need to run some tests…when you're ready, that is." The pillow in my lap was becoming more and more fascinating the longer he hovered over me.

"And my father. Does he know I'm alive?"

I shook my head. "No. No one does. Your people left after everything happened. And I was alone with Quinn when she did the spell. When it didn't work, I convinced my aunt to bring your body back here for a…proper burial. I didn't tell her what we did."

That was another conversation I was dreading. Unsanctioned spells performed by Witchlings were forbidden. Since Quinn had yet to turn eighteen, she would be punished for this. So would I, seeing as how I allowed it to happen.

My head throbbed just thinking about it.

When the bed dipped beside me, I begrudgingly turned to look at Kai. He reached for me and I went, allowing him to pull me into his lap. I sighed in content when he wrapped me up in his arms, holding me tight.

"I'm not mad at you. I'm just…overwhelmed. It's a lot

to process."

"I know. I'm sorry."

He stroked my hair. "Don't be. I would've done the same thing if it were you."

I pulled back to look at him. "Really?"

He smirked. "Fuck yeah. It was either that or take the bullet. I chose the easier option."

I swatted his arm when he chuckled. "Not funny."

"It's the truth. I'd rather it be me than you. I'd do it again if I had to."

"Please don't."

"No promises, Sorceress."

I never thought I'd be so happy to hear him call me that again, a tremendous weight lifting off my chest. Sliding my hand to his nape, I pulled him down until our lips touched. "I missed you so much."

"Mmm," he moaned against my mouth. "You won't have to anymore. I'm never leaving you again."

The excitement that heated my blood was unreal. Sinking my fingers into his dark hair, I parted my mouth for him, letting him control the kiss as his tongue surged inside. When he tilted his head, it was game over, his kiss sending tingles through my body.

His hand with my namesake tattooed to the back of it slinked up the middle of my chest and locked around my throat, guiding me where he wanted me. The more he leaned me back, the more I pulled him down, eagerly spreading my legs to make room for him.

Leaving my lips, his mouth descended lower, tongue and teeth driving me mad, sucking and nipping at my skin until it turned blotchy and red. His hand followed the same downward path, leaving my throat to roughly fondle my breasts. He pinched my nipple through the lacy fabric of my bralette, toying with the little nub until it pebbled, making me jolt beneath him.

A second later, his fingers slipped beneath the wire band, massaging my flesh with vigor, his touch just shy of being too rough. But I loved it. It prompted me to move my hips against him until his free hand crept inside my panties. A shuddering pant escaped me at the feel of his fingers gliding along my hot folds, gathering more of my juices as it pooled.

"Lift your hips," he demanded, his tone indicating he would do it for me if I didn't comply.

Pushing against the mattress with my feet, I elevated my hips off the bed, just enough for him to drag my panties down over my knees to my ankles. Tossing them aside, he returned his attention to my pulsating core. This time was different from the others. There was no hesitation on my part. No resistance.

I was *sooo* ready for him.

The moment he resettled between my thighs, I wrapped my legs around him and rolled us, putting him on his back. He grinned at the sight of me on top of him, his hungry gaze eating me alive, raking down my body with unbridled desire.

When he moved to touch me, I caught his hands and pinned them to the bed. "You've done enough touching. It's my turn. You can watch."

His pupils darkened, sending a chill down my spine. "I'm not much of a spectator, Sorceress. You get five minutes. Then the show's over and that ass is mine."

Oh, my…

The way this man made my heart beat wasn't normal. Just the promise of that threat had me dripping. Maintaining eye contact, I shimmied down past his legs to unfasten his jeans. He let me do all the work as promised, keeping his hands to himself even after I stripped him bare.

Having never seen him fully naked without the barrier of clothes, I took a moment to appreciate the view. My first glimpse of his cock, I did my best not to panic. *There's no way…*

"Something wrong?" he drawled knowingly.

Tearing my gaze from his cock, I looked up to see him smiling. He made my king-size bed look small, sprawled out with his hands tucked behind his head, legs bent at the knees.

"That thing is an abomination," I told him with the utmost seriousness. "There's no way it's fitting inside my mouth, much less my pussy."

He shrugged, annoyingly unbothered. "Let me worry about your pussy. What you do with your mouth is your business. I'm just here to watch for the next…" His eyes drifted over to the clock mounted on my bedroom wall. "Four minutes."

I rolled my eyes, hoping to play off the blush that tinted my cheeks. "I'm glad death hasn't affected your stellar personality."

Getting on my hands and knees, I crawled up his body, keeping my eyes on the task at hand. A very *large* task. His shaft laid on his stomach, the length of it going well past his navel. I made sure to hold his gaze as I wrapped my hand firmly around the thick base.

He groaned, a muscle ticking in his jaw. I straddled his legs again, going face-down-ass-up over his cock just to give him something to look at. His sharp intake of breath was like music to my ears. Bringing his cock to my lips, I tried not to let the weight of it freak me out. It was...*girthier* than I expected.

How did guys walk around with these things all day?

Pushing my thoughts aside, I sucked the bulbous head into my mouth, giving it a swirl with my tongue before releasing it with a *pop*.

Malakai hissed, his hips jerking off the bed.

Startled, I dropped his cock as if it had burned me, letting it flop against his thigh. "I'm so sorry! Did I hurt you?" Did my teeth nick him? I tried to keep them tucked away. Fuck. This was embarrassing. My first blowjob and I already suc—

His hand shot out faster than lightning, fisting my hair and steering my head back to his shaft. "No. It was good. Don't stop," he gritted out.

Smiling, I brought him back to my mouth and continued my ministrations. I teased him at first, little licks and sucks to test the waters until I felt brave enough to take down more of him. Though his hand stayed tangled in my hair, he didn't intervene, allowing me to move at my own pace. Every so often, I gazed up at him through my lashes to see the muscles straining in his neck as he fought to retrain himself. His eyes had grown darker, almost returning to their original color.

His brazen desire only spurred me on, pushing me to swallow a few more inches of his cock. I started off slow, trying my hardest not to gag when it hit the back of my throat. When I couldn't take any more, I used my hand, alternating between sucking and pumping. It wasn't long before I had a nice rhythm going, one he thoroughly enjoyed.

One vile curse after another fell from his lips as he watched me work. I took pride in every filthy word, sucking him harder and faster until my eyes watered.

Then it was over.

"Time's up," he growled.

The harsh tug on my hair was too quick to be painful. Then I was on my back with him looking down at me, his eyes hooded and glazed.

How did he move so fast?

My bra was the last piece of clothing separating us. Instead of unhooking it, he ripped it clean from my chest. Cold air kissed my nipples. I opened my mouth to scold him, but a moan slipped out instead. His skillful lips closed around my nipple, tongue flicking fast and hard. His cock probed my wet folds simultaneously, the head repeatedly dipping inside before receding, taunting me.

"Wrap your legs around me," he mumbled around the nipple in his mouth, carefully holding it between his teeth.

I obeyed, hooking my legs around his waist as he slipped his hands underneath my ass and hoisted me up into a sitting position. Then, in one fluid motion, he shoved me down onto his length. Crying out, my arms shot under his and latched onto his back, my fingernails scoring his skin. My tight vaginal muscles contracted around him, wanting him gone. He wasn't even all the way in, barely making it halfway.

I whimpered into his neck, second-guessing if I was truly ready for this. "It hurts..."

He peppered kisses along my neck to comfort me, whispering words of encouragement in my ear. His lean, cut muscles felt incredibly hard against my soft curves. The same was true for his cock inside of me.

"Just relax for me, baby," he said, pulling out to push back in slowly, plowing through any resistance he was met with. With each roll of his hips, he filled me, the tension easing from my body. "That's it. Just like that."

Fingers digging into my ass cheeks, he glided me along his shaft, showing me how to move, how to ride him. *Up and down. Up and down.* A few solid strokes later and the pain was gone, replaced with unrelenting pleasure.

"Oh...*oooh, God...*"

Malakai chuckled low in his throat, swatting my ass as I bounced with more confidence. "Praying to my god now, are you?"

"Shut up..." I panted breathlessly, eyes rolling to the back of my head.

My legs tightened around him with each snap of his hips, bringing me closer to release. He pulled my hair—a kink I was learning to love—forcing my neck back and my eyes to the ceiling as his thrusts grew harder. Wilder. His release chased mine, the two mixing together as we both came undone. Bliss filled me from head to toe, making my body go lax, stars exploding behind my closed lids.

Malakai collapsed backwards onto the bed, taking me with him. I laid on his chest panting, too weak to lift my own head. His cock twitched inside of me, remnants of his cum oozing out onto my inner thighs. His hand remained tangled in my hair, fingers massaging my scalp as if apologizing for the harsh treatment I had every intention of requesting more of in the future.

Minutes ticked by without either of us saying a word, just heavy breathing and soft caresses shared between us. But when his cock hardened inside of me again, I propped my chin up on his chest and shot him a devious smile.

He returned it with one of his own. "How sore are you, baby?"

Oh, how I loved hearing him call me that. It made my heart flutter, brightening my smile even more. "I can be sore later."

THIRTY-SEVEN

Malakai

"**I**'m the fucking greatest!" Quinn declared as she oohed and aahed her way around me, eyeing me down in a manner that would've made anyone else uncomfortable. "I mean, would you fucking look at him! I did it! I actually fucking did it!"

Oh, they were looking alright.

I was currently standing—unarmed, might I add—in a room full of witches who were probably bummed they wouldn't be burying my corpse tonight. After thoroughly having my way with Luna—for hours and in many positions—she decided it was time to come clean to her coven about what she and Quinn had done.

Let's just get it over with, she'd insisted while sprawled across my chest in bed. *Maybe it won't be that bad.*

Looking over at her anxious face now, she seemed to

be regretting her decision. She worried for the both of us because, personally, I couldn't be bothered by the opinions of these people. There were at least twelve witches gathered, including the leaders of the five covens. Luna had done her best to fill me in on who I would be meeting beforehand, but I failed to remember all of their names.

And yet, I wasn't the least bit intimidated. I felt...numb?

That didn't seem like the right word to describe it, though. A healthy dose of fear was normal for any hunter in my position. But I felt none. Zero. Zilch. And it wasn't because I was trying to be cocky or arrogant. Hand to God. I just wasn't fazed, even in the presence of the less-than-friendly faces that surrounded me. *They can't hurt me.* It wasn't rational, but I somehow knew it to be true. Deep down.

Luna, on the other hand, was a nervous mess. But she stayed glued to my side, her hand firmly intertwined with mine even as her aunt stared daggers at her.

"For fuck's sake," someone muttered with a scoff. "The Nightshade isn't going to shut up about this now."

"Fucking right I won't, bitches!" Quinn said, giving herself a clap as she continued to dance around me.

Luna's hand snapped out, latching onto the necromancer's arm and jerking her to a stop. "Enough with the merry-go-round routine, Quinn."

The pale-eyed blonde pouted. "Fine," she muttered, backing off immediately. From what I understood, her uncontrollable glee was due to the fact that I was her first, *successful*, resurrection to date.

"How do we know he's not a zombie like all her other failed experiments?" someone else chimed in.

Turning, I cocked a brow at Luna. She'd left that part out.

She looked back at me sheepishly, a nervous smile tugging at her lips. "You're not a zombie," she assured me quietly before turning to reiterate that fact to the others. "He's not a zombie! He's exactly as he was."

Her aunt stood leaning against a flaming hearth on the opposite end of the room. Straightening her posture, she sauntered through the crowd until she was standing before us, her disapproving gaze shifting between all three of us as if she didn't know who to lay into first.

She settled on Luna. "Exactly as he was, you say? What proof do you have of that?"

Luna sank into my side, her gaze lowering. "Well, we haven't run any tests yet, but from what I can see—"

"From what *you* can see?" a woman who looked an awful lot like Quinn stepped forward, a quiet fury simmering behind her pale blue orbs. "The Dark Arts are not your specialty, child. Both you and my reckless daughter have hung your hats where you cannot reach!"

Now it was Quinn's turn to shrink back, grimacing with her hands folded in front of her as she took her scolding like a champ.

"Do either of you have any idea the ramifications such a spell could have on a human long-term?"

I was beginning to wonder that myself. But I kept my mouth shut. For now.

"Whatever the ramifications," a male spoke up with a scowl on his traditionally handsome face. "There is none greater than him being a *hunter*. You've revived someone who is an enemy of our kind. Who would not hesitate to terminate our entire species if he could." He then muttered something in another language, his tone clipped and soaked in derision. A curse if I've ever heard one.

Someone doesn't like me very much.

My lips twitched as I refrained from speaking out of turn. Seeing as I was miles behind enemy lines, I had little ground to stand on. They had home turf advantage here, something I was trying to respect. But this motherfucker had been throwing jabs since he got here.

What was his name again?

I had a vague recollection of him from the battle, bits and pieces that were slowly coming back to me. He was powerful, from what I remembered, but even the mightiest of foes can be knocked off their pedestal. If old boy thought I was scared of his nineteen-hundreds-looking ass, he was about to learn otherwise.

Before I could open my mouth, Luna leaned into me, turning her face away from the crowd. "You killed his niece," she whispered for my ears only.

What? *When did I...*

Then it clicked. The witch I shot in the woods. Well, that certainly explained the *I-want-you-dead* glares the prick kept shooting my way.

"Why don't we just reverse the spell and put the human in the ground where he belongs."

"I second that."

"Double ditto."

Grinding my molars, I made no move to pinpoint the owners of those remarks and tell them to fuck right off.

They can try, a dark voice drawled from within. It sounded like me, but didn't at the same time. I agreed with it, nonetheless.

"No!" Both Luna and Quinn shouted, stepping forward simultaneously.

"I won't let anyone touch him!"

"This will look great on my resume! You can't just take that away!"

Luna and I both fixed Quinn with a glare.

She sputtered, quickly back-peddling. "I mean…killing him would be an insult to Hecate."

Several brows shot up, every expression in the room looking less than convinced.

"How would killing a hunter be an insult to Hecate?" someone asked.

"Because…" Quinn said, taking a long pause, clearly stalling for words. Then her pale orbs lit up as if she'd just solved the crisis of world hunger in the seconds that passed. "He's a gift, bestowed upon Luna from Hecate herself."

When no one challenged her logic, she continued, voice filling with bravado. She moved about the room with her shoulders back, looking each person dead in the eyes like a defense lawyer addressing a jury.

"Think about it. Why have all of my experiments failed until *now?* Until *him?* You all know I've done that spell hundreds of times with no successful outcome. So why was this different? If the Dark Goddess saw fit to return this mortal's soul from beyond the veil, who are we to question why? To return such a gift would be an inconceivable offense. A colossal *fuck-you*. And wouldn't insulting our Dark Mother have bigger ramifications than letting the hunter live?"

A resounding silence fell amongst the group. Everyone seemed to be at a loss for words, looking to the person beside them to disprove everything Quinn had just spewed from the top of her head. She glanced back at us with bulged eyes, proving that she was, in fact, talking out of her ass.

"As impulsive as my daughter is," the other necromancer said with a sigh. "She speaks true. It would be an egregious sin to destroy that which has been given by Hecate herself."

A low rumble of displeasure spread through the crowd, followed by several timid nods of agreement.

Shit. I can't believe that worked.

I now owed Quinn my life for a second time.

Luna stepped back into my embrace, sagging against my chest in relief. I enveloped her in my arms.

"Does this mean he can stay?" She directed the question to her aunt.

Canting her head, the female's pupilless eyes narrowed, searching her niece's face before moving to mine. I held her penetrating stare, refusing to cower. Whatever her decision, I had no intention of walking away from Luna. Even if I wasn't welcomed here, we would find a way to be together.

If death couldn't fucking stop me, neither could she.

It felt like hours before she spoke, a long, drawn-out sigh leaving her lips. Then she nodded. "For now, yes. We still need to run some tests before turning him loose into the world. Make sure he's as normal as you say he is."

She turned to me. "Think of it as payment for saving my niece's life."

I gave a curt nod, accepting her decision. With a delighted squeal, Luna spun in my arms and threw herself at me. Though I returned her affection, my eyes never strayed from the assembly of pissed off witches. The verdict had clearly left many with a sour taste in their mouths, especially the male with the perpetual scowl engraved on his face.

Luna's aunt waved a hand towards Quinn's mother. "Meet Ophelia Nightshade. She and I will be overseeing your tests starting first thing in the morning."

"Or we can start now."

All heads whipped towards the parlor doors that were flung wide by a gust of wind so strong it nearly took the thing clean off its hinges. A lone female figure stood in the doorway, her amber eyes and dark hair setting alarm bells off in my head.

Isn't that...

"Bella?" Luna gasped. Though no one else seemed to share her shock in seeing the once-dead witch up and about.

"Does anyone ever stay dead around here?" I muttered to myself.

The witch held her arms out, fire coiling up both limbs and burning from the inside out, much like they had the first time we met.

"Round two, asshole!" she shouted, arms going all flamethrower in my direction.

On instinct, I shoved Luna out of the way. I took the full force of the blast, flames engulfing my upper body, hitting my chest and face. I cried out, feeling my skin melt away, my vision blurring as heat seared my corneas, leaving me blind.

"Son of a bitch!" Pitching backwards, I fell against the wall, clutching my charred face. The smell of my own boiling flesh brought a wave of nausea up from my stomach, threatening to exit through my mouth.

"Malakai!"

Then, as quickly as the pain came, it left. *How...*

I blinked my vision back into focus, the sting fading from my eyes. Turning from the wall, a collection of shocked faces greeted me. Jaws were on the floor. But I gave it little thought. My gaze bypassed all the others to find the amber-eyed bitch still standing in the doorway, orange sparks retracting back into her arms.

She stood there gaping. "What the f—"

I was on her before she could finish that sentence, dashing across the room with a speed that stumped even me. My hand locked around her windpipe and squeezed. Her strangled wheezing brought me a sick sort of satisfaction, one I didn't typically feel while inflicting pain upon others.

"That was your one shot," I growled, inches from her face. "You won't get another."

Gasping for air, she clawed at my hand, eyes bulging until they rolled to white. I shoved her away when the color drained from her face, her complexion turning blue. She stumbled to catch herself, holding her throat as she coughed.

"Consider us even," I told her with a glare. I tried to kill her, and she tried to kill me. Clearly, neither had stuck. For a second, I forgot where I was. Forgot I had an audience wishing me dead.

"Kai…"

Luna approached me from behind, her eyes wide and disbelieving. "You're…healed."

Cautiously, her hand floated to my face, fingertips trailing from my eyes to my naked chest. Bella's flames had burnt my shirt to ash, leaving nothing behind. Covering Luna's hand with my own, I felt what she felt. Smooth skin. The burns…they were gone. I could've sworn I felt them sink into my flesh, laying waste to my muscles and melting away my skin.

"Just as he was, you say?" Freya drawled evenly. Her shock had worn off, and now she, and everyone else, were glaring something fierce at Quinn.

The blonde blew out a nervous laugh, scratching the back of her head. "Uh…oops?"

"I told you he was a fucking zombie!"

"What the fuck did you do, Quinn!"

"An attack like that would've easily killed any mortal."

"Does this mean he can't die?"

"Nice going, Nightshade. You created an immortal witch-killer who'll probably murder us all in our sleep."

"Let's see what else he can do!"

The chatter quickly grew into a competition of who could yell the loudest, voices overlapping until a shrill whistle pierced the air. I looked down to see Luna with her thumb and index finger between her lips, a stubborn crease between her brows.

"Will you all please shut up!" Then she spun to face

the witch who nearly shish-kebabbed my ass a minute ago. "When did you get back?" she asked nonchalantly as if the girl had just returned from Hawaii and not the fucking grave.

The other witch shrugged. "The night of the ambush."

Luna's brows shot up, eyes skirting around the room accusingly. "And no one bothered to mention this to me?"

"Oh, we're sorry," a young male scoffed from a sofa in the far corner of the room. He looked to be about Luna's age with wind-swept, ash-brown hair and electric baby blues—minus the pupils. "We were all a little busy trying to save you from the hunter who's dick you've obviously been riding. Forgive us."

Fucking prick. I tensed to lunge, fists clenching at my sides. *No one talks to her like that!* But Luna stepped in front of me, blocking my path to him as if she knew my thoughts were murderous.

"Fuck you, Tidus! Someone still should've told me. I've been back since yesterday."

"Yeah, crying in your room," another male added.

I was getting tired of this shit. "Who are these douchebags?" I asked Luna, not bothering to lower my voice in the slightest.

"My cousins," she deadpanned.

One of the boys stood from his chair in a huff, nearly knocking it over. "You got something to say, bitch? We can go right now."

Adrenaline pumped through me at the prospect of a fight, my body moving on its own, sidestepping Luna. Whatever was happening to me, I felt strangely at ease about it. Enough to use it to beat someone's ass if need be.

"You like hearing yourself talk, don't you, big man?" I smirked, cracking my knuckles. "Let's see how chatty you are without your fucking teeth."

The boy leapt forward with a snarl. "I'd like to see you fucking try!"

"Enough." Freya held up a stern hand, the quiet authority in her voice filling the room in a way that reminded me of my father. Strong and assertive. "Sit down, Marcus."

The command had the kid halting in his tracks immediately. Scowling, he spat out a curse and sat back down like a pouting toddler.

"I think that's enough excitement for one night. This meeting is adjourned. Everyone, please return to your respective covens."

It wasn't a request.

Only Freya and Ophelia hung back as the others began filing out. Taking my hand, Luna turned to guide me back up to her bedroom, waving goodbye to Quinn as the blonde booked it for the front door.

"Not you three," Ophelia called out sternly.

I exhaled a long breath. *Fucking hell. What now?*

The older necromancer pinned her daughter with a no-nonsense look. Her eyes were definitely the creepiest of the bunch—unsettling in the most haunting way. I almost mistook her for being blind with her pale milky gaze and pinprick pupils. "You're not going anywhere until you tell us exactly how you worded that little spell of yours."

Groaning, Quinn marched back into the parlor, stomping her foot as she went. "But I'm tired!"

"Yeah, trifling with the dead will do that to you,"

Freya muttered dryly, looking directly at me. "Have a seat, Malakai."

A chair dragged itself across the floor, spinning to a stop in front of me. Was the magic act meant to be intimidating? Gripping my hand, Luna smiled up at me, her expression apologetic. Going up on her tiptoes, she touched her lips to mine in a chaste kiss, not caring who was looking.

"Everything's going to be okay," she murmured. "We'll figure this out together."

God, I love her. It took me dying for her to realize it, but I was willing to endure any kind of torture if it meant I got to be with her in the end. To hold and touch and kiss her whenever the fuck I pleased, with no interference from anyone.

Nodding, I took the seat I was offered and pulled her into my lap. She squirmed and shifted around until she was comfortable, leaving me anything but.

I fought down the undignified groan warring to slip loose the more she pressed her perfectly rounded ass into my crotch, the delicious pressure making my cock surge. Trailing my nose along her nape, I inhaled her sweet scent, already craving the wet, tight comfort of her pussy. Feeling the hardness of my cock, she pushed back against it, her lips twitching.

The little minx.

She knew exactly what she was doing, turning me on while in the company of others, knowing damn well I couldn't do anything about it.

Yet.

I bit the back of her neck in warning, grinning

wickedly when a shiver rolled down her spine. Her hand sped to cover mine when I flattened it across her toned stomach, sprawling my fingers wide until my pinky was close enough to dip below the front of her sweats, grazing the hem of her panties.

Eyes narrowing, she threw me a look over her shoulder that screamed, *don't you dare*. Funny enough, her aunt was directing a similar look our way, catching on to our antics. So I relented.

For now.

Let's get this shit over with, I thought, nodding along to whatever these witches were saying so we could hurry up and be done with this. The sooner that happened, the sooner I would have my sorceress naked and pleading underneath me again.

THIRTY-EIGHT

Luna

I woke to find Malakai sitting at the edge of the bed with his back to me, bent forward with his forearms resting on his knees. It was such a strange feeling waking to a man in my bed, my body deliciously sore and still humming from the many positions he'd fucked me in.

Sitting up, I allowed the sheet to fall to my waist, unveiling my naked chest. A cool night breeze wafted in from the balcony doors, sweeping the sheer curtains aside to brush against my fevered skin, forcing a shiver from me.

"Kai?" He turned his head without looking at me. "You okay?"

Dumb question. Of course he wasn't okay. Mere hours had passed since his revival, during which he learned not only was he now an immortal who possessed amplified strength and speed, but he couldn't be killed.

After Bella had failed to roast him, Ophelia Nightshade ran every test imaginable to pinpoint exactly where Quinn had gone wrong during her resurrection spell. Everything from the incantation to her wording was dissected and picked apart. Malakai, bless him, sat patiently throughout the process, offering up his blood each time Ophelia needed to run another test.

The verdict?

He was no longer human. That part of him had died the moment that bullet ripped through his chest. Now his newfound strength and speed placed him on equal footing with most immortals. I almost couldn't believe my eyes when Aunt Freya made him bench press her Mercedes in the driveway, a feat he did with relative ease, proving he could lift heavier if he wanted to.

Then there was the rapid healing. Healing that outshined every witch in the five covens. Although we all healed quicker than the average human, we often needed more time to recover from graver injuries.

But the incident with Bella proved that Malakai did not.

The fire witches in the Blackwell Coven were known to burn hotter than the sun, yet he recovered from a dousing like it was as insignificant as a paper cut. The extent of his healing capabilities would only be revealed over time, but both my aunt and Ophelia were convinced he couldn't be killed, that he was somehow invincible.

Without meaning too, Quinn had indeed brought him back as a zombie. A fully functioning one with all the perks and none of the drawbacks.

News that hadn't sat well with him.

I would've been surprised if it had. For a mortal, turning immortal overnight was a daunting reality. Due to his rapid healing, he wouldn't age, wouldn't contract diseases. Everyone he knew and loved would pass from this life, leaving him behind.

All except me.

Without him saying it out loud, I knew those were the thoughts that plagued him the most.

"You'll always have me," I whispered quietly into the dark, hoping my words brought him some form of comfort in his despair.

Finally turning to look at me, his lips curved up into a half-smile. "I know, baby. That's the only thing keeping me sane right now."

I bit the inside of my cheek, afraid to ask him my next question. "Are you angry with me?"

His brows furrowed, pale gray orbs glowing in the moonlight that streamed in from the balcony. "What are you talking about?"

"You can tell me if you are. I would understand."

He twisted his upper body around to properly face me, resting one hand on the bed near my feet. "Why would I be angry with you?"

I bit down harder on my cheek, tasting the faintest bit of copper on my tongue. "For letting Quinn do that spell. I know she meant well, but I could've asked one of the others to do it, someone more experienced."

That never would've happened, of course. No amount of begging would've convinced anyone other than Quinn to perform that spell, to bring back an enemy from the dead. "If it was done properly, you would've been brought back normal, like Bella was. But I wasn't thinking...I didn't mean—"

"Hey." He leaned forward when my voice cracked, his hand locking around my calf over the thin fabric of the sheet that covered my lower body. "Come here."

Kicking out from underneath the covers, I crawled into his waiting embrace. Utterly unashamed of our mutual nakedness, I curled into his lap, looping my arms around his neck and nuzzling my face into his.

"I could never be angry at you for doing what I would've done in your position. I'm glad I'm here with you, that I get to hold you like this for as long as I want."

I played with the hair at his nape, gently scratching it with my fingers. "But your family..."

"Already think I'm dead. Best to leave it at that."

His somber tone broke my heart.

"If they were to see me as I am now, they wouldn't hesitate to pump me full of lead. For a hunter, death is a better alternative than becoming the very thing that we hunt. I'm already dead to them."

I pulled back to look at him, my thumb branching out from his nape to caress the hard cut of his jaw. "You don't know that. I saw the look on your father's face when that bullet hit you instead of me. He was devastated. He didn't look like a man who wanted his son dead."

He sighed, frustration hardening his voice. "He will once he sees me."

"You don't know that."

"Luna, please." Reaching up over me, he rubbed his tired eyes. "Can we not talk about this?"

I pressed my lips together, keeping the rest of my opinions to myself. It wasn't my place to tell him about the wants and needs of his loved ones. He knew them best, after all.

Leaning forward, I kissed the corner of his mouth, working my way to his lips. "I'm sorry. Let's not talk, then." I kept my kisses gentle and sweet, a silent message that I was here for him in any capacity he needed me.

But he didn't want gentle and sweet.

His hand slid beneath the curtain of my hair to grip the back of my neck, pulling me closer. His mouth slanted over mine, his tongue prying my lips apart so he could plunge inside. I groaned, surrendering myself wholeheartedly to him, his hands tracing my curves, squeezing and caressing every inch of me into memory. I shifted my legs over his lap until I was straddling him, wrapping myself around him like a koala bear.

Squeezing my ass in his calloused hands, he moved me along his semi-hard erection. I whimpered as it grew, gliding through my folds until moisture soaked the head.

"I'm the one who should be apologizing to you," he murmured against my lips, forcing me to roll my hips harder against his now fully engorged cock. "For mistreating you."

I gasped when his fingers slid down to my pussy, teasing my entrance before slipping past his cock to my clit.

"I forgive you." I choked on the words the moment he started rubbing, working my clit in slow, agonizing circles, compelling my hips to follow the same rhythm.

"You shouldn't," he growled against my jaw, my

breath coming in short, rough pants. "I should be punished for what I did."

"Punished?" My brows wrinkled, hips bucking against his hand in outrage when the rubbing stopped, seeking out more of the lost friction. Cracking my lids, I stared down at him incredulously. "What are you doing? Why'd you stop?"

He'd gone still, hands slipping from where I needed them most. Those pale eyes glinted up at me with a seriousness I wasn't expecting.

"Tell me what you want, Sorceress."

I blinked down at him, trying to understand his need for absolution. In truth, there was nothing to forgive. He'd redeemed himself the moment he saved me, choosing my life over his own, over his people. But death wasn't enough to absolve him of his guilt. He wanted to be punished.

So be it.

Grabbing his face, I squeezed his cheeks hard between my fingers, something he had done to me on numerous occasions. His eyes flared, taken aback by the roughness of my touch. Pressing my chest to his, my legs tightened around his hips to keep him in place.

"You're right, Kai. You do need to be punished." It was time I took what I wanted. "Do you want to know a secret?" I rasped seductively, running the tip of my tongue along the outer shell of his ear.

The shiver that rippled through him emboldened me, striking a fire in my veins that burned in the most exquisite way. I kept the trail going with my tongue, angling his head where I wanted it as I licked a path downward. His eyes grew hooded as he watched me, pupils darkening with lust.

That's it.

This was how I wanted him. His attention solely on me and nothing else. "I knew you were mine from the first day you rolled into town on your Harley, knew I would have you all to myself one day. And now, here we are. Hecate returned you to me, and I don't plan on ever letting you go."

A low, almost threatening, moan vibrated from his chest as my words went straight to his cock, the steel rod twitching against my entrance. He dug his fingers into the fleshy part of my thigh so hard I knew it would bruise, jerking me forward on his lap. With a surge, he broke free of my grasp and lunged for my lips, his big body thrumming with sexual energy.

He growled when I recoiled out of his reach, his predatory gaze narrowing dangerously. "Don't tease me, Luna." The sinister tone in his gravelly voice sent molten liquid pooling between my legs, dripping down onto his eager cock.

Giggling, my fingers sank into his dark hair, giving it a harsh tug. "I'm not teasing, hunter. I'm *punishing.* Now…on your feet."

Something animalistic flashed in his eyes, a primitive smirk stretching across his handsome face. "As you wish."

I slid from his lap to sit on the bed, watching as he stood to his full height in front of me. He peered down with utter reverence on his face, making me feel like a goddess in his presence.

Leaning back on my elbows with my knees raised, I took my time with the view, my appreciative gaze skimming down his hard, well-defined body. His dark tattoos only highlighted his corded muscles as they shifted and flexed under my shameless inspection.

I bit my lip, shuddering in anticipation at the very sight of him. He looked every bit the immortal he now was, the silver glow of the moonlight adding to his menacing image.

Meeting his gaze, I grinned, allowing my legs to fall wide at the knees. He sucked in a sharp breath, his greedy gaze lowering to my tender flesh. "On your knees, my hunter. It's time for your punishment."

He licked his lips, dropping to his knees before me. "As you wish, my sorceress."

Butterflies ran amuck in my stomach when his hands looped under my thighs and jerked me to the edge of the bed, bringing me closer to his mouth like I was a meal he was about to demolish.

I held his sinful gaze as he feasted, the pointed tip of his tongue slipping between my slick folds to taste me. Goosebumps tickled my skin, my heart pumping ten times faster as I reached for his head. Gripping his hair, I guided him, whispering my commands as he worked. Faster, slower, harder. There would be no teasing tonight.

Not for me, at least.

A half gasp, half moan escaped me when he licked from the bottom of my slit to the top, the sound of him slurping me down the most erotic thing I've ever fucking heard in my life.

"So wet," he murmured as if drunk off the taste of me.

"You taste so fucking good."

Sweet baby Lucifer…

My answer was another moan, my breath staggering when his tongue tortured my swollen clit, the tiny nub still sensitive from our earlier activities. But he was ruthless, alternating between licking and sucking, teasing and nipping until I was a shaky mess, my legs quaking uncontrollably as my release inched closer and closer. He was ravenous, utterly devoted to seeing me shatter.

And shatter I did.

"Oh, *fuuuck.*" I tugged at his hair as he sucked my tender flesh, drinking down every last drop of cum as a monster-sized orgasm tore me to pieces, leaving me wrecked. Sweat coated my skin by the time he was done, the stroke of his tongue switching from fast and hard to soft and slow, allowing me to ride out the last of my tremors.

I barely had time to catch my breath when Malakai flipped me onto my stomach, swatting my ass as he crawled up onto the bed and mounted me from behind.

I smiled with my face smashed into a pillow, my senses still floating back to earth when he nudged my legs apart with his knee and fed the length of his cock inside of my still sensitive heat, stretching me.

Fists grasping the sheets, I prepared myself for the mind-numbing fuck I was about to take, my inner muscles already clenching around his cock before he could take his first thrust. The forceful way he gripped my hips told me I wouldn't be able to walk straight come morning, that he would use my body until we were both blissfully sated and too sore to function.

I smiled. Nothing would make me happier.

THIRTY-NINE

Malakai

S trolling along the beaten path of the backroads in town, I was in no rush to reach my destination, blending in with the shadows to avoid detection. It would've been easier to borrow a car—God knows the Sinclairs had more than a few to spare lying about—but the cool night air was doing me good.

The quiet wasn't bad either.

It gave me time to think, to sort through the shit bouncing around in my head. To go from *hunter* to *hunted* overnight wasn't an easy pill to swallow, but I was trying my best to choke that motherfucker down regardless.

Though my memories were still foggy, they were creeping back slowly, the pieces clicking into place. Most came with a healthy dose of guilt attached to them, like the one of Luna being tortured, screaming in pain while strung up like an animal and electrocuted. I wish I could forget it, push it to the back of my mind until it eventually fades away, but it continued to haunt me.

The kidnapping, the drugging, the ambush. All of it was a nasty reminder of what a massive piece of shit I was to her in the beginning. And though she'd forgiven me, I was having a hard time getting there myself.

Stuffing my hands in my pockets, I ran a finger over the smooth links of the charm bracelet I bought her for her birthday—the same one she ripped off her own wrist and flung back at me after I'd taken her necklace. I couldn't believe I still had the thing, that it hadn't gotten lost in all the chaos.

I had planned on returning it to her tonight, but got distracted with worshipping her body until she was too weak to keep her eyes open. I grinned as better memories took hold, my greedy little sorceress taking every inch of me without complaint, squirming on my cock as she took her own pleasure while giving me mine.

She was definitely a screamer, and a loud one at that, my name falling from her pretty pink lips over and over again. An obnoxious part of me secretly hoped her coven had heard her cries of ecstasy, seeing as how none of them cared for my presence at the moment. I wanted to make it clear who she belonged to, because I wasn't going anywhere anytime soon.

So they better fucking get used to seeing me around.

Picking up my pace, I turned down the street leading to my final destination. I needed to get this done before daybreak. Before Luna wakes up. She'd fallen asleep while I was still inside of her and had no idea I was gone. She and her coven agreed that until they knew the extent of my...*abilities*, I should keep a low profile.

This was as low as I was willing to go.

Taking the next left, I crossed the street and approached the sign I was looking for. *Slade Auto*.

A deep sigh left me. It felt good to be home, even if it was just for a short while. Reaching the chain fence, I eyed the metal locks that looped around the bars on the end. I didn't have my key, and it felt wrong to break the fucking thing—which would be easy with my newfound strength. Instead, I quickly scaled it and vaulted over the top, landing gracefully on my feet on the other side.

Strolling across the salvage yard, I darted between the parked cars in the lot, using them as cover just in case anyone was here. I seriously doubted that, though. It would be unwise for my father and the others to return, seeing as how they knew the witches didn't live far. And I didn't have to worry about running into any witches either, since Luna assured me that her people weren't watching the place. The five covens were far too busy packing up their shit and preparing to move now that their homes and identities had been compromised.

Making my way over to the main house, I ambled along the side of the building to my bedroom window. It was locked. Using my elbow, I smashed the glass as quietly as possible, reaching in with my fingers to pop the lock and open things up.

Once inside, I looked around. I was always a minimalistic sort of guy, so the small space wasn't much to look at. Just a single queen bed—sheets neatly made just as I left it—a forty-inch TV mounted on the wall, a side table with a lamp, and a closet by the door. A simple place to rest my head until my father decided it was time for us to move again.

Now that time was here. Only this time I was on my own.

I had to breathe through the dull ache that settled in my chest. This wasn't my life anymore, and although I had to leave it all behind, there were some things I wasn't quite ready to part with.

Heading straight for the closet, I pulled down an army camouflage duffle bag from the top shelf and started packing. I stuffed in a few articles of clothing, just enough to tide me over until I bought new ones. The overly expensive brands I was currently rocking belonged to Luna's cousins, Marcus and Tidus. Neither were thrilled to see me in them, which actually filled me with a little bit of joy.

My weapons were next. Reaching for the long black case underneath my bed, I unlatched the two clips on each end and lifted the cover. Black velvet lined the inside, cushioning eight guns. But I only needed one. My Sig Sauer X-Five 9mm with the custom white pearl handle.

My first gun.

Zane had gifted it to me on the day of my first solo hunt.

If you're going to kill some monsters, might as well do it in style. Let those bitches know how we roll.

I smiled faintly at the memory, not allowing the sting to linger in my eyes for too long. Throwing the Sig into my duffle, I reached back under the bed and pulled out an old Nike shoe box. It was filled with memories I carried around but never looked at. But again, I only needed one.

Sorting through a stack of glossy photos, I plucked a single one from the bunch. A picture of me with my parents, taken several months before my mother killed herself. Growing up, people always told me I looked nothing like her, which was true enough. Her strawberry-blonde hair and dark green eyes were nothing like mine. I was my father's clone, after all. But she was tough and brave and unapologetically herself, all qualities that thankfully lived on through me. Bringing the photo to my lips, I gave it a kiss before tucking it safely into the duffle, laying it flat between some sweaters so it wouldn't bend or crease.

Zipping up the bag, I slung it over my shoulder and headed back to the window, grabbing a set of keys off my dresser on my way out.

I just needed one more thing.

Twirling the keys in my hand, I bypassed the garage and turned the corner, expecting to see my bike exactly where I'd left it. What I *didn't* expect to see, however, was the slender figure sitting on my Harley like she owned it, auburn hair blowing in the wind.

Luna turned and smiled at me, dimples on blast. "I figured you would come back for it."

Just the sight of her lifted my spirits. "Is that right?"

Her mischievous smile widened. "I know you better than you think, Malakai Slade."

Smirking, I made my way over to her, allowing the duffle to slip from my shoulder to the ground. "So it seems. How long have you been following me?"

She shrugged. "Since you left. I couldn't sleep without you."

I chuckled softly, tucking strands of flyaway hair behind her ear. "Noted. It won't happen again."

Her expression turned hopeful, her hypnotizing gaze holding me captive. "Really? Do you promise?"

Stepping into her, I slinked an arm around her waist and lifted her against my chest, her feet leaving the ground to meet my height. We moved so naturally together, her arms weaving around my neck to pull me closer. Burying my hand in her hair, I claimed her lips in a searing kiss, her head tilting with mine, perfectly in sync as we devoured one another as if this meeting would be our last.

Damn, I couldn't get enough of her. I never felt more at home than when my body was entwined with hers. I bent to lift her leg, hitching it to my hip. She quickly got the message and jumped to hook the other one herself, locking them both around me as I backed her into my bike.

"Why are you wearing a skirt?" I murmured against her mouth, my hands slipping below the short fabric to find her bare. "And no panties." It was far too cold out here for her to be dressed like this.

Her smile was nothing short of sinful. "You know why."

I groaned internally. *Fuck me.* I sat her down on my bike and spread her legs, rolling up the hem of her skirt until the material bunched at her waist. She grappled for my jeans, popping off the button in her haste to free my cock. I hissed when her hand closed around my shaft, the head pulsing as it thickened in her grasp.

When that familiar sensation trickled down my cock, I

gritted my teeth to hold it off. Unbelievable. She'd barely touched me and I was already on the verge of nutting! Needing a distraction, I reached for her throat, my hand closing firmly around it. This was another one of her kinks, being choked and held in place while I railed her.

My wicked little sorceress was a freak in the sheets.

She tipped her head back, throwing herself at my mercy, her eyes growing heavy-lidded and cloudy.

"You like it when I fuck you, don't you, witch?" I applied a little extra pressure to her throat when she only nodded, enforcing the rule she kept forgetting. "I can't hear you."

"Yes." She whimpered, her raspy voice filled with hunger.

Leaning down, I sank my teeth into her bottom lip, wringing a moan from her. "You should've waited for me to get back. It's dangerous out here." We had no idea where my father and the others were. For all I knew, they were on their way back here right now.

Luna leaned back on my bike, pulling me down with her by the collar of my shirt. I moved to stand behind the back wheel so I could hover over her. Lust swirled in her purple gaze, making it impossible for me to deny her.

"Then I guess you better hurry up and fuck me then, huh?"

I inhaled a breath through my nose. *Fucking enchantress.*

Though her powers didn't work on me anymore, she knew exactly how to rile me up. She had a fucking knack for it. Shoving my pants down, I plunged deep inside of her, sinking as far as I could go. No foreplay, no fucking around. She was already wet, her walls clenching and releasing around me. Keeping my hand locked around her throat, I used the other to steady my bike, white-knuckling the handlebar.

"Hold on tight," I told her, pulling out and plunging back in. Her grip on me tightened, her feet crossing at the ankles further up on my back so I could hit all her sweet spots.

My pace was punishing, fast and hard, my body seeking the comfort she was offering. She couldn't scream as freely as before, her breath hitching over and over again as her body jerked repeatedly against the force of my thrusts.

I eased my grip around her neck so she could suck down more air, but her hand shot up, covering my crescent moon tattoo. It reacted to her touch, the skin there heating as if it knew it was her blood that created it. It felt good having a part of her inside of me, linking us together.

"Don't stop," she panted, gazing up at me through dark lashes, eyes backlit by the moon above. Her fingers curled around mine, forcing me to tighten my grip again, needing to feel the pressure as she came.

Letting loose a growl, I rolled my hips faster, fucking her without restraint. A different side of me took over— the side that was no longer human—and she took it, her body going lax as she came, pussy spasming around me. I kept thrusting until I felt the tension coil all the way down to my balls, ready to explode. I came hard, back bowing as I lurched forward, grazing my teeth along her jaw as she milked me dry, my cum filling her. It gushed until oozing out of her was the only option, the sticky substance dripping down onto her glistening thighs.

We laid there for a minute or two, basking in one another while catching our breaths. Luna was the first to speak, her hand coming up to cradle my face.

"I love you."

I turned my face into her palm, laying a sweet kiss in the center. "I love you, too, baby." It was the first time I'd spoken the words out loud, but she wasn't surprised by them. I knew she'd felt it long before tonight, just as I had. Our connection was too strong for her not to. Hearing it was just a bonus.

Sitting up, I reached into the pocket of my jeans that were halfway down my legs and pulled out her bracelet. I admit, it wasn't the most romantic way to return it to her––with my cock still buried inside of her—but nothing about our relationship was conventional. The dangling gold charms glimmered under the moonlight, drawing her attention.

Frowning, she made a grab for the dainty piece of jewelry. "Is that my bracelet?"

I swatted her hand away. "It *was* your bracelet. You didn't want it anymore, remember."

With a playful glare, she lunged for it, nearly tumbling off the bike in the process. I used one arm to steady her while keeping the other tucked behind my back.

"Give it!" she pouted, poking out her bottom lip. "It's still mine!"

I smirked down at her, tempted to kiss those pouty lips. "If you want it back, you'll have to vow to never take it off again."

She rolled her eyes. "I only took it off in the first place because you were being an ass."

"Be that as it may, I'm gonna need that vow, Sorceress."

"Fine," she huffed, though it lacked any real irritation. "I promise to never take it off again."

I shook my head when she reached for it yet again. "No, no. I need you to vow it to that goddess you're always praying to. The one that brought me back to you."

She looked at me as if I'd lost my mind, eyes flaring wide. "Vows to Hecate aren't to be taken lightly."

I grinned darkly, glad to see she was catching on. "Yes, that's the whole point. I never want to see this bracelet leave your wrist again, no matter how much I piss you off. So, say the words."

Playing along with my little game, a slow smile broke out over her face as she sat up and scooted forward on the bike, her legs falling loose around my waist. "Okay. I vow to Hecate, the Dark Goddess herself, that I will never again remove this bracelet from my wrist. This I swear."

I grinned. "Good girl. Give me your hand."

Unable to contain her bright smile, she held out her hand. Unhooking the bracelet, I glided it around her slim wrist, bringing the two tiny clasps back together and securing it right below her pulse point.

"Now you're stuck with me forever, Luna Sinclair," I said, kissing the back of her hand.

Beaming up at me, she grabbed me by the nape and pulled my forehead to hers. "Oh, sweetie…that was always the plan."

FORTY

Luna

I t was moving day.

The week had been a long one with the covens working tirelessly to get their businesses squared away, tying up loose ends around town to make the move as seamless as possible. It was decided that we would continue running our operations here in Deadwood, it was just a small matter of hiring humans to deal with the day-to-day in our absence, keeping our involvement on a need-to-know basis. Wherever we ended up next, we would simply set up shop and continue as we were.

I was kind of looking forward to the fresh start, a strange feeling considering I'd been dreading this day for years. Before everything went to shit, I was content with my relatively mundane life, happy for everything to remain as it was. But change was inevitable.

Still, I'd be lying if I said I wasn't bummed about

missing my graduation ceremony. As pointless as it was to my future, it still would've been nice to walk across that stage and receive my diploma, to throw my cap in the air with the rest of the graduating class. And thanks to my royal fuck-up, the other Witchlings couldn't attend either. But most of them didn't care about the silly human tradition. Not like I did.

Packing up the last of my things from my bedroom, a loud crash sounded from downstairs.

"Oh, for fuck's sake!" Clay shouted.

"Would you stop touching shit, hunter," Marcus chimed in. "That's the third fucking box you broke."

I sighed. Malakai was still having a hard time adjusting to his amplified strength. Just yesterday he slammed Aunt Freya's car door so hard the glass shattered, the entire thing busting off its hinges.

She wasn't pleased.

"Luna! Come get your man!" Tidus hollered up the staircase. "Because if he drops my PS5, you best believe I'm gonna find a way to murder his undead ass!"

"You mean *this* PS5?" Malakai sang, his voice brimming with glee. Though I couldn't see him, I knew he was sporting a shit-eating grin on his handsome face.

Tidus's dramatic gasp echoed through our now-empty house. "Don't you *fucking* dare, freak!"

Then there was a scuffle, a sound I was growing used to when the four of them were together. I smiled listening to them bicker back and forth. None of them were ready to admit it, but they all secretly *liked* Malakai. He'd been a big help during the move, transporting any and everything that was too heavy for the rest of us to lift into the U-Haul. Even Aunt Freya was warming up to him, allowing him to stay with us indefinitely—a decision that William Blackwell did *not* take too kindly to. The man could hold a grudge with the best of them. And although Bella was alive and well, he still despised Malakai for killing her in the first place.

Bringing the boy with us is a mistake, I overheard him telling my aunt one night. But the argument had been a short one. Everyone knew where I stood on the subject. I had no intention of leaving Malakai behind, so the decision was simple. Either he stays, or we both leave. It was a sacrifice I was willing to make, one Aunt Freya was strongly against.

The Sinclair Coven will take full responsibility for the hunter. The decision has been made. Concern yourself with your own coven, William, and I will do the same for mine.

The wedge that formed between the two lovers had been painfully obvious since that night, and I couldn't help but feel wholly responsible. I didn't want to be the cause of any strife between them. I only prayed they worked it out soon.

A knock sounded behind me. I turned to see Kai leaning against the doorframe, wearing one of his dazzling smiles. "I think they're ready, Sorceress."

I inhaled and exhaled a breath. Time to go.

Before I could grab the last box sitting on my bed, he marched forward and picked it up. "I got it."

I smiled. "You're not going to crush it, are you?"

Leaning down, he gave my lips a quick peck. "Smartass," he mumbled, heading for the stairs. "Let's go."

My coven was waiting for us outside, the cars packed and ready to go. We were the last ones to leave. The other four covens were already on route to the new location.

Handing off the box to one of my cousins, Kai took my hand and led us over to his Harley. My arms snaked his waist as I got on behind him. "Are you ready for this?" I asked, discreetly slipping a hand under his shirt to rake my fingers over his washboard abs.

His chin dipped to follow the movement before throwing a look over his shoulder at me. A warning flashed in his eyes. "Careful, Sorceress. I won't hesitate to bend you over this bike and make your coven watch while I fuck you."

I shivered at the dark undertone in his voice, knowing damn well he didn't make empty threats. Immortality really suited him.

"Promises, promises," I purred against his ear, giving the lobe a playful nip with my teeth for good measure.

I giggled when he growled low in his throat, his grip tightening on the handlebars until the engine revved. To avoid scarring anyone with the X-rated show he would undoubtedly put on, I relocated my hand to less dangerous territory.

His grin turned cocky. "Wise choice."

One by one, the others rolled out, turning out of the swamp and onto the main road. I took the opportunity to give the only home I'd ever known one last farewell as Malakai and I brought up the rear, trailing behind Marcus's blacked-out Range Rover.

Laying my head against his back, I settled in for the

long drive ahead, inhaling the scent of his leather jacket and earthy cologne.

Every so often, he glanced back to check on me. "You sure you wouldn't be more comfortable riding with one of the boys?" he asked over the loud noise of the engine.

I shook my head against his back. "I'd rather be with you."

Pleased with my answer, he nodded and continued on. It wasn't until we reached the town border—meters away from passing the *Leaving Deadwood* sign—that I felt him stiffen against me. Before I knew what was happening, he veered off the road, making an abrupt U-turn in the opposite direction.

Frowning, I glanced back, watching as the rest of my coven continued on their journey, our sudden absence going unnoticed for the time being.

"What's wrong?" I asked, tugging on the front of his shirt.

Hesitating, he said, "I see smoke."

My brows knitted together as I looked around, trying to figure out what the hell he was talking about. Then I saw it. The swirl of black smoke drifting up into the air was barely noticeable at first, coming from a rather large woodland area.

"So what? It's probably just a bonfire or something. Who cares?"

His long pauses were beginning to worry me.

"Kai?"

"I just need to check something. Text your aunt and tell her we'll catch up to them soon."

Okay...

Carefully pulling out my phone with one hand while holding onto him with the other, I sent a quick voice message to my family group chat before slipping the device back into the front pocket of my hoodie. I refrained from asking him more questions until he pulled off to the side of the road and cut the engine. We were parked in front of a hiking trail, the path leading into the forest. I knew the area well. It was popular amongst the locals.

Staring down the pathway, Kai exhaled a deep sigh before dismounting his bike. "Stay here. I'll be back."

Oh, hell no.

Peeling off my helmet, I dropped it on the seat and followed after him. "Not happening. I'm coming with you."

To my surprise, he didn't protest. He simply took my hand and started down the trail. His expression urged me to choose my words carefully. He was entirely too serious, as if he was on some sort of mission that I wasn't privy to. Letting him take the lead, I kept my mouth shut and walked. And walked...

Then walked some more.

"Babe," I said, clearing my throat. "Do you have a destination in mind?"

"We're almost there," was all I managed to squeeze out of him.

Okay, then...

Trusting my man, we continued on until the path grew unpaved, taking us further from civilization. He moved like he knew the area well...like he'd been here before. As the stench of smoke grew more potent, he hustled us behind a cluster of trees.

I opened my mouth to ask another question just as he raised a finger to his lips, shushing me. "Keep quiet."

More confused than ever, I watched as he peered through the trees, totally engrossed by whatever was on the other side. I couldn't hear any voices, only the sound of running water and the crackling of firewood.

Leaning into his side, I tried to see what he was seeing. And it was the last thing I expected.

Eyes wide, I slapped a hand over my mouth to stifle the gasp I couldn't contain. There, in front of a serene and secluded lake, stood Malakai's father. And he wasn't alone. His uncle stood a few steps behind with two other hunters at his back. I recognized the one on the far right.

Well, barely.

His face was swollen and bruised, the black and blue bits already turning an ugly, yellowish color. He had a splint on his nose and a brace around his neck, but I recognized him just the same.

He was the one Malakai had nearly beaten to death for torturing me. They all looked haggard, like they hadn't slept in days. My gaze flickered over to Malakai's father, his sullen expression darkened further by the deep bags under his eyes and overgrown stubble across his jaw. His clothes were wrinkled and disheveled as if he'd been sleeping in them only hours before. He stared blankly at the burning raft drifting in the water, floating farther and farther away from the shore, his gaze devoid of emotions.

"What is this?" I asked, keeping my voice low.

"My funeral."

I blinked at the bluntness in his tone, unsure what to make of his detached demeanor. He didn't seem bothered or even surprised by the spectacle.

"What do you mean? You're not dead."

His smile didn't reach his eyes. "They don't know that, remember? When a hunter dies, we burn their corpse and send them out to sea, putting their soul to rest. We did the same for Zane."

"But they don't have your body. What are they burning?"

He shrugged. "Something that belonged to me, most likely. I'm guessing this was my father's idea. His way of..." He paused to swallow, finally showing a sliver of emotion. "Moving on."

I squeezed his hand in mine, offering my support. "I'm sorry."

"You have nothing to apologize for."

It didn't feel that way. It felt like I'd ruined his entire life, ripping him away from his family forever. My throat constricted as I prepared to say what I was about to, already dreading the answer. "Do you...want to go back to them?"

His eyes snapped to mine, looking a little peeved. *Dammit. Me and my stupid mouth!*

"We already discussed this, Sorceress. Even if I wanted to, they would never accept me as I am now. Not after what I did."

Biting my lip, my nervous gaze fell to his chest. "But *if* you could, would you?"

Slanting his head, he took one last look at his family before turning away. "Let's go," he said, tugging me along as he led us back the way we came.

We walked in silence. I didn't know what to say, and I

was too afraid to interrupt whatever he had going on in his head at the moment. I regretted my question. It was selfish of me to ask, to make him choose between a choice he didn't even have just to appease my own insecurities.

When we reached his bike, he grabbed my helmet from off the seat and pulled me closer so he could secure it to my head. It was on the tip of my tongue to tell him that I was fully capable of doing that myself, but I enjoyed him doting on me too much to care.

As he fastened the strap under my chin, he smiled down at me, this one reaching his eyes enough to make it sparkle. My breath hitched at the intensity in his gaze, the adoration.

"And to answer your *real* question," he said, gently tucking my hair in along the edges of the helmet so it wasn't sticking out. "I have no intention of going anywhere without you, Sorceress. It's me and you now, us against the fucking world. You good with that?"

A megawatt smile lit up my face, my heart exploding in my chest. No matter how many times he reassured me, I never got tired of hearing it.

Going up on my tiptoes, I stretched to meet his lips. "I'm more than good with that."

He met me halfway, arm circling my waist to lift me the rest of the way. His mouth came down hot and heavy over mine, kissing me like his life depended on it. The feeling was mutual. We were bound now, tethered together by fate, never to be separated again.

In this life or the next.

And, yeah, I was good with that too.

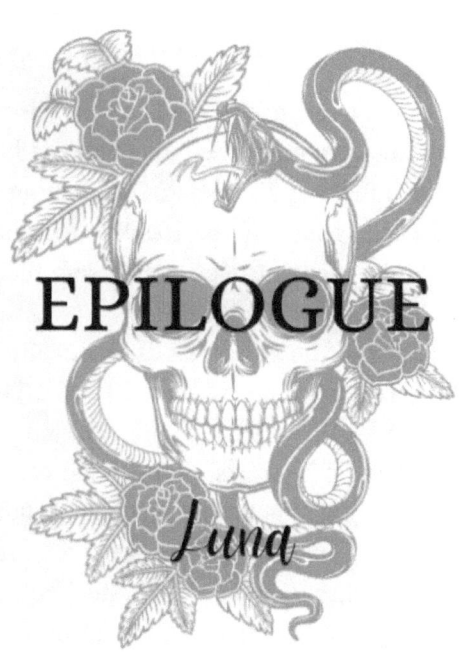

EPILOGUE

Luna

"Quinn, on your left!"

The Basilisk's poisonous tail missed the blonde by an inch, attempting to knock her off her feet. It scampered away, its green reptilian body moving too fast for me to follow.

But I didn't have to.

"I got it." Throwing up my hands, I cast an illusion around it, sending it careening into a brick wall. The creature panicked, slithering backwards as it whipped its scaled head in every direction in search of an opening in my deception. But it wouldn't find any. I had it trapped.

"Now!" I yelled.

On my cue, Quinn rushed it, impaling it with her spear. The creature squealed, a glass-shattering pitch that had me shielding my ear drums as the blade pierced its chest right through, rendering it lifeless within seconds.

Quinn's face twisted in revulsion as slimy yellow blood oozed down from her weapon and coated her hands. "Ewww! That's fucking disgusting!" Retracting her spear, she stepped back, allowing the Basilisk to collapse in a dead heap. "Fuck this shit. You get to stab the next one, Sinclair."

I laughed as she shook her hands frantically, trying to rid herself of the sticky mess. "No thanks. I just did my nails."

She flipped me off just as another one came hurtling towards us, leaping off the ledge of a nearby building and landing on its stomach. But before we could react, Malakai came plunging down after it, his boots slamming into the reptile's back, breaking his fall. In one swift motion, he captured the creature around the neck in a chokehold and wrenched it back until a notable crack echoed in the alleyway. The Basilisk's screams were short-lived as Kai outed his blade and plunged it through the creature's back, striking its heart from behind.

Quinn blew out a low whistle as he pulled his blade free, whipping it clean on the corpse before making his way over to us.

"Must be nice to pull Superman stunts like that without getting hurt. When was the last time you thanked me for that, by the way?"

We both rolled our eyes, knowing where this was going.

Even after a year, Quinn still refused to let anyone forget the miracle she had performed by resurrecting Malakai into the indestructible force that now stood before us. And, as annoying as she was at times, credit had to be given where it was due.

Even I couldn't help but marvel at the specimen Malakai had become. Since leaving Deadwood, he'd been my partner on every single mission I'd been assigned, watching my back at every turn. I tried to do the same for him, but he rarely needed it.

His ability to recover from just about any injury was truly remarkable. He'd been shot, stabbed, burned. Even drowned a few times. But he always got back up, rebounding like death was his bitch. And the more he endured, the faster he healed, the pain making him stronger somehow.

He truly was a phenomenon in our world, one Quinn couldn't seem to replicate. He was quite literally the only golden star on her resume, one no other necromancer could claim since none had ever risen a dead mortal into an immortal before. And an unkillable one at that.

Hence the bragging rights.

"I just thanked you by killing three of these things while you two fucked around with one," he said, nodding at the dead Basilisk Quinn had taken out.

Smiling, I leaned into him, craning my neck back for a kiss. "Don't be like that. You know I just did my nails."

"You and your fucking nails!" Quinn huffed from somewhere behind me.

Kai grinned, meeting my lips halfway before lifting my manicured hand to his mouth. "You're right. I much rather see them wrapped around my cock than stained with Basilisk blood."

"Oh, for fuck's sake!" Quinn shouted, her footsteps quickly receding down the alley. "At least let me leave before you two start fucking each other's brains out. That is *so* not something I need to see again." Her complaints faded the further she got, giving us some privacy. "Worse than fucking rabbits, I swear…"

I swatted Kai's chest once she was gone. "You did that on purpose, you brute."

He chuckled, not denying it. "We haven't been alone all day."

"We've been alone plenty."

He put extra emphasis on his scoff as if that was the biggest lie he'd ever heard. "What fucking house have you been living in, Sorceress? Between your sister and the three idiots, I barely have time to get you naked anymore."

Crossing my arms, I arched a brow. "And whose fault is that?" It certainly wasn't mine. Over the course of a year, my family had grown just as attached to Malakai as I was. From training Anya how to fight to playing Call of Duty with the boys, they all shared something personal with him.

And it wasn't just them.

Without trying, he'd become an integral member of our community. Whatever animosity anyone felt towards him had long since been forgotten. Even William Blackwell was able to tolerate his company from time to time. Bella, not so much. The fiery witch still held a grudge, keeping her distance for the most part. Not that Kai gave a shit.

I don't like the bitch, anyway, he'd say whenever I pleaded with him to play nice with the girl. It was safe to say the two would never be friends. But as long as they didn't try to kill each other anymore, it was a win in my book.

"Hmm." Sweeping me off my feet, he spun me to brace the brick wall of the ally. "You sound a little jealous, Sorceress. Have I been neglecting you?"

"You said it, not me." Damn, that sounded bitter even to my ears.

His grin was downright devilish. "Well, we can't have that, now can we." Bending slightly, he cupped the back of my thighs and lifted me to his waist, giving me no choice but to cling to him.

I shot him a glare, looking both ways down the alley. "What do you think you're doing? It's broad daylight out here."

Leaning in, he bit my neck. "That's never stopped us before."

True enough.

And there were many who could attest to that. Quinn especially. The necromancer had caught us in more compromising positions than I cared to admit. But I felt no shame for my growing promiscuous nature.

A girl has needs.

And I was feeling pretty needy right about now.

"Well...if you insist," I drawled, fingers sinking into his hair to yank his lips back to mine. The kiss was wild and frantic, just as I knew the sex would be. There was nothing sweet or tender about the way he hiked my leather skirt up past my hips and pushed my panties aside, his fingers exploring my wetness as I trembled in anticipation. I felt his cock a second later, the thick rod filling me before I could draw my next breath.

The deep growl that rumbled from his chest was a warning of what was to come, and I knew my back would be chaffed and bruised by the end of it.

My hips rocked at the thought, craving his aggression. *Needing* it. And just as he slid back out to the tip, preparing to absolutely *wreck* me, my lust-addled brain barely registered the voice that sounded somewhere in the distance before euphoria overtook me.

"Oh, for fuck's sake, you two!"

THANK YOU FOR READING!

Please leave a review on Amazon, Goodreads, or your favourite social media platform. Your feedback is greatly appreciated!

DON'T FORGET TO SIGN UP FOR MY MONTHLY NEWSLETTER!

Join for the chance to be a part of my ARC team and receive advanced reader copies of upcoming new releases. Plus get exclusive access to bonus scenes, giveaways and much more!

www.alessiaann.com

ABOUT THE AUTHOR

Alessia Ann is an author of Paranormal Romance books featuring demons, witches, shapeshifters, fey and more. Her dark, smoldering storytelling will leave you breathless and hooked from beginning to end. She has a university degree in English and Professional Writing, with a specialty in Creative Writing.

Alessia currently lives in Canada with her family where she spends her spare time spinning new tales to tell. Follow her on all social media platforms if you would like updates on her new releases and much more!

Connect with the author on:

www.alessiaann.com